IN THE
DEAD
OF THE
NIGHT

A NOVEL

NORTHSHIRE HERITAGE BOOK 3

JP ROBINSON

Publications

ignite faith

Visit Logos online at www.LogosPub.com.

Visit JP Robinson's website: www.JPRobinsonBooks.com

In the Dead of the Night

Library of Congress Control Number: 2021936121

Paperback ISBN: 978-0-9997793-7-8

Hardback ISBN: 978-0-9997793-8-5

Printed and bound in the United States of America

Published by: Logos Publications, LLC, **PO Box 271, Lampeter, PA 17537**

What Readers Are Saying

[In the Shadow of Your Wings] ". . . Robinson's eclectic array of characters and high-stakes scenarios make for an immersive beginning to a series that will appeal to fans of war dramas."
—PUBLISHER'S WEEKLY

[In the Dead of the Night] "It holds much food for thought, and will especially delight readers of Great War events who don't typically receive such a multifaceted, thought-provoking examination of the war."—MIDWEST BOOK REVIEWS

[In the Midst of the Flames] "Rich with political intrigue and subtle nods to the Bible, this novel's strength comes in the precise attention to historic detail and evocative imagery." —PUBLISHERS WEEKLY,

"A wonderful conclusion to trilogy and must-read for anyone who enjoys Christian historical suspense."—JEANETTE W, bestselling author of *Veiled Freedom*

[In the Shadow of Your Wings] "This story had characters from every walk of life-in all aspects of that time period. So beautifully written on how their individual stories intertwine. The author does a perfect job at setting a clear stage for so many stories, characters and their hardships. Absolutely mind blowing how the plot unfolds. Amazing! This is a must read for historical fiction lovers."-TARA

[In the Dead of the Night] "The story is exciting with spies, war, suspense and action throughout. I appreciated the depiction of the struggles a Christian faces and the reality of living in this world." -JANE

[In the Shadow of Your Wings] "Fantastic WWI historical fiction book. Fast paced, you won't want to put this book down.Great story, characters and believable. " -CAROLINE

"If there's one thing I've come to expect from Robinson is that he has a non-stop ride packed in his novels."-A.M. HEATH, Author of *Ancient Words*

"In the Dead of the Night is the fantastic finish to the action-packed, danger-filled Northshire Heritage series. If you like World War I fiction, I highly recommend this! I loved it."-STACEY

"This masterfully-woven historical novel is set during the Great War with a rich cast of characters, assassination plots, an infant held hostage, treacherous women spies, and a gripping tension-filled trial. Even a castle is at stake."- JOY, Author of *Leora's Letters*

[*In the Midst of the Flames*] "What an exciting story line with vivid characters! ... Once I started both books, I could hardly put them down. I knew my husband would like the books, and he read both straight through in a few days. (The benefit of having time during Covid 19 stay-at-home rules.)"-ELSIE

[*In the Shadow of Your Wings*] "Read this through in one evening. Suspenseful and entertaining. I enjoyed the storyline and look forward to the next book(s) in the series!!"

[*In the Shadow of Your Wings*] "Thank you for writing a clean book with Christian values that boys, as well as girls, can enjoy!"

[*Bride Tree*] "An enchanting romance woven with espionage, and a power struggle that will keep any historical fan charmed and mesmerized."—READERS FAVORITE

Dedication

To my children, spiritual heroes-in-training, whose brilliant faith continues to defy the night regardless of the terrors it may hold.

Cast of Characters

THE BRITISH
The Steele Family
Thomas Steele—exile and head of Northshire Estate
Malcolm Steele—Thomas's son
Leila Steele—Malcom's wife and former German spy
Michael Steele—Leila and Malcolm's son

The Thompson Family
Will Thompson—Malcolm's erstwhile friend
Eleanor Thompson—Will's wife and military nurse

Prominent members of the Northshire Staff
Greyson—butler and Thomas's personal assistant
Jenny Edwards—lady's maid to Leila Steele
Greta Bindau—Michael Steele's wetnurse

Prominent politicians
David Lloyd George—prime minister of Great Britain
Hughes—head of the British Secret Intelligence Service
Earl Curzon—member of the British war council
Arthur Hoffman—Swiss politician

THE GERMANS

The Haber Family

Fritz Haber—scientist, husband of Clara and Charlotte

Clara Haber—Fritz Haber's wife (deceased)

Charlotte Nathan Haber—Fritz Haber's former mistress now his second wife

MISCELLANEOUS:

Werner Jaëger—head of German Intelligence(deceased)

Elsbeth Schneider—head of a German espionage network

Gen. Paul Hindenburg—commander of Germany's military

Elijah Farrows—pastor on Northshire Estate

Lt-Col. James Stewart—Malcolm's commanding officer

M44—espionage agent under Elsbeth Schneider's command

Joseph Mara—barrister (lawyer) to the Steele family

Pierre LaRue—leader of a Geneva-based crime syndicate

Author's Note

One of the things I love about the Bible is that it doesn't just tell us the good parts in the lives of God's heroes. With brutal honesty, the Bible details the failures and struggles of its heroes as well as their victories, reminding us that they were human as we are.

In the Dead of the Night focuses on the battle within—the lifelong struggle against evil that faces every believer. To better illustrate this point, I have modified some parts of the historical record—particularly in regards to Elsbeth Schneider.

In his letter to the Romans, Paul the Apostle focuses on the conflict that raged within him in a voice that is humble yet inspiring. "I find then a law, that, when I would do good, evil is present with me." Romans 7:21 KJV

Finding Christ is not the end of our spiritual battles; it is the beginning. But like all good beginnings, there is the promise of a positive outcome—regardless of our faults—*if* we learn to depend on His strength alone.

Dear reader, as you enter the world of Northshire one final time, I pray that the characters' struggles will inspire you to keep fighting your own battles in Jesus's name. I pray that you will discover the strength that comes from committal. For only when we are willing to let go of our fears and of our own will can we experience the power of God.

Prologue

January 1918. Whitehall, London

Sir Robert Hughes stood in the rear corner of his office before a wall-length oval window. He counted as an army of raindrops slammed against the panes, spilling out their watery blood as though trying in vain to break through this translucent "front."

His eyes moved beyond the streaks carved by the raindrops in the grime, shifting to focus on the crenelated spires and rectangular rooftops that made up the administrative center of British government.

Whitehall.

It was just a road, really. A simple road that trudged through a host of brick buildings filled with snub-nosed politicians and draconian bureaucrats. All of whom impeded progress like an army of Goliaths.

Hughes shoved his hands in his pockets as he continued to count the raindrops that spattered against this one window into his clandestine world of secrets and lies.

Politicians.

The thought turned the lingering taste of his afternoon tea sour in his mouth. He wanted to spit.

"Let it go, Hughes." The voice of Britain's prime minister, David Lloyd George, interrupted his count.

I

"You've won your share of battles. Let Thomas Steele keep what little he has." David snorted as he shifted in his seat, a brown leather armchair. "Think of it, man. In the year since we released Steele's daughter-in-law, you've helped put down a rebellion in Ireland. Your men obtained vital information that helped us end the butchery of Passchendaele. You've redeemed yourself. Now let the past be."

Hughes turned around slowly, massaging the spot in his right leg just above the wooden prosthesis. "Nine hundred seventy-six."

"I beg your pardon?" The prime minister blinked.

"Nine hundred seventy-six raindrops died on my window in the last three minutes."

David stared at him, jaw slack, for a full thirty seconds before speaking. "You know, Hughes, there are moments when I truly question your sanity." He sat up straight. "W-why on *earth* are you counting raindrops? Aren't there more important things to count? Such as the rising number of our dead in this ghastly war?"

A momentary silence filled the space between the two men.

"The raindrops. They're our soldiers." Hughes gave a tight smile as he stumped to his desk. "A thousand raindrops ended their miserable lives in less than three minutes. Like as not, just as many of our lads have died fighting for law and order around the world while you sit here and insist that a man who has betrayed his king and country should go free."

David tilted his head to one side, eying him like a hawk might eye a potential rival. But Hughes had no interest in political games. Not anymore. One thought alone burned in his mind.

"What is it about Thomas that galls you? What is it, really?"

"Thomas is a transgressor." Hughes's jaw tightened into an inflexible line. "He broke the law. He must be punished."

"And . . . unless he is punished by law, you will not be satisfied?"

"How can I be satisfied?" Hughes laced his fingers together behind his back and began to pace, an awkward thumping rhythm, teeth gritted. David was a politician—a man whose personal standard of right and wrong was determined by the will of his voters. He could never understand Hughes's mind. "Every transgression, each tiny infraction of the law, must receive just retribution. It is the only way. The right way."

"I suppose the idea of mercy is a foreign concept?"

"Mercy?" Bile rose in the back of Hughes's throat. "There is no mercy. There is only the law. The law, Prime Minister!" He released a ragged breath. "Did you know that when my wife and I married, I took her last name?"

"Really?" David arched a silver eyebrow. "How very . . . progressive of you."

"Hm!" Hughes snorted. "It was part of our marriage contract. Her father insisted so his name wouldn't be lost when his only daughter died." He stared out into middle-space, lost for a moment in the fog of memory. "I wanted her inheritance. After the marriage I could have worked to change the situation. But, you see, every word of the original document had to be kept or my entire marriage would become a sordid affair."

"Every . . . word." His gaze shifted back to the prime minister. "That is why Thomas must face our justice. Not our mercy. In violating one part of the law, he is guilty of breaking the whole."

"And what of Thomas's son Malcolm? What part of the law has he broken?"

"None." Hughes spat out the word. "At least none of which I am aware. I have sent a message to his commander, Colonel Stewart, however. I want Malcolm Steele to answer some questions for me in London. If he is collaborating with the enemy, I *will* find out."

"I see." David leaned back in his seat, resting his forearms over his slight paunch. "But back to Thomas. You know he is beyond your reach. He's untouchable in Switzerland."

For the first time all day, the hint of a smile creased the corners of Hughes's lips. Yes, political figures stood in his way like an army of Goliaths. But that story had a happy ending.

"I am expecting a guest." He pulled out his bronze pocket watch, glanced briefly at the insignia of the British navy on its polished surface, and flipped it open. "He should be here . . . now."

A knock sounded on the door. Hughes turned to it, thrusting the watch back into his pocket. "Enter!"

The prime minister stood as a thin, pale man wearing a plaid jacket and maroon pants skulked into the room. A small, black briefcase hung loosely from the fingers of his left hand. With his right, he smoothed out his short-cropped moustache.

Hughes narrowed his eyes. The man was small and unimpressive like the giant-killer of biblical times. And like him, this man also carried a weapon that, if used correctly, would bring Thomas's world crashing to the dust.

"You are Sir Robert Hughes, head of British Foreign Intelligence?"

"Yes." Hughes leaned forward, peering at his guest through his monocle. Satisfied at length, Hughes nodded. The man before him matched the description and photograph he had received from his agents abroad.

"I am Arthur Hoffman of Switzerland." A leer twisted Hoffman's pointed, sallow face into a rictus. "And I have come to help you destroy Thomas Steele."

PART 1

November 1918

JP ROBINSON

Chapter 1

Geneva, Switzerland

The evening sky above Geneva swore the apocalypse
had come. Feather-like clouds curled upward, painted
various shades of red by the dying sunlight. To
Thomas Steele, it seemed the heavens burned.

As he moved away from the building that housed the
administrative department of his watchmaking facility, Thomas
caught sight of dark thunderheads on the distant horizon. They
scudded northwest toward Britain, pushed along by a stiff breeze.

With a sigh, Thomas tugged the lapels of his brown suit
jacket, picked up his briefcase, and stepped into the flow of
traffic on Rue Lombard.

Pedestrians and motorized vehicles shared the streets of
Geneva, sometimes with devastating consequences. The city's
population had more than doubled as refugees from both sides
of the war sought shelter and medical attention in neutral
territory. A kaleidoscope of languages buzzed in conversation
around him. French. German. Even Italian.

But not English.

Thomas fought a wave of nostalgia as the thought slipped
to the forefront of his mind. While business had often led to
extended stays in Switzerland over the past thirty years, there
had always been the assurance of a return to the quiet pastures
of Sussex County, England.

But now that assurance was gone.

Thomas's footsteps slowed as his mind rolled back through
the series of unprecedented events that had unraveled his world.
Last summer, Robert Hughes had arrested his daughter-in-
law Leila and had wrongfully concluded that Thomas was in

league with the Germans. The evidence against Leila had been overwhelming, and she had been condemned to execution.

In a desperate bid to save both Leila and his unborn grandchild, Thomas had used his influence in Switzerland's political spheres to pressure the British government into releasing Leila. London had ultimately relented, but Thomas had been branded a traitor. If he ever set foot in England again, he was a dead man.

Not that I regret it.

The joy of seeing his son Malcolm reunited with Leila when he had joined them in Switzerland last winter and the warmth that flooded Thomas's heart each time he held his grandson in his arms more than compensated for the grief of exile.

"But Northshire is our home. It will *always* be our home," Thomas said in a forceful whisper. He set his mouth in a grim line as he strode forward, wending his way through the crowds.

His every hope now lay in his son Malcolm. If only—

Someone jolted him from behind. Thomas staggered forward, losing his hold on his briefcase. His hands flew out to break his fall. He cried out as his knees slammed against the uneven cobblestones. Stabs of pain splintered through his shins and radiated up through his thighs.

"Oh, I'm so sorry!" a woman said in clear, unaccented German. Laying a gentle hand on his shoulder, she tried to help him up. "My thoughts were so far away, I didn't see—"

A gunshot echoed off the ancient buildings surrounding the square.

A puff of wind brushed past his head.

The woman's apology died in a gurgled shriek. Thomas whipped his head around. Clawing helplessly at her throat, she slumped across his back, pushing him down toward the unfeeling stones.

Rolling his shoulders, Thomas shrugged off her deadweight. He pushed himself up to a semi-crouch, ignoring the fire in his knees. Pulse hammering in his throat, he took in a barrage of details at a glance.

The green cross near the door of a pharmacy to his left. The woman in a nurse's uniform—white knee-length dress, gray striped shirt, a red cross emblazoned on the white patch across her chest—sprawled across its concrete steps.

Her life blood spurting out of a neat hole in her throat. Passersby screaming. Running in all directions.

Thomas snatched up his discarded briefcase and darted a few steps from the body. He took shelter behind the low-hanging branch of one of several plane trees that pushed up out of the cobblestones. Sucking in deep breaths, he ran his well-trained eyes over the crowd, looking for something—a furtive attempt to conceal a weapon, someone trying to quietly flee the scene—*anything*.

But he saw nothing.

"God have mercy on that poor woman's soul." Thomas glanced back at the body, remorse swelling within his chest. There could be no doubt that *he* was the target. If he hadn't stumbled . . .

"You!" Thomas grabbed the arm of a young man who darted past him. "Go get the police."

The man—an overgrown boy, really—blinked at him from behind a pair of wire-rim glasses. He looked from Thomas to the body and back again with wide eyes. "M-me?"

"I saw some not long ago." Thomas jerked a thumb toward the opposite end of Rue Lombard. "They're probably still there." Thomas spun him around and shoved him forward. "Go. Now!"

"Right. Right." The lanky teen licked his lips, then scurried away.

The square was largely empty now. A few bold pedestrians remained, staring at the body on the steps with morbid fascination. A clear path lay from the far end of the square to the victim's corpse as though an invisible hand had drawn an unseen line on top the stones, dividing the horrified spectators into two groups.

Thomas curled his fingers into a tight fist, teeth clenched. The shock of the attack had faded, melting into a familiar desire to find and destroy his enemy. He was a soldier. This was not the first time someone had tried to kill him. Nor was it likely to be the last.

Brushing a few strands of silver hair out of his eyes, Thomas leaned forward. *Where is he?* Thomas glared at a row of brick apartments that rose above the square like unfeeling collaborators. Any one of the dozens of curtained windows opposite him could have been the killer's vantage point.

Thomas grunted. Crime was not unheard of in Geneva. Many of the war's refugees were desperate people. With the increase in population had come an increase in robberies. But this was a different animal altogether.

His mind skimmed through the details, picking up facts as though they were pieces of some invisible puzzle. Thomas laid the irrelevant aside, sifting through the barrage of information until only two main points stood out in his mind.

One: The shooter had uncommon skill. Rue Lombard wasn't a wide street, but a moving target in a crowd was difficult at best. Only someone very skilled—or very desperate—would attempt it.

4

Two: Thomas was a man of wealth, power, and politics. The kind of man that attracted enemies like a dog attracted fleas. A skilled assassin would not have come cheaply. But two governments—Britain and Germany—could potentially benefit from his death. He had outmaneuvered both of them, an act that neither party was likely to forgive.

So which one stands the most to gain from my death?

"Get out of the way. Move!" Rough voices from the far end of the square cut through the crowd. Bystanders quickly stepped aside as five Swiss *polizei* rushed to the scene. A few moments later, a tan ambulance screeched to a stop behind them.

Thomas waited until their milling bodies temporarily obscured the view from the apartments from which the shot had been fired. Then he quietly slipped into the crowd, his mind still churning.

Could this killer have been hired by someone in Switzerland? It was possible. His manipulation of Arthur Hoffman had certainly ruffled some high-ranking feathers. But Switzerland stood to lose much if he died.

A sick feeling akin to nausea rose in his gut as he allowed the most obvious thought to surface. Had the killer been commissioned by London? Had the British empire decided assassination was the only way to chastise its wayward son?

Thomas quickened his pace, turning off Rue Lombard into a small, quiet park, then made his way toward a bench that lay between two plane trees. Women chatted amiably nearby. Children played at a small fountain in the park's center. Apparently, none of them knew that murder had been committed just a short distance away.

Thomas looked upward once more. The orange in the sky had yielded to a morbid red as though the heavens reflected the blood that had been shed on earth.

"Quite beautiful, isn't it?"

Thomas stiffened as Arthur Hoffmann's unwelcome face came into view.

Hoffmann had been the pawn that Thomas had sacrificed to secure Leila's release. Publicly named a disgrace, Arthur had been expelled from the Swiss government. The man had disappeared for the better part of a year, and Thomas had hoped that the river of life would push them in separate directions.

Apparently, he was to be disappointed.

"What do you want, Arthur?" Thomas straightened, every sense alert. Had Hoffman come to finish the botched job on Rue Lombard? Thomas doubted the spindly erstwhile-politician had the gumption to use a gun, but one could never be too careful.

"Oh, not much." Loosening the buttons of his black suit jacket, Arthur sat on the unoccupied part of the bench. "Just to talk. After all, that is what we politicians do best." His gaze slid to Thomas's face. "But you'd know all about that, now, wouldn't you?"

"If you're implying that we're alike, you are sorely mistaken. I am a businessman, not a politician. For you, time is a way to buy support. For me time is—"

"Running out." Arthur tapped his fingertips together as if he were praying and looked up again at the gory sky. "Such a sight! I could almost believe today is Judgment Day."

"I thought you don't believe in God."

"Oh, I do." Arthur's lips twitched. "But your God is an invisible being with intangible power whereas I . . ." He leaned forward, eyes glittering. "I *am* a god."

"You are sick, Arthur. You need help." Thomas shook his head. "I have neither the time nor the inclination to debate with you."

"There's no debate." Arthur sniggered—a thin, wheezing cross between a cough and a laugh. "Doesn't your God make things happen through words?"

Thomas hesitated. "Yes."

"So do I. With words, I bend situations to my will." Arthur paused. "I may have left politics, but believe me, Thomas, my influence is still very real."

"And this has something to do with me?"

"Oh yes." Arthur's voice dropped to a silken whisper. "But to continue, doesn't your God punish the wicked?" He spoke louder now, his voice rising with each syllable. "Doesn't He bring down the proud and destroy every liar?" He didn't wait for Thomas to reply. "Yes! He does."

A sense of foreboding gripped Thomas, building on the nausea. "As I said before, my time is valuable. If you have something to say, spit it out and be done." He stood up, gripping his briefcase. "If there is nothing more, I bid you good day."

"Thomas, you are about to see that I have the same power." Arthur rose, jerking a newspaper from the pocket of his black pants. "When you *do* find the time, take a look at the article on page 21. You'll find it most enlightening." His thin lips angled into a vicious smile.

Thomas said nothing.

Hoffmann tossed the paper onto the bench, then rebuttoned his jacket. "I leave you with the words of Saint John the Divine. 'For the day of His wrath is come and who shall be able to stand?'" Hoffmann sniggered again. "Judgment Day is here, Thomas. And now it is *you* who will fall."

Chapter 2

Château des Aigles, Switzerland

Streaks of auburn gold streamed through patches in the clouds that floated across the evening sky. Filtering through the glass dome of the castle study, they came to rest upon the upturned face of Leila's son. Propped upon a supporting cushion, Michael squealed as he tried to catch the solitary rays in his chubby fists.

"Just look at the young master!" Jenny stopped dusting a bookshelf at the far end of the study, her narrow face wreathed in a smile as she placed one hand on her hip. "Just a few months old and reachin' out as if he owned the castle and everythin' in it already!"

Leila squatted next to her son, dangling a small wooden eagle that Thomas had carved a few inches above his face. "That's because he's a man who knows what he wants. Isn't that right, Michael my angel?"

With a loud chirp, Michael lurched forward and gripped the eagle.

"You see?" Leila let him have it and straightened, smoothing out the skirt of her simple ivory dress. "Once Michael makes up his mind, he doesn't stop until he gets what he's after."

"Just like his father." Jenny came closer, the white feather duster tucked beneath her arm.

Leila let out a deep breath but didn't respond.

"Oh, forgive me, Lady Steele. I . . . I wasn't thinkin'. I shouldn't have—"

"No." Leila stopped her maid's apology with an upturned palm. "It's all right, Jenny. Really."

Jenny gave a sympathetic cluck, shaking her head. "All *will* be well, you'll see!"

"Yes, it will. I know that." Lifting her head a fraction of an inch, Leila forced a smile, pushing past the fear that clawed at her insides. Much like the shadows that darkened the skin beneath her emerald-green eyes, fear was a constant companion.

Malcolm was doing his duty at the battlefront. Defending his country. His family. His honor. But the cold reality that every second of every day could end her husband's life kept Leila praying long into the lonely nights.

"It does seem that this ridiculous war just goes on and on." Jenny puffed out her cheeks. "What are they out to prove exactly? By the time they decide who owns the stupid patch of earth, they'll all be dead!" Dropping the duster, she cupped both hands over her mouth. "E-except Lord Malcolm, milady."

Leila slanted her a wry smile, this one a little more genuine. "Well, there's been no word from Mr. Mara. And that's a measure of comfort."

Joseph Mara, Thomas's erstwhile legal advisor at the Bank of England, had quicker access to the British casualty lists. If the worst should happen, he would get word to them in Switzerland.

"That's right, milady. You know what they say. No news is the best kind in times like these."

"You're right, Jenny. But it's harder on us. Most women get constant letters from their husbands while they're at war."

"But you can't write to Lord Malcolm because that curmudgeon in Whitehall might accuse him of bein' a traitor?" Jenny brushed back into place a strand of chestnut hair that had somehow escaped the prim bun behind her head.

"Exactly. Hughes and British intelligence monitor all mail to and from the Front. If there's any hint of communication between myself, Thomas, and Malcolm, he could use it to fabricate charges that Malcolm is working with the enemy." A hard edge crept into Leila's voice. "With . . . me."

For a moment, Jenny's face screwed into a tight ball. "Oh, of all the hairbrained, foolhardy notions! Let the old cripple think what he likes. You've seen worse than this. Why, only this time last year you were locked up in the Tower, expectin' death at any minute."

"I remember," Leila said. She'd spent weeks in the Tower, waiting on Hughes to carry out his threat of execution. It was in the cold, damp cell that Leila had learned she harbored new life within her womb.

"But was Hughes able to do it? Of course not." Jenny, who had become more of a sister than a servant, grabbed Leila's hand. "Then there was the time when those Irish savages came screamin' up the lane, bent on murdering us all back home at Northshire. Did it happen?"

"No."

"Right. So, since things have worked out this far, let's just believe that nothin' bad will happen now." She jerked her pointed chin in Michael's direction. "At least you're here. With the young master. Just as a mother should be."

"A mother." Leila winced. She turned back to her son, who had now rolled on his side and was gumming the soft edges of his blue-and-white blanket. "A mother who's robbed her son of any chance he has for a future."

"Milady! What are you sayin'?"

"You see, Jenny, I never expected this." Leila's voice hitched. "I never thought I would become . . . a mother."

"Well." Jenny's angular cheeks reddened. "'Tis only natural. Every wife should—"

"Natural?" Leila whirled around, a fist clutched to her heaving chest. "No, Jenny. It's not natural. Not when you've been sterilized."

"What?" Jenny recoiled, jaw slack.

A coldness rose up in Leila's gut, wadding itself into a tight iron ball. For a long moment, Jenny, her surroundings, even the glittering lake on the other side of the window faded out of sight, suppressed by a tidal wave of dark memories. Once again, she stood in the narrow corridors of Antwerp's espionage training center, the *Kriegsnachrichtenstelle*.

Once again, she faced a nondescript door outside a medical room in the basement. Faced down the fear that made her wipe her moist palms on her skirt. Today would be the final operation. The first two sessions had been brutal. The recovery had been prolonged. But *this* was what she wanted to do. What she *needed* to do if she wanted to be the best. And she would do anything to be the best.

"They took me into a room with no windows." Leila's voice was quiet. Small. "Dark. It was so dark." She closed her eyes. "I lay down on a steel table. Just like I had done before."

The surgeon had insisted she remove all her clothes from the waist down. The cold had been numbing, permeating her bare skin. "Only one bright light shone down from the ceiling."

That light revealed the gleam of lust in the surgeon's eyes. Only the stoic presence of her mentor, Elsbeth Schneider, kept Leila from leaping off the table, grabbing the vicious needle filled with formaldehyde from the surgeon's hairy paw, and ramming it down his fleshy throat.

But Elsbeth had promised she would remain at her side throughout the entire operation. Once Elsbeth gave her word, Leila knew she would be safe.

"He used ether as his anesthetic." Leila's eyes flickered open. "When I woke up, it was done. I was no longer a woman."

According to the surgeon, the series of injections would produce internal scar tissue that would prevent conception. If the pain was an indication of progress, the treatment was a success indeed.

Jenny's face was the color of bone. "You mean they... But... *why?*"

"I was a spy, Jenny. Did you know that?"

No. Of course Jenny didn't know. Only Malcolm and Thomas knew the full truth of her past. But Leila was beyond caring now.

Jenny's hand flew to her throat. She gawked at Leila, mouth opening and closing wordlessly. "So it was true? What Sir Robert Hughes said when he arrested you last year? It was all true?"

"Yes," Leila said slowly. "I was a German spy. The sterilization process was still new, but my superior wanted it done." She paused, glancing at the floor. "You see ... we often used our bodies to get the information we needed. A procedure like this would prevent unwanted consequences."

Silence spread between the two women. After a moment, Leila looked up. "I can't make excuses for what I did, Jenny. It was wrong. Dead wrong. But God gave me a new beginning, and Michael is my proof that everything is made new."

Bending down, Leila scooped her son into a protective embrace and kissed the fuzz on top of his head. His tufts of hair were a mixture of her own mane of gold and Malcolm's shaggy brown, but his eyes were the same shade of green as her own.

He's perfect, Malcolm. I want you to see him. To hold him. To love him as I love him.

"I-I can see that, milady," Jenny said at last.

"This child is a miracle, Jenny. A miracle in every sense of the word. If Malcolm dies—"

"Please! You mustn't say that."

"I have to consider all possibilities. If my husband dies, Michael will ultimately stand to inherit Northshire Estate." Leila paused again, steeling herself against the dread spawned by the thought of Malcolm's death. But this was her way. To distance herself from the emotion of the moment and impassively consider the facts.

"Forgive me for askin', milady, but can that happen? With us in exile and all?" Jenny bobbed out a quick curtsey. "Beggin' your pardon."

"Don't apologize for speaking your mind, Jenny." As a girl who had grown up in a primal German village, Leila had never accepted the strict hierarchy of British aristocracy. Truth was truth no matter who said it. "Besides, you're right."

"Thank you."

Leila shifted Michael into the crook of her arm. "Elsbeth said a woman could never be both a mother and a spy. Not if she wanted to be the best." She let out a ragged breath. "Because I was determined to be the best, I almost lost my chance to bring life into this world."

"Well, that Elsbeth sounds like a right cheery old dame to me!" Jenny leaned forward, her hands angling like the crooked arms of a teapot on her thin waist. "The sheer cheek of it! I mean, what gives that old crone the right to say what you can and cannot be?"

"I know what I am, Jenny. I am the reason we're in exile. Were it not for my past, Michael would have a future in England." She swallowed. "God alone knows if we'll ever be able to go home."

"Don't think like that, Lady Steele. You really mustn't."

"But it's the truth!" Stepping toward an immense bay window that jutted over the blue waters of Lake Thun, Leila stared out into the distance, the gentle sound of Michael's coos kissing her ears.

For the past year, Leila, Thomas, and two trusted servants from Britain—Jenny and Greyson—had been forced to remain as exiles in Thomas's castle in Switzerland, known as the *Château des Aigles*, or Castle of the Eagles. Thomas had acquired the castle over a decade earlier as a second property, hoping that the pristine alpine climate would help his beloved wife recover her health. He was to be bitterly disappointed.

Leila could endure the exile without complaint. It truly was no hardship. But the real struggle lay in knowing that Northshire Estate was lost to their son. *Because of me.*

Leila let out a deep sigh. "Did I make a mistake, Jenny? Am I wrong to love Malcolm as I do?" Life was complicated. God had forgiven her past, but it seemed that those made in His image would not. One mistake had spawned a litany of consequences that she couldn't outrun no matter how hard she tried.

"'Tis never wrong to love." Jenny stood next to her. "And if Lord Malcolm were here, he'd not abide such words."

"But Lord Malcolm is *not* here." Leila's voice took on a sharp edge. "I owe it to him and to our son to set things right."

Leila rubbed her cheek against the soft top of her son's head, savoring the fragrant mixture of life, hope, and new beginnings. She would not—*could* not—allow him to pay for her sins. Which had led her to this point.

Leila had not been idle during the past year in exile. She had analyzed the situation from multiple angles, poring over the news from the various warring nations. In that time, one thing had become clear. The Great War had shattered her dreams for a future. Only the Great War could rebuild them.

While Leila wanted peace more than anything, the truth was that it offered her a chance to clear her name. If the war ended and London still considered both herself and Thomas to be traitors, the entire Steele family would bear the stain of treason for generations. The possibility of peace was real. Which meant one thing.

"Time is running out," Leila said.

"But there's nothing you can do, milady. You can't fight the whole British government."

Leila stiffened. "For my son, I would fight the whole world."

The first step was to buy credit with the British government. To prove that she was working with them by providing credible information London couldn't afford to ignore. Her mind rolled back to the fateful night when her former handler, Werner Jaëger, had issued her orders.

Leila had been chosen to spearhead a high-profile assassination plot of the Allied leaders should it become clear that the Germans would lose the war. She had passed this information on to the British spymaster Robert Hughes, but he had refused to accept her intelligence as credible.

Leila's brow furrowed. It was likely that the assassination plot—or some version of it—was still alive. It was a contingency plan in which the *Oberste Heeresleitung,* or German High Command, had invested heavily. Now, the German position was more tenuous than ever. The Americans had entered the war, and the newspapers claimed widespread riots rocked Germany from within. But the German army remained strong. Under the direction of an unscrupulous military leader such as General Hindenburg, the possibility of an unsuspected attack on the Allied world was very real indeed.

"Forgive me for askin', milady, but would Lord Malcolm approve of your tryin' to right the wrongs done to your family all alone?" The tips of Jenny's ears turned pink. "He is your husband, after all."

The ghost of a smile touched the corners of Leila's mouth. It was forward of the maid, but Jenny only asked out of concern. Leila knew from personal experience that not all men were as understanding as Malcolm.

"My husband and I work as a team, Jenny," she said. "Each of us supports the other—regardless of the situation. Restoring the family honor *is* Malcolm's duty. But it is also mine. In his absence, I must carry on. But don't worry. I know my husband will approve of my decision."

Her mind shifted back to her original thoughts. It was time. The Allied powers were on the brink of victory—or so they thought. She had to unearth fresh intelligence that would benefit the Allied cause before the war ended. If she provided London with useful information, her success might earn her a small measure of trust. Trust that she could use to pave the road for her son's future.

But Leila would need the backing of the British government. And only one man could give her that—the British prime minister, David Lloyd George. *If* she could somehow convince him that she was a valuable asset to the empire, he might override Hughes's authority.

Lips pursed, Leila turned back to the window. Direct communication with the prime minister was impossible now. She needed an ally. Someone close to him. *Who can I trust?*

Her mind shifted to Thomas's old friend, Lord Curzon. It had been Curzon who had brought her to Switzerland after her release from the Tower. It was Curzon who had managed to carry out Thomas's wishes while keeping his own reputation intact. Of all the men in the prime minister's war council, Curzon was the most likely to consider the plausibility of her innocence. He was also the most likely to present her proposal to the prime minister in a favorable light.

"Well, tears serve no purpose unless they're the seeds of change." Jenny's voice snapped her back to the moment. "'Tis what my mum always said."

"And she was right," Leila said. *Change.* She would ask to spy for Britain in areas under German control. Success could alter everything. "Against all odds, I became a mother. Against all odds, I'll ensure my son has a future."

"What will you do?" Jenny took a step back as though she feared the next words that would leave her mistress's lips.

Lifting her chin, Leila met her gaze. "Change everything."

Chapter 3

Geneva, Switzerland

The room was little more than a small, windowless closet built behind a false concrete wall. Situated at the rear of a dank cellar, it was crowded with empty beer bottles, discarded trash, and rats. The *plop, plop* of leaking sewage echoed in Elsbeth's ears like the tolling echo of a church bell.

Elsbeth knew it was safe here. Despite this morning's murder, no one was looking for *her*. She had lingered in the shadows of the crime scene long enough to determine that Geneva's police didn't have the faintest idea who was behind the woman's death.

It was possible that Thomas would clue them in. Fox that he was, he had gone back to his den, where he would find shelter behind his castle's walls. But if Thomas Steele was a fox, he was a chivalrous one. By now, the upstanding Brit had probably told the police that he believed himself—not the girl—to be the real target.

But Elsbeth wasn't worried. This subterranean shelter would defy the best of police units. Or counterespionage teams for that matter.

She smirked. Even if some overpaid government agent happened to stumble across her safehouse, he would be dead before he could blink twice.

She had done it before.

All the same, Elsbeth refused to light a lamp, choosing to feel her way in the darkness. Only by constant practice could she keep her skills at the cutting edge. And she would need to be at her best for what lay ahead.

She reached for the telephone in the inky blackness. As her fingers kissed its wooden handle, she ignored the silky touch of a rodent that skittered past her calf. After a long silence broken by periods of static, a male voice answered the phone.

"Is it done?"

Elsbeth breathed out a humorless laugh. Already the impatient fool on the other end had broken protocol. "You see, this is precisely why I will never take you as a lover, Hindenburg. You are always in too much of a hurry. What if it wasn't me on the phone? A British or French plant, for instance?"

"You are the only one who can reach me here."

"General, you were born for the brutality of the battlefield. Not the delicate world of espionage. Your predecessor, Werner Jaëger, would not have made such a mistake." She paused, letting the subtle insult work its way into his mind.

Hindenburg scoffed. "Jaëger is dead as you well know. He is hardly a good example. Jaëger failed. That is why I have chosen you to finish the job."

"Werner did not fail to kill Leila Steele because of a lack of skill. He failed because he did not know her as well as I do. Jaëger had to learn the quarry while he was already on the hunt. I, on the other hand, know her as I know myself." Elsbeth's eyes narrowed. "All the same, if you were one of my students, I would have you dismissed."

Hindenburg's voice hardened. "But I am not your student. I am your master. And this is *not* the

Kriegsnachrichtenstelle where you train pretty little women to pull secrets from men. This is war. So do not presume to lecture me, Elsbeth Schneider!"

"My master?" Her laughter bounced off the concrete walls. "If you were my master, I would obey you."

"And so you shall!"

Elsbeth didn't reply, choosing instead to reach across the narrow bed—the only furniture in the room—and unclasp the hinge of her pocketbook. Her fingers groped for a slim packet of Russian cigarettes, which she lit in the darkness with practiced ease. The shadows were her home, a refuge from which she dealt death to those unfortunate enough to know her.

"*Hallo?*"

Elsbeth sucked in a deep breath, letting the smoke build up in her mouth before breathing it out again.

"*Hallo?*" Hindenburg's voice was tight with fury.

Still she waited, enjoying the tidal wave of Hindenburg's anger. Like a siren, Elsbeth lived to toy with men, manipulating their emotions with the skill of a puppet master. It was this unique ability and her penchant for discipline that had earned her the rank of lieutenant in Germany's army.

Elsbeth mentally calculated the rising arc of Hindenburg's emotions. He was about to give in to his anger. A few moments later, when the storm of his emotional energy was spent, he would realize berating her was useless. Then she would mold him to her will.

"*Fräulein*, you would do well to remember that I am the Kaiser's right hand."

And yet you and the other generals are conspiring against him?

Elsbeth decided not to reveal her knowledge of his secret plans. Instead, she exhaled again, loud enough for him to hear.

"I am a man of considerable influence."

Elsbeth cocked her head to one side. The slight quaver in his voice could only mean that he was giving in. Already. *He continues to disappoint me.*

"All right, all right. Have it your way. I will follow your ridiculous protocol." Hindenburg grated out a sigh. "It seems that the weather has been unpredictable lately."

Elsbeth's lips curved upward as he muttered the prescribed phrase. This wasn't about protocol. It was about ensuring that he understood she would only play the game if he agreed to her rules.

"We've seen our share of storms this past week."

"Really?" Hindenburg's voice had the enthusiasm of a tombstone. "How strange. So have we."

"Now that wasn't so difficult, General, was it?"

"Is it done?" He ignored her taunt, repeating his question.

"No."

Static crackled on the line. "And why not? My orders weren't clear?"

"I missed."

"What?" Hindenburg spit out the word like a curse. "Since when does Elsbeth Schneider miss her target?"

Elsbeth cradled the receiver between her head and shoulder while reaching into a little pocket just above her left breast. Retrieving a small dart, she followed the sound of the shuffling rat, then flicked her wrist forward.

Schlunk. The sound of metal piercing a small body. A series of sharp squeaks split the air. Seconds later, the noise died.

"Elsbeth Schneider misses whenever she likes."

"You *let* Thomas live?"

"Yes." Elsbeth moved the receiver away from her ear, anticipating his bellow.

"Why? You told me he would be dead within two days."

"So I lied," she said. "It's a most convenient habit. You should try it some time."

"Listen to me, *Fräulein*. Thomas Steele sabotaged our country's pending agreement with Russia. Were it not for his meddling, this war would already be over. Our armies would be victorious." He paused just long enough to suck in a short breath. "I want both Thomas and his daughter-in-law dead!"

Elsbeth rolled her eyes. Not for the first time, she realized that the supreme commander of Germany's army had positively no imagination.

"If I killed Thomas, Leila would be on her guard. She's no fool, Hindenburg, no matter what you think."

"So what did you do? Besides lie to me?"

"I killed someone else instead. Thomas is a clever man. He'll realize the bullet was meant for him. That will set his nerves on edge."

"What good does that do?"

"Men who are afraid make mistakes. Don't worry, General. He'll soon be dead." Elsbeth adopted a patronizing tone as though he were indeed her student. "Thomas will soon go to London where the jackals that run the British parliament will tear him to shreds."

"What do you mean?"

"I saw him in the park today with Arthur Hoffmann."

"What of it?"

"I was close enough to hear them speak. Arthur handed Thomas a copy of the National *Zeitung* and advised him to read a specific article. I got my hands on a copy. Britain has signed the *Deprivation of Titles Act* into law." Elsbeth paused to draw again on her cigarette.

"Explain."

Elsbeth leaned back against the rough wall, relishing the feel of the coarse stone beneath her thin, gray cotton shirt. "Under the Act, those perceived as being enemies of the Crown will lose their status as a peer of the realm. Anyone charged with such a crime must appear in a British court to defend himself or lose everything."

"Do you think Thomas is a fool? Why would he leave the security of Switzerland to face trial in England?"

"You're not listening." Elsbeth heaved an exasperated sigh. "Under the Act, all property belonging to enemies of the state becomes the property of the government unless the accused appears *in person* for trial."

This time the silence was on his end.

"So you see, my *master* . . ." She let the sarcasm in her voice linger before continuing, "Thomas, who loves his little country estate more than his life, will have no choice but to trot off to England and stand trial. Otherwise his name will go down in infamy. His heirs will be left with nothing. It was quite a clever move on Arthur's part."

Elsbeth extinguished the cigarette and rolled it beneath her bare heel. The sting of the burn made her spine tingle.

"Fine!" Hindenburg acquiesced. "Let Thomas die at the hands of his own people. But the girl must be silenced."

"Kill the girl and you get rid of your greatest asset."

"Asset?" Hindenburg barked out a laugh. "She is married to a British officer. She has turned her back on all that is German. How could she possibly be an asset?"

"Because Leila Steele is unlike any woman I have ever trained."

Hindenburg snorted. "You mean, you don't want to accept the fact that you've been tossed aside for marriage and family."

A muscle worked in Elsbeth's jaw. "Believe me, Hindenburg, I have taken the lives of men while they slept in my bed. If I decide Leila must die, I will put a bullet in her brain myself."

"What is your plan?"

"I will give her a chance to return to the fold. Eventually, she will either see the light or die."

"And the advantage to our cause?"

"She has her husband's trust. Leila's father-in-law adores her. Logic says Leila will want to earn the trust of the British government so she can end her exile in Switzerland. She's perfectly placed to achieve our larger goals."

"With all that in her mind, how do you expect to command her obedience?" Hindenburg demanded.

"Leave that to me, General." Despite her flippant approach, Elsbeth knew well that she needed Hindenburg's permission to alter the plan. She had humbled him. Now, it was time to give him something in return.

Elsbeth lowered her voice to a throaty whisper, the kind that would make him wish she were within reach instead of a thousand kilometers away. "My master, do I have your permission?"

Chapter 4

Château des Aigles, Switzerland

Dawn found Thomas in the same clothes he had worn the previous day, still clutching the paper with which Arthur Hoffman had shattered his world. The scope of Arthur's retaliation wasn't surprising. Given the nature of Thomas's own actions against him, it was only natural that Hoffman form an alliance with Robert Hughes to bring down a common enemy. What *did* surprise Thomas was his willingness to walk this road, knowing it could only lead to a dead end.

Forking a hand through his silver hair, Thomas turned to an oblong mirror that hung above a dark cherrywood dresser. Shoulders slumped beneath an unseen weight. His eyes were bleary, his face pale. But the mirror's observations could only go so far. His reflection could not show the emotional price of exile. Northshire was part of his soul. It would always be his home.

Not only mine.

It was Malcolm's home. One day it would belong to his grandson, little Michael. The generations to come should not be cheated of their heritage by the capricious nature of feeble men.

Thomas straightened slowly. The battle for Northshire could only be waged in England. He had left active service decades ago. But the call to battle sounded once more.

Thomas jerked his chin downward in a sharp nod. "So be it."

Harold Greyson rarely found himself at loss for words. But looking at his master, Greyson found that for once speech was impossible. Thomas had shaved his beard. His salt-and-pepper hair and eyebrows were now a dark shade of brown.

Instead of the tweed suit Greyson had prepared the night before, Thomas wore a pair of dingy, gray overalls that covered most of a stained pale shirt. A worn, dark French beret slouched at a low angle above Thomas's creased brow. Black, scuffed boots disappeared beneath the frayed cuffs of his pants.

"Amazing what a change of clothes and some hair coloring can do to a man, isn't it?" Thomas stuffed his military uniform—one worn only on the most formal of occasions—into a black carpetbag, then snapped the clasps shut.

He pulled off his hat and Greyson flinched. The corners of Thomas's eyes were tinged with red. Shadows darkened his eyelids as though he had not slept. A thin sheen of sweat hung over a face set in rigid lines.

But although his eyes were bloodshot, they blazed with a vehemence Greyson had not seen since the last time Thomas left for war in India.

"A-are you quite well, Your Lordship?"

"Come inside, Greyson. Shut the door."

Hesitating only a moment, the butler stepped through the threshold into Thomas's bedroom.

"I'm going on a journey," Thomas said simply.

"A journey?" Greyson's brow furrowed. "Forgive me your Lordship, but I must have forgotten. How careless of me! If you will give me just a few moments, I will—"

"No, old friend." Thomas shook his head, his expression showing regret. "The fault is not yours. This trip has come up rather unexpectedly."

"I see." Greyson considered this, disliking the uncharacteristic nervousness that turned his stomach into knots almost as much as he disliked his master's evasiveness. "Will you travel alone?"

Thomas hesitated, glanced at a gilded portrait of his late wife, Isabella, then turned back to Greyson. "Yes."

"Are you certain, Your Lordship? It will only take a few minutes to be ready." Greyson suppressed a shudder. The note of resignation in Thomas's voice hinted that something was happening, something that would shatter the fragile tranquility they had salvaged thus far.

"I am." Pulling in a deep breath, Thomas laid a firm hand upon his shoulder. "But I will need your help."

"Of course, Your Lordship. You have only to ask."

Reaching into the breast pocket of his dark blue jacket, Thomas retrieved a few pages of a newspaper. It had been meticulously folded and folded again as if the pages contained some secret his master wished to keep contained. "I'm going home, Greyson."

"Home, Your Lordship?"

"Back to England." Thomas motioned for him to take the paper. "Parliament's passed a decree. In brief, I must face trial on British soil or lose Northshire."

"I see."

I see? What exactly do I see? That if his master faced trial, nothing short of divine intervention would keep him alive. That if Thomas died, Leila would hold herself responsible for the rest of her life. *I see.* Two innocuous words that could not remotely express the sudden turmoil in Greyson's heart.

Greyson cleared his throat. "When . . . when can we anticipate your return?" The question needed asking if only to evoke some semblance of normality.

Thomas didn't answer. "Contact Joseph Mara," he said. "Let him know I'll make my way to his home in London after lying low in Dover for a few days."

"Of course, Your Lordship." Greyson dipped his head, as much in deference as to hide the moisture that collected in the corners of his eyes. When he was sure his emotions were in check, he looked up. "I presume, Your Lordship, that the guards you've engaged will remain during your absence?"

"Of course. Five men in a place this size doesn't sit easily with me, Greyson. Not after today. God knows I wish I could have taken on more. But the Swiss government is our only ally at the moment." Thomas's lips twitched. "We don't want them thinking we're raising some sort of an army on their soil, now do we?"

"Indeed, Your Lordship."

Thomas moved for the door but paused. "There's a note for Leila in my office. Don't wake her. It's better this way."

"Of . . . of course."

"Take care of her, Greyson. Outside of Malcolm, there's no one I trust more than you."

Greyson bowed slowly. "I am honored by your trust."

Thomas extended his hand. "Thank you. For everything."

"An honor." Greyson gripped it with his own liver-spotted hand. "But—forgive me Your Lordship—is there something *I* can do? Northshire has been my home for forty years, you know. I'd like to be of assistance, but all this cloak-and-dagger activity seems rather dodgy, if I might say so."

The corners of Thomas's mouth turned up, if only slightly. "You will hear from me when I need you. Give Leila and little Michael my love, will you?"

"Of course."

Thomas's glance shifted from his steward to the painting of his wife. "In the end, Greyson, all that matters is that we have loved. Not only have I loved, but I have been loved in return. Nothing means more than that."

Without another word, he passed through the doorway, strode down the long hall, and stepped outside into the morning light.

Chapter 5

Château des Aigles, Switzerland

Leila lurched upright. Filtered sunlight streamed in through a window on her right. It was bright. Too bright.

What time is it? Twisting, she craned her neck to see a grandfather clock in the corner. *Half past seven.* Normally, she was up before dawn. But writing various drafts of her letter to Lord Curzon had kept her awake long into the night.

Sitting up again, Leila swung her legs off the side of her oversized poster bed, then padded over to a small water closet in the far corner of the room. Her bladder ached. A few moments later, she ran her hands beneath a stream of cold water from an ivory-handled faucet, then walked over to the window.

The glittering waters of Lake Thun reflected the azure of a clear sky. As she watched, a gust of wind tossed handfuls of leaves into the air, scattering them like miniature boats onto the lake. Life was full of change. Just a few weeks had robbed the trees of their lush foliage. Perhaps the time for change had now come to her as well.

The sleeves of her white cotton nightgown ended just below her shoulders. Leila rubbed her bare arms as a slight chill worked its way from the window, raising the pores on her skin.

"*Nutze den Tag,*" she said. *Seize the day.*

Turning from the window, Leila changed into the lavender skirt, white vest, and amethyst cardigan that Jenny had laid out the night before. Then she slipped toward the door that opened into a hallway of gray stone. The hall separated her room from Michael's nursemaid. At its far end stood a second door of heavy oak.

The castle had been built in a time where lords and ladies held full expectation of their own privacy—and offered none to their servants. All the locks were therefore on Leila's side of the door.

"Gretna?" Leila rapped on the door. "Is it all right to come in?"

There was no response.

After a moment, Leila slid back the second latch and pulled the door open. The room was empty.

Making her way back to her own room, Leila stepped outside into the castle's main corridor. "Gretna?"

A short, wiry man at the far end of the hall—one of Thomas's new hires—turned. He began walking toward her.

Her gaze swept over him, registering details with each step. A navy-blue uniform with four dark buttons down its center. Polished black shoes. A holstered gun—most likely a Luger. Hair that grayed at the temples and faint crowfeet in the corners of his eyes indicated he was too old for the current draft. Some former servicemembers who were past the age of active service made a living hiring themselves out as private security.

"Is everything all right, Lady Steele?" The guard slowed to a halt.

"Yes, everything is fine," she said. "It's just that my child's wetnurse doesn't seem to be anywhere around."

"Why don't you stay here while I look for her downstairs? The less you move about, the better. In a castle this size, you never know where danger could be lurking."

Leila tilted her head to one side. "Hans, isn't it?"

"At your service." Hans clicked his heels together and snapped out a sharp salute.

A faint smile tugged at the corners of Leila's mouth. She appreciated his enthusiasm. Though since Switzerland hadn't been involved in any war for almost seventy years, she couldn't help but wonder how prepared he was for action. Should the need arise.

"Thank you, Hans," she said. "But I'd rather get her myself."

Leila eased her way down the wide staircase. She appreciated Thomas's heightened security, more for his sake than her own. While Thomas hated to admit it, there was no denying that age and hardship had taken their toll. He had only barely survived the recent attempt on his life. As far as they knew, the assassin was still at large.

Her brow furrowed. Where *was* Thomas? Or Greyson for that matter?

At the bottom of the stairs, she turned left and made her way toward the butler's office. The castle staff had traditionally been kept to a minimum as Thomas had never lived permanently on the grounds prior to his exile. After relocating to Switzerland, he had still refused to take on more personnel than was absolutely necessary.

Both he and Leila were high-profile targets on the lists of both the British and German governments. Acquiring staff in a foreign country could expose them to risks that neither wanted.

The low murmur of voices in hushed conversation drew her toward Thomas's office.

"I tell you I've only seen such a look on his face once before."
Greyson's voice wafted toward her.

Jenny spoke next, her own voice shrill. "When?"

"In India. Just before he walked outside a fortress to face
an army of violent rebels singlehanded. But this time it was
worse." Greyson sighed. "Mark my words, this is no ordinary
journey His Lordship has taken."

Leila's heart stopped. *Thomas is gone?* In Britain, he had
often left on short notice. But the stench of treason had not
clung to him then. Rounding the corner, Leila spoke without
preamble.

"Where has he gone, Grayson?"

Three heads pivoted in unison toward her. Michael cooed
contentedly in Gretna's arms, his eyes wide and a pudgy finger
stuck in the corner of his mouth.

"Lady Steele!" Jenny swung wide eyes from her to Grayson
and back again.

Leila ignored her, focusing on an open newspaper in Grayson's
hand. "Let me see it," she said.

Without a word, the butler handed over the paper. Suppressing
a shiver, Leila pulled the sides of her white cardigan closer
together, then took the paper. She skimmed through the details,
her heart sinking lower with each word. Their meaning was clear.

The implications were even clearer.

"Dear God," she breathed.

Leila turned away. Moving toward the window, she gazed
out at the lake. The waters no longer glistened. Instead, small,
choppy waves scudded by in chaotic lines of white froth, propelled
by brisk wind.

Thoughts sped through her mind like bullets, each a merciless
reality.

One. She was the reason Thomas was in this predicament.

Two. Although he was skilled at evasion, it was only a matter of time before Thomas was caught. Truth be told, the only way to retain his hold on Northshire was to give himself up and stand trial. Which led Leila to her final, inevitable conclusion.

Three. Thomas was going to die. She slammed her eyelids shut. But an image of Thomas being led before a firing squad battered its way into a deep corner of her mind.

Silence swelled in the room behind her. Pulling in a deep breath, Leila opened her eyes and turned. "Greyson, bring in the remainder of the staff."

"At once," he said.

When Greyson had gone, Jenny stepped closer. "A letter from Mr. Mara, Lady Steele," she said in a low voice. It was only then that Leila noticed the small silver tray in her maid's hand. On its smooth surface was a small letter in a cream envelope.

"It's addressed to His Lordship, but seein' as he's not here . . ."

Leila's mouth went dry. Could it be news of the worst kind?

Then her eyes swiveled to the center of the envelope just below the castle address. *There!* A miniscule cross, drawn to look like the stray mark of a pen, revealed that the sender was not Joseph Mara at all.

"Thank you, Jenny." Leila resisted the urge to snatch up the envelope. Keeping her voice emotionless, she calmly lifted the letter from the tray and slipped it into a thin pocket of her lavender skirt.

Greyson returned, followed by the remainder of the staff. In the absence of the Steele men, the staff would look to her for leadership.

"His Lordship is gone," Leila said simply. "We trust he will return to us shortly. I ask you all to remain vigilant. Remember, a killer is on the loose. He may come here, hoping to finish what he started."

She looked at Hans, the leader of the security team. He shifted his feet but held her gaze. Again, Leila wondered if he had ever drawn his weapon in a moment of crisis, let alone used it. "Be alert but do not be afraid. All will be well in the end."

＊＊●＊＊

Elsbeth Schneider coasted her bicycle off the main road and onto the narrow path that marked the entrance to the trail snaking upward to Thomas Steele's castle. Perched on top of the mountain, it sat apart from the world of mortals. She smirked. It was a precarious position.

From a practical standpoint, Elsbeth could see the wisdom of Thomas's decision to own property in Switzerland. Her mind spun through the facts that surrounded the British tycoon.

Over the past thirty years, Thomas had used his vast wealth to develop a string of manufacturing plants in Switzerland. His factories specialized in the fields of metallurgy and precision engineering. He employed at least a thousand Swiss workers in various cantons across the small country.

Elsbeth clucked her tongue. "So although your mother country wants you dead, you still have economic value to Switzerland."

With a wary glance down the empty road, Elsbeth pedaled into the shade of a leafy scrub oak. Dismounting, she wheeled her bicycle behind the tree.

A thrill of adrenaline shot through her as she checked her rucksack once more. Dark clothing, mask, and a small assortment of weapons met her experienced eyes. Tonight marked a milestone in her career. Elsbeth had trained dozens of women. Some had succeeded and others not. But to win back a spy who had fallen from grace? *That* took the art of persuasion to a whole new level.

Nestling against the tree trunk, Elsbeth focused on her prodigy-turned-prodigal. Leila was the kind of woman who had untold potential.

Withdrawing a pair of high-powered, dark binoculars, Elsbeth began a meticulous examination of her target. From her vantage point, she had an unobstructed view of the castle's gate and southern points of entry.

"That's the problem with big houses." She lowered the binoculars, shaking her head. "Simply too many doors and windows to guard."

Four soldiers, garbed in the dark-blue uniform of Switzerland's active militia, or *Landsturm,* leaned idly against the wrought-iron gate at the base of the hill. Switzerland's government might be neutral, but it was clearly willing to protect its financial benefactor. It was also rumored Thomas had hired private security after the attempt on his life.

Leaning back against the base of the tree, Elsbeth pulled a small notebook and pencil from her pocket on which she sketched her planned invasion. As she did, her mind rolled back through the years, analyzing her memories of Leila. Physical combat training. Intense lessons in observation, deductive reasoning, and assassination. They had all transformed the emotional wreck into a deadly beauty.

Elsbeth grunted. Perhaps there had been a grain of truth to Hindenburg's accusation. Her pride had been hurt when Leila abandoned the cause. And for as stupid a reason as *marriage?*

Bile rose in the back of Elsbeth's throat. But still, there was the chance that Leila could be redeemed. Hindenburg was a butcher. He couldn't understand. Killing Leila would mean a waste of both time and talent. No, Leila's murder was only to be considered if there was no other choice.

Her mind shifted back to the plan. A few strategic questions posed to the right people had yielded a goldmine of information about the daily operations of the Steele household. Leila used a wet nurse for her infant son. Elsbeth's lips curved upward as she put the finishing touches on her plan.

"Yes, that will do nicely." She settled back among the tree's roots, secure in the knowledge that her plan was simple, practical, and diabolical.

Elsbeth smiled. All she needed to do now was wait. Wait until the night swallowed the day and unleashed her true potential.

Chapter 6

Château des Aigles, Switzerland

"Will you need anythin' else, Lady Steele?" Jenny primped a white pillow one last time, then stepped back from the bed. The room was largely empty, almost spartan. There was only a bed—made too large by Malcolm's absence—a nightstand, a looming armoire, and Leila's writing desk. Thick rugs helped thwart the chill of the oncoming winter.

"No," Leila said. "I'm fine. Thank you, Jenny."

Jenny shivered as thunder reverberated across the sky. "Ooh. I think we'll have a bad one tonight and make no mistake about it!"

"We'll be fine, Jenny. It's just another storm in the mountains." Leila tried to hide the impatience in her voice. Malcolm's letter burned in her pocket, begging to be read.

"Right." The maid rubbed her hands together, then dipped out a slight curtsey. "Well, good night, then."

As soon as the heavy door swung shut, Leila strode over and slid the bolt into place. Then, pivoting, she hurried to her cherrywood writing desk and pulled the letter free. Her desk was free of clutter, just as she preferred. Clear spaces made for a clear mind. And she needed that more now than ever.

Opening the bottom right drawer of her desk, Leila slipped her fingers into a set of slight grooves on either side and tugged upward until the false bottom came free. Then, removing a silver key that dangled lightly around a thin chain on her neck, Leila slid it into a miniature keyhole at the bottom of the drawer.

The compartment's lock slid back with a soft *click*, and she withdrew a small, dark gray notebook.

Then she picked up the letter. For a moment, she just held it close to her heart. It was from him. From Malcolm. Inhaling slowly, she closed her eyes, remembering her husband's scent and the security she felt whenever he wrapped his strong arms around her body.

"I need you, Malcolm," Leila whispered. "I need you." Slowly, she opened her eyes, leaving the fantasy and accepting cold reality. Malcolm wasn't here but at least she had a letter from him.

Her gaze snapped to the cream envelope. Leaning over, Leila pulled a bronze-hilted letter opener—a small dagger, really—from the drawer. The sharp blade sliced through the envelope.

She pulled out a few sheets of cream paper, her trained eyes scanning for the telltale marks Malcolm knew to include. An extra comma halfway through the seventh and tenth line. A double period three-quarters of the way through the fifteenth. *Yes, it's from him.*

Satisfied now, Leila set the letter down on the desk and eased into a chair. Wiping her palms on her skirt, she pulled in a deep breath, then flipped open the notebook to a clean page and began to decode Malcolm's hidden message.

"My good friend, Thomas . . ." She muttered softly as she worked. As she had told Jenny, Malcolm couldn't write to her—at least not openly. So they had devised a simple yet effective system that would slip beneath the radar of anyone in British intelligence.

Malcolm wrote to Joseph Mara, who oversaw the family's business and legal affairs. Knowing that his letters would be opened by the censorship department—and that he was already at the top of Robert Hughes's watchlist—Malcolm restricted his letters to casual enquiries about the estate. However, Joseph Mara knew that every third line of Malcolm's letters was to be copied verbatim and included in his own correspondence to Thomas.

Specific letters of the transcribed words came together using a cipher combination that Leila and Malcolm had devised. Though Malcolm's letter was written in English, the cipher translated his words into French—a language in which they were both fluent.

"*Femme de mes rêves.*" Leila paused, resting her forehead on the heel of her palm. After all they had been through, despite the litany of hurt and betrayals, Malcolm still thought of her as the woman of his dreams. She worked feverishly now, desperate to know his thoughts.

The castle was quiet. The room was still. Only the gentle swaying of the pendulum in the grandfather clock, the scratching of the pen, and the rustling of the paper she held broke the silence.

There were occasional oddities. A few incomplete fragments she had to finish. Some words were missing letters. But the message was a treasure. Finally, Leila straightened, replaced her notebook in the drawer, and examined her work.

Woman of my dreams. Each day apart from you and our son is torment. I am alive, which is to say I am well, unlike too many others. I have been hit in the head by some shrapnel, but it is nothing serious.

The pa—

Leila sat straight in her chair as the groan of a footstep on a floorboard reached her ears. Her fingers curled over the hilt of the letter opener as she dimmed the light of the lamp. *One of the guards on patrol?*

She waited immobile, her eyes glued to the heavy door for several seconds.

Nothing.

Relaxing her hold on the knife, Leila shifted her attention back to Malcolm's letter.

The papers are full of news about Parliament's latest edict. I'm sure Father realizes it's a trap, but I'm worried he'll go anyway. Tell him to remain in Switzerland. Northshire is not worth his life.

She put the letter down slowly. "You're too late, Malcolm. We were both too late."

Do your best not to worry. I am safe. This war will be over soon. God will bring us all together again.

I love you forever.

Rising, Leila devoured the letter once more with her eyes. Then, gathering both the original letter and her translation she held the papers over the edge of the lamp. This was always the hardest part. Walking to the fireplace, she tossed the blazing papers inside and watched as the licking flames turned everything to ashes.

"It would have done no good, Malcolm," she whispered. Once Thomas made up his mind, there was no changing it. Thomas was a warrior. He would die before abandoning the field without a fight.

Thunder rumbled, closer now. It was a slow-moving storm, one that blanketed the air with a heavy fog this high in the mountains. Once, long ago, she might have feared it.

But life had hardened her. Like the flames before her, Elsbeth's brutal training had consumed whatever lingering tenderness she had possessed, leaving only a shell of a woman buried in its cold embers. It had been Malcolm who stirred her will to love . . . to live once more.

But life was a fickle blessing that demanded everything and sometimes still more. Times like these called for strength. The strength to face challenges that were sometimes unseen yet were always felt. The strength that had faith as its source.

So Leila no longer feared the storm.

She stepped to the large window, questions humming through her mind. *God, what can I do to save Thomas's life?*

Her room stood high above the lake. From this viewpoint, she could see clearly-defined shadows cast by the overarching mountains as thick bolts of lightning shattered the night.

Leila tapped the sharp edge of the blade against her palm. "Am I making the right choice?" She had sent the letter to Curzon this morning. "Do I—"

A clap of thunder pulsed through the room, but not before Leila heard the dull *click* of the bolt on her door slide back. The lock had been opened from the outside!

Pivoting, Leila instantly dropped into a crouch, hiding the bulk of her body behind the wooden bedframe. Grasping the blade by the hilt, she darted toward the desk and snuffed out the lamp just as the door eased open.

Someone was in her room.

"Good, Leila. *Good.*" The voice was a sinuous whisper that turned Leila's blood to ice. The door settled into place with a heavy thud. "I'm so relieved to see you haven't forgotten everything I taught you."

Impossible.

But there was no time to consider. Leila shifted away from the window, then slashed the hem of her nightgown open to mid-thigh so she could move unhindered.

Elsbeth?

"Did you think that your past died with Werner?" Elsbeth's mocking voice drifted toward Leila from the right. "Or did you really imagine that a few walls and that pathetic gaggle of men outside could stop me from reaching you?"

She's near Gretna's room!

Dread slowed Leila's heart to a crawl. Scrambling to her feet, she shifted left. To speak would be to reveal her location. But at all costs, Leila had to draw Elsbeth away from her child.

"You killed them?" Leila said. It was more of a statement than a question.

"Only two. You see, I'm working on my self-control." While the darkness hid Elsbeth's face, the sound of her voice kept moving. "The rest have no idea that I'm here. I imagine they'll find the bodies in a few days."

Like a frenetic spider, Leila's mind spun through possibilities. The ancient stone walls, thick carpets, and heavy bedroom door of her spacious room would shut in most of whatever noise she might make.

The storm outside had now begun in earnest. No one would hear a thing.

Hans, the guard, might be outside at the far end of the hall—assuming he wasn't dead of course. But, calling for help would mean leaving Elsbeth with free access to Gretna's room . . . and Michael.

"I'm a new woman, Elsbeth. Everything from the past is dead."

"So I hear." The voice sounded from behind her. Leila ducked, then slammed her elbow backward. Elsbeth's fist shot above her head, but Leila's own attack was blocked by Elsbeth's other forearm. "But I don't believe it."

Elsbeth's fingers coiled around her wrist. A muted cry slipped past Leila's lips as the other woman jerked her backward. "You see, Leila, I heard rumors that you became religious when you abandoned our cause. But I believe all this talk of changed allegiances is just that—talk."

Elsbeth yanked harder on her arm. The blade clattered to the ground. Elsbeth kicked it to one side. "Deep down, the real Leila is just biding her time. Deep down, she's just waiting for the right *push* to bring her back to the top." Elsbeth flung her wrist outward, sending Leila staggering forward. The side of Leila's head slammed against the bedpost.

Leila rose, chest heaving. Adrenaline pulsed through her. Gingerly, she probed her temple. A trickle of warm blood moistened her fingertips. She pushed past the fury that coiled like a ball of fire in her chest, letting her mind rip through the years to the endless sparring matches with Elsbeth.

Be where you're not expected. Do what shouldn't be done. Everything with Elsbeth was backward. If she feinted left, she would strike with her right fist. If she struck at your feet, her real target was the head.

"You're wrong." Leila had to keep Elsbeth talking so she could pinpoint her location in the room. "Everything *is* different now." Thunder exploded, bringing with it an echo of Elsbeth's laughter.

47

"Really? Somehow I'm not convinced." Lightning flashed, illuminating the sneer on the other woman's face.

In an instant, Leila was there.

Leila flung her forearm upward, blocking Elsbeth's jab. Scooped up the blade with her left hand. She swung the blade towards Elsbeth's ribs. Elsbeth caught her wrist mid-swing and wrenched it from Leila's grasp.

"Too slow, Leila," she taunted. "Time away has made you soft." Elsbeth tucked the blade into a belt at her side and dropped into an orthodox fighter's stance.

Leila shook her head. If Elsbeth put the knife away, it could only mean one thing. "You're not here to kill me."

"If I were, you'd already be a corpse."

"Then what do you want?" Leila edged a few steps to the right. "I told you, I'm done with the Fatherland."

Elsbeth clucked her tongue. "You thought you were the exception to the rule."

"What rule?"

"Oh, you remember. Motherhood isn't for us."

"You were wrong. The sterilization failed." Ducking, Leila slammed her fist forward, following the blow up with a sharp chop to Elsbeth's neck. The woman's winded gasp flooded her with a cold satisfaction.

Elsbeth staggered backward. Taking advantage of the situation, Leila planted her left foot on the ground, then swung out in a front kick. But in that moment, Elsbeth shifted.

"Oh, you managed to conceive," Elsbeth said, panting slightly. "But to what purpose? Your child will always be an outcast. A grandfather who's a traitor? A mother who's a foreign spy? You know the British can't let go of anything. Society will hate him after the war."

"I'll find a way."

Elsbeth stepped into Leila's reach. Slamming her fists into Leila's abdomen, she sent her former protégé sprawling backward. "And your son will hate *you* when he's old enough to understand."

The words ripped into Leila's heart, in part because she knew they were true. Unless she altered the present, Michael would have no future.

"And what about you, Elsbeth?" Leila lashed back, each muscle in her body contracted as she stalked forward. "What will the world say about you when this is all over? I'll tell you what they'll say—nothing! No one will even know you existed."

"Oh, I'll leave my mark on history. But you've already scarred your son." Elsbeth's laughter dripped scorn. "You ruined his life just by being you. It would've been better if you *had* been sterilized."

"Enough words!" Leila snapped. She ducked as she leaped forward. Punched. Jabbed. Lightning flickered, providing just enough scattered light to illuminate the room while thunder roared above.

Elsbeth staggered back, then spun left, slapping Leila's throat with the back of her hand. As Leila reeled, Elsbeth placed her ankle behind her opponent's heel, sending her crashing to the ground.

"Well done. Well done indeed." Elsbeth's words coiled around Leila's mind. The voice was calm. Too calm. "Nothing has changed." Fire glinted off the edge of Leila's letter opener as Elsbeth slipped it from her belt and pressed it against Leila's throat. "You see? The evil. It's still inside you."

"I will never . . . serve Germany again," Leila grunted out as she squirmed beneath Elsbeth's iron grasp.

"Won't you? You've forgotten something." Elsbeth's even teeth gleamed in the demonic firelight. "Collateral."

Michael! The thought slammed into Leila's mind with the mercy of a freight train. "Leave my son out of this!" She lurched upward, ready to tear into Elsbeth again, but the pressure on the knife increased.

"Stay down!"

"Why, Elsbeth? Tell me why!"

"Because I know your true worth, Leila." Elsbeth's voice hardened. "You're my creation. Mine! And I'll not let Britain—or Christ—destroy what I've spent years building."

"I owe you *nothing!*" Leila spat out through clenched teeth.

"You owe me everything. You're a child of the shadows."

"You sold your soul to evil."

"Evil? Oh, that's rich! I saved you." Elsbeth bared her teeth. "You came to me, broken after the husband who tried to kill you ended up dead! But I saw strength behind the pain in your eyes. Cunning behind your tears."

"You just wanted someone you could use. Someone to build your empire. Well I'm not her. Not anymore!"

"Think what you like." Elsbeth ground out the words. "But I'm saving you from *yourself*, Leila. And if you can't see it now, you will. One day you'll understand."

In a sharp movement, Elsbeth flipped the blade around and slammed its bronze hilt into Leila's temple.

Leila felt her jaw working. Felt her mouth struggling to protest. Heard a distant groan that sounded like a foggy echo of her voice. Then, unable to stop herself, she slumped downward. Into the waiting arms of the abyss.

Chapter 7

Château des Aigles, Switzerland

"**L**ady Steele? Wake up. Lady Steele!"

The voice, so familiar yet so foreign, wooed her back to the land of the living. Blinking, Leila slowly pushed herself upright, wincing at the thunder in her skull.

"Greyson?" Daylight filtered through the curtains on her window. Her brow furrowed. Why was she on the floor?

"Thank God you're all right." The butler pressed a cup against her lips. His hands trembled. "Here, drink this."

Leila tasted the bitter mixture, then pushed it away. "What . . . happened?" It was more an unintelligible groan than a coherent question.

"You had a visitor in the night." It was Jenny's voice, but something was different. It was sad. Quiet.

"A visitor?" Leila frowned for a moment. Memories flooded her mind, barging past her disorientation and pain.

"Michael!" She swayed as she shoved herself upright, waving off Jenny's arm. "Michael?" Leila staggered toward the gaping hallway that led to Gretna's room.

"No, Your Ladyship, don't go in there, I beg you!" Greyson stepped forward, but she stopped him with a glare. The door to the corridor between her room and Gretna's swung open with a dismal groan as though reluctant to reveal its dark secret.

Hushed male voices came from inside the wetnurse's room, but they died as Leila appeared on the doorway. Leila's eyes rolled over the room.

Five of Thomas's security guards crowded the small space. Their drooping shoulders and averted faces triggered an alarm in the back of Leila's skull. But there was no broken furniture, no smashed windows. Everything was as it should be—everything except Gretna's corpse.

The young woman's body lay prostrate on her bed. Her caramel eyes stared vacantly at the ceiling. A pool of dark blood congealed below a neat hole in her skull.

"Michael?" Leila's eyes skittered toward a bassinet in the corner of the room. She leaped toward it. *Empty.*

Panic threatened to choke her. She swallowed, eyes shifting from the dead woman to the bed in which her son should be lying. "Where is he?"

"W-we've looked everywhere, Your Ladyship," one of the men spoke up. "I'm afraid your son is . . . nowhere to be found."

Leila opened her mouth, then closed it without saying a word. *Michael's gone. I let her take him.*

"I've already questioned the staff, Lady Steele," Greyson spoke up from the door. "What with that storm last night, no one saw or heard anything."

"Hans, our leader, is gone too," another guard said. "Him and Lars. The pair of them have gone missing."

"Start in the cellar." Leila's voice was cold. Detached. Odd, given that the only thing she wanted to do was scream herself hoarse. "If you don't find him there, check every closet. Or beneath every staircase with enough space to fit a corpse."

"A-are you saying—?"

"Get out," Leila said. "Just . . . just leave."

Sucking in a deep breath, she closed her eyes until the last of them exited the room, muttering their feeble apologies. She couldn't stand the sight of them. They had failed to protect her son. But so had she. And that hurt worst of all.

Michael gone? In those few seconds, Leila teetered on the brink of insanity. How could she rationalize the impossible? How could she deny the truth? But there was another question. One even more pressing.

What can I do?

Nothing. Nothing but strip herself of every feeling a mother could have. Nothing but force every ounce of her pain into a chest much too small for it and bury it all deep within her heart. Only when her emotions were conquered could she hope to track Elsbeth down and find her son.

Leila's eyes flickered open as Greyson cleared his throat.

"Would you like me to ring for the police?" The butler sounded as though he had aged a decade over the past day. Not surprising. The past twenty-four hours had seen Thomas leave on a suicidal mission, Michael kidnapped, and innocent servants murdered within the castle walls.

"We have no choice," Leila said absently. She forced herself to think past the blanket of ice that smothered her mind. "Word about what happened here will spread once those men reach the village. But the police will never find my son."

Leila glanced at the window. Elsbeth had always emphasized caution. She would have waited until both Gretna and the baby had fallen asleep. Then, using a silenced weapon, she would have murdered the wetnurse.

She must have left one of the castle's many side doors unlocked and made her escape under the cover of darkness.

"I-I'm afraid I don't understand," Greyson said. "Why wouldn't the police be able to help?"

Moving to the bassinet, Leila traced with her finger the outline of the slight indentation where Michael's little head had lain. *He's so small.* Too innocent to understand the world of violence and intrigue into which he'd been born.

"They'll never find Michael," Leila said softly, "because she won't let them."

"You know who did this?" Greyson sucked in a sharp breath.

Turning back to the body, Leila gently closed Gretna's eyes, avoiding his question. "Gretna had no immediate family?"

"No," Greyson said after a slight pause. "The Spanish influenza took both her husband and child. The poor girl was spared."

"Only so she could die in her sleep."

A momentary silence filled the small room. In that silence, Leila's mind flew beyond the present, examining the situation from a different angle. Elsbeth had called Michael something. What was it?

The answer flew into her mind, making the back of her neck burn. *Collateral.* There was something Elsbeth wanted. *But what?* Leila's thoughts turned to the letter she'd sent to Lord Curzon yesterday. She had offered to serve the British empire's needs, hoping to prove her innocence. But Elsbeth would have abducted Michael only if she planned to force Leila to work *against* the Allied cause.

"Jenny, I'm leaving once I've spoken with the police." Leila turned from the bassinet. "I need you to prepare my things."

"Leaving?" Jenny glanced from Leila to Greyson. "But won't—"

"Greyson, see to the poor girl's funeral arrangements," Leila called over her shoulder, ducking as she passed beneath the stone archway at the end of the corridor. "Take care of things here until you hear from me again."

Stalking over to her nightstand, Leila yanked open a drawer and pulled out her Luger. She dropped the magazine. It was already filled to capacity. "Do either of you have any questions?"

"W-where will you go?" Jenny moved around the bedpost and stood in line with the window.

Where indeed? Leila replaced the magazine. Holstering her gun, she stepped over to the desk, eyes skimming its dark surface. Elsbeth would have left some clue, some instructions on where they should meet. A slip of paper near the lamp on her desk caught her eye.

Café du Soleil. Noon, the day after tomorrow. Michael's hungry.

Leila lit the candle in silence, then held the note above the flame.

"Where will I go?" she repeated. Striding to the hearth, she tossed the paper inside. It writhed in the flames, twisting, and jerking like spasmodic fingers. "I'm going back to the heart of darkness. To the place where only the dead can live."

Chapter 8

London, Great Britain

The cab jostled through the busy London streets. War fever gripped the city, but it was not the same enthusiasm that had driven hundreds of thousands to enlist when the war first began. This was the tail end of the disease—the weary point at which everyone only wanted the devastating conflict to end.

It had taken the better part of three days to make the trip from Geneva to Dover. There Thomas had lain low for another two days before deciding it was safe to make the trip to London. He'd ditched the grimy dock worker's outfit he'd worn out of Geneva, choosing to make the trip to London disguised as a librarian.

As he bounced around in the backseat of a Unic cab, Thomas realized he didn't miss London's afternoon chaos. Pedestrians—mostly women who held umbrellas overhead to ward off the light rain that misted the ground—scurried under looming posters that decried the evils of the "barbaric Hun" and demanded all able-bodied men enlist. To his right, the ruins of a series of burned-out tenements gave mute evidence of the German *Luftstreitkräfte's* brutality.

"Been a hard year for our lads." The cabbie spoke around the butt of a chewed-up cigar.

"Yes, it has." Thomas pushed the pair of false spectacles back onto the bridge of his nose. His gaze dropped to the paper in his lap. He had purchased a copy each day since returning to England. Malcolm's name still did not appear in the casualty lists. *God, keep him safe!* "Like as not we've still many hard battles to fight," Thomas added.

"Mebbe. But the real danger isn't the Hun, says I." The cabbie braked hard at a crosswalk, then glanced at Thomas through his rearview mirror. "You might think ol' Muggins is a bit barmy, but it's traitors that's the real problem, says I!" He let the cigar drop from his thick lips. "Take that banker Steele, for instance." Hawking up some phlegm, Muggins rolled down the window and let fly.

"Oi! Watch it!" A plump, red-faced woman jumped back. Scowling at the cabbie, she grabbed her child by the arm and dragged him across the street, muttering under her breath.

Ahead of Thomas's return, Hughes had put millions of eyes to use. Thomas had seen the various posters around London. *Beware this enemy. The wolf still wears wool. Judas lives among us.*

The wording varied, but each poster sported an easily recognizable image of himself as Hughes had last seen him. Bearded. Light-haired. The exact opposite of his current appearance.

"Traitors are indeed a menace," Thomas said carefully, passing a hand over his freshly-shaven chin. "No matter who they are."

"And here we all were, a lot of barmy goons, thinkin' Steele was one of us. A true patriot. A right and proper hero." The cabbie's face darkened. "Head of the Bank of England and a Hun-lover? It's a cryin' shame, says I." Leaning to one side, he jerked a crumpled-up paper out of the pocket of his gray trousers. "I keep one of these posters right close. I get about, yeah? If I happen to see Steele in these parts, I'll know him. Doing me duty as a citizen, see."

"I would expect nothing less," Thomas said calmly. "Each of us must do his part for King and Country."

"I've done more than me share." Muggins clutched the paper to his chest between a hammy fist. His lower lip trembled. "M-me two boys. Lovely lads. The pair of 'em. Shot to bits at Passchendaele."

Pain knifed through Thomas's heart. "I'm so sorry. I can't imagine . . ."

Muggins swiped a fist over the corner of his eyes. "If I ever lay eyes on that treacherous snake, I'll rip him to pieces with me own hands!"

"I'm sure you will."

Horns sounded behind them. A copper blew his whistle and motioned for them to get moving. With a grunt, Muggins chugged forward, weaving his way through the traffic.

Thomas leaned back, resting his elbow on the stack of books beside him. *I'm too old for this, Isabella.*

First the attempt on his life in Geneva. Then the shock of Hoffman's retaliation. Now everywhere in London, he saw himself branded a traitor. He couldn't deny the accusation. But the circumstances were misunderstood. And that hurt worst of all.

Thomas lifted sagging eyes to the street sign that was still visible in the evening light. *Fenchurch Street.* "I'll get out here."

"Right you are guv'nor."

Thomas paid the cabbie and stepped out onto the cobblestone sidewalk. To his right, the ominous Tower of London dominated the skyline. At this time last year, Leila had awaited a death sentence in one of its cold cells. Would he do the same?

He shook off the chill that snaked down his back. In so dark a time, his friends were few. Only one man might stand by him now. Hiking his shoulders together, Thomas pulled the brim of his hat still lower and began walking in the direction of the setting sun.

Joseph Mara, barrister and former legal counsel of the Bank of England, planted a kiss on the forehead of his sleeping daughter. He continued standing there, gazing in wordless admiration at his only child. Hadassah slept beneath a thick coverlet of white with light blue stripes at each end. A beam of light kissed the pendant, a Star of David, that dangled loosely around her neck.

If only I could sleep as soundly.

But the peace of childhood had proven to be an illusion. Now, whether asleep or awake, Joseph was plagued by the harsh reality of a world gone mad.

"Goodnight, darling." Stealing softly to the door, he kissed the mezuzah, then shuffled down the carpeted stairs of his Tudor-style cottage to the drawing room below.

Despite his indulgence toward his daughter, Joseph was a practical man. Parliament and the King had officially removed Thomas from his former position as head of the Bank of England. Joseph had always been careful not to vocalize his support of Thomas Steele. When it became clear that Hughes would target those whom Steele had appointed as members of the bank's leadership commission, Joseph felt it only prudent to resign before his private loyalties became public knowledge.

He had just reached the last step when a furtive sound reached his ears. Joseph froze. It was coming from his drawing room!

Pulse spiking, Joseph shrugged off his gray Savile Row jacket and draped it over the banister. Then he slipped toward a tall cherrywood hutch on the opposite side of the hallway.

Easing open the uppermost drawer, he withdrew a black Webley revolver and forced a deep breath through his lungs. London was not the place it had once been—especially to suspected friends of Thomas Steele.

Mounting death tolls and lethal bombardments by the German air force had created an atmosphere of rabid hatred for anyone suspected of collaborating. Thomas had once been a national icon. Now he topped the list of wanted men in Great Britain.

Joseph's mind flashed to his daughter upstairs as he pulled the hammer back and eased toward the door. No one would harm his child. Not while he lived.

Again, the sound of quiet, shuffling feet. The sun's dying light revealed the bulk of a man through the beveled glass panes in the study door. Joseph ran a moist palm over the grizzled stubble on his chin. A thief? An assassin?

There was only one way to find out.

Pointing the gun straight ahead, Joseph leaned forward and jerked the door open.

Thomas blinked as the light in the hallway behind Joseph Mara glinted off a revolver that was pointed at his forehead. "Hello, Joseph."

"Thomas?" Joseph's lips twisted into a smile as he released the revolver's hammer. "Thomas Steele! But how—?"

Chuckling, Thomas clapped him in a warm embrace. "I can't tell you how good it is to see you again, Joseph."

"I only wish it were under better circumstances, my friend." Joseph smiled, then took a step back, eying Thomas carefully.

"You haven't lost any of your old skills, I see. Completely transformed. Appearing in my home like a ghost in the night."

Thomas gave a nonchalant shrug. "I thought it best not to use the front door. Like as not, Hughes is taking an interest in any visitors you may have."

"Quite right." The smile faded from Joseph's lips. "Everything in London has changed. But please! Sit down. I'll return in a moment with some port."

Murmuring his thanks, Thomas shuffled into the drawing room and sank into an inviting leather armchair near a bright fire. With a sigh, he leaned backward and let his eyes wander around the room.

He and Joseph differed in their religions but also had much in common. Both had a healthy interest in business. Both had served in the military. Both were widowers. But whereas Thomas dreaded little and feared none, Joseph was naturally more cautious.

Which is why he's the perfect man for the job.

"Thank you for everything you are doing for my family, Joseph." Thomas attempted a smile as the barrister returned with a decanter and two glasses. "I know the risk is great."

Joseph shrugged, set the glasses down, and began to pour. "It is the least I can do for a friend."

"Friendship can be dangerous." Thomas swallowed, letting the sweet amber liquid warm him from within. "Especially in times such as these."

"I may not openly advocate your cause, Thomas. But I doubt there's much speculation as to where my loyalties lie. When the King officially removed you from serving as the head of the Bank of England, acting on the advice of David Lloyd George, the government claimed it was purely a proactive measure for national security. That was no surprise."

Joseph raised a thin finger. "The real surprise was the lack of protest. Whereas many in the upper classes and lower classes supported you, believed in you, now they all want someone to blame for the millions of dead. You're a scapegoat, Thomas. Once you were their hero. But now you've become the enemy."

"So I realize." Thomas fell silent for a moment, then changed the topic. "Hadassah, how is she?"

Light flickered in Joseph's dark eyes. "My daughter is doing well. She is sleeping. I'd wake her but I'd rather she not know you were here."

"I understand."

A comfortable silence stretched between the two men.

"So, old friend," Joseph said after a few moments, "why return to London?"

"Northshire."

"Ah." Joseph tapped the tips of his fingers together. "The Deprivation of Titles Act."

"Exactly." Thomas leaned forward, eyes intent on Joseph's face. "Unless I appear in court, Northshire will become the property of the Crown."

"But to appear in court is to die. You know they're after your blood. If you show up in the assizes, they'll crucify you. Trust me, I'm a Jew. We know a thing or two about lambs being led to the slaughter!"

"Never mind that." Thomas waved off his protests. "Let's focus on the core issue. I've combed through the act myself and . . . there is a flaw."

"What?"

63

"The act mandates the defendant appear in court or forfeit his lands. It does *not* mandate that the defendant *win* his case in order to maintain his property." Thomas tapped the arm of his chair with his finger. "I appear in court. I present my case. The law is satisfied. Even if I'm condemned, the land will still belong to Malcolm."

Lips pursed, Joseph stood and moved toward a writing desk in the corner. Pulling open the top drawer, he withdrew a packet from a cream dossier.

"A copy of the act." He waved the paper under Thomas's nose by way of explanation, then dropped back into his cloth armchair. Placing the pince-nez that dangled from a silver chain around his neck back on his nose, he began to read.

Thomas waited in silence as Joseph's lips moved in mechanical tandem with his reading. His mind had already shifted to the next piece in the puzzle. He needed to get to Northshire before turning himself in to Hughes. It had been a long time since the staff at the estate had seen a member of the household. Joseph's reports that Thomas had received while in Switzerland had stated that most staff had left. Some because of new opportunities in the city. Others because they didn't want to be associated with a family of suspected traitors. If Thomas was successful in keeping Northshire in the family, Malcolm would need a loyal following with which to rebuild when the war ended.

But the times had changed. The strict social order that Thomas had seen all his life was fracturing. Thomas knew that cultivating renewed trust with Northshire's staff demanded a step that most aristocrats would consider radical. He would make his servants his equals.

"Ah," Joseph commented at length.

Thomas leaned back, squaring an ankle over his knee. "You see my point."

The lawyer shook his head. "It only reads that the accused must appear in the assizes, not *win* the trial. In his rush to get this bill passed through Parliament, Hughes must have overlooked this technicality."

"I don't believe it is entirely an oversight," Thomas said. "Hughes is obstinate, but his stubbornness is born of patriotism not hate. His quarrel is with me."

"You think this in intentional, then?"

"It is possible. Malcolm is not under suspicion of treason. I am. There will be no need to confiscate the estate once I'm dead."

"There is that." Joseph gave a dubious nod. "Then there is the matter of public opinion. Many already suspect the government of abusing its wartime privileges. I doubt they would take kindly to the idea of the government actually confiscating the property of private citizens. The upper classes would have an apoplexy!"

"The fact remains that, win or lose in court, I triumph in the greater picture."

"Make no mistake, Thomas. To go to court *is* to die."

Thomas held his gaze. "I am under no illusions."

"But you will need an experienced barrister to argue your case." Joseph slanted Thomas a shrewd glance. "That *is* why you are here, is it not? To ask me to represent you in court?"

"I value your friendship too much to ask anything you are not willing to freely give. There is your daughter to consider. Your reputation. I'd not ask you to endanger either for my sake."

"My daughter is leaving at first light to join my sister in the country. London has become too much of a magnet for German bombs these days. She'll be safer there."

The corners of Joseph's mouth turned downward. "As to reputation? Well, every Englishman deserves a solid defense."

"Even a traitor?"

"Even a traitor." Joseph stroked his gray-spangled beard. "But I ask you to consider your options carefully, Thomas. It is not as though Malcolm will be penniless. You already have assets that you can leave to your descendants. So why fight this battle? Why not retire to Switzerland permanently?"

For a moment, Thomas didn't answer. His family would agree with Joseph. Malcolm would argue against his decision. Leila would be furious with him for even thinking about it. It was why he had left Switzerland without saying goodbye. He couldn't abide Leila's anger.

"Because . . ." Thomas cleared his throat. "Because Northshire is more than land. It is a promise. A heritage. A promise from father to son that must never be broken."

"And if Malcolm dies? It will all have been for nothing!"

"Malcolm *will* come home." Thomas set his jaw. "My son and I were estranged. But God brought us together. I doubted. I questioned the possibility of such a miracle. But He did it anyway. He put Malcolm through the fire, beat out the dross, and gave me a man of honor. Since He has done that, I know God will bring Malcolm home."

"I don't mean be the doubter here, Thomas, but in my opinion, you're asking for too much. It's as impossible as Moses at the Red Sea."

"That ended rather well, I think."

Joseph slanted him a wry smile. "You know what I mean."

"I know what I *believe*."

"All right. All right. So . . . *when* Malcolm returns, he will be the owner of the estate. I will work with him to ensure that his hold on Northshire is secure."

"He will need Leila's wisdom to help him manage the estate."

"Thomas, have you gone completely insane?" Joseph stared at him with wide eyes. "If there's one point on which the Germans and the British agree, it's that your daughter-in-law must die. How could you *possibly* think that she'll be able to return to England and openly live with her husband?"

Joseph held out his hands in a pleading gesture. "Suppose—just suppose for a moment—that Leila managed to sneak back into Britain. Do you think that Robert Hughes would give her one moment's peace? No! He wouldn't rest until she was a corpse."

"I know what you are saying is true, Joseph. But if I bothered to consider impossibilities, I could never be who I am. Everything about my faith defies our understanding of what is possible." Thomas hiked his shoulders together. "A virgin giving birth? A crucified Man killing death itself? Impossible. Yet true. True enough to change the hearts of men. True enough to revolutionize the world."

"But the risk, Thomas. The risk!"

Thomas stood slowly and walked over to a dark-green marble hearth, above which hung a portrait of Joseph's late wife. Resting his elbow on the smooth stone, he stared into the amber flames. "Battle and business have much in common, Joseph. Both must be carefully planned. Both hold the possibility of failure. Both have a price that must be paid."

"Your life?"

Thomas turned around, locking eyes with his friend. "Yes, my life. Remember that I am not only a father. I am also a son. If I falter in my duty now, then I fail my forefathers as well as my descendants."

"I understand the emotional attachment, my friend." Joseph rubbed his forehead wearily. "But we're talking about piles of dirt and stone. Not flesh and blood!"

"Not to me. Joseph, a century ago, my family came to this country as fugitives who fled a civil war in France. We had nothing. From those ashes, we became peers of the realm." Thomas set his jaw in a hard line. "Northshire was my father's legacy. A heritage that was entrusted to me. Should it all be for nothing?"

Silence claimed the room again, broken only by the crackling of the fire.

At length, Joseph stood and stepped across the dark wooden floor. "As governor of the Bank of England, you surprised many when you chose a Jew as your legal counsel. This country has not always been kind to my people."

"I judged you for your abilities not your faith."

"All the same, you took a risk. Now it is my turn."

"Are you certain?" Thomas drilled his friend with a hard stare. "Once the die is cast, there is no turning back."

Joseph didn't hesitate. "I am certain."

Thomas clasped his hand. "Believe me when I say that one day the Steele name will rise again. One day, all of my family *will* come home."

Chapter 9

Geneva, Switzerland

The outdoor dining area of the Café du Soleil was not very crowded. More than likely this was due to the chill in the autumn air. The café was a small, single-story rectangular building that was lined with a brick façade. A brass sun emblazoned above its door caught the light. The café itself was situated on the northern side of Geneva, close enough to *Lac Léman* to catch an occasional cool breeze and the odor of fish.

Strolling to one of the empty tables, Leila forced a floating image of Michael's face to the back of her mind. The past two days had been a nightmare. She had found herself twitching every time a child laughed or cried. Caught herself staring at children being pushed along in prams, wanting to make sure that the child wasn't hers.

The irony was bitter. Just two days ago, her mission had been to find a way for Michael to claim his future inheritance at Northshire. Today, her mission was to find him. Period.

I'll find him, Elsbeth. Even if it means following you to the lowest pit of hell itself.

Leila slipped into a straight-backed wicker chair away from a small, round wire table in a far corner of the patio. From this angle, her back was to the building and she was in a better position to see all passersby.

Flicking aside the edge of the white tablecloth, Leila crossed one leg over another as her mind ticked through the facts. Elsbeth had always been obsessed with caution, neither totally trusting her agents or her superiors. She wouldn't show up in a public place like the café. Instead, she would probably send one of her agents with orders.

The woman to my left, perhaps?

Leila's gaze shifted to a slender woman in a black skirt and matching blazer who sat at a nearby table, a teacup in one hand and a book in the other.

It's possible.

With the Kaiser's blessing, Elsbeth had built a shadow network of female spies and assassins over the past fifteen years. She had pulled them from every walk of life, training those with potential and discarding those without it. And therein lay Leila's challenge. Find her son while outmaneuvering a woman with a curated network of agents at her disposal all across Europe.

"*Bienvenue au Café du Soleil.* May I offer you something to drink? Lemonade, perhaps?" The waitress, a middle-aged blonde woman with sad gray eyes, looked down at Leila.

"A mineral water. With lemon, please." Leila replied in French.

With a slight nod, the waitress moved off. The woman in black Leila had been surveilling chose that moment to close her book. Rising, she moved over toward Leila.

"It's a beautiful day, isn't it?" she said, her lips curving upward.

Leila motioned toward the chair. "A bit frigid for my taste."

"A bit," the other woman agreed. The smile was still plastered on her face. "I'm Janelle, by the way."

Slipping into the seat Leila had indicated, Janelle reached her right hand across the small round wire table. Leila tilted her head to one side, hesitating a moment before reaching out to shake the other woman's hand. As expected, something small—it felt like a wad of paper—passed from Janelle's palm to her own.

"A little something from our mutual friend," Janelle said in an even voice.

She started to pull her hand back. But rather than release her hold on the other woman's hand, Leila tightened her grip, pulling Janelle forward. With her left hand, Leila eased her Luger out of its holster on her thigh.

"One wrong move and your ugly little heart will never beat again," Leila said quietly. She straightened, letting just the tip of the gun show above the table.

Janelle's smile dropped. "You wouldn't dare. Not in public."

Leila spoke rapidly in hushed German. "Werner Jaëger equipped us well. A silencer can be a girl's best friend. Tell me what I want to know or I'll send you to give Jaëger my thanks."

The two women glared at each other for several long moments. Somewhere on the brick wall that lined the café's patio, a skylark trilled, the cheerful sound contrasting sharply with the naked violence Leila had just proposed. Then the sound of approaching footsteps reached Leila's ears. Easing eased the gun back out of sight, she released Janelle's wrist.

"Your water, *Madame*." The waitress placed a clear glass on the table.

Leila slanted her a bright smile, keeping Janelle within her peripheral vision.

"Can I get you anything else?"

"Not at the moment," Leila said. "Not unless my friend here would like something?"

Janelle flicked auburn curls out of her face. A thin sheen of perspiration dotted her brow. "No. I'm fine."

With a dutiful nod, the waitress turned and plodded away.

"I thought you had become a peaceful person." Janelle jerked her chin in the direction of Leila's hidden gun.

"Clearly, no one has ever kidnapped your child. Right now, I'm in the mood to kill. How about I start with you?"

Silence. Then, "What do you want?"

"What do you know of my baby?"

"Nothing." Janelle spread her hands, palms outward. "I have no idea what you're talking about. I'm just here to deliver a message."

It was possible. Elsbeth would share information on Michael's kidnapping with as few people as possible. But that didn't mean the woman across the table had nothing to offer.

"Elsbeth. Take me to her."

"S-she wants to meet." Janelle licked her lips, eyes darting from Leila to the gun, then back again.

"Where?"

"It's better if you just follow me."

Leila tilted her head to one side. Elsbeth had passed up on multiple opportunities to take her life, so it wasn't likely this was a trap. All the same, in this arena dynamics could change by the minute.

"If you so much as twitch in a way I find suspicious, this will be the last conversation you'll ever have."

"Just follow me," Janelle said.

"Believe me," Leila said as she slipped the Luger back into her holster, "I will."

Chapter 10

Geneva, Switzerland

Elsbeth pulled a white curtain aside as she gazed out the window overlooking *Rue de Berne*. The street cut through the heart of Geneva's red-light district and was bordered by brothels on both sides. Elsbeth had chosen to base her operation here for the simple reason that few would speculate at the sight of women coming and going late at night.

A ghost of a smile slid across Elsbeth's face. She let the curtain slip back into place. "She's here. Let the game officially begin."

The young, blonde woman at her side, codenamed M44, stepped forward. "Are you sure Leila will cooperate? I don't think—"

"Have I asked for your opinion?" Turning, Elsbeth silenced her subordinate with a level glare. "A clue—no."

Elsbeth shook her head, questioning momentarily her decision to give the girl this opportunity. Then again, M44 had a proven record for compliance in the four years that she had been under Elsbeth's tutelage. It was time to entrust her with more responsibility. After all, unpicked apples spoiled on the branch.

"Like most of your generation," Elsbeth said, "you have intelligence but not the sense to know how to control it."

The girl's face tightened, but she dipped her head. "My apologies."

Elsbeth made a humphing noise in the back of her throat. Perhaps all the girl needed was a warning. "I'll excuse this slip as it is the first time you're serving as my second in command on a mission. Remember, I value initiative, but I despise a lack of discipline. Question me again, and your future will be short-lived. Do we understand each other?"

"I understand," M44 said quietly.

Elsbeth lifted her chin. "Good. Now, quickly, is there news from the *Abhorchdienst?*" More commonly known as the Listening Bureau, the *Abhorchdienst* was an emerging division of German intelligence that had become adept at intercepting Allied telegrams and radio messages.

"A telegram was sent to Malcolm Steele's commanding officer."

"And the message?" Elsbeth checked a surge of impatience. "What is it?"

"Robert Hughes wants Malcolm Steele back in London. He's been recalled."

"Ah!" Elsbeth said, turning back to the window. "It was only a matter of time. Well, let us hijack Hughes's plans. Initiate the London operation."

M44 nodded once. "I will."

Elsbeth drummed her fingers lightly on the windowsill as Leila entered the building. All that remained was to bait the trap.

"It's showtime," she said.

━━━━━━━━━━━ ◆◆●◆▶ ━━━━━━━━━━━

"Wait." Leila's command, sharp as the switchblade strapped to the underside of her forearm, jerked the woman before her to an abrupt halt. They stood on a small landing inside a dimly-lit apartment that was wedged between two brothels on *Rue de Berne*. Thin, wood-paneled walls failed to keep out raucous noise from the adjoining buildings—sounds that made Leila's stomach clench.

It was hard to believe there had been a time when she saw nothing wrong with exploiting human instincts to get what she wanted. In her world, information had been the most coveted of currencies. But her change of heart, along with Malcolm's confession of infidelity, left a lingering hatred for places such as these.

Leila skimmed the area with her eyes. A short flight of stairs ran up on Janelle's right, leading to a closed, tan door. Could Michael be hidden somewhere in this viper's nest?

"What's the matter?" Janelle threw her a caustic look, one hand on her hip. "Lost your nerve?"

"I just—"

"You think you're clever, don't you?" Janelle stepped closer, eyes burning with malice. "Well, you've got it all wrong. I wanted you here. You see, I have a secret all my own."

Leila's left hand slid toward the blade that was concealed by her long, white sleeve. "Keep your distance."

"Oh, don't worry. I'm not going to hurt you." A leer twisted Janelle's face. "At least . . . not physically."

"If you've got something to say, spit it out. I *am* busy."

"So was your husband."

Leila froze. "Excuse me?"

"A brothel in Etaples, France." Janelle leaned closer, lowering her voice to a crooning whisper. "Your loving husband . . . Malcolm? Well, I really enjoyed getting to know him."

Leila took a step back, her lips tightening into a firm line. Malcolm had been broken after his return to Northshire. In truth, they had both been. But with their marriage razed to its foundations, Malcolm and Leila had decided to rebuild instead of abandoning their relationship. Janelle's words stunned her, not because she was unaware of Malcolm's past infidelity, but the odds of actually *meeting* the other woman were next to none.

"That's not possible," Leila said at length, more to flush Janelle out than to deny her insinuation.

"Possible?" Janelle barked out a dry, cruel laugh. "He has a scar on the right side of his lower back." The wretch was clearly enjoying this. "You see, there are no coincidences. Elsbeth has everything planned out."

Leila refused to give in to the fury that welled up within her. Elsbeth was clearly targeting her marriage. But she wouldn't have known that Malcolm had already confessed his infidelity. So, who better to tell all than the other woman?

"Oh, I can see that clearly." Leila shoved her face inches from Janelle's. "But there's this incredible thing about love that neither you nor Elsbeth could ever understand. It's called . . . *forgiveness*. And that makes my marriage indestructible."

"Well, well." A sinuous voice floated toward her. "What a deliciously awkward conversation."

Shoving a garish image of Malcolm and this woman out of her mind, Leila turned. "Elsbeth. We need to talk."

"Really? I thought you were done talking." Elsbeth stood in the frame of a doorway, flanked by a younger woman.

Leila stalked up the stairs, stopping just below her son's abductor. "I want Michael. And I want him now."

"Wait here, both of you," Elsbeth said to the two women. Then, "Come inside, Leila."

The heavy door closed with a firm *thud*. "Welcome." Elsbeth motioned to a table that sat between two plush armchairs. "Have a seat."

Leila glanced around the room as she moved forward. Pale yellow wallpaper accented by lurid scenes of men and women reached from ceiling to floor. Thick, golden curtains lined two large windows that faced the street. At the center of the room on the dark hardwood floor lay the tawny skin of a lion.

"I do hope the risqué decorations don't offend you, Leila," Elsbeth said in a dry tone. "Now that you've become—how should I put this?—spiritually enlightened? It came with the apartment, and I haven't had the time to redecorate. I've been rather busy, you see."

Ignoring her taunt, Leila sat in a hardback chair. This was life as she had once lived. Hard. Unforgiving. Relentless. Three years away from the madness had altered her understanding. Northshire was heaven compared to the filth and decadent violence that filled Elsbeth's world. And, lost somewhere in the midst of it all was an innocent child. *Her* child.

"Why, Elsbeth?" Leila sat, stiff-backed and erect.

"*Deutsche bitte.* German is the only language that you and I should speak." Elsbeth arched a finely-plucked eyebrow. "So why did I take your son? Well, I should think that was obvious. Motherhood makes a woman weak." Her eyes hardened. "I don't like weakness, Leila. Not in myself. Not in you."

Leila leaned back in her chair, considering the woman before her. Elsbeth's dark hair fell to her shoulders, curling around an oval face that boasted a strong jawline. Her brown eyes sold none of their secrets. She was slightly built yet carried an almost feline aura of power.

"Where is Michael?" Leila said again.

"He's safe." Elsbeth reached into the breast pocket of her gray business suit and withdrew a thin case of cigarettes. "For now."

Leila's fingernails dug into the chair's wooden handles. "If I thought it would do any good, I would carve the truth out of your lying throat."

"But we both know it *won't* do any good. Neither of us respond to threats." Elsbeth inhaled, then let the smoke curl around her face. "We only fear one thing."

"And what is that?"

"Loss."

"I haven't lost Michael," Leila said in a quiet voice. "I will find him. Then, for the good of humanity, I will kill you."

Elsbeth's lips twitched. "I'd expect nothing less. But let's focus on the present. At the moment, your greatest fear is losing everyone you love. Your husband. Your son. Your father-in-law. For them, you'll do anything."

"Get to the point, Elsbeth."

"I want you to help me. You should know that my orders were to kill you, Leila. As long as you live, you are a threat to Hindenburg and his bunch of bungling idiots."

"You went against orders from General Hindenburg, the supreme commander of Germany's army?"

Elsbeth threw back her head with a snort. "Supreme buffoon if you ask me. If you want to blame someone for our losses in this war, start with him."

"Why, specifically, is Hindenburg interested in me?"

"After Werner Jaëger was executed by the Kaiser, Department 3B was brought under Hindenburg's command. Hindenburg knew Jaëger had failed to eliminate you. Your former status with German intelligence makes you more of a liability than an asset in his eyes. So he ordered me to finish the job."

"It took you a year to find me?" Leila stalled for time, her mind racing. Hindenburg wouldn't care if she lived or died if the original assassination plot was indeed a moot point. After all, there was no way to prove anything. But the fact that Germany's supreme commander wanted her dead . . .

"I knew where you were all along." Elsbeth's lips curved upward. "I was waiting for the baby's arrival. Collateral, remember?"

Leila's fingers twitched. "I—"

"Oh, come now, Leila. It's only natural for people in our line of business to exploit weaknesses wherever they exist." Elsbeth shrugged. "I will do whatever it takes to secure Germany's future. Right now, Germany's future centers around you."

"Germany's future centers on its army. If you're losing the war, there's nothing I can do."

Rising, Elsbeth moved to the window. "A week from now, Hindenburg will overthrow the Kaiser and declare himself the new leader of the Fatherland."

Leila caught her breath. It was no secret that social unrest gripped Germany—this was the age of revolution, after all—but a military coup? "Why are you telling me this?"

"Because the days of the country we knew and served are numbered, Leila, and that number is seven." Elsbeth shook her head. "You need to understand these shifting dynamics if you are to carry out your mission."

"And what exactly is my mission?" Leila stood, pulling the slip of paper that Janelle had given her from her pocket.

"*Our* mission is to bring Switzerland out of neutrality and leverage the playing field."

"Gaunt and Field Bank." Leila held up the note. "You want me to organize a strike on the bank run by the Swiss government. Why?"

"A little chaos never hurt anyone." Elsbeth took another long drag on her cigarette.

Leila folded her arms across her chest, considering. "You want to create social unrest."

The move was bold but logical. Switzerland's population was divided into pro-German and pro-French factions. Protests had marked the country as the war shifted one way and then another.

"After enough acts of terror, humans will freely give up their rights for the illusion of security," Elsbeth said.

"You want me to terrorize the population," Leila said. "But let me guess. You want it to look as though French supporters did the job."

"Precisely." Elsbeth tapped a few ashes into a steel tray on the windowsill. "When the pro-German factions in Switzerland have had enough, they will retaliate. Faced with rising pressure from within and with Thomas no longer in a position to argue for neutrality, the Swiss government will see the wisdom of forging an alliance with Germany."

Leila began to pace, her pulse spiking. "So when Thomas prevented Arthur Hoffman's bid for an alliance last year, he unintentionally created a political crisis for Hindenburg." Thomas had acted to save her life, but his actions had also prevented what would have been a major setback for the Allied powers.

"Suffice it say that your father-in-law made some powerful men in Germany very angry." Elsbeth sniffed and inspected her fingernails. "I did him a good turn the other day."

"You were the assassin!" Leila went rigid. "Clearly there was a reason you let him walk away."

"His death wasn't necessary."

"But killing an innocent bystander, murdering my household staff, and kidnapping my son is?"

Turning, Elsbeth stared her full in the face. "Yes. Before you ask why, understand that Hindenburg *needs* the Swiss on his side. Without an alliance with Switzerland, once in power, Hindenburg will be the head of a bankrupt republic. And we know how that will end."

"So you want Switzerland's economic strength to bolster Germany's post-war economy," Leila summarized.

"I may hate Hindenburg, but I do love my country. The riots swallowing Germany now will be nothing compared to what will happen if the money doesn't start flowing . . . and soon. I will not stand by and watch my country fall into anarchy. Not when I know that its salvation is within reach."

Leila crumpled the note. "If I carry out these missions, I'm working against everything Thomas wanted. He fought *against* a treaty between Switzerland and Germany."

"So I want a little cooperation. Is that too much to ask from an old friend?" Elsbeth gave a non-committal shrug. "Your choice is simple, really. Help me or your son dies."

"I just want Michael back."

"You were born for this, Leila. Think of your future."

"My future is with my husband and my son," Leila said flatly.

"You need to dream bigger." Elsbeth clucked her tongue. "This is your only chance to secure a future for yourself . . . and for your son. Britain is out to kill you, but Germany stands ready to receive you—our prodigal daughter—with open arms. Serve well, and I will secure clemency from Hindenburg on your behalf."

As if I'd take it, you witch. Leila remained impassive. Her mind rolled to the letter she'd sent to Lord Curzon.

London would benefit from this intelligence. Elsbeth had revealed a well-planned operation that could be devastating for the Allies. But Leila needed proof. Proof that the British government would accept her offer to serve. Proof that not even Robert Hughes would be able to deny.

"One day it could be *you* who heads the *Kriegsnachrichtenstelle*," Elsbeth said. "Have you ever thought of that? Leila, I'm offering you the chance to *really* live. Not as a housewife on some miserable patch of dirt in dreary England but as queen of an intelligence network more powerful than anything Robert Hughes could ever conceive."

Leila shook her off. "Never—"

"Say never. There's always hope you'll see sense tomorrow."

"What I want to *see* is my son." Heat rose on the back of Leila's neck. "I'm not doing anything without proof that he's alive."

Elsbeth looked at her intently. "I'm not unfeeling. I understand." Crushing the smoldering cigarette butt in the ashtray, she strode to the door and pulled it open. "Janelle, bring in our guest."

Leila's heart leapt to her throat. She waited, eyes glued to the door, her breath hanging in her throat. Each second spanned an eternity at last the door swung open and—

"Michael! My baby?"

Janelle gripped him roughly in the crook of her arm. Michael gurgled as he caught sight of his mother. Waving his arms, he cupped his fingers together as though calling her.

"Oh, thank God!" Relief swallowed Leila. "Thank God!" She started forward but skidded to a halt when Janelle pressed a gun to Michael's temple.

"Stay back." Janelle cocked the hammer. Her mouth curved into a pout. "Or my finger might slip."

Elsbeth sidled alongside her. "Satisfied?"

"Yes." Leila didn't trust herself to say anything else. Her mind spun through various scenarios. With the knife in her sleeve, she could take Elsbeth down. But there was no way she could get Michael out of Janelle's arms before the harlot pulled the trigger and snuffed out her baby's life. "Yes," she said again.

"Get him out of here," Elsbeth said.

"Wait!" Leila started forward, her heart clenching. Michael cocked his head to one side, then stuck his chubby fingers in his mouth.

"Back!" Janelle snarled.

Leila blew Michael a kiss. "Mommy loves you. Mommy will come and get you." She kept whispering the words as the door slammed. *Mommy loves you. Mommy will come get you.*

"Let me make this perfectly clear," Elsbeth whispered in her ear. "Hindenburg wants you dead. I'm the only thing standing between you and death. Fail me and Michael dies. Then those parasitical servants of yours, Jenny and Greyson. And I'll keep on killing until you're the only one left. Then I'll deal with you. Is that understood?"

"I want proof of life each week." Leila's nails bit into the fleshy part of her palm. "Is *that* understood?"

"I think we've always understood each other perfectly, Leila," Elsbeth said. "At least, until someone else got in the way."

Leila said nothing.

"I want that bank destroyed by sunrise tomorrow."

"Hurt my son," Leila said, "and I will follow you to the very gates of hell itself and kill you there."

"I'll be waiting, Leila. That is my home after all."

Spreading her arms wide, Elsbeth pulled the reluctant spy into a lifeless embrace. "*Willkommen zurück, Tochter.* Welcome home . . . daughter."

Chapter 11

London, Great Britain

"We've done it!" British prime minister David Lloyd George whooped as he smacked his palm on the surface of his walnut desk. He leapt out of his chair, clutching the latest military report against his chest.

As the man who had steered Great Britain through the darkest period of a brutal conflict, David had read the report with the excitement of a child opening a Christmas present. Finally—after years of devastating losses and harrowing political calamities—the war's tide had turned.

David himself turned as the white, double-paned doors of his office swung open. "Ah, Hughes! Come in, my good man. It's a fine day, isn't it?"

Flanked by three members of David's war cabinet, the saturnine spymaster scooted into the office on his modified version of a child's toy, then skidded to a halt. Leaning his kick-scooter against the wall, he jerked a black walking stick from beneath his arm and thumped forward, his wooden prosthesis scraping David's glossy hardwood floors. "Yes, Prime Minister. It has been a very fine day indeed."

"Gentlemen." David dipped his head in the direction of his advisors. "Welcome to—"

The words died on his tongue.

Hughes was smiling!

Something akin to dread swirled in David's gut, smothering the elation he had felt. Robert Hughes, director of Britain's Secret Intelligence Service, *never* smiled. The fact that he did so now—after relating how good his day had been—could only mean that something was very wrong.

"You were saying, Mr. George?" The voice of his exchequer snapped David back to the moment.

"Yes, I, er, hmm . . ." David tugged at the lapel of his tan suit jacket. "We're on the march toward victory and the end of this dastardly conflict."

"Yes, so I've heard." A trace of boredom tinged Hughes's voice. "The German offensive has been broken. Our troops have been victorious in Amiens, France."

David's thick moustache twitched. "Amiens is the beginning of the end! As many as seventy-five thousand Germans killed and another thirty thousand surrendered. Our own losses were substantially lower." His eyes swung from one face to another. "Gentlemen, I believe we are nearing the end of this war. I believe the enemy is destroyed at last."

"Amen." Hughes's smile returned in full force as did the chill that worked its way from David's spine to his toes. "Precisely why we have come."

David tossed the sheaf of papers back onto his desk. Casually, he folded his arms across his chest as he eyed his director of espionage. He was about two inches shorter than Hughes. His own stocky build contrasted sharply with the spymaster's eel-thin frame. As always, Hughes wore a blue uniform that harked back to his days in the navy.

Poor health had led to Hughes's dismissal from active service. The insult had driven the man to an unhealthy obsession with espionage and conspiracy theories. Nonetheless, Hughes's efforts in this war had been vital to the empire's survival.

"Why have you come, Hughes?" As he locked eyes with the man before him, taking in the Frankenstein-like grimace, David had the distinct impression his spymaster would enjoy this latest round in his game of shadows.

Hughes coughed once, then stroked his clean-shaven chin with his fingers. "As you said, the enemy is about to surrender. In fact, the enemy is here."

"Get to the point, Hughes, sharpish. I have no time for idle jests."

"Very well." Hughes leaned forward, eyes boring into David's skull. "Thomas Steele is *en route* to his estate at Northshire."

David felt the blood drain from his face. "How do you know he's in England?" The question was a desperate bid for time.

"A little bit of money in the right circles does wonders. Not even the members of Thomas's staff are immune."

David hid his dismay behind a display of anger. "You interrupt me at a time like this to tell me *that*? The war is almost over, man! Who cares about Thomas Steele?"

"I do." Hughes's voice was as hard as the expression on his face. "These men do." He gestured to the politicians behind him. "Every loyal Britisher does." He paused, then added, "We hope that you are in that number."

"Just what are you getting at, man?" The hairs on the back of David's neck lifted.

Hughes peered at him through his monocle as though examining David's face for evidence of the truth. "Thomas saved your life. Perhaps, Prime Minister, you hesitate to enforce the rule of law in his case. Hmm?"

The grin was back. Evil. Predatory. David resisted the urge to smash his fist between those glistening, perfectly-even teeth. Only now did he see the deadly scope of Hughes's plan. Hughes had brought members of David's own war council to force him into action.

Hughes leaned back, letting his monocle drop. David's mind spun through the facts as he watched it twist like a condemned man on a noose.

One: He had used his influence as prime minister to hinder Hughes's attempts to bring Thomas down over the past three years. But that was no longer possible after Thomas's open rebellion against the Crown.

Any hesitation on David's part now in front of these men could be turned into a charge of partiality or even treason. It had been difficult enough to keep his war cabinet together. Some had blatantly stated that they were more capable of running the government.

Two: Thomas had left the security of Switzerland, no doubt because of the infamous Deprivation of Titles Act, pioneered by Hughes for this very purpose. In so doing, Thomas had condemned himself. When he fell—as fall he must—it would be best for David to be as politically distant as possible.

Three: The evidence against Thomas was indisputable. These very men had been present when Thomas claimed responsibility for a diplomatic crisis that had almost sent Switzerland into the arms of Germany a year ago. Any attempt to hinder Thomas's arrest now would be political suicide.

"Don't ever question my loyalty." David's lip curled back in a snarl as he glared at Hughes. "You are the law. Do what you must."

"I am grateful for your unswerving commitment to justice, Prime Minister."

David was startled to hear a chorus of agreement from the other members of the council. He spread his arms in a pleading gesture. "What, did you all think I would stand in the way of justice?"

Hughes did not give the men any time to answer. "Reassurance is all we seek."

David bit back an angry retort, and Hughes spoke again. "Thomas Steele will be arrested. He will be tried. Thanks to your impartial testimony and the testimony of the other members of the war council, Thomas will be found guilty of treason and will be executed in the Tower square." The spymaster leaned heavily on his cane. "I know we can depend upon your support. In truth, unless you support our efforts to rid the empire of this traitor, you are no friend to the King."

David stared at him, teeth clenched. Overpowering his thoughts was the dismal sense of futility. He was in no position to argue. The political atmosphere of London was fraught with tension and suspicion. After months of abysmal defeats, British morale was finally rising. If the newspapers announced that the prime minister was unwilling to execute a traitor, the uproar would tear the city—if not the country—apart. Would it not be better to forfeit one life than to jeopardize the entire nation?

David spoke slowly as though each word were a bullet from a gun. "I remain unswerving in my commitment to the King's justice."

"We would expect nothing less." Hughes dipped his head then turned toward the door. "Good day, Prime Minister. God save the King."

The members of the war cabinet preceded Hughes to the door. He let them go on ahead, lingering as though expecting David to call him back.

"Shut the door, Hughes," David growled.

After a moment's hesitation, the spymaster complied, turning around with a bemused expression on his face. "If you're about to lecture me, David, spare us both the trouble. You and I both know this needs to be done."

"Must it?" The prime minister stalked forward. "For whose benefit? England's or yours?"

"Let us not quibble about details." Hughes made a dismissive gesture. "If England benefits, then I am content. We cannot let a traitor live."

"Under the circumstances, I find it hard to see Thomas Steele as a traitor. You forced his hand. You held his daughter-in-law prisoner in the Tower. The girl was with child! What was he supposed to do? Let you murder her?"

"I am the law!" Hughes slammed the tip of his cane against the floor. "There is no mercy here, no absolution. Thomas became guilty when he chose to welcome a Hun into his own family. He chose them over his own people. Now he must pay the price of his own wrongdoing."

The spymaster leaned forward, his blue eyes blazing with an intensity that made David take a step back. "I swear to you that if you stand in the way of justice, your days in office will be numbered." As an afterthought he added, "And that number will be very small."

"Don't make an enemy of *me,* Hughes." David bunched his hands into fists.

"I don't want to, David, believe me. But beware. Since you have risen so high, of all concerned, you have the greatest distance to fall."

David closed his eyes, sucking in a deep breath. Hughes was right. He could not afford to let his emotions dictate his path.

There were no winners in the game of politics. There were only those who survived . . . and those who did not.

"Fine." His eyelids snapped open. "I wash my hands of the entire affair." He thrust a finger in Hughes's face. "Do what you want. But *do not* ever presume to bully me into submission again! Is that understood?"

Again the slight pause. Again the twisted smile. Then Hughes spoke in a low voice like the rustle of a serpent through dry leaves. "Yes."

"Good." With a grunt, David strode over to his desk, then glanced back at the man. It was time to change the subject. "Now, what do you know of a German plot called *Herkules?*"

Hughes's ears pricked up. "Nothing. Where did you hear of it?"

"I had a rather interesting conversation with Lord Curzon earlier today. Apparently, he received a letter from Steele's daughter-in-law."

"His daughter-in-law?" Hughes's eyes narrowed into slits.

"Yes." David sat on the edge of his desk, letting his legs dangle over the side. "Come, now, you remember Leila. The spy you took on as your cleaner?"

The sight of Hughes squirming was gratifying. It was also a warning. If Hughes denounced him for being partial to Thomas, David would make Hughes's blunder public. It was, after all, the reason the spymaster wanted the girl dead. As long as Leila breathed, Hughes would live under the shadow of a major threat to his otherwise spotless reputation.

"According to Curzon, the girl claims that once negotiations have been hammered out and all parties are ready to sign an official treaty, the Huns will unleash some sort of attack. The plan is called *Herkules* or some such rot."

"She is lying." The reply was crisp and terse, a sure sign that Hughes had understood David's underlying threat. "She's obviously trying to endear herself to our government for her own welfare."

"Curzon doesn't seem to think so."

"Then Curzon is a fool!"

"And yet it wasn't Curzon who gave her a job," David said drily.

Hughes clamped his mouth shut.

"What you say is possible." David tugged at the edges of his drooping moustache. "She is willing to procure intelligence for the empire."

"You cannot accept! That area is under my jurisdiction."

"And you answer to me," David said softly. "But it appears you have forgotten that detail."

Hughes adjusted his strategy. "If this attack were true, why didn't Leila say something about it when on British soil?"

"The fact is, Leila writes that she told you everything. While you kept her locked up in the Tower." David arched a frosty eyebrow. "But you just said you've never heard of this plot."

Hughes stiffened. "So now you're trying to decide which of the two is more trustworthy—a *German* spy or the head of your national intelligence networks. Have we really come to this point, David?"

"Truth and beauty have much in common. Both live in the eye of the beholder." David tucked his arms tightly across his chest. "The better question is, would you have listened if the girl told you of this plot? You, who have repeatedly denounced her as unworthy of trust?"

"I have every reason not to trust her." Hughes sniffed. "Let's start with that German we captured on Steele's property last year, Werner Jaëger."

"The head of German espionage, wasn't he?"

"Yes. Jaëger emphatically stated that Leila was a plant. That she was a spy sent to deceive us into trusting her. According to him, once she was accepted into British circles as a turncoat, Leila would feed us false information."

"A prospect you readily accepted," David observed.

"Well, was I wrong in doing so?" Hughes's knuckles went white on the handle of his cane. "The man had nothing to gain by lying. He was begging to die!"

"No, no. Of course, you're right, old chap," David stood up. "In truth, this conversation is all moot. The girl is no longer in England."

"Yet here we are, debating whether she or I is more worthy of your trust."

The prime minister paused, raising a stubby finger. "My mind goes back to Ypres. We were warned by a German source, if you recall—a warning we failed to heed. Tens of thousands paid the ultimate price because of our negligence."

"This is an entirely different circumstance."

David nodded once. "Quite right. All the same, keep your ear to the ground. This is the 'war to end all wars.' I don't want it to become the end of humanity as we know it. If those devilish Huns are up to something, I plan to strike first!"

"And what of Leila's offer to gather intelligence?"

"You said she's not reliable," David said, locking eyes with him. "Would I trust a German over my right-hand man?"

Chapter 12

Northshire Estate, Great Britain

The sun had just begun its decent into a pool of blood as Joseph Mara's black Rolls Royce crested the hill that overlooked the farthermost boundary of Sussex County's heart. For Thomas, the moment was unforgettable.

Home.

The castle's spires glimmered just above the thick copse of trees that lined both sides of the dirt path.

Home.

Each verdant acre, each blade of grass was soaked with poignant memories that made the back of Thomas's eyes sting. He wanted nothing more than to spend his remaining years in this place. But he had not returned to live. He had come home to die.

"Stop the car, Joseph."

Reaching over to the backseat, Thomas grabbed a pair of high-power glasses. He focused in on the castle's main gate, a good distance down the road. "As I expected."

"What?" Mara pulled the car to a halt.

"It looks like Hughes has an entire convoy blocking off the main entrance. Soldiers. A few trucks. Even a tank."

"What about the other entry points?"

"Oh, he'll have blocked those off too," Thomas said calmly. While it wasn't surprising that Hughes would take such a step, such an overwhelming amount of force could only mean that he expected Thomas to show up at any time.

Thomas sighed. "Someone's grassed about our arrival. Probably one of the staff." It was as he had planned. Tonight he would turn himself in, which meant that Hughes needed to know he had come home.

"So we're going to turn around, right?" Joseph said, a hopeful tone in his voice.

Thomas lowered the glasses. "We've already discussed this, Joseph. I'm not turning myself in until I've seen the place one last time."

"But there are men *everywhere*. What, do you think that you can just walk up and demand they let you in?"

Thomas slanted his friend an amused glance. "Every experienced commander has a back door, Joseph." He motioned to the woods on their left. "It's a bit of a trek in the woods, but that path leads to a hidden entrance to the castle."

"Ah," Joseph said. "Well then."

Thomas twisted in his seat, staring hard at the road behind them. It was empty. "Let's get the car into the brush and cover it up. I'm ready to go home."

Robert Hughes stared at the black telephone on his desk, lost in the hypnotic silence that filled his office. The rest of the staff had gone home. By rights, he should have as well. But like the tawny owl, Hughes functioned best in the dead of night.

His eyes drifted to the row of three starched white shirts and navy pants that hung in the open closet on the far end of his office. This was his home. This was his world.

Rising, Hughes hobbled over to a window. Darkness threatened to swallow London and the rest of the free world. Only committed citizens like himself held the evil at bay. But playing the part of the empire's savior was no easy task. It demanded long nights. Bloody political feuds. Hughes's mind drifted to Thomas. And a willingness to destroy all who threatened what he valued most.

The telephone's shrill cry shattered the silence.

Turning, Hughes limped back to his desk. Picking it up between thin fingers, he cradled the receiver to his ear and waited in silence.

"Sir! Lieutenant Jefferies here."

Hughes's forehead tightened. Jefferies was a capable young officer, charged with managing the stakeout at Thomas's home in Northshire.

"I'm here, Lieutenant," Hughes said.

"Sir." Jefferies paused. "Our informant, the caretaker, has reported us that Thomas Steele is *inside* the castle! I-I don't know how to explain it. I mean, we've had this entire place locked tighter than a sultan's harem! There's no way he could have given us the slip, sir."

Hughes pressed down on his cane as he sat down heavily in his chair. So the pigeon had come home to roost. Come home to be betrayed. *No surprise there.*

The times had changed—whether or not Thomas and his aristocratic cronies realized it. Now the common caretaker wanted the same rights as a peer of the realm. With Thomas a branded traitor, inducing one of the staff to cooperate had been child's play.

"I'm requesting permission to execute his arrest." Jefferies's taut voice broke through his thoughts.

"Permission denied, Jefferies," Hughes said after a moment.

"Sir?"

"Send a few men to comb through the woods. There must be some other entrance. I want you to keep the rest of your men in position until I arrive. It will be a few hours, but I'm sure you'll manage. *Then* we'll arrest him."

"Sir!"

Hughes hung up without another word. Then, rising with a grunt, he shuffled to the door. By the time he reached Northshire, night would have completely fallen. And nothing would be the same again.

───────◆◆●◆▶───────

Thomas stood in the center of about a dozen staff members. They stood in a loose circle in Northshire's open foyer. White tiles brought stunning contrast to the dark wood of the double staircase that spiraled upward to a landing supported by a dozen massive columns.

"Beggin' your pardon, Your Lordship." Jamison, Thomas's chauffeur, knuckled his head in a salute. "But none of us expected to ever see you again."

"Jamison!" Marjory, Northshire's cook, wheeled on the younger man. "What a thing to say! And to His Lordship's face!"

"Well." Jamison fell back a step, his face reddening. "Not any time soon, is all."

"It's all right, Marjory." Thomas's resonant voice rolled over them all. "The truth is . . . I won't be with you very much longer."

Silence sliced through the murmurs like a hot knife through butter.

"We heard about the situation . . . *Thomas*." This from one of the groundskeepers, an older fellow whose chin was covered with graying stubble. Lewis. "Why are you here?" Resentment dripped like acid from the man's voice.

Marjory sucked in a sharp breath. "You'll address the master properly, Lewis." She brandished her ladle as though it were a sword. "Or I'll give you a right proper taste of Soup Slayer!"

Thomas set his lips in a firm line. It was clear that some of the staff harbored suspicions. But that was why he had insisted on coming. To allay their fears. To prepare the way for Malcolm to face a changing world with loyal staff at his side.

"I've come to stand trial," Thomas said evenly. "To fight for my home."

"You expect us to believe that?" Lewis's face screwed up into a tight ball. "I think you've come back to continue working for the Kaiser. To get more of our lads killed." He jerked a thumb toward his chest. "Just like my Horace."

"I've never worked for the Germans," Thomas said sharply. "And if your son has been killed, I am sorry. But that is no fault of mine."

Lewis elbowed his way forward. "Right! And I'm the king of Scots, I am!" He sneered. "If you're not working with the Huns, then why've you been in hiding?" He didn't bother waiting for a reply. "There's posters all over the county about you. You're the devil. A real Judas!"

"Don't believe the lies, Lewis," Thomas said. "Not after—"

"Oh, you and your kind. You think you're so high and mighty. Well, I think you're lower than a slithering viper!" Lewis brandished a meaty fist. "That's why I did it."

"Did . . . what?" This from Jamison.

A smirk twisted Lewis's face as he glanced from Jamison to Thomas. "Oh, you'll find out soon enough." He spun on his heel. "And then you'll pay, Your *Lordship*. You'll pay!"

"I-I'm sorry, Your Lordship," Jamison said after the echo of a slamming door faded away. "Since his son was killed, Lewis has been angry with the world."

"That does not matter. You are what is important. All of you." Thomas's gaze flickered over the small gathering. A gamut of emotions was reflected on their faces. Caution. Fear. Sorrow.

"Some of you have served this household for more than thirty years. You honor my family with your devotion," Thomas said. "It's almost supper. Tonight I would like to break tradition. I want you all eat with me. Tonight, there will be no 'upstairs' or 'downstairs'. We will share a meal."

There were twelve frozen statues in the room.

"Sir?" Jamison spoke first. "Are you . . . quite certain?"

"Yes, Jamison." Thomas turned to an elderly woman who wiped the corners of her eyes. "Who was it that nurtured Malcolm when he was ill as a child but you, Elaine?" To a balding, tanned man on his left, "Elijah Farrows, who but you spoke to our villagers, planted our fields, and led my daughter-in-law to a new life?"

He spread his hands outward as though embracing them all. And he meant every word. "Each of you is a part of Northshire. When my son returns, serve him as you have me. My son is now defending hearth and home against the onslaught of enemy oppression. If you believe in me, then believe in him. Stand with him and all will yet be well."

———————◆◆●◆◆———————

Hughes waited until his driver pulled open the door of the black Vauxhall, then jabbed his walking stick on the hard cobblestones and struggled upright. Elation swelled within his chest like a living thing.

Tipping his head backward, he let his eyes roll over the Steele eagle that glowered down from its perch on a marble pillar at the military convoy crowding the courtyard of Thomas's precious castle.

"Arrogant sot!" Hughes smirked as his gaze drifted from the proud bird to the reserve special operatives who trotted out of four lorries, taking up defensive positions around the courtyard. The entire perimeter was ablaze with searchlights. The reverberations of the truck engines and the tramping of boots would make a deaf man wince. But this long-awaited moment of triumph must be nothing short of unforgettable.

"Come on lads!" His lieutenant, Jeffries, waved the front line of soldiers forward. "Look lively now."

Hughes beckoned to the man. He jogged over then, snapped out a crisp salute.

"Are the men ready?"

"Yes, Sir!" Lieutenant Jeffries clicked his heels together.

"Good." Hughes pointed to the woods. "I brought a hundred men. Last time I was here, this place was as deadly as any battlefield in France. Thomas's private army against the Irish."

"He has a reputation, sir," Jefferies said. "I still can't understand how he gave us the slip."

Hughes's grip tightened on his walking stick. "That's the thing with Thomas. You can never tell what he's up to. He might even have another gang of hoodlums holed up in those dastardly trees. Some of the peasants from the village."

"With respect, sir, every precaution has been taken." Jefferies pointed to a tank that rolled into position as he spoke. "Besides the infantry, we have four tanks that will cover the road and forests. Standing orders are to destroy anything that moves."

Hughes craned his neck, peering over the rumbling vehicles. "The journalists. Where are they?" Armed with their portable cameras and sketchpads, the press was the deadliest weapon in his arsenal. He had enough firepower to reduce Thomas's precious castle to a heap of rubble, but the havoc wreaked by skilled writers would eclipse anything done by tanks and rifles.

"There they are, sir." The lieutenant pointed to a car sliding to a screeching halt a few feet away. The doors flew open. From the vehicle's rear, three skinny men leapt out, dragging their equipment behind them.

"Well done, Lieutenant. Well done indeed."

A public demonstration of the arrest, trial, and subsequent execution of Thomas Steele would unify the country. Britain needed unity as the war lurched toward its belated end. The press would be Hughes's instrument.

He turned back to Jefferies, anticipation coiling in his gut. "Be sure the journalists are close enough to hear his every word. Let the jackals glut themselves on the lion's corpse."

The soldier did not hesitate. "Of course. Will that be all, sir?"

"Yes." Hughes's mind shifted to the orders he had sent to Malcolm Steele's commanding officer. Malcolm would be in London for his father's trial. If the son shared his father's corruption, Hughes would root it out once for all.

Hughes turned toward the looming castle, fondling the head of his cane. "Checkmate, Thomas."

◆◆ ● ◆◆

Thomas heard the commotion outside. "It's time."

"Don't go out there, Your Lordship. Please don't!" Jamison jumped back from the table, letting his chair clatter on the floor. "We have weapons on the property. We can hold them off!"

Thomas stood slowly, wiped his hands on his napkin, then tossed it onto the table. "Don't you think enough British blood has been spilled, Jamison?" He leaned forward, pressing his clenched fists on the white tablecloth. "This is why I have come home."

"To die?" Marjory stared at him, her rotund cheeks flushed.

Thomas looked at her kindly. "One day, Malcolm will return as lord over this house. He will need you to stand by him. Until that day comes, do as you have always done."

The cook hung her head. "But your Lordship—"

He stepped away from the table and pushed it back in its place. "Better times *will* come, I swear it." The noise of tramping boots made him raise his voice. Thomas breathed in deeply, trying to calm the racing of his heart. *It has to be this way.*

He didn't fear death. As a soldier, he had lived with the reality that his life could end at any moment. It was the thought of dying a *criminal's* death that made him shudder. He had devoted his entire life to the service of the British empire, only to be executed by his own people.

Lifting his head, Thomas motioned to his lawyer. "Joseph, with me."

A fist banged on the door. Thomas and Joseph stared at the door for a moment, heedless of the staff that watched from the side corridors.

"Open in the name of His Majesty, King George!"

"I . . ." Joseph glanced at him, licking his lips. "I will open it."

Thomas nodded once, then turned to look over his shoulder at the portraits of the three generations of Steele men who had forged this heritage. They had sacrificed everything to transform a ruined swamp into a paradise. Now he would ensure that their work had not been in vain.

"I will not fail you." He whispered the words even as his gaze shifted to the empty place next to his own image where Malcolm's portrait would one day hang. "And Malcolm will not fail me."

Pulling a deep breath in through his nose and letting it out through his mouth, Thomas turned back toward the door just as Joseph pulled it open.

In a moment, dozens of black-clad soldiers poured into the castle foyer. Cordoning off the servants, they pointed rifles first at Thomas, then at the staff. "Back! Back!"

"Leave them alone!" The veins in Thomas's neck bulged. "They've nothing to do with this."

"Well . . . Sir Thomas Steele at last." Hughes's voice, dry and grating, was punctuated by the clacking sound of his cane on the tiled floor. "Well met, old chap."

Thomas's head swiveled toward him. Every instinct urged him to protest this invasion of his own home. But this was war. A battle for the future of Northshire. As he had faced down death with stern resolve countless times before, so now he would yield to the law in order to defeat it.

"Well met? I wish I could say the same." Thomas jerked his head toward the soldiers. "You come here with soldiers and weapons as though I were some criminal?"

Hughes's nostrils flared. "You *are* a criminal, Thomas. The worst kind of criminal. You're a toff who has somehow managed to sink lower than a rat. You are one of a breed of rabid leeches who suck at the veins of the empire with the goal of bleeding it dry."

"Well, you'd know all about vermin, now, wouldn't you?"

Hughes's nostrils flared. "You had everything, Thomas. Influence. Power. Wealth. But it wasn't enough. You weren't sure which side would win the war. Being a businessman, you chose to make alliances with both sides."

He limped closer, drilling Thomas's face with narrowed eyes. "But we both know how that sort of thing turns out. The game is over. And I'm afraid you've lost."

"You're wrong, Hughes," Thomas said. "More wrong than you can know."

Heaving a dramatic sigh, Hughes turned away. "Yet another spy loses to the man with the cane." Snapping his fingers, he said, "Take him."

Thomas did not struggle as soldiers grabbed his arms. But furious shouts erupted from his staff.

Thomas clenched his teeth. They dragged him outside. Forced him to stand in front of a trio of piranhas whose popping flashbulbs blinded him as they photographed and assaulted him with questions.

He closed his eyes, visualizing the faces of those he loved more than life. Malcolm—dark-haired with his mother's high cheekbones and eyes the color of a foaming sea. Leila—blonde with eyes the color of Northshire's lush grass in summer. Michael—a bundle of innocent joy.

And, as the jeering crowd pushed him along, one prayer reverberated in Thomas's mind.

God, bring them home. Bring them all home.

PART 2

November 1918

Chapter 13

Passchendaele, Belgium

Dawn.

The naked landscape, twisted and barren like a mother robbed of her children, was covered with a fine layer of frost. Despite the early hour, the steady chatter of machine guns crackled through the still air, accompanied by the rhythmic thuds of exploding mortars. Both sides knew the war was almost over. So both sides had redoubled their efforts to claim the final victory.

Lieutenant Malcolm Steele did his best to ignore the clamor. He hunched his shoulders together, keeping his head low as he made a routine inspection of the few men under his command. This section of the trench was about a mile long—a mile of muck and stink.

Trench walls rose about eight feet high on either side, lined with catwalks and barbed wire. Aside from occasional breaks away from the front lines, Malcolm had sweltered during the summer's heat, frozen through winter's cold, and endured the spring rains in the open—as had ten thousand other men in Britain's 28th Division.

Malcolm nodded to a group of men who cleaned weapons, played cards, and smoked. Life in the trenches was either the absolute chaos of battle or absolute boredom. Given the choice, he'd take the latter any day.

A sharp November wind swept unhindered through the treeless countryside. He pulled his greatcoat closer as it knifed through his wiry frame. Malcolm slipped his hands into his pockets, his fingers brushing against a pair of gloves Leila had made for him during his two-week leave in Switzerland last year.

Leila.

He pulled the worn gloves from his pocket, holding them tightly as a smile hovered about his lips. The stitching was off in places—Leila was never much for sewing—but in his eyes, they were perfect.

Like the mist that hovered above the barren ground, the words she had whispered in his ear while gripping the lapels of his coat floated through his mind once more.

You will *stay alive. You* will *come back to me . . . and our child.* Time had made those words almost sacred.

"How's the leg, soldier?" Malcolm squatted on the frozen ground next to an infantryman whose swollen calf sported an ugly gash on the side.

"Not too good, Lieutenant." The soldier struggled to stand, but Malcolm shook his head.

"At ease." Malcolm clapped him on the shoulder, rising. "The war will be over soon, and we'll all go home. You're a good man. Don't let the Huns get you down."

"Thank ye, sir. Thank ye."

Malcolm straightened, startled to see the glint of tears in the wounded soldier's eyes. *A few words can do so much good!*

He resumed walking, gaze shifting from side to side.

"Keep your head down, Jackson," Malcolm hailed an infantryman who kept watch on no-man's-land through a periscope. "The war's almost over. Stay alive and get home to that pretty lady of yours."

With a grin, the soldier knuckled his forehead. "Aye, and that'll be the day."

Murmuring words of encouragement to those around him, Malcolm let his mind roll over the more personal aspects of this conflict. He stroked the stubble that darkened his chin as his thoughts shifted back to his last conversation with his father in Switzerland.

At all costs, Malcolm had to keep his reputation spotless if the ultimate battle—the return to Northshire—was to be won. His responsibility was clear. It fell to Malcolm to rebuild what his father had destroyed.

But Malcolm himself had not escaped the shadow of Thomas's treason. His own career was blotted by his father's actions. Despite a proven record of heroism *and* the recommendation of his commanding officer, Malcolm had repeatedly been denied promotion.

The news of Thomas's treachery had long spread through the ranks like wildfire. Most of the fifteen men under his command respected Malcolm enough to not mention it—at least not in his presence. But Malcolm refused to cower before the often outright hostility of other soldiers. In truth, he wondered if it was only his undeniable gallantry in face of the enemy that kept Robert Hughes from slamming him in the Tower.

Pausing, Malcolm slowly massaged the back of his neck. Promotion was clearly impossible. How then could he manage to repair the damaged Steele legacy? He had prayed long and hard about the situation, but Heaven remained as silent as the grave.

"Lieutenant Steele!"

Malcolm turned, catching sight of a slim, beardless soldier barreling toward him.

"Lieutenant!"

"Easy, soldier." Malcolm tilted his head to one side and laid a hand on the breath-stricken boy's shoulder. "No need to hurry. Unless, of course, you've come to tell me an armistice has been signed."

A crooked grin broke out on the messenger's face as he saluted and gulped down a lungful of air. "No, sir. Regret . . . to say that's . . . not the case. Lieutenant Colonel James Stewart commands your presence, sir."

"I'll follow you." Malcolm jerked his chin forward as he fell in step behind the frenetic young man.

Malcolm ducked as he stepped under a wooden overhang. His mind rolled back to the day he had first entered a trench. Feces, lice, and vermin. The realities of trench warfare had once been as unimaginable as the dark side of the moon. Now a deadly pandemic swept through the ranks, adding to the soldiers' list of worries.

He had changed. War had played a part, but the true change had come from Christ. Christ who had killed the evil within and claimed Malcolm for His own.

Other memories elbowed their way to the front of his mind. His selfish pride had cost others dear. Others like Will Thompson.

Just after his arrival at the Front, Malcolm had lied to both Will and Will's wife Eleanor, unleashing a string of tragic circumstances that had ended in Will's capture. Will had disappeared—doubtless blown to an ignominious death like so many unknown others.

Remorse sliced through Malcolm as he slowed to a halt outside Stewart's hut. Pulling in a deep breath, then exhaling slowly, he cleared his mind. If Lieutenant-Colonel Stewart had ordered Malcolm to his tent, it was likely for one purpose.

They were going to attack.

———————————◆◆●◆►———————————

Lieutenant-Colonel James Stewart, commander of Great Britain's 28th Division, thumped the detailed map before him with his index finger, then glared at his Belgian counterpart, an eel-thin wisp of a man with sunken cheeks and jutting teeth.

"No, you bawface! We *must* send a platoon here to Harelbeke after crossing the river." Stewart's lips curled back in a sneer. How the man had managed to become an officer was nothing short of a mystery. The Belgian looked like a human sheep.

Aye, and he acts like one too!

The pair were surrounded by three other British and Belgian junior officers. All were armed with a need to cement plans for an imminent assault of the last German-held towns in Belgium. As he stared down the buffoon before him, Stewart couldn't help but wonder if he'd be better off shooting the wretch and seizing command of the Belgian troops himself.

"Bawface?" The Belgian recoiled. "What is this that you call me? I do not understand this word." His forehead crinkled as he struggled to mimic Stewart's Scottish twang. "What is this baw . . . face?"

Fury made Stewart choke. "It means you're a blitherin' goon!" He slammed his fist on the solid desk, scattering papers. "The British government has ordered me to free *your* Belgian city of Courtrai. But you want me to pull back when we've finally got the Huns scramblin' sideways? Listen you little parasite. I'd rather *bosie* the devil himself!"

The Belgian commander looked positively ill. "The . . . devil? You call on the devil?"

"Get *oot* of here!" Stewart shoved the man to one side, jabbing a fist toward the door. "I'll send an orderly with the plans once we've made them *without* you—bawface!"

The officers at Stewart's side punctuated his words with mocking laughter.

The Belgian colonel's face went white. Staring at Stewart with bulging eyes, he opened, then closed his mouth like a fish in distress. "Th-this is an insult!"

Flanked by his subordinates, he turned and lurched toward the door. He had almost reached it when Malcolm Steele pushed the door open and saluted. The door slammed into the lieutenant's cheek with a *thunk*. The Belgian stumbled backward, colliding with his men behind him. The trio went down in a tangle of legs and arms.

Stewart held his belly as hearty laughter rumbled past his lips. "Aye, and the next one will be my fist *skelpin'* the other side of your face!"

"My . . . my government will complain about this treatment, *monsieur*." The Belgian staggered to his feet, sucking in shallow breaths, clapping a trembling palm to his bruised cheek. "This is harassment!"

"Ah, go boil your head." Stewart belched out another unsympathetic laugh as the colonel and his men scurried out of the room.

Malcolm let them pass, then closed the door. "I apologize if I offended your guest, sir."

"Nay." Stewart scoffed and shook his head. "'Twas the perfect endin' to a pointless conversation with a true *eejit*. The man doesn't have a porpoise's smarts when it comes to leadership."

Sobering, he gestured to the map that sprawled out on the wooden desk before him. "Now Lieutenant Steele, cast your eyes here a moment."

Malcolm stepped closer, nodding to the officers who stood around him at the table. Stewart followed his gaze, noting that the men refused to acknowledge Malcolm's presence. Instead they lifted their chins and pulled back as though something repulsive had entered the room.

Aye, the poor lad will have to deal with that and more. It was why Malcolm had been demoted from the rank due his social station and now was condemned to remain in a rank lower than he deserved. Steward had fought for Malcolm's promotion. But the promotion board had been adamant. *Keep Steele in a position where he can't do much harm.*

Stewart's blue eyes flickered back to the young man before him. Judging by Malcolm's rigid posture and crinkled brow, he too had noticed the unvoiced insult. It was to Malcolm's credit that he kept his head high, rising above the stain on his father's name. A stain that Steward didn't believe was just.

"Gentlemen." Stewart glowered at the other soldiers. "Has the British army forgotten how to show respect?"

"With respect, sir." The foremost sneered at Malcolm. "You can't expect us to look at a traitor's son? Why, he should be shot as a precautionary measure!"

Malcolm's face darkened, but he kept silent.

"That's enough!" Again, Stewart slammed the table with his fist. "Get ye gone. I've no further need of you."

Tightlipped, the pair saluted their superior, then brushed past Malcolm without a word as they filed out the door.

Every soldier in Malcolm's regiment knew that he was Thomas Steele's son. Stewart himself had made no secret of it early in Malcolm's career. He had hoped that the stories of Thomas's past victories would inspire the men to follow the legend's son. But everything had backfired when news of the "Steele Scandal" ripped through the army with the mercy of a thousand bayonets.

And now this last bit.

"You . . . sent for me, sir?"

Stewart gave an appreciative grunt. Steele clearly understood that duty took precedence over pride. Malcolm resembled his father in more ways than one. Dark hair spilled over a strong forehead, angular jaw, and somber gray eyes. The same air of command, even when speaking to a superior officer.

"Aye, Lieutenant, that I did." Stewart sniffed, then cleared his throat. "Some news came through in the wee hours of the morning. Unfortunately, those baboons already know what's happened. Given the respect I have for your father, I wanted you to hear it first from me."

A muscle ticked in Malcolm's jaw. "What news, sir?"

"It's your father." Stewart laid a heavy paw on Malcolm's shoulder. "He was arrested last night."

Malcolm sucked in a sharp breath. "He went to England, then."

Stewart nodded wordlessly. He didn't have to say the obvious. Thomas's betrayal had sent shockwaves to the very heart of British society.

At length, Stewart released his breath in a long sigh. "Right now, I'm hopin' that you have some answers for me."

"He doesn't deserve this," Malcolm said.

"*Och,* I can't explain it, lad." Stewart sighed again, scratching the back of his head. "All I can say is that your father is one of the best men I've ever met. But it seems he has enemies in very high places."

Stewart tapped his chin. "This Robert Hughes, for instance. I was told he had journalists and photographers ready when your father was taken." He shuddered. "Nothin' like a picture to sway the masses."

Shaking his head, Stewart added, "No, lad. Mark my words, this whole thing's been planned out. And quite carefully too."

"Where does that leave me?"

Stewart jerked a white envelope from the breast pocket of his olive uniform. "On your way to London."

"London?"

"I've been ordered to send you back forthwith."

"Ordered? By whom?"

"The same man who arrested your *da.*"

Malcolm barked out a sardonic laugh. "So Hughes wants to interrogate me? Even if I wanted to help him, I have nothing to say. My father and I have not corresponded since last year."

"That's just as well, or they'd have already arrested you too. The only reason you're not already in the Tower is because they can't find anythin' to pin on you yet. That and the fact that we need all the help we can get." Stewart's eyes bored into Malcolm's face. "Even so, laddie, you're under constant watch with only a handful of men under your command. The simplest question of German sympathies and—" Stewart finished by cracking his neck. "Do you take my meanin'?"

"Oh, I understand," Malcolm said. "All I've done for King and Country doesn't matter." His voice took on an edge. "Four years of cold, wet, and blood. And it counts for nothing."

"I've no doubts of your loyalty, laddie," Stewart said. "I've seen you lead your men. I've watched you fight. But you'll have to work harder than a nursin' housewife to keep yourself clear of the whole mess. Do you take my meanin'? You'll have to keep on *provin'* you're innocent. Not just today. For the rest of your life."

Malcolm scoffed. "The Americans believe in innocence until proven otherwise. What went wrong on our side of the pond?"

"We grew up," Stewart said. He laid a hand on Malcolm's shoulder. "There's a heart of steel beneath that shirt, Lieutenant. But, right now, the war's taking you in a different direction."

Malcolm tilted his head to one side. "There's something else, sir."

"What is it?"

Malcolm drew in a deep breath. "As you know, two years ago my wife turned to the British cause. But Hughes refuses to believe that."

"Well, I can't exactly blame the man." Stewart snorted. "They're a bunch of sausage-eatin' barbarians! Did you know they blew up the cathedral at Rheims? A *church*! I mean, who does that?"

"Please, sir." Malcolm held up his hands in a pleading gesture. "That's not the point. You'll remember I told you about the plan she uncovered before she defected—"

"Oh, not that again." Stewart's bushy eyebrows hiked together. "Listen, lad, I presented that information to my superiors. They almost laughed me *oot* of the room!"

"With respect, sir, is this something to joke about?"

"They all agree that intelligence from a woman wanted for crimes against the Crown is not worthy of their time."

"And what do *you* think, sir?"

"I—" Stewart stopped short. He turned away, rubbing the back of his thick neck.

"I'll tell you what I think." Malcolm stepped around so that he was in Stewart's line of sight once more. "I think of all the twisted, broken bodies at Ypres. The sightless eyes of the men who drowned on dry land as the gas filled their lungs. I think of the article in *The Times* that was printed two weeks before the attack. You remember?"

"Yes." Stewart's voice was tight. "It stated London had received warnin' from a German about an attack if our men continued to advance."

"Here again, a German—who happens to be my wife—is trying to warn our government." He paused, then added. "Now that we're so close to the end, isn't it possible that the Huns just might still have a trick like this up their sleeve? The plan my wife warned about—it was to come into effect if the Germans were plainly losing. And that's certainly the case now."

"*Och,* there's no need to lecture a Scotsman about the thick-headedness of the British government. Just ask Sir William Wallace!" Stewart shook his head. "You've done all you can for the moment, laddie. And so have I. Whatever happens now is on their heads—not ours."

Stepping around his desk, Stewart clapped Malcolm in a strong embrace. "You're real *braw.* You've made me proud. And whatever happens, I know you'll make your *da* proud. Nothin' is worth more than that."

Chapter 14

Dover, Great Britain

Malcolm stood inside the crowded train as it pulled away from the Dover depot, away from the devastation that lay just across the Channel. Two days after he had left the Front, an armistice had gone into effect. The effect was electrifying.

Crowds of Britons waved the national flag on all sides. The throngs were peppered with military personnel from the various Allied countries that had already begun to demobilize. Boys in red uniforms scurried about the depot, armed with tin bugles. Cheers ripped through the air as the train picked up speed.

In theory, the armistice was just a temporary end to the fighting. But Germany's crippled economy and the military pressure brought on by the Americans meant that—as far as Europe's general population was concerned—the war was indeed over.

As the train chugged into the countryside, Malcolm spotted clumps of sheep dotting pastures and feeding on the stubborn greenery that clung to the earth. He blinked away tears. After the barrenness of Belgium, he could see grass as nothing short of a miracle.

He squeezed into a corner as soldiers milled about the packed train. Parliament's demobilization plan allowed for soldiers who had been serving since the war's beginning to be discharged earlier than men who had enlisted later. While the general population was exuberant, the atmosphere around the soldiers themselves was a curious mix. Some men laughed. Others cried. Still others just stood mute, their faces an unreadable conglomeration of emotions.

I fit best with that lot.

But Malcolm's pensiveness wasn't only sparked by the armistice. The coming battle for his father's life weighed heavily on his mind. He glanced around. At least here he could blend in with the other men in greatcoats. No one knew he was Malcolm Steele—and for that he was thankful.

"Pardon me, soldier." A gruff voice sounded in his ear. "The missus and me are coming through."

Malcolm squeezed further into the corner as a tall, lean, muscled man in black trousers and a white shirt tried to force his way through the crush of soldiers. Then he suddenly stopped and took a step back. The tall man's head was turned away so Malcolm couldn't see his features, but surely . . .

"I said 'excuse me.'" Impatience tinged the soldier's voice as he pushed another step forward, his elbow now jostling Malcolm's chest. "Could you kindly step aside—"

Malcolm remained immobile as though his feet had suddenly sprouted roots. He couldn't move even if he'd wanted to. Not now. He hadn't been wrong. It really was the man who'd once tried to kill him. "Will? Will Thompson?"

"Malcolm?" The tall soldier tilted his head to one side as he took in the sight of Malcolm. "Huh. Fancy seeing you here." If Will felt any surprise, the thick layer of disdain in his voice masked it well.

"Malcolm?" A feminine voice spoke up from Will's elbow. Malcolm pulled his eyes away from Will as Eleanor pushed her way forward and grabbed his hand.

"Oh, it *is* you!"

"Eleanor! I . . . I can't believe this."

She was thinner than he remembered, but that was no surprise. Food served at the gates of hell was often little more than a gooey mass of shredded beef in a can. And as a volunteer nurse, Eleanor had served at the front lines, often running under enemy fire to pull a hemorrhaging soldier to safety or tourniquet a shattered leg with bullets whistling around. Malcolm knew firsthand why the men called her the Angel of the Trenches. If it wasn't for Eleanor, he would be dead.

"So, you're alive," Will said in a dry voice, reclaiming Malcolm's attention.

Malcolm tensed. "I'm sure you wish otherwise."

"That would've been one thing the Huns did right," Will said under his breath.

"Now that's enough." The smile melted off Eleanor's face. She glowered at Malcolm first, then at Will. "Listen to the pair of you! You've both survived the worst fightin' the world has ever seen—four years of it, mind you—and that's all you've got to say?"

"El, I—"

Eleanor rounded on her husband. "Will, we promised there'd be no lookin' back. Remember?" She pinned him with a frosty glare.

At length, Will dipped his head in a reluctant nod. "I did say that."

"I want the pair of you to shake hands." Eleanor folded her arms across her chest.

Malcolm hesitated. There was nothing he wanted more than to ask Will's forgiveness. In his mind, he'd rehearsed this moment a thousand times, never believing it would actually happen. Now that it had, he didn't know where to begin.

Eleanor cleared her throat. "Before we all *die* of old age."

Malcolm thrust his hand forward. "I'm sorry, Will. For everything."

Will sniffed.

"Mr. Thompson?" Eleanor elbowed her husband. Hard.

"Oi. Watch it!" After hesitating another moment, Will clasped Malcolm's hand.

"Right, well." Eleanor said, clapping her hands on her hips. "That's a fine beginnin'." She pointed to a narrow space on a seat across the aisle. "Oh, look at that, Will. There's an open seat." Her eyes glinted with mischief. "Suddenly, my legs are just achin'. Now, it's a long ride to London, so let's all just get comfortable, shall we?"

An hour later, Malcolm leaned back against the iron pole. He occasionally snatched glimpses of Eleanor and Will. He couldn't make out their murmured conversation—not with the clamor of soldiers, nurses, and other travelers jammed into the railway. But he imagined Eleanor was continuing to work her magic on her husband, healing his wounded pride as she had healed wounded bodies on the battlefields of France.

She caught his eye. Leaving a saturnine Will, Eleanor made her way over.

"It's unbelievable, isn't it?" she said.

He looked down at her, remembering again what a pivotal role she had played in his life. In one of life's paradoxes, this penniless woman from London's slums had irrevocably altered his life. Eleanor had pointed him in the direction of the cross. She had pushed him to reconcile with Leila, ultimately saving his marriage. It was Eleanor who had shown Malcolm that social class didn't determine the value of human life.

"What do you mean?" he said.

"Everythin'." Despite the lines of fatigue and perpetual dark shadows beneath her eyes, Eleanor glowed. She still wore the blue uniform, overlaid by a white apron and emblazoned with a red cross on its sleeve. But as she looked at him, emotion flitted across her high-cheekbones and darkened her brown eyes. "Us meetin' here. Like this. The fact that we're finally goin' home. It's a miracle, Malcolm. A right and proper miracle."

Malcolm clutched the metal post next to him, steadying himself against the train's jarring motion. It was as Eleanor had said.

"How's Will?"

"He'll mend."

"He's not the man I remember." Four years ago, disgraced and disinherited, Malcolm had enlisted in the army without his father's knowledge and without the rank or privileges that would normally have been his due.

Will had been part of his platoon. While their relationship had been initially strained by Malcolm's priggish aristocratic habits, over time they had developed a mutual respect. A respect that had lasted until Malcolm shattered both Will's and Eleanor's world with a lie.

"Will's not the only one who has changed, Malcolm," Eleanor said. She shrugged. "We all have our stories to tell."

"I want this one to have a happy ending," Malcolm said. "Will he talk to me?"

"There's only one way to find out."

Malcolm considered this a moment, then crossed the space between them. "Will, I'm going to get some air."

Malcolm jerked his head toward the rear of the car, where an open window let blasts of cold air into the train. The immediate area around the window was empty. Malcolm assumed that was because of the cold. "Care to join me?"

Will tilted his head to one side, then nodded. Malcolm stepped aside to let Will go first, then followed his lead, elbowing his way through the crowd. For a few moments they stood by the window in silence.

Then Malcolm spoke. "Will the war ever truly be over, Will? For us, I mean?"

"You mean, are we going to stop hating each other?" Will's voice was low and hoarse.

"I don't hate you, Will. I never have."

"What, you call wrecking my marriage an act of love?"

"I didn't mean to—"

Will cut him off. "But you almost *did*, Malcolm. Everything could have gone horribly wrong. You told her I was dead. She trusted you. We both did."

"I—"

"Eleanor could have remarried. Gone back to London and had children with some other man." His grip tightened on the railing. "All because of *you*."

Malcolm was silent. Truly, there was nothing he could say. Nothing that could undo the pain he'd caused. Even now, the memory of the pain in Eleanor's eyes when he spun the lie that Will had died splintered Malcolm's heart.

Then Will spoke again. "But El's right. We have to keep moving forward."

"I hate what I did, Will."

"So do I." Will blew on his hands, then rubbed them together. "But we both know my hands aren't too clean either."

Malcolm absorbed this in silence. The admission of guilt was telling. After learning that his infant daughter had been killed in a German zeppelin attack, Will had hardened into a man without mercy. He had earned the name "the Butcher" as he made it a point to end the lives of wounded enemy soldiers after each battle, ramming his bayonet into his victim's temple. Much had clearly changed since their last encounter. Malcolm shifted the conversation's focus. "How do we move past the war itself?"

"You mean, will we ever get over the memories? Stop reliving the deaths of our friends? Forget the last expression on the faces of the men we killed?"

Malcolm's gaze drifted to the passing fields. Patches of snow covered the ground in places. "Yes."

"It'll never go away. That last night together. When we raided the German trench. I got taken prisoner and was away from it all for over a year." Will stared into middle-space. "It was just as bad in Germany as it was in France." Blinking, Will turned to Malcolm. "But that doesn't mean you and I can't end our own war."

Malcolm met his gaze. "Will, I can't tell you how sorry I am. I was a real beast to you both."

"Yeah," Will grunted. "It was pretty rotten. But I *did* almost kill you, for that matter. That was pretty low of me too."

"Yes, it was rather . . . unpleasant."

Will looked out the window. "Before I was captured by the Germans, I swore that I would hate all Germans because of what they had done to my daughter. My little Abby." He drew in a slow breath, then released it. "It wasn't until one of them took me in and treated me like his own son that I realized how wrong I was."

The steady chugging of the train and the low murmur of voices filled the silence that followed Will's words. Malcolm dropped his head, overwhelmed by a sense of gratitude. "Thank you."

"Forget it."

"What will you do when we get to London?"

Will rubbed his hands together, then blew on his fingertips. "Don't rightly know. Me and El, we'll try to find a place after we visit Abby's grave. I have some back pay coming, so we should be able to rent a flat in the East End."

"Why not come to Northshire?"

"Me?" Will chuckled. "What, are you offering me a job, now?"

"I'm serious, Will." Malcolm leaned back against the window frame. "A good number of men who used to work the estate either died in the trenches or took off for the cities. I need allies." He met Will's gaze squarely. "I've a lot on my mind right now and could use your help. There's an empty cottage with ten acres of land on it that you and Eleanor can call your own."

Will slanted him a cautious glance. "I'll not accept a gift."

"I wouldn't ask you to. Come on to Northshire as my foreman and work off the price. There are good men there. Men who were too old to go to war. They can teach you what you need to know. What do you say?"

"I'd say it's right generous of you," Will said with a thoughtful expression on his face. "Alright. We'll try it out for a few months and see how things go."

"Glad to hear it. I've neglected this estate my whole life. More than anything, I want to continue my father's work. But now that I'm finally ready, life has become . . . complicated."

Images of his wife, his son, and his father crowded Malcolm's mind. He gripped the window frame, squeezing until the backs of his knuckles turned white. "Whatever God has planned seems too much for me."

Will stepped up beside him, staring out the window. "In Germany, I felt the same way. There were times I questioned if I could win the fight against myself." He grew quiet, then added, "Until a German woman showed me that God gives His hardest battles to His strongest soldiers."

"That's hard to remember that when all you can see are the bullets flying toward you and the enemy gaining ground."

"True enough." Forking his fingers through his shaggy brown hair, Will slanted Malcolm a thin smile. "You've only got one option whenever that happens."

"What's that?"

"Close your eyes . . . and stand your ground."

Chapter 15

Geneva, Switzerland

Leila pushed open the sagging door of the abandoned warehouse and staggered inside. It screeched as it swung on its hinges, a sound that echoed the groaning of her heart.

She turned slowly in the direction of the distant horizon.

It was three o'clock in the morning, but a patch of the night sky carried the orange glow of a premature dawn. The light didn't come from heaven. It was the hellish hue of earthly flames that consumed the west wing of the Geneva Opera House. And she was the arsonist, driven to calculated acts of violence by a ghost from her past.

"God." Leila's breath escaped in a chopped-up sigh. "Show me another way out of this."

So far she had not been forced to kill anyone, but it was only a matter of time. Her voice trailed off, but she could still hear the sounds of sirens and distant shouts as men fought the blaze that she had ignited.

By dawn they would find the message she had sprayed in bold, red paint across the backstage wall.

Victoire aux Alliés! Sus aux allemands! Victory to the Allies! Death to the Germans!

By noon there would be another riot, just as there had been the last time she had struck. Fears of an impending German defeat stoked fears among the pro-German population of Geneva. What revenge would the pro-French factions unleash if Germany's forces were defeated across Europe?

The question haunted Geneva. It became even more pressing when calls for "Death to the Germans" began appearing on scenes of arson. After Leila's last attack, thousands of Swiss Germans had crowded around the state capital, demanding a closer alliance with Germany as well as protection from French radicals in their neighboring cantons.

Unable to bear the sight any longer, Leila closed the door. Rubbing her hands to warm them, she lurched toward the corner where a thick layer of rotting straw and mouse droppings hid her clothes and personal belongings. Squatting, Leila carefully slid the straw to one side, then pulled a loose floorboard out of its place. Underneath lay a simple navy-blue valise.

With a grunt, she tugged it free and pulled out her clothes—a dark-brown calf-length skirt, leggings, and a thick, faded cream sweater. Sighing, she stood, jerked the black balaclava off her face, and shook her blond hair free. Then she pulled her Luger from its holster in the small of her back and tossed it on the straw before peeling off the boots and clothing Elsbeth had provided for her covert operations.

Leila blew on her numb fingers. She had filled a rusty tin bucket with river water late last night. The water had become an ice crust that she cracked open. She plunged the black shirt into the icy water, then wrung it out, letting droplets fall onto her shoulders and neck. The shock was a pleasant relief.

Clean. I need to feel clean again.

Once, she would have considered the mission to be a brilliant success. Her orders had been carried out to the letter, and no one had witnessed her crime. But now she felt no joy. Instead, she pushed down a gnawing sense of guilt. *Michael. It's for Michael.*

Carefully, Leila dipped the cloth into the bucket again, wiping away the grime and sweat that covered her body. Then, shivering, she hurled the black shirt on top of the rest of Elsbeth's discarded uniform and quickly pulled on her own clothing.

Pulling a rectangular flashlight from her pocket, Leila flicked it on and stalked toward the rear left of the warehouse. She was in the appointed meeting place. Tonight, one of Elsbeth's agents would meet her here with new instructions.

Taking a lighter from her valise, Leila tossed a few fragments of dried kindling into a discarded clay bowl and lit it. Then, prying open a can of corned beef, she squatted, sending chittering mice scurrying for safety. As she forked down the salty meat, Leila analyzed her situation.

Elsbeth thought Leila to be vulnerable. In a sense, with her son's life at stake, she was. But Elsbeth had revealed Germany's plans for Switzerland.

As she had predicted, the radio broadcasts had broken the news that the Kaiser had abdicated his throne, ousted by his generals. Leila's chewing slowed. Hindenburg knew that he was playing a losing game in terms of the war. An armistice had been signed, and a formal treaty was forthcoming. So why would he go to such lengths to gain power unless he had some strategy in place to keep it?

Leila swallowed. Hindenburg could still accomplish Germany's goal of conquest—if he still planned to assassinate Europe's leaders. And she was willing to bet that the proud general intended to do just that.

Leila shoved another forkful of cold beef into her mouth. Her mission was two-fold. First, to find her son. Second, to find indisputable proof of Germany's intentions.

Putting down the can, Leila pulled the telegram from her pocket and read it once more. Greyson had passed it along the last time she made contact. The message was only ten words. But they gave her the first touch of hope she had felt in a long time.

I am listening. Need proof. Find me at Versailles.

The British prime minister had signed the note with his initials. *DLG*. Leila slipped it back into her pocket.

With news of Thomas's arrest dominating newspaper headlines across Europe, she somehow doubted David Lloyd George had informed Hughes that he had accepted her offer of espionage. But this tiny scrap of paper gave Leila a sense of legitimacy. Elsbeth had brought her back into the game. So Leila would play to win. And for the first time, she had support.

Her head snapped up as the faint creak of the door swinging open cut across the warehouse. Leila slid slowly to the right of the dilapidated door. The warehouse was dark except for the faint glow of the small flame in the bowl. Squinting in the dim light, she made out a slight figure that slipped through the small space in the partially-opened door with practiced ease.

Her pulse hammering, Leila made herself small in the corner, slowly pulling back the handle on her Luger and propping her extended left arm on her left knee.

Only one.

Not police then. She focused her breathing, waiting as the intruder inched forward, ruling out the possibility of a vagrant. This person moved like a woman. Most likely Elsbeth's contact.

"State your name and business." Leila's voice was raw with bruised anger.

"M44. Elsbeth sent me."

Keeping her gun centered on the agent's chest, Leila reached out with her left hand and grabbed her flashlight. She flicked it on and shone the light on the intruder's face.

The girl did not flinch. Leila recognized her as the second woman who had been in Elsbeth's apartment at their first meeting. She was young. Perhaps twenty. Blonde like herself with a lean, tawny build. She wore a gray coat, belted at the waist.

"You've come with instructions?" Leila rose, index finger still curled around the gun's trigger.

The young woman just stared at her, blinking for several moments.

"I asked you a question." Leila stalked closer, hardening her voice.

"I brought orders." The girl lifted a small bag. "And I brought this."

"What is it?"

"Oh." M44 licked her lips. "Food. Some money. Feminine things."

Leila paused mid-step. "Elsbeth sent you?" Such consideration wasn't Elsbeth's way.

"Yes." M44 dropped her gaze. "That is . . . she sent *me*. Not the supplies. "

Leila cocked her head to one side, her attention drifting from the bag to the woman herself. A distant memory tugged at the corner of her mind but refused to come into the light.

"Toss the bag on the ground and build up the fire," Leila said, shrugging off the impression. "You're armed?"

M44 shook her head as she unbuttoned her coat and held it open. Her white collared shirt was tucked neatly into an ash-gray skirt. "No."

"You came to see me with no weapon?" Leila said. "I don't know whether to be impressed or insulted."

The younger woman emptied her pockets, then turned so Leila could see there was no weapon tucked behind her back. "I'm clean."

Leila eased the hammer off her own Luger and slipped it back into its holster. "Sit."

Cautiously opening the rucksack, Leila saw at once that the girl had brought more than just a few things. Canned goods, carefully-wrapped packages, even some first-aid equipment lined the bottom of the bag.

She turned to M44. "Why?"

The girl smiled faintly as she squatted near the fire. "You don't remember me, do you?"

Leila sat across from the newcomer, eyes probing the girl's oval face. She could see now that the other girl's eyes were blue. They still retained an innocent quality that was rare in their line of work.

Perhaps that's what makes her so confident.

No one could possibly suspect that this girl was an efficient killer.

"No, I don't," Leila said at last.

M44 tossed another clump of straw on the fire. It flared up brightly, then just as quickly began to die down. "That's all right. I'd be surprised if you did. I was young, the last time we met. It was at the *Kriegsnachrichtenstelle*. You sparred with Elsbeth one day. You almost won. Remember?"

Leila gave a slow nod. "She called all thirty cadets together to witness the match."

"I made myself a promise." M44 paused, drawing her knees up tight against her chest. "I promised myself that one day I would be just like you."

"You've come up in the world since then," Leila observed. "You're among Elsbeth's elite."

The girl's face remained impassive. "What do you mean?"

Leila scoffed. "Out of all her agents, Elsbeth selects *you* to join her on a critical mission. Clearly, you've clawed your way into her inner circle."

"So I'm good at what I do."

"You've come with orders. Perhaps you know then that this mission isn't just about reclaiming my rogue soul." Leila leaned back, eying the other girl thoughtfully. "You're someone Elsbeth can rely on. Someone willing to take unauthorized action." She nudged the rucksack with her foot. "Could it be that you hold some kind of authority in Elsbeth's den of snakes?"

For a moment, M44 didn't respond. When she did, it was with a question. "What made you leave us, Leila?" She tilted her head to one side. "You knew the risks, but you did it anyway. Why?"

"Is that Elsbeth asking? Or you?"

"Me."

Leila hesitated, then said, "I fell in love."

"With the enemy?"

"He wasn't the enemy. At least not to me." Leila closed her eyes for a moment, losing herself in the memories. "With Malcolm, I felt free. For the first time in my life, I realized love is not a weapon. He taught me that."

"That must be a wonderful feeling." M44's voice was small. Wistful. "Did you ever tell your husband the truth?"

Again, Leila hesitated, reluctant to share this personal part of her story. "Yes," she said at last. "Yes, I did."

"And he forgave you?" M44 leaned forward, eyes wide. "He still loved you?"

"Not at first. Not till he found Jesus. As I had."

The girl's brow darkened, her mouth twisting as though she tasted something foul. "Jesus?"

"Our new beginning was founded in the love of Christ. He set us both free when we didn't even know that we were slaves."

"I don't think Christ has done you much good. You're in trouble but . . . where is He now?"

"He doesn't keep us *from* trouble. But He promises to face it with us." Leila set her jaw. "Somehow, He will lead me to my son."

"Brave words. But that's all they are. Just words. Sometimes He fails those who believe." M44's voice dropped. "I should know."

At that moment, insight flooded Leila's mind. M44 was a living reflection of the twisted woman she had once been. Of what she would have remained had Christ not changed everything.

Leila shifted closer. "What happened to you?"

For a moment, M44 stared at her with too-bright eyes. Then she shot to her feet and pulled her coat tight again around her body.

"Here are your orders. You strike again tonight. The Federal Palace in Bern. Destroy the meeting room on the second floor." She cinched her belt around her waist.

"Another strike?" Leila gaped at her. "It's too soon! Besides, the Federal Palace is the capital building of Switzerland. After what I just did, that place will be swarming with security."

M44 spoke in short, clipped tones. "You'll have to travel during the day to get to Bern in time. Railway tickets are in the bag." She jerked her chin toward the rucksack.

"What is Elsbeth doing?" Fury roiled in Leila's gut. "She knows that after a mission I need to lay low."

"I don't know Elsbeth's mind," M44 said evenly. "But those are her orders."

"Tell her I want fresh proof my son is still alive," Leila said, rising. "She gives me nothing, she gets nothing."

"I'll tell her." M44 took a step back. She turned to leave but paused. Running a hand wearily over her pale face, she said, "Leila, sometimes we're just not strong enough to escape the evil. No matter how much we wish we could."

Leila folded her arms across her chest. "I almost beat Elsbeth once. You know that."

"Yes," the girl said softly. "*Almost.*"

Then she was gone.

Chapter 16

Geneva, Switzerland

The predawn air was crisp. Leila's breath congealed in small puffs as she moved down the narrow, dark alley that opened up to a side street in Geneva's Pâquis district. A thick fog had moved in from Lac Léman, making visibility poor. Her shoes clicked out a quick tattoo on the deserted cobblestone streets, echoing off the dilapidated buildings that stood like cautious sentinels around her.

Refuse lay in small clumps among worn doorframes of stone, partially hidden beneath clusters of dead leaves. As Leila walked the leaves skidded about the lifeless street, retreating from the urgent force of her footsteps. Somewhere in the distance, a dog yipped.

The area was a fitting home for the man she was hunting. Dismal and decrepit on one hand yet adjacent to a bustling center of commerce. Wolfgang Siegrist—now known by the distinctly less German name of Pierre LaRue. Like the neighborhood he haunted, LaRue was a dichotomy. On one hand, he was charismatic and efficient. On the other, he was the calloused leader of a crime syndicate in Geneva with ties to the 'Ndrangheta, a powerful Italian mafia.

He was a heartless killer with a weakness for a beautiful face. The former head of an organized crime unit based out of Berlin, Pierre had been wanted on several counts of murder and civil unrest by the Kaiser's government before the start of the war.

In all honesty, Leila didn't expect to find Pierre as much as she expected his men to find her. His control of Geneva's underworld could be invaluable in helping her find Michael. If he didn't kill her first.

Leila turned a sharp right, then flattened herself against the rough exterior of a pub and slowly craned her neck to see around its corner. Squinting, she peered through the mist for several seconds. *No one's following me.* She'd taken every precaution, but when dealing with Elsbeth, one could never be too cautious.

Leila heard a soft footfall behind her. Before she could move, a voice spoke. "You're up early, *Madame.*"

The voice behind her was smooth but contained more than a hint of menace. The press of a gun in the small of Leila's back didn't help. "Why is such a beautiful creature wandering about in such a lonely place? And at such an ungodly hour?" The thumb of his right hand brushed lightly against her neck.

"I'm here to see a friend." Leila pulled as far as possible from the man's touch. "Pierre LaRue." Her mind sped through possibilities. This man spoke in French, but there was a slight trace of an accent.

Italian?

"Then I'm afraid you've come to the wrong place." Her assailant increased the pressure on her spine. "There's no one here by that name."

"I know he's in this area." Leila lifted her chin. "I've spent the past two weeks tracking his operatives through this part of Geneva. I need to speak with him. As I said, I'm a friend. If you don't know Pierre personally, perhaps you know someone who can get a message to him?"

The man leaned forward, his hot breath passing through a few strands of the brown wig that covered her hair. "I've heard it said that this Pierre LaRue *has* no friends."

"Leila Steele née Durand. Berlin. 1914. Tell him that."

Silence.

Leila waited, still feeling the pressure of the gun. Then another voice, quiet but authoritative, spoke from further back. "Bring her."

Quick footsteps sounded behind her. Leila didn't resist as someone jerked her head back and stuffed a wad of cotton in her mouth. She forced herself to hold still as male hands patted her down in deliberately slow but efficient movements.

"She's clean," the first man said at last.

Someone jerked a hood over her face while someone else slapped tight handcuffs on her wrists.

"This way, *Madame*." The voice of the first man was slightly muffled. Leila allowed them to prod her back into the alley, her pulse racing. Between the mist and unlit alley, it was unlikely anyone had seen the quick exchange. Even if anyone had noticed, who would be foolish enough to get involved?

They had waited for a few minutes when Leila heard the sound of a car easing to a stop at the mouth of the alley. Once again, she let her abductors steer her forward. She heard the sound of a car door opening, then rough hands shoved her inside.

God in heaven, make this work. Make a way through this sea of turmoil.

So much depended on the silent prayer.

On the one hand, she had the tacit approval of the British prime minister to obtain intelligence for London. On the other, the German government was forcing her compliance. It was only a matter of time before she would have to take a life while carrying out Elsbeth's orders. She couldn't do that. And yet to fail would mean Michael's death. Her only hope was to locate Michael before it came to that. To do so, she needed the help of Pierre LaRue—a man she had once been commissioned to kill.

Her mind ticked off the risks.

One: She was wedged between two men who clearly had no aversion to violence or worse. Two: She was vulnerable. Unarmed, bound, and blindfolded. Three: Her fate would soon be decided by an international terrorist.

But she was a mother. And her child was worth any risk.

A throaty engine purred as the car rolled over bumpy roads. With each turn of the wheel, one thought pulsed through Leila's mind. While she had been surprised by the unexpected twists of life, God had not been surprised.

She had survived torture, imprisonment, and attempts against her life in times when she would have been the only casualty. God had brought her through although she deserved her fate. But her son had done no wrong! Now that her child—her sweet, innocent Michael—was at risk, surely God would intervene.

And, if for some reason, He chooses not to help. . . then I'll die trusting Him.

—◆◆●◆◆—

"It's been a long time, Leila Durand. Or I suppose I should say, Leila *Steele*." Pierre LaRue leaned back in his chair. They sat at opposite ends of a rectangular table of glass set in a bamboo frame. Between them lay several white trays of croissants, jam, fruit, and poached eggs. "The world has gone mad since we last saw each other."

Leila wiped her mouth with a white cloth napkin, then laid it gently on the table. "The world has always been mad. This is only the newest stage of its insanity."

Pierre threw his head back and laughed. It was a soothing sound that suited its charismatic owner. He was about forty, slim but muscular, and about an inch shorter than Leila herself with a slight patch of gray shading each of his temples. A white shirt, open at the collar, was offset by a pair of black slacks whose tailored hem hung just above Pierre's spotless black shoes.

"You know, that's one of the things I've always admired about you. You adapt course like"—Pierre paused, searching for the word— "like a falcon in flight."

"What do you mean?" Leila tipped a steaming cup of black coffee to her lips, her eyes flitting to the two armed guards that stood at each of the doors. Despite Pierre's show of hospitality, Leila knew they wouldn't hesitate to end her life if he so much as snapped his fingers.

"I mean, my men bring you here bound like an animal." He shrugged. "Yet you take breakfast with me and trade jokes as though nothing was wrong." Pierre wagged his index finger. "You're a falcon, Leila. A ravishing, untamed creature."

Leila set the cup down. "An interesting comparison. Especially given that the falcon is renowned for its ability to hunt . . . and to kill."

"Yes." Pierre's eyes never left her face. "There is that." He speared a grape with a fork, sending some crimson juice droplets spurting upward. "So what exactly are you hunting in this part of the woods?"

Instead of answering, Leila hiked her eyebrows in the direction of the closest set of guards.

"Ah." Pierre popped the grape into his mouth, eyeing her thoughtfully as he chewed. "Giovanni," he said at last, dabbing his mouth on his napkin. "Take your men and wait outside."

Giovanni gave a few curt orders in Italian. Within moments, the apartment was empty.

"So, Leila," Pierre said, leaning back and spreading his arms wide. "I am at your mercy."

"I'm the one who is unarmed."

"Quite right." Tossing the napkin on the table, Pierre started to rise with an unmistakable gleam in his eye.

"How is your wife, Bernadette?"

Pierre stopped short. "Ah . . . my beloved wife. S-she *is well.*" A silver watch gleamed as he rubbed the back of his neck. "You must forgive me, Leila," he said, sitting down again. "The men in my family, we struggle with our passions. It is a hereditary weakness."

Leila pounced. "I know you love Bernadette. If it weren't for me, you know she would be dead."

"I haven't forgotten." His mouth twisted into a grimace as though the grape had been sour. "We were trying to escape Berlin. The *polizei* almost had us cornered."

"You know it wasn't the police who pushed for your arrest."

"No. It was Elsbeth. For years, that witch privately benefited from a casual partnership with my startup branch of the 'Ndrangheta in Berlin. Money. Connections." Pierre waved a hand in disgust. "Then she gets promoted to head of the *Kriegsnachrichtenstelle,* and she has something to prove to the

Kaiser. All of a sudden, her business partner becomes the lamb to be sacrificed on the altar of Elsbeth's prestige."

"If it were only the police, you would have escaped."

Pierre snorted. "Of course. It was you who tracked me down then. You who found me again now."

"You were at the entrance to a tunnel beneath a safehouse in Berlin when I found you." Leila prodded his memory. She wanted the details fresh in his mind before unveiling her scheme. "You were halfway down the tunnel, but Bernadette hadn't yet entered. I was alone and ready to shoot. The *polizei* had the place surrounded." Leila paused, then continued, "Bernadette was at my mercy."

"You spared her life," Pierre said in a soft voice. "And then you lied to your government. To Elsbeth. You said you hadn't seen us. Why?"

Leila stared into middle-space, reliving the moment. "Bernadette. The look in her eyes. It wasn't fear. It was sadness. And then your wife turned to me and said, 'I don't want to leave Pierre to face life without me.'" Leila blinked, and his face slipped back into focus. "I knew how hard it is to be alone."

"And now you've come to collect on the debt," Pierre said calmly.

Leila shifted to the edge of her seat. "Elsbeth has my son. I want him back. If anyone is powerful enough to pull secrets from the night . . . that man is you." It was flattery, but like pearls, truth looked better when set in a case of silver.

Pierre said nothing.

"I need your help, Pierre." Gripping both sides of the table, Leila rose halfway. "I'm a mother whose child has been stolen. There's nothing I won't do to find my son."

"Nothing?" His eyes wandered over her body.

"Stop it, Pierre," Leila snapped. "You know you don't mean that."

Pierre sighed. "You're right. But the real question is, *why* would Elsbeth abduct your son?"

Leila had anticipated this question. She couldn't tell him the full truth. Not if she wanted to walk out of here alive. "Retaliation. I've betrayed Elsbeth. The war is almost over, and she has come to settle old debts." Leila sat back down. "And now, so have I."

"Hm!" Pierre rubbed his chin. "I believe there is more to it than that. But that is irrelevant. What *does* matter is this—whatever debt I owed you is already paid."

She stared at him. Hard. "Explain."

"Leila, I left you alive in your castle on the mountain. You know it wasn't out of the goodness of my heart. You are the one person in Switzerland who could compromise me. Could expose my real identity." His voice dropped to a whisper. "In this game, we both know that today's ally can be tomorrow's foe."

The fingers of Leila's left hand tightened around the hilt of her fork. Pierre was undoubtedly armed, but there was no way she was going down without a fight.

"In spite of everything," Pierre said, "I would have killed you long ago were it not for one thing." He held up a finger. "The fact that you—like me—were being hunted by the Germans. If they hate you, then perhaps you can be useful one day to me. The enemy of my enemy . . ." He bared his teeth in a brilliant and unexpected, smile.

"We can never be friends, Pierre," Leila said, holding his gaze.

"True enough," he said. "Friends are expensive. Besides, my beloved Bernadette would probably die of jealousy."

"Will you help or not?" It was time for straight answers.

Picking up another grape, Pierre rolled it between his thumb and middle finger. "I will go hunting with you," he said at length. "Not because I owe you a supposed debt of gratitude, but because I owe Elsbeth a debt of revenge. There is, however, a condition."

"I'm listening."

"These *supposed* random acts of terror in Geneva." He popped the grape into his mouth. "If it continues, life will become quite difficult for me. The pro-German cantons and the government are idiots. They think this is the work of the French sympathizers." He shook his head derisively. "Anyone with half a brain can see this is the work of professionals. The jobs are too clean. Too perfect. Which makes me wonder which group is behind them."

"How is this your problem?" Leila kept her voice steady. "I presume your men are not involved."

"Involved? Not at all! God knows I've no love for Deutschland. If the pro-German factions gain control of Switzerland, it will be only a matter of time before that dog Hindenburg controls Switzerland. Hindenburg knows my past. All that I have rebuilt will be destroyed. And I refuse to run anymore."

It made sense. Pierre had as much reason as anyone to resist a Swiss alliance with Germany. Like her, he realized that what would start as an alliance would end with Switzerland becoming an extension of a reformed German empire.

"What do you want from me?"

"You are *Leila*!" He threw his arms open as though stricken with awe. "Deadly spy. Lucious assassin. Trained by the best minds in Germany. Recruited by Werner Jaëger himself." Pierre moved closer, stopping about a foot away. The musky scent of his cologne filled the small space between them. "You know what I want."

"Information." Leila said evenly.

"I will find news about your son's whereabouts while you will discover who is staging these attacks. I'll find you when I have word." Pierre held out his hand. "Do we have an accord?"

Chapter 17

Bern, Switzerland

The russet-colored roof of the Federal Palace, Switzerland's seat of government, angled sharply beneath Leila's black boots. The Palace—a massive structure topped with a green dome at its center—sprawled out in all directions, its two rectangular wings reaching out like the grasping claws of a crab. A steady breeze, stiff and sharp, sliced through the balaclava that masked everything but her eyes, making them smart.

Overhead, a full moon clearly illuminated both the rooftop and the sprawling cobblestone plaza known as *Bundesplatz Bern*. The plaza was still full of Swiss border guards who had been recalled to the capital city due to the recent violence.

Elsbeth had chosen the worst possible night for an act of sabotage. Either time was running out, or the witch was deliberately pushing Leila to the limits of her conscience. So far, Leila had avoided bloodshed. But her luck—God's mercy, really—would only last so long. The question haunted her.

Would I kill an innocent to save my son?

Leila cringed within herself. She wouldn't hesitate to defend herself or those she loved. But Michael's life wasn't at stake tonight. Just Hindenburg's plans to rebuild a paper-thin empire. To kill while on a mission for Elsbeth would be an irreparable stain on her conscience.

Which is exactly what she wants.

Leila stiffened as a pair of soldiers walked by below her feet, chatting amiably as they paused to light up their cigarettes. The moon shone on their green uniforms and rounded helmets as they loitered in the area. They passed directly below her, then stopped.

So did her heart.

It was only the angle of the roof that let her see without being noticed by those below. Leila waited, immobile. Forcing her thoughts away from the imminent danger, she chose instead to flip through the events that had precipitated this moment.

Pierre. She had struck a deal with a demon to defeat the devil that had kidnapped her child. Her situation couldn't be more precarious.

Elsbeth wanted the pro-German faction of Switzerland to seize power. Pierre LaRue wanted things to remain as they were. David Lloyd George wanted her to uncover fresh intelligence of Germany's military intentions. All parties were determined to take advantage of Leila's skills. And all parties could turn on her at a moment's notice.

Leila held her breath as one of the soldiers below glanced upward.

Did I make a noise?

Experience taught her to remain motionless, defying the instinct to escape. Humans saw what they expected to see. Nothing more.

True to form, the Swiss guard glanced back at his friend, slapped his shoulder, and the pair meandered back toward their comrades.

Leila eased a pair of ebony field glasses from a pouch at her side. She had not slept in more than twenty-four hours. Pressing the glasses to her burning eyes, she looked for the window that had seemed slightly ajar. After arriving in Bern, she had spent the daylight hours furiously working out a plan that could get her inside the palace, blow up the council's meeting room, and escape unnoticed.

"Impossible." She hissed the word through teeth that were clenched to keep them from chattering. It might be impossible. But she was about to do it.

Her mind flitted through the details that could mean the difference between success and failure. Getting in was not the problem. The problem would be getting back out. She would have to wait to ensure that the explosion went off. By that time, it would be too late. The palace would be full of angry men.

Angry men with guns.

Pulling back the edge of her black glove, Leila angled the watch on her wrist so the moonlight spilled upon the silver hands. It was the dead of the night—three minutes to 4 a.m.—the time when most watchmen were usually the least alert.

Three minutes.

A tingle of anticipation slithered up and down Leila's spine, electrifying every pore. She was up against immense odds tonight—odds that both infuriated and exhilarated her. But as she planned out the next few steps, a part of her mind drifted back to M44's parting comment.

Sometimes we're just not strong enough to escape the evil. No matter how much we want to.

What exactly did the girl mean? She had been fascinated when Leila spoke of Malcolm and the new life they'd made together. Could it be that the girl *wanted* to be free of Elsbeth? If so, could she be turned into an ally?

Leila pursed her lips, riveted by the thought. M44 was highly placed in Elsbeth's circles. Turning her into a reliable asset was unlikely. But all options had to be explored if she wanted to find her son and destroy Elsbeth. Thomas had paved the way for her freedom, buying it at an immense cost. But now Leila needed to act upon his sacrifice.

How? She didn't know. Perhaps the girl was the key.

The moon escaped the blanket of shifting clouds and shone upon her masked face. Her eyes flitted to her watch.

Showtime.

———————◆◆●◆▶ ——————

Felix Calonder, president of the Swiss Federal Council, stroked his graying, short-clipped moustache as he eyed his predecessor, Edmund Schulthess.

His eyes flickered to the clock behind Edmund.

Four o'clock in the morning.

Felix didn't bother hiding a groan. He was worn out from the never-ending political debates about Switzerland's response and the terrorism that plagued Geneva. But equally concerning was how to navigate the political turbulence brought on by the prospect of peace between the Allied and Axis powers.

What attitude should Switzerland take toward a defeated Germany? This was the question that hounded him. And it was one that Edmund believed Felix could not answer.

After a late dinner and a quick shower, Felix had snatched a few hours of sleep. He'd returned to his office, expecting to find a quiet place in which he could draft legislation that would soothe the country's fears.

Instead, he had found the cantankerous former president of the Swiss Federal Council waiting outside his office with arms folded. How the garrulous old man had known he would come back to his office that evening was a mystery. All Felix knew was that, an hour after Edmund had started talking, he was ready to commit murder.

"It is a mistake to even *think* about developing trade relations with Germany after the war." Edmund's whine niggled its way into his troubled thoughts. "You *can't* give in to the will of the pro-German faction, Felix. You can't!"

"Edmund, I'm telling you these indiscriminate acts of violence will tear this country apart. We *must* make a clear statement that assures our citizens of German descent they will not be punished for their loyalty to Germany during the war." Felix blinked rapidly, then rubbed his eyes. He needed to sleep. But he continued, pushing past his exhaustion. "Don't you see, Edmund? They feel targeted because they're of German ancestry. They feel marginalized!"

"They'll get over it."

Felix ignored him. "The German-speaking cantons have taken to the streets. They're accusing their French-speaking neighbors of terrorism while the leaders of the French-speaking cantons deny everything. It's only a matter of time before full-scale violence breaks out. Is that what you want?"

"Let the police do their job." Edmund nodded sagely. "That's my advice."

Felix threw him a hard glare. "The police have found nothing. But *somebody* is responsible for blowing up our bank and burning our opera house. God knows what they'll do next. All in the name of some medieval notion of avenging France's honor!"

He slammed his fist against the table, no longer willing to let this ape control the conversation. "We *have* to give the pro-German citizens something. At least until we find out who's responsible for this barbarism. Otherwise, Switzerland may not survive this war!"

"And what kind of *statement* do you intend, exactly? A promise that we'll seek a rapprochement with Germany?" Edmund removed his round glasses, wiped them with a white handkerchief, then jammed them back in place. Apparently, he too could get tired.

A flicker of hope flared in Felix's chest. Perhaps getting to bed wasn't a fanciful dream after all.

"I know that in your time as president you fought long and hard against any form of allegiance with Germany," Felix said. "But—"

"But now that an armistice has been signed and Germany has clearly lost, we should seek some sort of absurd alliance? What sense does that make?" Schulthess snorted, leaning backward in his plush leather seat. "If I was still president, this conversation would never have happened. That is the problem with our law—it only allows a man to hold the office of president for one year!"

"Some would call that a blessing." Felix massaged his temples, feeling the onset of a headache.

"Like you, for instance?"

Felix didn't respond. The old man was nothing short of a political deadweight, an anchor that clung with ironfisted tenacity to prehistoric principles, refusing to let the ship of state sail forward.

"You ask what sense lies in a memorandum of understanding with Germany?" Felix leaned forward, pressing his index finger hard on the small desk that separated them as he thrust his face inches from Edmund's. "I'll tell you. First, it will reassure our German-heritage citizens that they are *not* forgotten. Second, it will promise them that they will not be persecuted. Finally, it will open the door for trade with Germany as it recovers from the war. There is no harm in that!"

"And how do you think the Allies will respond?" Edmund arched his bushy unibrow. "With parades and flowers? We almost lost our status as a neutral country when Arthur Hoffmann proposed a similar deal. A status that has kept our economy strong in these horrific times. You *do* remember the Thomas Steele affair?"

Felix threw up his hands in the air and expelled an exasperated breath. "That was entirely different. The war is over now, Edmund. *Over.*"

"You do realize that this treaty is only buying time for another war? France, England, and the United States will *crush* Germany in whatever treaty they draw up." Edmund curled his lower lip in a cynical leer. "If you lead Switzerland toward a political alliance with a defeated nation, you'll drag us into the mud. And whenever the next round of fighting begins, the Americans will remember that *we* aligned ourselves with their enemy."

Felix spoke through clenched teeth. "Age has blinded you to reason, Edmund. You're missing the realities that stare you in the face."

"Then why don't you go ahead and teach me, *boy?*"

Felix almost choked. He glared at Edmund in speechless silence for a few seconds, then held up three fingers. "First, we will hunt down the terrorists responsible for these attacks on Geneva. Second, we will reassure our citizens that Switzerland will foster warm relations with Germany. Third, we will begin normalizing business operations with Germany on terms that are favorable to us. Germany *has* to rebuild, Edmund. Loans issued to them now will only benefit Switzerland in the future."

"And that is where you stand?"

Felix held his gaze. "That is my final word. I have no doubt that the council and legislative assembly will bow to reason."

"Then I have nothing further to say." The former president's chair scraped the ground as he rose. "I've changed my mind, Felix. Our law that limits a president's term to one year is a good one."

"Yes?" Felix stood, stifling a yawn. "And why is that?"

Edmund grinned, a cold smile that held no humor. "Because it means you'll be out of office before you can do too much damage." With those words, he stormed out the room.

Felix shook his head as the door slammed shut. "What an arrogant *dummkopf.*" He shrugged on his coat, slipped the document he had drafted into his bottom drawer, then stepped out of his office into the spacious hallway of the Federal Palace.

Dark carpet covered the stone floors while gracious columns rose on all sides. It was an architectural masterpiece, designed to commemorate Switzerland's glorious past while embracing the changing needs of the future.

Only a few lights shone in the hallway at this hour, but it was enough to reveal the massive statues that protruded from the alcoves carved into the stone walls. A surge of pride struck

Felix's heart as he began his descent of the long, carpeted staircase that led outside.

This is what our country does best. Build for the future.

His gaze drifted from the iconic statue of three men with hands outstretched to the statue of Arnold Winkelried, the farmer who had given his life for Switzerland.

Sacrifice.

Now that was—

Felix skidded to an abrupt halt, eyes glued to Winkelried's statue. He blinked rapidly, then rubbed his eyes, trying to convince himself that they deceived him.

Did it . . . move?

He glanced around. The hallway was empty with only a few guards at the distant corners. Schulthess was nowhere to be seen. Besides, crazy as the old man was, Felix doubted he had taken to scaling walls. Brow furrowed, he edged closer to the stone banister, eyes intent on the statue that hovered in an alcove about ten feet away.

Whoosh!

He opened his mouth, but no sound came out. Like a demon, a shadow slipped out from behind the statue of Winkelried and leapt for his throat.

"Argh!" Felix held up his hands to ward off the attack, but the man's feet slammed into his chest, throwing him backward onto the carpeted stone stairs. He fell hard on his side. "Ugh!"

He rolled upon the impact, fumbling for the revolver he carried at all times. "Guards!" His shout was hoarse, and the assassin—for it could only be an assassin—sprinted toward the arched doorway. "Guards!"

At his second shout, the black-clad intruder whirled. Jerked a pistol from his waist.

Felix's heart forgot to beat. He pulled back the hammer on his own gun. Lifted it.

Pfft! The assassin's bullet ripped into his right shoulder.

Felix screamed as he spun backward, arms flailing wildly. His gun roared to life just as the doors to the outside burst open and a group of soldiers dashed into the hall, weapons ready.

"Mr. President, are you all right?"

"F-forget me!" Felix writhed on the ground, pointing with his gun in the direction of the door. "Get . . . him!" A shadow in the massive hall, the assassin had disappeared into the gloom. "Find him!"

Soldiers poured into the hall, scrambling in all directions. Most were concentrated in a landing at the base of the staircase when a blinding flash of light erupted from the second floor and waves of fire came roaring down the stairs.

"Look out!"

"Move, move!"

Prone on the ground and pressing his necktie to his bleeding shoulder, Felix watched in horror as the soldiers milled around, coughing, sputtering, and staring at the unexpected conflagration. The flames illuminated scrawling words in red that dripped like blood on the far wall. Words that caused more pain than the bullet in his shoulder.

Victoire aux Alliés! Sus aux allemands!

This time, the extremists had struck at the heart itself of Switzerland's government. *Victory to the Allies! Death to the Germans!* Felix trembled at the implications of the graffiti, for a moment oblivious to his wound. Flames licked at the interior of the Federal Palace. Unless he acted at once, those flames would consume the entire nation.

Chapter 18

Bern, Switzerland

Leila hugged the stone wall, letting her body melt into the shadows as dozens of guards dashed by. The swift stomping of their boots kept pace with the mad pulsing in her ears. She eased around the corner of an immense column, waiting for the explosion that would provide the distraction she needed to cover her escape. Her exit, a set of wide double-doors directly ahead of her, was only a few yards away. But between it and her were at least twenty armed men. *With many more probably outside.*

She inched forward, every muscle taut. *Komm schon!*

Silently Leila urged on the explosion, hoping it would provide enough of a distraction for her to sprint through the doors. Slowly, she turned, craning her neck to see over her shoulder. The man she had shot still writhed on the floor.

Remorse hit her. She hadn't meant to attack him. Whoever he was, he had simply been in the wrong place at the wrong time.

At least he's not dead.

The soldiers scattered about the room, fracturing the darkness with the crisscrossing beams of their high-powered flashlights. It was only a matter of time before someone turned on the hallway's main lights and—

Whoomp! Whoomp!

Fire belched out from the meeting room on the second floor, sending shards of wood, metal, and glass raining down in a hurricane of dust and flames. The concussion bowled over the men, knocking them off their feet like toy soldiers swept away by a child's hand.

But no child had done this.

Now!

Covering her eyes with her forearm, Leila hurtled toward the door, slamming it open with the side of her body. Alarmed cries rose on all sides. She lowered her arm, taking stock of her surroundings as she ran.

Six soldiers. Scattered about the plaza. Weapons drawn.

"Stop!"

She ducked as a bullet pinged near her ear.

"*Arretez-vous!*" Another voice repeated the command in French.

Leila threw herself to the ground and rolled, knowing another shot would follow.

Sparks lit up the night sky as a salvo of bullets bit into the stones where she had been seconds before.

Leila leapt to her feet, chest heaving, and bit off two shots. Then she pivoted. Darted for the closest street.

The plaza opened into a main throughway that was currently empty, whether because of the late hour or the gunshots she couldn't tell. Across the street, dozens of high-rise apartments loomed, buildings that could offer shelter.

Smack! Smack! Her feet pounded the pavement as she ran, desperate to gain the shelter of the buildings.

Thirty yards.

"*Fermati!*"

She ignored the command in Italian. There would be no arrest. There would be no trial. To stop was to die.

A bullet split the air near her face. Were it not for the sailing clouds that occasionally blocked the moonlight, she would be dead.

Fifteen yards.

Her lungs burned, but she lowered her head and ran faster.

Almost there—

"Agh!" Leila screamed as a bullet ripped into her side. She stumbled, pressing her hand to her burning ribs, then threw a glance over her shoulder. Guards who had been patrolling the palace grounds as well as those who had been inside were now pouring into the plaza. At least a half-dozen had caught sight of Leila and were hard on her heels, at most fifty meters and closing. They surged forward, doubtless realizing she had been hit.

Leila lurched upright, clenching her teeth against the pain as she forced herself onward. If she died, hope died. Malcolm would never see her again. Michael would be lost. Thomas would die.

"No!" she grunted, stretching her legs into an unsteady sprint. She had to stop the bleeding. Blood loss could kill in as little as five minutes. "I won't die . . . not today."

She whirled around, sighted, then pulled the trigger. A short scream. The closest of her pursuers went down, writhing as he held his injured leg. Leila fired twice more before breaking again into a run.

Gasping now with the growing agony of her wound, Leila ducked into a dark, narrow alley that led toward the River Aare. There was no time to seek shelter. No time to concoct a proper escape plan. The river was her only option.

Just a little further.

She had slowed to a staggering trot by the time her feet hit a narrow dirt path that cut through a thick cluster of trees lining the river. The blood loss was making it hard to focus. But at least she seemed to have lost her pursuers with the last turn. As the shouts behind her grew more distant, she allowed herself to slow long enough to draw a deep, shuddering breath into her laboring lungs.

Then a dog's howl turned her blood to ice. If her pursuers had brought in the blood hounds, there was no time to lose. Pivoting, Leila forged ahead through the tree line, which thinned near the water's edge. The river was narrow here, its current sluggish. On the opposite bank, she could make out trees, then a few scattered lights that hinted at some kind of small town.

"I can do this." Leila muttered. Then with another deep, shuddering breath, she dove in.

Shock numbed her. The freezing water temporarily dulled the pain. But as she swam through the dark water, each motion rekindled the burning in her side. Swimming sapped energy, and she had precious little to spare.

Leila surfaced, took a deep breath, and went down again. But not before spotting the flashlight beams of soldiers reaching the bank behind her. She'd made it about a third of the way to the far side.

Kicking hard, she continued swimming underwater while also letting the current push her downstream beyond direct line of sight from the bank behind her. Blood leaked out of her body with every stroke. So did her strength. Motion became harder. Her strokes less coordinated.

Air. Need . . . air.

Teeth clenched, Leila broke surface once more. The men behind her were distant shadows now, visible only because of the moon and their swerving flashlights. But a dog's staccato barking made clear they'd spotted exactly where she'd entered the water.

The current pooled about her, tugging her further downstream. Sucking in a fresh lungful of air, Leila dove again. The water closed over her head. Each stroke was sheer agony, an effort of supreme will.

I . . . can't make it.

Muscles trembling, she pushed against the current, aiming now for the far bank. Her lungs began to burn. But this time she doubted she had the strength to make it to the surface.

I just . . . can't.

Just then, a flailing hand touched clayish soil. Dimly aware of what this meant, Leila scrabbled onward. Seconds later, her head broke the surface. Coughing, spluttering, she dragged herself onto the muddy bank. She had made it!

Every part of her body *ached.* Leila rolled onto her back, arms spread wide. Breath came in short bursts. Her teeth began to chatter. The moon was a blurry blob overhead.

Then she heard the approach of running footsteps.

They've found me!

"No," she moaned. "N-no."

"Leila, hold still." A woman's voice reached her.

Leila squinted at the blurry face. "You?"

Ripping a piece of gauze off with her teeth, M44 squatted beneath the trees. She probed Leila's side, stopping when she heard Leila's grunt of pain.

"Hold still!" M44 stuffed the gauze into the wound, then secured it. "That'll hold. At least for a little while. Come. I know a safe place."

Rising, she pulled Leila to her feet and looped Leila's arm around her neck. Then they moved away from the river's edge and disappeared into the shelter of the trees.

Leila's eyes flickered open. She lay still, trying to gather her scattered thoughts. She was stretched out on top of a blanket in what looked like an underground cellar. A flashlight tucked into a crack in the wall opposite her partially illuminated the room. Leila closed her eyes, feigning unconsciousness as she tried to think past the pounding in her skull.

"How are you feeling?"

Her eyes snapped open.

Slowly, Leila pushed herself to a sitting position. "M44?" She groaned as she blinked to clear her eyes. The girl's blurry face came into focus.

"You were lucky." M44 pointed to Leila's side. "It was only a flesh wound, no bullet inside. I changed the bandage, cleaned it out, and bound it properly this time. It looks like the bleeding's stopped."

Leila pulled up her black shirt and probed the neatly packed gauze with her fingers. "What were you doing there?" Her gaze shifted to M44's face, taking in the neat, blond ponytail that hung down her back, the babyish face, and innocent blue eyes.

"Elsbeth sent me to observe and report back. I saw what happened. I saw you dive into the river. There's a bridge not too far down and I got there before the soldiers did. I wasn't sure I'd find you first, but then I heard you coughing." M44 looked away. "I know I should say I did it for the Fatherland. But the truth is . . . I think some part of me wanted to work with you. The great Leila Steele."

"So, you *again* took it upon yourself to act beyond the scope of your authority." Leila hardened her voice. "Or . . . *is* it beyond your authority? Somehow, I get the feeling you're more than you let on."

The girl met her eyes. "I'm Elsbeth's second."

"Ah. Well, that explains a lot." Wincing, Leila stood up. Her mind hummed with the possibilities of what she'd just learned. But she wasn't ready to take action—not just yet. Her eyes flickered around the room. "Where are we?"

"In a cellar beneath an abandoned apartment."

Leila nodded. The room was about ten feet long and just as wide. "How did you find this place?"

"It's a safehouse I've used before."

"Are there any supplies?" Leila said. She had hidden her own kit with her clothing before the strike on the palace.

"Some clothing, bandages, dried food." M44 pointed toward a small box in a far corner. "Here." She tossed over a metal key.

Leila turned to the trunk. "Elsbeth sent you to monitor the situation. But she didn't order you to help me."

The girl hesitated. "Like you said, this mission didn't give you much time to prepare." She shrugged. "I thought I'd help you even the odds."

"I see." Leila pulled out a tan skirt and sweater. They looked big for her frame but would have to do.

"You don't mind, do you?"

The corners of Leila's mouth twitched. "Not this time," she said, pointing to her wounded side.

The girl was silent for a moment. "Was it true what you said the other night? About finding freedom?"

"Every word." Turning her back, Leila changed quickly. She had been wearing pants last night. A man's garment. Therefore the police would be searching for a man, not two women. She would get her kit and head back to Geneva.

"But look at you now. You're back in your old life."

"You see, that's what Elsbeth can't understand. I can't go back because I am a different person. All I want is my baby." Adjusting the sweater, Leila turned around. "But motherhood is something Elsbeth never understood."

"I can see that."

Leila paused. There was something in M44's voice, a slight inflection that said more than the words themselves. "What do you mean?"

"Nothing, I . . ." The younger woman blinked rapidly.

"Look, you need to be honest with me," Leila said. "You're clearly competent. You have Elsbeth's trust. And it seems you know something about her personal life." She took a step closer, stopping only inches away from the girl. "I'm asking you one more time—who are you?"

"My name is . . . Mercedes." She jerked the flashlight from the wall. "We should go."

Leila caught her arm. "We're not going anywhere. Not until you explain. Everything."

The girl tugged at her braid. "Look, just forget it. I-I shouldn't have said anything. I'm just tired, all right? I'm just . . . just sick of it all."

"Sick of what, exactly?"

Mercedes set her jaws. "The lying. The betrayal. The violence. I hate it. I'm eighteen! I have a right to live how I want. And what I *want* is a normal life."

Leila remained silent, trying to force her tired brain to absorb the facts. "How did you get involved with Elsbeth?"

Mercedes sighed, rubbing the back of her neck. "I was orphaned before I can remember. The elderly couple who raised me died a few years ago." Her face tightened. "Despite my prayers."

A surge of compassion swelled in Leila's heart. Grief had shattered whatever faith Mercedes had possessed. She understood that feeling all too well.

"So I was thirteen and on my own, trying to find answers to life's tough questions. Eventually, I saw a poster calling for women to join the *Kriegsnachrichtenstelle*."

"*Women,*" Leila said. "Not girls."

"In our world, is there a difference?"

When Leila didn't respond, Mercedes continued, "The war broke out about a year after I joined the *Kriegsnachrichtenstelle*. I was fourteen then. Too young for Elsbeth's world. But she didn't think so. Elsbeth thought my innocent look made me the perfect spy."

Mercedes covered her face with her hands, speaking through her parted fingers. "I lost that innocence the first time Elsbeth sent me to get information from a British lieutenant on leave. Now there isn't anything I haven't done."

"You were so young!"

A bitter laugh broke through Mercedes's lips. "Too late, I learned that this kind of a life is slavery. Once you're in, you're never really out." The hands slid downward, slowly. "I hate her."

"But you were smart enough to hide your feelings."

"Oh yes. I learned to obey. To pretend compliance until I finally get close enough to break her." Fire glinted in the girl's cobalt eyes. "You see, I'm not doing this just for myself. I'm going to stop her from ruining any other girl's life."

"I understand."

"When I saw you again, I realized that now is the time." A note of eagerness crept into Mercedes's tone. "With you, I have a chance at winning. At finally being free."

"I didn't become free because I left espionage. In fact, everything I did to free myself only made my life became more complicated. It was only when I finally realized the power of faith that freedom found me."

Mercedes's tone hardened. "Don't ask me to trust God, Leila. I trust my wits and my gun."

"I know." Leila paused, weighing the possibilities. On one hand, the girl's story was plausible. On the other, she could be Elsbeth's ploy to flush out Leila's next move.

Can I trust her?

Mercedes pulled back from Leila and stiffened her shoulders to the stance of a trained soldier. But the light from her flashlight reflected on what might have been tears before she quickly wiped a hand across her eyes. "I-I've never told any of that to anyone."

Leila smiled as the first tendril of warmth she had felt in a long time curled around her heart. Mercedes—if that *was* her real name—had taken a bold step in sharing her identity. But Leila needed more reassurance.

"Then I'm doubly honored by your trust." Leila chose her next words carefully. "But *my* trust is something that must be earned . . . slowly."

Mercedes met her gaze. "I understand." Her voice was small and tight as though baring her soul had taken an immense amount of energy. Leila understood.

"Then you know what will earn my trust."

"Leila, I have no idea where Elsbeth has hidden Michael. She wouldn't share any information like that with me. There are times where I think she mistrusts her own shadow."

"But you can find out." Leila moved closer. "Mercedes, if you want to be free, you need to hit Elsbeth hard. My infant son is at the heart of an international conspiracy. No child deserves that! Get Michael to me and Elsbeth's whole scheme will fall apart."

"I . . . I'll try," Mercedes said.

Leila's eyes narrowed. Up to this point, she hadn't revealed anything to Mercedes that Elsbeth didn't already know. If the girl was a plant, she'd have nothing to report. If, on the other hand, Mercedes was genuine, she could be invaluable in discovering the truth about Germany's military intentions.

"Get me something actionable, Mercedes," she said. "It will be the first step toward earning my trust . . . and my friendship. Will you do this?"

Mercedes's glistening blue eyes met her own. "Yes."

Chapter 19

Geneva, Switzerland

lsbeth drew deeply on her cigarette, considering the woman before her. They stood alone in her apartment. Leila held a photograph of her son. The front page of a newspaper offered proof it had been taken that morning. In the picture, Elsbeth held Michael in her arms. The wretched creature gaped as widely as any drooling infant could, little suspecting that the woman who held him was only days away from snuffing out his pathetic life.

"So, the prodigal returns," Elsbeth said at last. "Tell me you didn't enjoy the action, the heart-pounding adrenaline."

"I didn't," Leila said, tearing her eyes from the photograph.

Elsbeth blew a ring of smoke and leaned back in her divan, one elbow propped on its wooden trim. The newspapers claimed that the soldiers around the palace had shot the terrorist, but Leila looked none the worse for wear.

More fake news.

"You should be proud, Leila," Elsbeth said. The fire had been brought under control in only an hour, but the political chaos Leila had unleashed would take far longer to bring to heel. "The odds were against you. Yet heroine that you are, you return victorious. Already that idiot President Colander has begun drafting legislation from his hospital bed that will cement a deal with Germany after the war."

Tossing the cigarette into an ashtray, Elsbeth rose and draped her arm over Leila's shoulder. "Don't you see? You've succeeded where anyone else would have failed."

"I don't consider shooting a man who did me no harm—or blowing up part of a palace—to be marks of success."

Ignoring her, Elsbeth turned to the large window. "I pushed you hard, putting obstacle after obstacle in your path. Little rest. High security. No time to scout and plan." She whirled around, pride flaring within her. "Still, Leila, you exceeded even my wildest expectations." Pressing a fist against her own chest, Elsbeth moved closer. "Can't you see it's your *duty* to continue my legacy when I'm gone?"

"No, Elsbeth." Leila's voice cut through Elsbeth's heart with the mercy of a stiletto. "The day you die, humanity will rejoice. *I* will rejoice."

Elsbeth recoiled, stung. "You don't know what you're saying. Why, if I had to be a mother, I would want a daughter like you."

She stepped over the lion skin that covered part of the wooden floor and threw herself into the divan, seething at life's injustices. How she wished that Leila was at her side instead of that doll-faced brat!

Mediocre Mercedes. True, the girl was dependable. Give her orders and she would carry them out. She had the skills, the wit, and the beauty to stand in second place. But time and again, Leila had proven she had the ability to lay the world at Germany's feet.

"Give me my son," Leila said. "This is over now."

Elsbeth slanted Leila a glance. "Perhaps I should keep him. Raise him as my child. Wouldn't that be delicious?"

Something akin to panic flared in Leila's eyes. "You know you wouldn't."

"Why not?" Elsbeth lay a finger thoughtfully on her slightly parted lips. "Perhaps one day he will lead a *Kriegsnachrichtenstelle* of his own."

The wretched boy was alive only because Elsbeth knew his mother would turn outright against her if he died. As long as he lived, there was a chance that Leila would repent of her betrayal and return to the shadows. But Hindenburg's warning flashed through Elsbeth's mind.

The girl must be silenced.

If Leila continued on this course of persistent obstinance, there could only be one outcome—her death.

"Give him to me." Leila dropped to her knees, hands clasped as though praying. "I'm begging, Elsbeth. Give me back my son! You've got what you wanted."

Elsbeth propped one elbow on her knee, leaning forward. "Have I?"

"Yes!" Leila leaned back on her haunches. "An alliance between Germany and Switzerland is forthcoming—you said so yourself."

Elsbeth smiled.

"There's more to this sick joke, isn't there?" Leila regained her feet and drilled her with a hard stare. "It's not enough that I've created a crisis. It's not enough that I risked *my life* for you. You want more. You always want more."

Elsbeth studied her evenly filed fingernails. "Hm, yes. Something I quite forgot to mention."

"What?"

"Oh, nothing major. Just . . . an assassination."

"What?"

It was the same word, but this time horror flooded Leila's voice. Why, Elsbeth couldn't fathom. What could possibly be more empowering for a woman than to see a man slumped dead at her feet? Nature had given men strength. Science had given women guns.

"I want someone killed." Elsbeth shifted her gaze to Leila's stricken face. "In London."

"London? You're insane!"

"Aren't we all, *Tochter?*" Elsbeth spread her hands outward in a helpless gesture. "We've spent the past four years butchering each other over scraps of land no one really needed. Millions are dead. What can you call that but *insane?*"

She stalked toward the window, hands clasped behind her back. "But when the entire world is mad, only the crazy are sane. So there is only one way to win this game—be mad enough to gamble it all."

"No," Leila said.

Elsbeth whipped around, thrusting her finger in Leila's face. "No? This is the only way for world peace. One leader over all the nations. One nation over all others."

"Germany."

"*Ja.*" Elsbeth thrust her hand upward in a sharp salute, fingers together and palm facing down. "*Deutschland über alles!* Germany above all others." Lowering her arm, she said, "The end of the war will bring just that—global peace."

"By slaughtering the opposition?"

"Well, what else would you have us do? Hold hands and pray?" Moving closer, Elsbeth said, "Doesn't your Bible claim that one ruler will reign with a rod of iron?"

Leila was silent.

"So this is prophesy then. Prophesy in the making. And you have a part to play. Eliminate a man who threatens our vision."

"I cannot kill for you. Not anymore."

"Hope for the best, plan for the worst," Elsbeth said. "I taught you that the first day you entered my school. Naturally, I hoped for the best in you—that you would do this voluntarily. But I've planned for the worst."

Elsbeth eyed her dispassionately. "It's the moment of truth, dear. You decide. Your conscience . . . or your child? Which one dies?"

Leila closed her eyes.

"There is an armistice in effect across Europe," Elsbeth continued. "With the number of travelers returning from the war, British security will be lax. They won't expect a spy to come *into* the country. Not now. All the same, you will enter Britain in disguise. I will, of course, see that you receive the needed documents."

"My target?" Leila said in a monotone voice, eyes fluttering open.

"Male. Mid-thirties. Dark hair. M44 will fill you in."

"The location?"

Elsbeth's lips curved upward. This was going to be *delicious.* "Saint Paul's Cathedral in London."

Leila sucked in a sharp breath. "In a *church?* You're an animal!"

"And here I thought I was being humane." Elsbeth heaved a dramatic sigh. "What better place to die but in the house of God? He'll already be halfway to meet his Maker." She smirked.

"That's—"

"Just do your duty and all will be . . . forgiven."

Leila's face darkened. "I already made it clear what my duty is."

"You did," Elsbeth snapped, serious now. "Your duty is to your son. By eliminating this man, you *serve* your son."

"And if I don't kill him, then everyone I care about dies." Leila's voice was flat. Dull.

Good.

She was resigning herself to the mission. Elsbeth arched a pencil-thin eyebrow. "I'm sorry, was that a question?"

A muscle jerked in Leila's cheek.

"Of course, you won't be alone. M44 will go with you to make sure you don't stray from the path. If I don't hear a successful report, the extermination begins." Elsbeth drew a slim finger across her throat. "Starting with Michael the archangel."

Without another word, Leila pivoted and stalked out the door.

Elsbeth waited for several minutes, then moved toward an ornate, bronze telephone in the corner of the room. A few moments later, a female voice sounded in her ear. "*Allo?*"

"Is everything ready for the London operation?"

"*Oui.* Your instructions have been followed to the letter. He will receive the telegram once he returns to his London residence. Do not worry. He will be at the church."

"Good." Elsbeth let the receiver drop back into place, then glided to the window.

The wheels of history turn on tiny hinges.

Leila and Mercedes moved quickly in the direction of the *hauptbahnhof,* or train depot.

"Go to London, Leila," Elsbeth murmured. Leila would never recover from the crime she was about to commit. But a barren conscience produced the most fruitful spy. And Hindenburg demanded solid evidence of her loyalty to Deutschland. What better proof could there be than the death of the man who'd seduced Leila from her true calling?

Elsbeth's eyes narrowed into slits. Leila's judgment had been clouded by the empty promise of forgiveness and a new beginning. The coming encounter would shatter her faith. Once his father was dead, Elsbeth would see to it that little Michael swiftly joined the angelic choirs. Then—when Leila was broken and alone—Elsbeth would gently woo her back to the life she now shunned. It had happened before. And humans never changed.

"Do your duty, Leila," Elsbeth said again. A cold smile touched her lips. "When Malcolm is dead, then you will truly be free."

Chapter 20

London, Great Britain

"Peace be with you, Rabbi." Joseph Mara removed the blue-and-white *tallit*, or prayer shawl, from off his head and waved farewell to the leader of his synagogue. The rabbi, a kindly man with a face that had more lines than a map, smiled through his thick beard. "*Shabbat shalom.*"

It was the afternoon of *shabbat*. For the first time in the decade since his beloved wife had left, Joseph felt the need to return to the synagogue. The decision was not based so much on a desire to reconnect with his Jewish roots as it was to find the answer to the question that had hounded him since the night Thomas had been arrested

Are there still miracles in this world?

Thomas's blind faith had unnerved him, making him question the power of his own convictions. What gave this man—this follower of a false messiah—the ability to believe when every scrap of evidence conspired against him?

While he had hoped to find answers in the synagogue, Joseph was to be disappointed. Thomas had brought out the best in him, challenging him with his raw, undiluted faith.

"May *Hashem* reward him." Squaring his shoulders, Joseph rubbed his hands together as he began the short trek back to his

183

home. He had not overtly identified with his Jewish heritage since becoming an adult. While Jews had lived in Britain for over half a millennium, social stigmas continued to make life difficult. Keeping his faith private made him less threatening in the eyes of his clients.

Thomas had been different. Like Judah Maccabee, Thomas had taken a bold stance against the prejudices of his class, claiming Joseph's expertise was the only thing that mattered.

That is why I'm ready to risk everything for him.

Since taking on Thomas Steele's case, he had received a slew of nasty letters, including three threats against his life. Joseph frowned as he loosened the gun that hung in a concealed holster beneath his left arm. In times like these, he could not be too careful.

He had just reached the bottom of the steps when a muscular, dark-haired man stepped out of the small space between his home and the adjoining house.

"Joseph Mara," he said in a low voice.

Startled, Joseph reached for his gun. He stopped abruptly, hand on its hilt.

"Malcolm?"

Malcolm nodded, then glanced around. "It's good to see you, Joseph. Can we talk?"

"Yes." Joseph pointed to the door. He pulled his key from his pocket and mounted the flight of stairs. "Quickly. Come inside."

Malcolm spoke as Joseph unlocked the door. "My father, he is well?"

"As well as one can be in the Tower." Joseph kept his voice low. The street was still empty, but one never knew who watched from the shadows.

"I can't imagine how he feels, caged up like some vicious beast." Malcolm's fist clenched. "They didn't even have the decency to offer him house arrest."

"It's serious, Malcolm." Joseph shook his head. "I am very concerned."

Within the house, he motioned for Malcolm to take a seat by the fireplace and closed the door. "I'm afraid we don't have much time. I must get to the Tower to confer with your father."

Malcolm pointedly eyed the folded *tallit* in Joseph's arms. "On the Sabbath?"

"Yes, well, acts of mercy are the will of God." Joseph tilted his head back and forth. "I believe it was Jesus of Nazareth who taught it was permissible to rescue a donkey from a ditch. I'm sure we both agree your father is more important than a donkey."

Malcolm sighed, rubbing his forehead. "I've been ordered to report to Hughes's office in Whitehall by noon tomorrow, but I wanted to see you first."

"It's good that you did. I have news, shared with me by your father."

"Of Leila?"

"Yes." Joseph nodded.

Malcolm leaned forward, eyes intent on Joseph's face. "Tell me. Everything."

"Before I do, since this is the first time I'm seeing you since the birth of your son, please accept my heartfelt congratulations. When Thomas left, they were both safe and healthy."

"Thank God," Malcolm said. He smiled, but Joseph could still see worry in his eyes. "You don't know how much it means to me to know they're both safe."

Joseph raised a warning finger. "I urge you not to communicate with her at all. Especially now. Thomas's case already hangs by a thread. One call, one telegram to Switzerland could seal his fate."

"I understand."

"Now." Joseph leaned back in his chair, fingers folded behind his head. "I sent tickets to your father's butler, Greyson, asking him and the maid Jenny to come to London post-haste. They may be valuable in establishing a credible defense. Unless I miss my guess, they will soon be at your London home—if they are not already there."

"Good." Malcolm's eyes glinted. "Now I need to see my father. Can you make that happen?"

"Yes. As Thomas's barrister, I can arrange it. Meet me at the Tower Bridge tomorrow at noon." Joseph rose. "I managed to gain an adjournment, but the Crown wants a speedy resolution on this case. He goes to trial in two days."

"So soon?"

"Malcolm . . . this case has all but been decided," Joseph said sadly. "There are powerful witnesses on the side of the prosecution."

"What of the defense?"

"Lord Curzon has agreed to testify on your father's behalf," Joseph said.

"Curzon is a privileged member of the acting government and a man who knows Father well. I imagine he's your strongest witness."

"The entire case may rest on his testimony," Joseph said, nodding. "I cannot promise victory, Malcolm. But I promise that I will not stop fighting until this is over."

———————————◆◆●◆▶———————————

"This . . . *this* is your home?" Eleanor's brown eyes swiveled from the Steele town home to Malcolm's face and back again.

It was a large Georgian-era mansion. White stucco covered the upper level while a pale-red brick lined the bottom of the house.

"Will." Eleanor shook her husband's leg. "Will, do you see this? Tell me I'm not dreamin'. Tell me that I'm goin' to sleep tonight in a house fit for King George himself!"

Will whistled as Joseph Mara's car slid under a brick archway and slowed to a standstill. "A man couldn't get tired living here, that's certain."

A valet hurried to open the door for Malcolm. "Thank you, Jonas," he said. Turning back to Will, "Given that Northshire is a good distance away and Father was constantly in London on business, he thought it best to acquire the property."

"Welcome home, Lord Malcolm."

Malcolm turned at the familiar voice. "Greyson!"

Greyson, dressed as always in his impeccable black swallowtail uniform and spotless white shirt, bowed deeply. "I can't tell you how good it is to see you again, Your Lordship."

Malcolm gripped his butler's hand. "Nor can I." His gaze shifted to the maid beside the butler. "Jenny, it is good to see you as well."

Jenny flushed, eyes darting to the gray stones below. "Thank you, Lord Malcolm."

Malcolm moved forward, clapping Greyson on the shoulder, then addressed them all. "As we all know, these are somber times for Northshire with both my father's reputation and the status of the estate in question."

Greyson shifted closer, his deep voice filling the small space between them. "We are with you, Your Lordship. You are not alone."

Malcolm locked eyes with the intuitive butler. "And for that I am grateful."

"All the same, I must speak with you."

"I'll join you in the study." Malcolm turned to Will and Eleanor, who waited in respectful silence. "Jenny will help you get sorted. We'll be in London until after the trial, so make yourself comfortable."

Then, pivoting, he followed Greyson inside.

◆◆●◆◆

Joseph Mara leaned back against the corner of the hearth, contemplating Malcolm's reaction to the news with which Greyson had shattered his world. It was something Joseph couldn't understand.

There was anger, yes. His son had been abducted.

There was also an understandable measure of fear. His face had gone white when Greyson informed them that Leila had gone after Michael.

But throughout an ordeal that would have sent an ordinary man into a fit of rage, spewing profanity and swearing vengeance, Mara had observed only a calm, steady determination.

This was not the Malcolm he remembered. This was not the son who had repeatedly shamed his father, running headlong through life as though it was something meant to be wasted. This man . . . was changed.

But Joseph knew from years of defending criminals that humans never changed. Reformed? Perhaps. For a while. But never truly changed.

Yet here Malcolm stood, speaking words that defied everything Joseph understood about human nature. Words of faith in a time that deserved only doubt.

"It's all right, Greyson. It will be all right. I'll get them both back, and we *will* all come home." Malcolm's voice was tight, but Joseph couldn't miss the confident undertone.

This illogical approach—shared by both Thomas and his son—left Joseph confused. He knew that Malcolm had shifted from complete disbelief to a life of faith. But years of experience had taught Joseph that religion was often a matter of convenience instead of the heart. Still, the question that had lingered since the fateful night of Thomas's arrest tormented him.

Can their Christ truly change men's hearts?

Like Gideon of old, Joseph needed a clear answer. Only then would he have peace. His eyes flickered closed, and his lips moved in soundless prayer. If their faith was true, he needed a sign.

"Make the impossible happen, *HaShem*, if they speak the truth. Bring the wife and child home. Then I will know . . . and I will believe."

He exhaled slowly, opening his eyes to see Malcolm standing at the ceiling-high window .

"Thank you for the news, Greyson." Malcolm lifted his chin, clasping his hands behind his back. They trembled slightly. "At least now I know how things stand."

"Is . . . is there anything we can do, Your Lordship?" Greyson took a step back as though unsure himself if the man before him was indeed the boy they had once known.

Malcolm turned toward the two men, a strange light smoldering in his dark eyes. "Yes," he said. "You can pray."

◆◆●◆▶

The evening sky above London was a thick blanket of gray. A low-lying fog slithered across the courtyard, wending its way like a serpent toward the building itself. Hours after Greyson had broken the news about his son's abduction and his wife's disappearance, Malcolm still stood before the window, seeking answers that seemed not to exist.

His heart clenched. Two situations pulled him in conflicting directions. On the one hand, he couldn't leave England with his father's trial pending. But to remain here while his wife faced the crisis of their kidnapped child alone?

Unthinkable.

Greyson's voice broke into his troubled thoughts. "Excuse the intrusion, Your Lordship."

Malcolm turned. On the other side of the drawing room, a crackling fire radiated heat from the confines of a marble hearth. "Don't apologize, Greyson. My problems will still be there waiting after we've finished our conversation." He forced a smile. "What is it?"

"A telegram."

Malcolm took the proffered plain cream envelope and opened it. For a few moments, he stood stock still, reading the note multiple times.

"Is everything all right, Your Lordship?"

"I don't know, Greyson," Malcolm said without lifting his eyes from the paper. After a moment, he added, "I saw Will walk across the courtyard a few moments ago. Please. Fetch him."

After the butler had gone, Malcolm read the note once more, then tossed it into the fireplace. Leaning forward, he rested his forehead on the cool marble slab that sprawled out on either side of the hearth.

Questions hummed about in his mind like a swarm of German bullets.

How could Leila be in England? Had she found evidence that Michael had been smuggled out of the continent? If not, what else would make her leave Switzerland and ask him to meet?

Malcolm loosened the gray cravat around his neck, then unbuttoned the collar of his white shirt. On the battlefield, he had learned that the difference between life or death often lay hidden in the details. Years of war had made him cautious. Was this message truly from Leila?

He would meet her. Of that there was no question. But he would take precautions. And for that, he needed backup.

Footsteps outside the drawing room were followed by a series of quick knocks.

"Enter," Malcolm said.

Greyson entered first, dipping his head in a slight bow. "Will Thompson, Your Lordship."

Malcolm nodded his thanks, then said, "Will, come in."

Will, dressed in faded brown trousers and a loose white sweater, stepped past Greyson, who exited and closed the door. Will's eyes rolled around the room. "It's hard to believe one man can own all this."

"Yeah? Well, you might think owning it all is grand, but believe me, hanging on to it is quite another animal altogether." Malcolm waved him over. "I need to talk to you about something that's come up."

"You're asking my advice?" Will asked quizzically. "Not quite the normal procedure for the gentry. No offense."

"None taken." Malcolm slanted him a humorless smile. "I've always been quite the rebel. Besides, you and I fought together before you even knew who I was. You even saved my life once." He paused. "You and Eleanor showed me that everyone had value, regardless of parentage or status." His eyes snapped to Will's face. "I think that gives your opinion merit."

"You plan on running for office? Quite the speech, that."

"I meant it, Will."

"Well, glad I've had some impact on the world," Will said, sighing as he sank into a plush leather armchair and stretched out his legs. "Ah . . . a fellow could get used to this, you know." He rolled his head in Malcolm's direction. "Got any more of these lying around? I could use one in my bedroom."

"Don't get too comfortable. We're leaving soon."

"Leaving?" Will arched an eyebrow. "You mean, to visit your father? I wouldn't reckon you'd want company given the circumstances and all."

Malcolm dropped into the chair across from him. "I've had word—a telegram—from someone claiming to be Leila. I'm to meet her at Saint Paul's Cathedral at midnight."

"So . . . you want me to tag along while you go on a midnight rendezvous with your wife?"

"Are you even listening, Will?" Reaching over, Malcolm jerked the pillow from behind Will's head, letting it smack against the wooden frame. "A little easier to focus now, is it?"

"Oi, all right. All right." Will sighed as he sat up, rubbing the back of his head. "So, you're thinking that this meeting might be a trap. Is that it?"

"It's possible. I mean, think about it. The Germans know Leila is my wife. If this whole assassination bit is still in the works, like as not the Huns have me high at the top of their 'to-be killed' list. What better way to rub me off the ledger than to set a trap with Leila as the bait?"

"I see." Will stroked his chin. "And it's not as though you can take this to the authorities."

"No! My hands are tied, and they know it. If it *is* Leila, the last thing I want is for Hughes to find out she's back in England. I've no other choice but to handle this on my own. Unless—"

"Unless I come with you."

"That decision is totally up to you," Malcolm said, spreading his hands wide. "And Eleanor."

"Again, you ask my opinion. I'm flattered." Propping his elbow on the armchair's side, Will rested his chin on his knuckles. "I don't know what to make of this. I'm not just a hired hand?"

"I prefer to think of you as an ally."

Will considered this for a moment. "Well, there is the odd chance that the Germans do plan to commit murder. If there's a threat to King and Country and I don't do my bit in stopping it, El will string me up herself. The woman's quite the patriot." Will paused, serious now. "Just keep in mind, Malcolm, I'm doing this for our country—not for you."

"I understand," Malcolm said. Will was a good man, but it would take time to regain his trust. Malcolm knew he deserved no less.

"Once we're clear." Will rubbed his hands together briskly. "So I'm in. What's the plan?"

"Pack your bags," Malcolm said. "I'll tell you on the way."

Chapter 21

London, Great Britain

Robert Hughes's scooter clattered to a stop on the uneven limestone that formed the foundation of the British empire's most infamous prison—the Tower. But even these ancient stone walls could not keep out the noise of Londoners celebrating victory.

Victory. It was a weak word—anemic really. A phrase that in a rather myopic way focused on the outcome of a fight rather than the actual cost of the struggle itself. Who knew how long the armistice would hold? A month? A few years? But those who had sacrificed everything to gain this victory would soon be nothing more than illegible letters on a granite tombstone.

With a soft groan, Hughes clambered down from the scooter and limped toward the prison cell of a man who was once the empire's perfect son. Now that same empire purposed to kill him.

"You know, Thomas, this all seems so familiar. What do the French call it? *Déjà-vu?*"

His lips parted in a craggy smile despite the dull ache the moist air provoked in his severed joint. "A year ago, your daughter-in-law was chained to that same wall. Now I have you."

Silence, broken only by the *plop, plop* of water that trickled down the rocky walls to the murky puddles of sewage on the floor.

"Ironic how history repeats itself, isn't it?" Hughes said. "Four centuries ago, Thomas More betrayed his king. He was contained in this very cell. Now another Thomas—another peer of the realm—does the same."

Hughes steepled his fingers, tapping them lightly together. "I know I should be happy. I'm the villain of the story, am I not? Evil always rejoices when good is crushed underfoot."

His eyes narrowed. "But that's the problem. *You* are the evil one here—not me. Your mother must have mixed up her disciples." Hughes thrust a finger through the bars, his voice rising to an angered hiss. "Thomas may have doubted, but he still held a scrap of loyalty. But you? Well, you're nothing but a Judas!"

Thomas sat, draped in a simple gray-and-white-striped prison uniform, on a small rocky ledge that protruded from the uneven surface of the cell's jagged walls. Somehow, he still managed to lend an irritating air of dignity to the cell.

"What? Nothing to say? Well, consider this." Hughes glared at him. "I'll get Leila. Somehow, I'll get my hands on your precious daughter-in-law."

Thomas rose slowly and stepped toward the set of massive iron bars that separated him from the outside world. "You'll never get what you want."

"What I want?" Hughes's nostrils flared. "What I *want* is to exterminate every wretched traitor in the empire. This is about patriotism, man! But you've forgotten what that word means."

"I sweat drops of blood for King and Country." Thomas gripped the iron bars, glaring down at his captor. "Nothing can destroy my love for England."

Hughes scoffed. "You mean, nothing but German gold and German promises! Promises that turned out empty in the end.

How does it feel, I wonder, to lose everything?" He limped backward, leaning heavily on his cane.

"I haven't *lost* anything."

"The evidence against you is overwhelming. Your friends have abandoned you. The nation's rage is focused on you, Thomas." Hughes flicked his wrist. "After your trial tomorrow, you *will* die."

"And then you'll hound my son, hoping to find some evidence of a conspiracy that does not exist."

"Ah . . . yes, your son. Malcolm Steele, hero of Passchendaele. The man who saved an entire mud-bogged platoon single-handed." Hughes's voice rose with every word. "The man who held the Germans off until reinforcements could arrive with nothing more than two machine guns. And yet, he has never been promoted."

Hughes thrust his face inches from the bars. "You'd better believe I'm going to watch him. One wrong move and the Steeles will be the best customers the undertaker ever had!"

Thomas cocked his head as muted shouts reverberated through the walls. "Do you hear the noise outside? The shouts? The cheering?"

"I'm a cripple. I'm not deaf."

"The armistice has been signed," Thomas said. "Soon the powers that parliament has given you will expire. You won't be able to conduct random searches or arrests at whim. Law and order will reclaim Britain."

The look on Thomas's face made Hughes's blood run cold. It wasn't hate or animosity. It was . . . pity.

"Get to the point, Thomas."

"The war will never end for you, will it? You will continue to fight to prove your infirmity will not hold you back.

As long as you are thus driven, the war will rage in your mind." Thomas's gaze drifted to Hughes's wooden leg. "For you are your own worst enemy."

Hughes recoiled, flinching before the accuracy of Thomas's words. He was about to bite off a vicious reply when the tromp of approaching boots reached his ears. Hughes turned to see his lieutenant, flanked by Thomas's pet monkey-turned-barrister Joseph Mara.

The barrister was shadowed by another man who carried himself like a soldier. Hughes squinted, recognizing him as he stepped into a patch of filtered light.

Malcolm.

"Speak of the devil, and he'll come running," Hughes said.

With a contemptuous glare in his direction, Malcolm shoved his way past Hughes and gripped his father's hands through the iron bars that separated them. "Father, are you all right?"

"Malcolm." Thomas clung to his arms, saying nothing for several moments.

"Beggin' your pardon, sir." Lieutenant Jefferies gestured to the men behind him. "But these two have business with yourself and the prisoner."

"You mean, with His Lordship, *Sir* Thomas Steele." Malcolm turned around, a muscle twitching in his jaw.

Leaning on his walking stick, Hughes stepped around his lieutenant and faced the slim-built soldier. Hard living had suited Malcolm. Muscle strained against the shirt of his khaki uniform. His dark hair was cut low. His bearing was erect, his piercing gaze sharp.

"Well, if it isn't the little tomcat back from the war. I must say, from what I hear of your exploits in the field, it appears you *do* have nine lives." Hughes chuckled. "They say God has a sense of humor. The fact that you managed to come home when millions of good men did not must be part of a divine jest."

"Believe me, I know how high the butcher's bill has been. Unlike you, I was there!" Malcolm's hooded blue-gray eyes bored into Hughes's skull. "While you were dreaming up ways to imprison my wife, arrest my father, and destroy my family name, I was protecting our shores from the Huns!"

"Malcolm!" Thomas called out from the cell. "Don't!"

"Oh, believe me, boy, I have been fighting." Hughes's lips curled back in a snarl. "As you'll see tomorrow, there are many ways to wage war."

"I was ordered to report to you in London." Lifting his narrow chin, Malcolm folded his arms across his chest. "What do you want to know?"

"All in good time, Steele."

"Ahem. One moment, Lord Malcolm." Joseph Mara laid a hand on Malcolm's shoulder. "The law grants the accused time to confer—in private—with his barrister. I therefore must ask you, Sir Robert, to leave us."

"Oh yes." Hughes dipped his head. "But remember one thing, Mara. No matter what legal tricks you conjure up, Thomas Steele will die." He threw a mocking salute in Malcolm's direction and mounted his red scooter. "Have a pleasant evening, gentlemen."

◆◆●◆◆

As soon as Hughes disappeared around the corner, Thomas lurched toward the bars of his cell, grabbed Malcolm, and pulled him as close as he could.

"Malcolm!" His heart threatened to burst with pride, with joy, with a thousand other feelings too wonderful to identify. "My son, home from the war." Emotion made his voice hoarse.

Millions of sons had not come home. But here, in the flesh, was the pride of his life.

"It's over, Father." Malcolm held him. "I'm home. Home for good."

Thomas pulled back, eyes roaming over him. Malcolm was every inch a soldier, as tall as Thomas, and resplendent in his freshly pressed tan uniform.

"So!" Thomas said. "I know you haven't seen your son yet, but how does it feel to know you're a father?"

Malcolm dropped his head. Something was wrong.

"What is it?"

It was Joseph Mara who answered. "It would be best if we did not discuss the situation at the present." He looked pointedly in the direction that Hughes had taken. "One never knows just how many ears the walls have."

"I see." Thomas made some rapid mental assumptions. Whatever troubled Malcolm obviously had to do with his son and Leila. But Malcolm would not have been in direct communication with Leila. Greyson, Jenny, or perhaps both must have returned to England with news from Switzerland. But they would never abandon Leila or little Michael, which meant that they were either missing or . . .

No! He lurched forward. "How are you coping?"

"It's all right, Father." Malcolm gestured to the bars. "Let's focus for now on getting you out of here."

Joseph stepped closer, lowering his voice. "Your trial is set for tomorrow at noon. It'll be held at the Old Bailey."

"The most notorious court in London." Thomas grimaced.

Malcolm's voice was grim. "With the armistice going into effect today, it's clearly no coincidence that your trial is tomorrow."

Thomas snorted as the pieces fell into place in his mind. "Hughes wants this done quickly while the people's anger at the Germans is still at fever-pitch."

Joseph gave a slow, sad nod. "There will be no appeal. We win or we lose the first time around."

Thomas focused on Malcolm. When he spoke, his voice was iron. "You must not try to defend me, Malcolm."

"What? You think Hughes will use whatever I say about you as proof that I was somehow involved in a plot that never existed?"

"Why else do you think he wants you here for the trial?"

Malcolm stared at his father. "I was summoned to answer his questions."

"Questions he'll ask during the trial." Thomas gripped the bars. "Believe me, I know how Hughes thinks. He doesn't plan to question you personally. He'll put you on the prosecution's witness stand and make you testify against me. That is his way of testing your loyalty to the empire."

Malcolm's face paled. "So if I speak for you, he'll accuse me of treason."

"Anything you say in my defense will be used against you personally. There is no saving me, son. You *must* save Northshire. If you do not, Hughes will win and everything I have fought for will be lost." Thomas held his son's gaze for several long moments. He knew he was asking Malcolm for the impossible, but there were times when only the impossible would suffice.

"You know why I came back to Britain, don't you?"

"For Northshire." Malcolm folded his arms across his chest. "To make sure that your descendants will be able to claim their inheritance."

"Exactly." Thomas nodded his approval. "So if the Crown calls you to the witness stand, you must go. You must tell them *everything* in order to keep your name clear with Hughes. Only then will we be able to start to rebuild."

"Then . . . there is no way we can win this trial." Malcolm pulled in a deep breath, held it, then released it slowly. "If I testify for you, everything is lost. If I speak against you, then you will die."

Thomas gripped his hand. "If your testimony condemns me, so be it. I know you love me. Speak the truth no matter what happens. If you perjure yourself, you will be arrested. Shot. Northshire will go to ruins. Leila and little Michael will never come home. You must be blameless."

"Your father is right." Joseph tugged at his salt-and-pepper beard.

"But how can I—?"

"It's an order, soldier!" Thomas pulled back and lifted his chin. Everything hinged on Malcolm's choice. There could be no weakness. No hesitation.

"Pursue victory relentlessly," Thomas snapped. "Nothing else matters. Will you fulfill your duty?"

Malcolm straightened and flung his shoulders back. Eyes glistening, he snapped out a crisp salute. "Yes, sir!"

Chapter 22

Saint Paul's Cathedral. London, Great Britain

"Okay, Leila, I'm done." Mercedes tossed the pencil onto the stone floor. She stretched as much as she could in the small room—a large closet, really—that wasn't visible from the main floor of the crypt in Saint Paul's Cathedral. She and Leila had waited hidden since early morning in the dry, cramped space. A few rays of light passed through a ventilation duct near the ceiling, illuminating the sheet of paper that lay between them.

"So these are *all* the places you've seen Elsbeth go in the past month." Leila sat cross-legged, scrutinizing the rough map that Mercedes had drawn. Ten squares occupied seemingly random places in the girl's rough sketch of Geneva.

"I think so. But I can't say that her trips have anything to do with your son. Elsbeth changes his location at random times. And she never takes him anywhere. Someone always comes to get him. Sometimes a man. Sometimes a woman. But they're always people that I've never seen before. She trusts me only up to a point."

"But she'll need to keep Michael in Geneva so she can easily assure me he is still alive."

Mercedes tilted her head to one side. "Possibly. With Elsbeth, you never really know." She leaned forward. "But I managed to slip inside her office before we left Geneva. Inside her desk, I found a locked drawer."

"And?" Leila's gaze sharpened.

"There was a small compartment beneath a false bottom. I found a piece of paper with one word. *Aufseherin.*"

The word described a female warden. "A gatekeeper?" Leila's pulse spiked as she mentally probed the implications. "You're suggesting she has a point of contact who coordinates Michael's movements."

Under normal circumstances, it would be safe to assume that such a gatekeeper was female. But Elsbeth might deliberately have tried to disguise the warden's gender. Just in case the note fell into the wrong hands.

"I think so," Mercedes said. "There was part of an address. Just a street. *Rue de Veyrier.*"

"I don't know it. When we get back to Geneva, we'll track down this warden. I don't know if this will take us anywhere but at least it's a start." Reaching over, Leila squeezed Mercedes's arm. "Thank you."

It was the first tangible piece of trust-building evidence the girl had brought to the table. Which was why her reaction now was puzzling.

Instead of responding, Mercedes averted her gaze.

"What is it?" Leila asked.

"There's . . . there's something else. Something you should know."

"About Michael?"

"About this mission. I-I've been trying to find a way to tell you since we left Geneva. You see . . . this is not what you think."

"If you've got something to say, spit it out."

"Leila . . . I'm sorry. This is all my fault."

"Tell me." Leila's grip tightened on her arm.

"A few days ago, the *Abhorchdienst,* the Listening Bureau, intercepted a telegram from Robert Hughes." Mercedes lifted her eyes slowly. "It was orders for Malcolm Steele to return to London. I shared this information with Elsbeth, and she told me to initiate this operation."

She leaned forward. "Leila, the man we're supposed to kill tonight. It-it's your husband."

The crypt of Saint Paul's was a massive tribute to the architectural genius of its designer, Christopher Wren. The largest mausoleum of its kind in Western Europe, it held the bodies of almost two hundred history-makers within its limestone walls. As he slipped soundlessly toward the curved dome of the chapel in the crypt's east end, Malcolm pushed aside an ironic thought. What if he survived four years of war just to die in a church surrounded by the bones of Britain's heroes?

Illuminated by electric lights, the crypt was a mixture of light and shadow. Statues protruding from walls or mounted on coffins cast larger-than-life silhouettes. Moving from one decorated pillar to another, Malcolm pressed against the cool blocks and peered around the corner.

Clear.

He gestured for Will to join him.

"I don't like this, Will," he said in a hushed whisper. "We've staked this place out for hours. Nothing."

Visitor traffic had been slow in the crypt. They had waited, hidden in an obscure corner of the mausoleum, until a caretaker had switched off the lights at closing time. After still a few more hours in gloom broken only by a few shafts of moonlight,

Malcolm had made his way to the switch and flipped on the lights in the main area of the crypt.

"I know what you mean." Will peered around his side of the column. "The problem is the sheer size of this place. Between that and all the statues, columns, and graves, a chap could hit you up from anywhere." He paused, then added. "Of course . . . it could just be your wife out there."

"Well, Leila knows what she's doing," Malcolm said. "If she's here, we won't see her until she's ready." He glanced at his watch. *Three minutes.* "Right. Well, you're all set then?"

Will eased his revolver from its holster and counted the number of bullets in the chamber. "Right as rain."

Drawing a deep breath, Malcolm craned his neck once more around the column. Horatio Nelson's tomb lay west of him at the center of the crypt, surrounded by eight pillars. That was where he was to meet Leila. But from the moment he stepped out of the shadows, he would be completely exposed.

Malcolm mentally ticked once more through the precautions he had taken. They had arrived early and swept the area. Will would continue to survey the area from his vantage point, remaining hidden unless something went wrong.

Closing his eyes, he whispered a quick prayer. Then, jaw set and shoulders thrown back, Malcolm stepped out into the light.

◆◆●◆◆

Leila prowled through the crypt's collection of tombs, moving east toward Nelson's memorial. Elsbeth had been right to order this hit to take place in a crypt. For tonight, Leila knew her own heart would die.

Swathed in black from head to toe, she was invisible in the gloom. Her mind subconsciously registered the columns and life-sized statues of Britain's heroes that provided ample cover as she padded forward.

Mercedes moved to her right, silent as the tombs around them.

Leila's grip tightened on the G98 rifle in her left hand, her mind churning. This assassination was itself a desperate bid for time. But Malcolm's life was the price.

If she failed to carry out the mission, their son would die. But carrying out the mission could buy her the time she needed to get back to Switzerland and go on the   offensive. The information Mercedes had shared could change everything. But now she was forced to choose between the man she loved more than life and the child she had brought into the world.

What would Malcolm want me to do?

She knew the answer.

Leila touched Mercedes's arm, then pointed to the base of an imposing statue.

"Will you do it?" Mercedes's hoarse whisper was barely audible. She settled her back against the statue's base. "I'll tell Elsbeth you did even if you don't."

"No." Leila shook her head. "My father-in-law's trial is tomorrow. Malcolm will have to testify. Elsbeth will find out."

"Then let me do it for you." Mercedes's whisper was urgent. "You love him. Don't do this to yourself."

"It's because I love him that I must do this." Leila peered around the statue's base, sighting through the scope, an eight-millimeter lens that grew blurry at the sides. She blinked away the moisture in her eyes. "If someone has to take Malcolm's life . . . it should be me."

Her mind shifted back to the cathedral's floorplan that Mercedes had produced. The cathedral had been built in the shape of a cross with Admiral Lord Nelson's tomb at its heart.

"We'll stop her." Only the outline of her forehead and the shadows of Mercedes's eyes were visible. "I promise, we'll find a way to destroy Elsbeth."

Leila didn't respond.

Glancing at her watch, Leila screwed on a cylindrical silencer, ignoring the erratic pounding of her heart, the voiceless screams of her soul. Ripping off the black combat gloves, she wiped her sweat-slick hands on her pants. Then, letting out a ragged breath, she adjusted the height of the rifle's stand to allow for a clear shot with numb fingers.

A salvo of scattered memories that summarized their turbulent story of love, betrayal, and forgiveness slammed into her mind.

Malcolm insisting that we get married.

She slid a large round into the rifle's chamber. Her chest constricted, making it hard to breathe.

Malcolm coming home a changed man.

She rested her weight on one knee and slipped deeper into the shadow of the tomb.

Malcolm promising he'll never leave me again.

She snapped the bolt into place.

Malcolm holding me close in the night.

The distinct echo of footsteps reached her ears. Leila tried to shut down her mind. Tried to pretend he was just another man.

Malcolm promising to be a true father to our son.

She pressed her eye against the scope as he stepped through the columns that ringed Nelson's tomb. A haze of light cast by the iridescent bulbs made her wince. Malcolm walked closer, resting his hands on the black-and-gold-trimmed base of Nelson's tomb, head slightly bowed as though praying.

"Forgive me, Malcolm," Leila whispered, waiting until the tears that blurred her vision streaked down her cheek. "Forgive me one more time." She held her breath, her finger curled around the trigger.

Then he looked up.

Will Thompson stole forward, wending his way through the massive columns that lined the chapel toward the cathedral's treasury. His gaze darted between Malcolm, who now stood by Nelson's tomb, and the area around him. Will's job was to make sure the perimeter was secure.

Not that I owe rich boy anything!

Will's brow furrowed. That wasn't quite true. Not anymore.

Jobs were scarce in England, as many discharged soldiers had already found out first-hand. Whether Malcolm had made the offer of employment because of his wounded conscience or because he genuinely cared, it would have been folly for Will to turn it down.

Will turned right, then paused, surveying the area.

All clear.

He stalked forward. But tonight wasn't just about Malcolm or his own future, for that matter. It was about England. Will had taken an oath to protect his country from all threats. If that meant dying in an underground cemetery, well—

A slight movement to his far right.

Will instantly dropped into a crouch, easing the revolver from his belt. Something had shifted in the shadows.

There again!

Squinting, he padded forward, keeping his body pressed against the three-dimensional wall reliefs. Ten yards. Eight. He inched closer until he was close enough to make out the outline of a kneeling man.

Realization hit him like a punch to his gut. Will turned his gaze, drew a mental line from the statue to . . .

"Malcolm!" Will threw himself forward as the words exploded from his mouth. Running now, he shouted again. "Malcolm, get down!"

Will had just reached the outermost column around Nelson's tomb when the world exploded. Pain mushroomed in his left shoulder, spreading through every corner of his chest. He staggered backward, then crashed, landing hard at pillar's base.

"Elean. . ." He tried to speak but his mouth refused to obey him. "El—"

Sucking in deep breaths, he clamped his right hand over his shoulder, trying to slow the spurting blood. But something was wrong. Everything was wrong. The world spun in a slow arc with the darkness swallowing the light.

"E-el . . ."

Then the darkness claimed him.

———————————— ◆◆●◆▶ ————————————

Malcolm ducked behind the tomb just as a bullet ripped out of the night. Gun in hand, he waited a few moments, then retreated to the shadow of the outer columns, breathing hard. Will was down.

Hurt? Dead?

Whoever did this would pay. Malcolm slowly picked his way to the edge of the intersection around Nelson's tomb, noting that silence had claimed the crypt once more. He peered around the corner of a column.

A body was on the ground, arms and legs spread at odd angles. *Will.*

His gaze hardened. Kneeling next to Will was another man, cloaked in black with a rifle at his side. Malcolm had seen enough of the Gewehr 98 rifles in the hands of his enemies to recognize the German gun on sight.

He inched closer, his teeth bared. A dark hood covered the assassin's head. His back was to Malcolm as he leaned over Will's body.

Verifying the kill.

A feral rage clawed up inside him. Malcolm cocked his revolver, silently edging forward. Then he stopped, leveling the gun with the killer's head. "You deserve to die with a bullet in your spine like the rat you are. But I'm not without honor. Get up."

The figure stiffened. Then he stood, hands slightly raised.

"Turn around!" Malcolm's finger curled around the trigger.

The killer hesitated, then slowly turned. Small hands reached up and tugged off the balaclava. A mound of blond hair spilled around a woman's shoulders.

"Malcolm."

Chapter 23

London, Great Britain

Leila tore her eyes from Malcolm's stricken face, focusing on the man whose blood pooled onto the gray stones. "Who is he?"

Dropping to her haunches, she felt for a pulse once more. *Alive. Thank God he's still alive!*

Will's unexpected shout had startled her. The bullet had gone wide, striking below the shoulder.

"His name is Will Thompson." Malcolm squatted next to Will. Jerking a knife from his belt, he sliced a strip of cloth from his left sleeve. "Here, let me."

"Thompson?" Leila shifted, giving him space to work. "Is he connected to Eleanor?"

"Her husband." Malcolm nodded, glancing at her briefly, a strange light in his eyes. It was the first time he'd seen her in action, and the expression on his face was unsettling. "The bullet's still inside?"

She held it up between bloody fingers. "No. It passed right through."

"Good. Help me with this."

They worked together in an awkward silence, Leila putting pressure on the wound while Malcolm bound it tightly. She blew a stray hair out of her eyes, trying to gauge her husband's reaction. His face was a mask, his body language ambiguous.

Malcolm could have no doubt of her intentions. She had pulled the trigger, knowing he was at the other end of the rifle. A thousand questions probably burned in his mind, but he was silent.

Is he angry? Resentful?

Nothing.

"Malcolm, look, I—"

"We'll talk later."

Will stirred, then groaned as his eyes flickered open.

"You're still alive, soldier," Malcolm said. "Let's get you back on your feet.

Will groaned again as Malcolm slipped an arm beneath his shoulder. "Feels like a hot poker . . . got jammed through my chest." His glassy eyes shifted to Leila. "Wh-what's this?"

"No time to explain now," Malcolm said briskly. "Right, let's get him out of here."

"We can't take him to a hospital. It's too risky."   Pulling a gray cloth from her pocket, Leila wiped her hands, then offered it to Malcolm. "If someone asks the wrong question . . ."

He took the cloth. "We'll go straight to our place in London. I'll ring for Eleanor to come up from Northshire tomorrow. She's treated worse in France."

"Leila." Mercedes stepped out of the shadows of the long corridor. "We have to go. Elsbeth expects a report. I'll confirm the mission a success to buy a little time."

"Thank you." Leila pulled her into an embrace, holding her tight as she would a daughter. "But if you do that, there'll be no turning back. When Elsbeth discovers the truth, she will hunt you down."

"I've already crossed the line in my mind," Mercedes said, lifting her chin. "This is my decision. I choose to be free."

"So be it." Pulling back, Leila stooped and snatched up her gear. Then, slinging her rifle over her shoulder, she turned back to Malcolm and Will.

Malcolm caught her eye and nodded once. It was his first unspoken gesture of reassurance. A thread of warmth spun through her core, making the corners of her lips twitched upward.

"Let's go," Leila said. "We have a lot to do."

◆◆●◆◆

Malcolm closed the door to his bedroom with a soft *thud* and let his eyes devour the woman before him. Leila reclined against the wooden headboard of their bed, her eyes closed and her breathing even. She'd exchanged her morbid uniform for a simple, light-blue nightgown.

He inched forward, the cuffs of his black, silk pajamas making a slight *swishing* sound, then stopped just a foot away from the bed.

A kaleidoscope of emotions pulsed within him. Her face, so beautiful and so serene, made his heart ache. How long had it been since they had said goodbye in Switzerland? *One year.*

A year in which they had endured a hurricane of circumstances—situations that would have broken any couple who did not have God as their rock. There was a time when he had run from his father's faith, determined to shut the light of faith out of his life. But when his world had shattered, faith alone had given him the ability to endure.

But their struggle wasn't over.

"Mm . . ." Leila shifted in the bed, then her eyes fluttered open. "Malcolm?" Blinking, she sat up. "I didn't mean to fall asleep."

"It's all right." He sank onto the edge of the bed next to her and slipped an arm around her shoulders. "I doubt either of us has slept more than a few hours in the past few weeks."

"How's Will?"

"As good as can be. Mercedes is keeping an eye on him. When I last saw him, he seemed to be sleeping."

"And . . . what about you?" She looked up at him, her golden mane forming a soft halo around her face. He understood her unspoken question. They'd talked out everything that had happened since they last saw each other before she'd taken time for a bath or change of clothing, including the excruciating choice she'd been forced to make.

"It was my life or Michael's." Malcolm reached for her hand, gently cupping it between his own. "You did the right thing. It was the choice I would have wanted you to make."

Pulling away, Leila stood, wrapping her arms around her body as though the fire that glowed in the hearth was suddenly unable to ward off the cold.

"We're running out of time, Malcolm. Mercedes sent a message confirming the hit. But once Elsbeth realizes she's been betrayed, she'll kill Michael."

"I know. But we can't give in to our fears."

Leila gestured toward the glass doors that opened onto a veranda behind him. "Michael is out there, lost somewhere in the cold and dark. Is he hungry? Is *he* afraid?" She clutched the sides of the black robe Malcolm wore over his pajamas. "His hands, Malcolm, they're so tiny, so . . ."

She choked back a sob. "Whenever I close my eyes, I see him. His green eyes. His soft hair."

Malcolm stood, closing the gap between them in two deliberate strides. He held each of her shoulders but said nothing, letting her talk.

"It was my fault." Turning away, Leila folded her arms beneath her chest. "My sins brought this on us. My past did this."

"And what of *my* sins? It's not as though I was some innocent." Malcolm turned her to face him. "But even our wrongs can produce something good in the end. Leila, if it wasn't for your past, we would never have met. We would never have a marriage that I treasure more than my life." He wiped her moist cheeks with the balls of his thumbs. "The evil here isn't in us. It's in Elsbeth. Don't hold yourself accountable for that."

"And your father? Thomas may die!"

"He knows that. And he is at peace. His greater purpose is working out. That's what matters."

"Will we ever be a normal family, Malcolm?" Reaching up, Leila touched his cheek with a moist palm. "In my dreams, we're always together. You and me. Holding each other. Loving each other. Laughing with our son between us." She looked away. "Then I wake up and the world has no color."

Tilting her head back, Malcolm gently brushed a golden strand from her eyes. "We are the ones who turn dreams into reality." His lips caressed her temple. "Leave tomorrow for Switzerland. Do whatever it takes to track down our son. I'll join you in Geneva once this trial is over."

A slight tremor ran through Leila's back. "I don't know. Things will be dangerous in Geneva. You remember what I said about Pierre LaRue? The man is unpredictable—especially when he feels threatened."

Malcolm mentally rifled through the briefing Leila had given of her encounter with the leader of the German crime syndicate. By her account, the man was violent, greedy, and amoral.

His heart clenched. He was sending his wife into the line of fire, but he knew there was no keeping her in London. The path was treacherous. And yet it was the only way.

"Leila, listen to me." Malcolm lifted her chin, losing himself in her emerald eyes. "For years, I endured the stink and mud of the trenches. There were times when I was sure I'd never see you again. But I prayed. I fought. I survived. And each day I repeated the last words you said to me before I went back to war. Do you remember them?"

"I ordered you to stay alive," Leila said, the faintest of smiles touching the corners of her lips.

"And now I'm telling you the same thing," Malcolm said. "No matter what comes your way in Switzerland, you *will* take it down. And, in a few days, I will be right there with you. We will get Michael back. And we will all come home to Northshire."

Closing her eyes once more, Leila wrapped her arms around him, nestling against his chest with a sigh. "Hold me, Malcolm. Just hold me tight and never let me go."

"Oh, I'll never let go, Leila." Malcolm pulled his wife close, savoring the feel of her soft warmth. "Never."

Chapter 24

London, Great Britain

Joseph Mara removed his black top hat, glancing upward as he trotted up the stone steps of London's most infamous criminal court— Old Bailey. "Excuse me." Condensation from his breath collected in small clouds around his mouth. He wound his way through the masses that thronged the courthouse steps despite of the bitter cold. It seemed that all of London had come to spectate at Thomas's trial. Like vultures, they waited to gorge themselves on the news that a great man had fallen.

"Look, it's the Jew!" a snide voice called from the crowd.

"Come to defend a wretch just like yourself, are we, Mr. Mara? They do say misery loves company!"

"Make way, please. Make way, I say." Setting his jaw, Joseph ignored the guffaws of the heckling crowd. Antisemitism had always been a harsh reality in England as well as elsewhere in Europe, but recent months had seen a sharp uptick in open displays of prejudice.

"Let him pass!" A police officer forced the bystanders back with his billy club.

Nodding his thanks, Joseph pressed forward.

The massive rectangular building was faced with gray stone. Its roof was edged with a smokey-white railing. Soaring above the entire structure stood a gold statue called the Lady of Justice. A pair of scales dangled from one of her graceful hands while the other held a glittering sword.

Joseph paused, tilting his head backward as a sense of foreboding seized him. Never before had he realized how fine the line was between justice and revenge. In Thomas's case, he doubted if the line existed.

The Crown at the behest of Robert Hughes sought to avenge itself against Thomas while claiming that it wanted only justice. But was it just to take the life of a man whose only desire had been to save his family? A man who had been forced to action by the Crown itself?

"Ah, Mr. Mara."

Joseph looked sharply to his left at the unexpected voice. His eyes narrowed as he took in the black robe, gray horsehair wig, and fleshy jowls of another barrister. "Mr. Boulton, I presume?"

"One and the same." The prosecution's portly barrister made an exaggerated bow. "A pleasure to meet you at last, good fellow. Although I would have preferred less odious circumstances." He straightened, fondling the smooth hilt of his black walking stick. "You know, I've heard quite a bit of good about you in the past. A pity your reputation will take a hit today."

Joseph hid his growing irritation behind a cold smile. "What makes you so certain you will win?"

"Well, isn't it obvious? You will lose because I am your opponent." Boulton blinked several times, then pointed to the statue above their heads. "You will have noticed, Mr. Mara, that in most cases the statue of justice is presented as being blindfolded. At Old Bailey, however, it is not."

"Your point?"

"Only this." Boulton leaned heavily on his stick, his thick lips parting to reveal crooked teeth. "Justice is not blind. Not in this case. The Crown sees quite clearly what your client has done." He gestured to the murmuring crowd behind him. "The people of London see that millions of Britain's sons have died fighting against the very nation that Thomas supported."

Joseph's blood ran cold. Boulton had just confirmed his darkest suspicions. Thomas's fate was sealed before the trial had even begun. He jutted his chin. "I believe in British justice. It is the jury who will decide his fate. Not you. Not the people."

"Oh believe me," Boulton purred, stroking the hilt of his walking stick. "The eyes of the jurors have been opened." With a grunt, he turned and began climbing the stairs. "Justice is never blind Mr. Mara. The only one here who cannot see the truth . . . is you."

———————————◆◆●◆▶———————————

Malcolm entered the courtroom caught up in an odd sense of detachment from the harsh reality around him. It was as if his mind had shut down. It had endured enough and was now resigned to accept whatever the future held. Straightening his shoulders, Malcolm pressed through the milling crowds as he followed Joseph Mara.

He had dressed for the occasion. On the left side of his chest dangled the Victoria Cross—the honor he had received early in the war before his father's alleged treason became public knowledge. Perhaps this subtle evidence of loyalty and courage would help persuade the jury that treason did not run in the Steele family.

His mind shifted to Leila. By now, she was well on her way to the continent, continuing the fight to find their son. War hammered at their home from all fronts. Could they possibly win every battle?

Malcolm took his place in the witness stand, which faced a row of twelve leather-backed chairs in which the jurors were seated. They were all middle-aged men. Men who had likely sent their sons to war and would be unlikely to sympathize with a man accused of treason. He didn't recognize a single one of them.

Scanning the room, he noticed the prime minister, David Lloyd George, taking his seat in a balcony reserved for spectators of the better class. His face was pale and grim. Thomas had once saved the man's life.

And this is how he is repaid.

David Lloyd George could influence the trial in Thomas's favor. But diplomatic gain always outweighed loyalty. To stand with Thomas now would be political suicide. And so, the prime minister would wash his hands of the matter.

"All rise in honor of Lord Chief Justice, the Honorable Sir Rufus Isaacs." The sharp voice of a court official was followed by a rumble of scraping chairs and shuffling feet.

Malcolm's eyes were riveted on the man whose curved nose and angled features were covered by a snow-white wig that fell to his shoulders. As the Lord Chief Justice, Sir Rufus was responsible for the oversight of the entire judicial system of Britain. The fact that he had chosen to sit in Thomas's case was a clear indication of its national significance. Whether his presence boded ill for Thomas or not, Malcolm couldn't tell.

"Bring in the accused." Sir Rufus sat as he gave the command, his black, fur-trimmed robe billowing around him. Malcolm and everyone else turned their eyes to the far corner of the courtroom. Four armed soldiers stomped forward, followed by Thomas, then by another small contingent of armed men.

At the sight of his father, the crowd exploded. Shouts rose on all sides.

"Traitor! You betrayed us."

But some voices rose in Thomas's favor.

"Set 'im free! Down with government oppression!"

"Order!" Sir Rufus rapped his gavel twice, his strident voice punching through the air. "Order!"

Malcolm gripped the rails of the barrister before him, tightening his hold until his knuckles turned white. Joseph Mara sat a few feet away behind the dock in which Thomas stood. He caught Malcolm's eye and gave a slow, encouraging nod.

For his part, Thomas ignored the heckling crowd, standing with his shoulders back, chin thrust forward, and legs spread slightly apart. Were it not for the fact that he stood between two armed guards, an onlooker might have doubted that he was a prisoner.

His silver hair was neatly combed. Not a wrinkle appeared anywhere on his brilliant scarlet jacket. Gold epaulets perched atop his shoulders, and a series of medals identifying his rank covered his chest. Black, freshly-pressed trousers emblazoned with a thick, red stripe on one side completed his uniform.

Malcolm's eyes swiveled to the prosecution's desk to his left. Hughes leaned back in his chair, a cunning smile snaking across his lips as his eyes drifted from Malcolm to Thomas and back again. He slid his index finger across his throat in a swift motion.

"Sir Thomas Steele, Earl of Northshire." The judge cleared his throat. "You stand accused by the Crown of three offences which violate the law of the empire under the Defense of the Realm Act. One: giving classified information to an enemy of the empire. Two: giving food, shelter and aid to a German agent on British soil." He pinned Thomas with a stern glare. "Three: attempting to seduce a neutral party, Switzerland, from its wartime status of neutrality. How do you plead?"

Thomas said nothing. His silence was filled by a wave of overpowering shouts from the crowd.

"This is all a conspiracy! The government's seizing private property!"

"String 'im up, guv'nor!" Fists pumped in the air.

The judge again slammed his gavel against his desk. "The court demands order!"

After a few tumultuous moments, the riotous crowd settled down.

The judge motioned to an overweight barrister seated next to Robert Hughes. "In light of the defendant's refusal to cooperate, the Crown's representative, Mr. Boulton, is invited to step forward."

"Thank you, Your Honor." Boulton tossed a sheaf of papers onto his desk, then ambled toward Thomas, his hands clasped behind his back. "Gentlemen of the jury, we have before us a most dangerous man. A villain whose treachery is eclipsed only by his cunning."

He thrust a finger at Thomas. "Today I will show beyond any doubt that this man conspired against the Crown. And I will prove that—were it not for the dedication of the Crown's loyal servants—Thomas Steele's duplicity would have led the Germans to victory." Boulton drew in a long breath. "Sir Thomas,

I understand that you are a man of influence, not only here but also abroad."

"Whatever influence I possess has been earned on the battlefield in service to His Majesty King George V," Thomas said.

"Service?" Boulton froze, midstride. "You consider asking a neutral country to arm itself against our great empire an act of *service* to our sovereign?"

"Objection!" Joseph Mara shot to his feet. "There is no evidence that the defendant made any attempt to convince Switzerland to break its neutrality."

Judge Isaacs leaned back in his chair. "Do you have any evidence to support your claim, Mr. Boulton?"

Boulton dipped his head. "Indeed, your Honor. The Crown calls upon its first witness: Arthur Hoffmann, politician and former member of the Swiss government."

Dread rolled like an iron ball through Malcolm's gut as the thin, goateed man angled his way to the witness stand. Hoffmann turned to Thomas, a smug smile plastered on his oily face.

"Mr. Hoffmann." Boulton stepped closer. "Did Thomas Steele convince you to approach the Swiss government with the idea of breaking its neutrality with Germany and arming itself against Britain and her allies?"

"Yes, he did." Hoffmann punctuated his words with an emphatic nod. A wave of angry murmurs swept through the courtroom. But Bolton wasn't finished.

"And may I presume that the defendant threatened you if you refused to comply?"

"Yes. He said he would use his financial clout to pressure members of the Federal Council to boot me out of office." The murmurs swelled into an angry growl, prompting Judge Isaacs to reach for his gavel. "And then—"

"Thank you, Mr. Hoffman, that will be all." Boulton cut him off with a stern glance.

Malcolm grunted in disgust. It was a bold-faced lie, and Hoffman knew it. The Swiss politician had been illegally orchestrating an alliance between Switzerland and Germany. Thomas had encouraged him to speak publicly about it to the Federal Council—Switzerland's governing body—but had withdrawn his support at the last minute, effectively aborting Hoffman's political career.

That snake is using this trial as an arena to settle an old score.

"Objection!" Joseph shot to his feet again. "This accusation stems from a time when the defendant was out of the British empire. It therefore cannot be admitted as evidence in a British court of law."

Malcolm's eyes swiveled to the Lord Chief Justice as appreciation for Joseph's keen wit rose within him. Thomas had been in Switzerland when he had negotiated the fateful deal with Arthur Hoffmann. How could he be tried in England for a crime that wasn't committed on British soil?

"The defendant knew his actions would affect the empire regardless of his then-present location." Judge Isaacs leaned forward, a hard light in his eyes. "Objection overruled!"

But Mara wasn't finished yet. As soon as Boulton vacated the center of the room, he stepped forward to cross-examine the witness.

"Mr. Hoffmann, you claim that Sir Thomas took advantage of your political connections."

"That is correct." Hoffman sniffed imperiously.

Joseph pulled himself to his full height and stared into Hoffmann's eyes. "Did Sir Thomas—a peer of England and venerated commander of British forces—*actually* attempt to persuade the Swiss government to violate the terms of its neutrality?"

Hoffmann opened his mouth, but Joseph stopped him. "Before you speak, I must warn you that I have a legal copy of the transcript of the entire meeting." He held up a cream folder. "A meeting in which *you* demanded that Switzerland ally itself with the Germans."

Shocked whispers rippled through the courtroom. Hoffman glanced around, licking his lips. "I . . ."

Joseph seized this moment to drive his point home. "After reading the transcript, I find it difficult to understand why the Crown has chosen to name this man" —he thrust a finger in Hoffmann's face— "a man who repeatedly called for an alliance between Switzerland and our hated enemy as a *witness* on its behalf."

Silence swallowed the room, a silence broken only by Hoffmann's stuttering. "I-I—"

"Mr. Hoffmann!" Joseph slammed his fist onto the railing. "Did Thomas Steele support your efforts to break Switzerland's neutral position? It is a simple question. Yes or no?"

"No."

"Did Thomas Steele speak against it?"

"Like the snake spoke to Eve." Hoffmann's face twisted in a snarl. "Steele said forging the alliance was a mark of patriotism. He even threatened to close his businesses if I didn't comply. Do you know the impact that would have on the Swiss economy?"

"Answer the question, Mr. Hoffman. Did Thomas Steele speak against the alliance?"

Hoffmann spoke through clenched teeth. "Yes."

"I'm sorry, but could you say that a bit louder?" Joseph cupped his ear with his hand. "I'm sure the court couldn't hear you."

"Yes!" Hoffmann glared at him, his face reddening.

"Ah." Joseph turned, shaking his head in the direction of the prosecution. "So Mr. Boulton is accusing a man for the horrific crime of persuading Switzerland to *keep* its promise of neutrality." Cynicism dripped from his voice. "How worthy of you."

A faint smile tugged at Malcolm's lips. Thomas had been right to ask Joseph to take his case. The barrister had proved himself to be a cunning force in the financial sector, but it was here in the courtroom that his true genius was revealed. In targeting Hoffmann's German sympathies, Joseph had destroyed the Swiss politician's credibility.

"Will that be all?" Judge Issacs rubbed his chin.

"That is all, Lord Chief Justice." Joseph dipped his head.

Boulton hurried forward, no doubt eager to shift attention away from his suddenly unpopular witness. "Ahem, the Crown summons the prime minister, Mr. David Lloyd George."

Malcolm's heart sank as the prime minister moved in brisk steps to the platform.

"Prime Minister, we all know you to be unwavering in your devotion to King and Country—"

"This is an unpleasant business, barrister," the prime minister said. "Let us not prolong it."

"Very good, sir." Boulton sniffed. "Last year you received a phone call while meeting with your war cabinet. Please tell this assembly who was at the other end of the call."

"Sir Thomas Steele."

"And what was the purpose of the defendant's call?"

David Lloyd George locked eyes with Thomas. "He demanded that we release his daughter-in-law from the Tower."

A rumble swelled in the courtroom. Boulton waited for it to die down before continuing.

"And if you did not?"

"Thomas swore that he would cause Switzerland to violate its pledge of neutrality."

Malcolm had often seen his comrades die in battle. Each time, a sense of helplessness swallowed him. It was the fatal certainty that he could do nothing to keep life within the broken body. That same sense swelled within him now, dulling the outraged roars of the onlookers.

"Sir Robert Hughes." Boulton's whine snapped Malcolm back to the moment.

The spymaster limped to the center stage. Hughes was dressed for a funeral. Instead of the blue uniform typically worn by former navy officers, he wore a sharply-pressed black suit. His cheeks were sunken, his shoulders slumped.

"Sir Robert, is it true that the accused was privy to classified information?"

"Yes." Hughes winced and leaned heavily on the rail, easing pressure off his amputated leg.

"And is it true that, because of your suspicions of his loyalty, you once gave him false intelligence known only to yourself and the prime minister?"

"Yes."

The barrister scratched his skull as though confused. "But then your men intercepted that same message on its way to Germany?"

"Yes." A muscle ticked in Hughes's jaw.

"And there was no way anyone else could have sent that information?"

"No. Not unless the prime minister is a Hun-lover."

A smattering of chuckles rippled through the audience, but dread coiled around Malcolm's heart. Thomas had never been able to explain how Hughes's message had ended up in German hands. Leila believed her now-deceased handler Werner Jaëger had stumbled across the information and relayed it to German High Command.

"Thank you, Sir Robert. That will be all." Boulton bowed, then sat down.

Malcolm held his breath as Joseph moved to question Hughes. The barrister had warned Malcolm that the leaked intelligence was one of the prosecution's strongest points.

"Sir Robert." Joseph clasped his hands behind his back. "You claim that only the three of you were in the room when you deliberately gave false information to Sir Thomas."

The spymaster's thin eyebrows hiked together. "Yes."

"It is possible that the information you *claim* was leaked to the Germans was never sent by Sir Thomas, is it not?"

"Just what are you implying?" Hughes leaned forward, fists clenched on the railing that separated them. "Are you suggesting that I planted evidence? That *I* sent the false information to the Germans? That I *wanted* to bring down a peer of the realm? Need I remind you that, like many here, I once counted Thomas Steele among my friends?"

Joseph raised both hands, palms outward. "I am merely pointing out that the evidence is circumstantial and—"

"Objection!" Bolton's fleshy jowls trembled as he rose, eyes flashing. "The witness is not on trial here."

"Objection sustained." The Lord Chief Justice shook his head. "If there is nothing else, Mr. Mara, then sit down."

"That is all." Joseph pulled in a deep breath. Lips set in a thin line, he made his way back to his seat.

Boulton rose, eyes fixed on Malcolm's face. "For its final witness, the Crown summons . . . Mr. Malcolm Steele."

Chapter 25

London, Great Britain

Malcolm rose slowly, his mouth dry. Each step to the witness stand was an interminable journey. From the stand he had a clear view of his father, the prime minister, Sir Robert Hughes—all the key players in this charade of justice.

"Mr. Steele." Boulton rubbed his hands together as though he were a wolf about to take supper.

A fitting description.

Malcolm lifted his chin, leveling a stern glare in his direction. "Mr. Boulton."

"First, the Crown thanks you for your service." He pointed to the medal on Malcolm's chest. "Your heroism inspires us all."

"You didn't summon me here to pay me compliments."

The barrister tilted his head to one side. "Ah . . . regrettable but true." He paused, then asked, "Regarding your wife, is it true that your father knew she was a German spy but allowed her free reign in your family home?"

Malcolm eyed him coldly even as his pulse hammered in his ears. "Sir Thomas is a man of integrity."

"Yes or no, Mr. Steele. Yes . . . or no."

Malcolm couldn't speak. He glanced at his father, stalling for time while knowing that time had run out. Thomas gave an imperceptible nod.

Slowly, Malcolm shifted his gaze back to the prosecuting barrister. "Yes."

"But you didn't know your wife was a foreign agent as you met only"—Boulton scanned his notes—"a few days before your wedding."

"No. I didn't know."

"Hm. A true case of marrying in haste only to repent at leisure." Boulton sniffed. Again, raucous chuckles spattered the crowd.

"It is no crime for a man to love his wife." The back of Malcolm's neck grew hot.

"No." Boulton thrust a finger in his face. "But it *is* a crime to help an enemy of the state! Sir Hughes found a cache of radio equipment, notes in *German*, and other tools that only a spy would know how to use on your father's property. Is that true?"

"Leila was trying to find information that would help *our* side!"

"How convenient." The barrister stepped back, chuckling. "And then, no doubt, she would have passed her findings along to the defendant, who we all know has the best interests of Britain at heart."

"He does." Iron tinged Malcolm's voice.

"Balderdash!" Boulton smacked his fist into his other palm. "We have seen other peers betray the empire. We remember the Duke of Gotha—a peer of Britain who became a general in the German army. We cannot forget the Duke of Cumberland, who also sided with the enemy." He whirled around to the jury. "Thomas Steele welcomed a German spy into his home. He gave her whatever she needed—money, clothes, radio equipment—is this true?"

Malcolm was silent.

Boulton pointed at Thomas. "Is it true?"

Malcolm swallowed. *He's twisting my words.*

"Mr. Steele?"

"Yes." Malcolm ground the word out between clenched teeth. "He welcomed Leila into our home. He trusted her and gave her free reign. But you have to understand—"

"Thank you, Mr. Steele. We have no further questions."

Judge Isaac's voice sounded from behind him. "Does the defense wish to cross-examine the witness?"

"Mr. Steele," Joseph said as he regained the floor. "You claimed that your wife's true purpose was to gain information that our great empire would find useful. Is that correct?"

"Yes."

"May I remind the court that this would not be the first time an enemy agent has become a valuable asset to the Crown." Joseph began to pace, his gaze sweeping the jury, the spectators, and Judge Isaacs. "Our warning of the ghastly attacks at Ypres did not come from a Brit but from a *German* whose conscience would not permit him to keep silent."

He stood still, then turned to Malcolm. "Mr. Steele, I understand your wife shared intelligence directly with Sir Robert Hughes himself. Is that true?"

"Yes."

"Information that was rejected out of hand *by Sir Robert.*"

"Objection!" Boulton leapt to his feet, cheeks jiggling. "Classified information of military nature is not admissible in court."

"Objection sustained."

Joseph dipped his head. "I have no further questions, Your Honor."

As Malcolm stepped from the podium, his eyes slid to Thomas's face. Fierce pride burned in his father's gaze. Thomas dipped his head in a slow, approving nod.

Joseph spoke again, this time to the jury. "The man on trial today has led a life of ongoing dedication to the empire. In India and Africa, Sir Thomas gained a reputation that none can deny." He gestured toward Thomas. "The defense contends that any actions taken by Sir Thomas were with the empire's best interests at heart. In proof of this, the defense would like to call the First Marquess of Kedleston, Lord Curzon as its first witness."

Malcolm leaned forward in his seat, every muscle in his body taut as the thin man with a receding hairline took the stage. Joseph had emphasized that, given Curzon's prestige and record of service, he was their most valuable witness.

"Lord Curzon," Joseph said. "You know Sir Thomas to be a man of honor. Is that true?"

"Yes." Curzon flicked a speck of dust off the gold epaulets that glittered on the sleeves of his darn navy waistcoat. "When I was newly appointed viceroy of India back in '99, a small army of rebels attacked the garrison where my wife, myself, and our troops were stationed. We were outnumbered. Thomas walked outside alone and singlehandedly convinced the mob to back down. Saved all our lives that day, I imagine."

"Very good." Joseph nodded as he tapped the railing. "And would you say that this man—this *hero*—would lightly betray his own country?"

"Lightly?" Curzon sniffed. "No. Not lightly."

Joseph froze. "I beg your pardon?"

"Thomas Steele would never *lightly* do anything at all. Especially not betray the empire."

"Thank you, Your Lordship," Joseph said hurriedly. "And—"

"But he *did* betray the empire. Not lightly. After careful consideration. You see, I know because I was present when he spoke with the prime minister. I personally delivered his daughter-in-law to him in Switzerland. I owed him a debt, you see. He saved my life, so I was honor-bound to pay my obligation."

Malcolm sat ramrod straight, his mind numb. Joseph had vetted these witnesses. Curzon had agreed to testify in his father's favor! To testify that Leila had written to him, sharing intelligence. *Why betray him now?*

"Your Lordship—"

But Curzon continued, relentlessly overriding Joseph's attempt to stop him. "Since Thomas had gotten what he wanted, he promised that he would now work to stop the Swiss from forming a treaty with Germany. *That* is why he spoke against an alliance." Curzon turned to the jury. "There you have it, gentlemen. The truth."

He pointed an accusatory finger at Thomas. "Such a man threatens the very order of our society. To do anything less than take the life of Thomas Steele would show the Crown a weak and insignificant instrument. And I have given too many years of my life to the Crown's service to see the insult he has rendered go unpunished. The natural order of our society is crumbling. Peasants revolt. Earls flaunt the authority of the King. Do your duty, gentlemen, and find him guilty."

For several fleeting moments, utter silence claimed the room. Then chaos erupted.

Screams for Thomas's death echoed off the rafters. Someone shoved a bystander. Fists started flying. Soldiers waded into the crowd, forcibly escorting onlookers from the room.

Malcolm didn't hear the rest of the trial. He was dimly aware of Joseph's attempts at salvaging his case. The barrister called Greyson, Jenny, and one or two souls still brave enough to support Thomas. But it was over.

All too soon, the Lord Chief Justice announced that the jury would retire to deliberate on Thomas's sentence. All too soon, the jury returned with a verdict.

The crowd waited as the judge rose and motioned for Thomas to be brought directly before him. "Sir Thomas Steele. After due deliberation upon the testimony presented in this court, the esteemed men of the jury have reached a unanimous verdict.

Malcolm stood, his breath hanging in his chest.

"They have found you guilty of all charges."

No, no. It can't be true!

But it was.

The vengeful shouts of the crowd. The shrieking howls from Arthur Hoffmann. The grim satisfaction in Robert Hughes's eyes. The sickened look on the prime minister's face. The ache in Malcolm's own heart. All of it testified that his father had been condemned.

"For aiding and abetting the enemy. For transmitting classified information." The Chief Justice's voice hardened. "And for attempting to coerce His Majesty's government, you are hereby stripped of your title and sentenced to immediate execution. I hereby sign the order."

Isaacs scribbled his signature on a piece of paper, then broke the nib of his pen. "May God have mercy on your soul."

Malcolm stood slowly, his mind spinning through scattered fragments of his life. How many times had his father been there, loving him even when he spurned his affection? How many evenings had Thomas waited at the door, looking with longing down Northshire's winding path for his prodigal son to return?

"Father!" Malcolm thrust his way forward. The guards tried to stop him, but Hughes's voice sounded sharp above the hubbub.

"Let him through. He's earned it."

They parted, and Malcolm staggered forward. There was so much to say, so much he needed to know. But time was the real master here.

He reached out, and Thomas clasped him in his arms. "It's over, Malcolm."

Malcolm gripped his father's neck. "I won't let this be the end. I will clear your name if it takes the rest of my life."

"I know you will."

The Lord Chief Justice's voice sliced between them. "Carry out the sentence."

Malcolm stepped back as Thomas was ripped away.

His father paused and looked back at him with a smile. Then he straightened, clicked his heels together, and saluted his son.

———————————◆◆●◆◆———————————

Thomas clung to the bars of his prison cell in the Tower of London. It was here in a courtyard of this stone palace that he would end his life. There was no fear in the thought of dying. But a part of him rebelled at the thought of a life of honor and glory ending in such ignominy. The world would watch him die as a criminal, never understanding it was love that had compelled him to act.

And yet the knowledge that he was about to be reunited with his beloved Isabella sparked a sense of anticipation.

He was tired, worn out from years of struggle. The thought of eternal rest with the woman he had never stopped loving filled him with longing.

"So it ends like this." The dry voice sounded from his left.

Thomas turned as Hughes limped out of the shadows. "Yes. It all ends here."

Hughes nodded, then looked at the uneven floor. "I have thought on what you said."

Thomas waited.

"You were right." Hughes patted his wooden stump, heaving a sigh. "It is time I stopped fighting." With a grunt, he straightened. "I plan to retire."

"Does that mean you will cease your persecution of my family?"

Hughes made a *humphing* sound in the back of his throat. "You were the traitor, Thomas. It was you all along. Your son testified against you. I am willing to accept that he had no part in this sordid affair. For the moment."

Hughes paused, then added, "You'll be glad to know that your barrister has somehow managed to convince the Lord Chief Justice that Malcolm should retain the rights to your estate. He will also inherit your title."

A wave of gratitude washed over Thomas. This was what he had wanted—what he was willing to die for.

But then his brow furrowed. "Why are you telling me this?"

"Consider it my attempt to retain my humanity," Hughes said. "We were friends once, Thomas. Even now, I don't hate you. I just hate the evil you have become."

Thomas pressed his face against the bars as Hughes turned to leave. "You're wrong. I'm not evil. But I will not die a prisoner of hate. So I forgive you."

Hughes paused at the door. He was silent for a moment. When he spoke, his voice was thin and tired. "But I cannot forgive you."

———————◆◆●◆▶———————

A small procession gathered at the door of Thomas's cell, headed by a chaplain and completed by an escort of eight armed soldiers. The gate groaned as it swung open. Thomas took his place between them, lifting his eyes toward the rocky ceiling. With each step, he breathed a prayer for his family, for Northshire, and those he would leave behind.

Soon, the procession passed beneath a stone archway and moved outside to a walled firing range. Gray, somber skies reflected the solemnity of the moment. Thomas inhaled, savoring the fresh tang of the wind.

Death. He had escaped it in countless skirmishes in India and Africa, but it had caught up to him at last in his native land.

Thomas was bound to a pole on the far end of the range. A guard offered him a blindfold, but he shook his head.

"Our Father who art in Heaven, hallowed be Thy name." The chaplain mouthed the prayer in a quavering voice. Thomas whispered in unison. How many of his prayers had been answered?

Countless.

". . . as we forgive those who trespass against us."

The words were true. At the heart of every conflict was human fallibility. Misunderstandings. Jealousy. All humans were born into a fallen condition that made each of their decisions prone to error.

"Ready!" A strident voice bellowed out the order.

Thomas's eyes drifted from the eight men who cocked their rifles to the gloomy skies above. He was about to die. And yet today he had achieved his greatest victory.

"Lead us not into temptation but deliver us from all evil."

The evil of war would surely gather again. His last prayer was that his descendants would join the fight against evil in their own generation—and win.

"Take aim!"

He saw the men lift their rifles to their shoulders. Heard the sound of guns snapping into position. The wooden stake to which he was bound thrust hard against his back. A cool breeze whipped a few wisps of his shaggy hair around his forehead.

Any moment now.

"For thine is the kingdom and the power and the glory forever and ever—"

A roar sounded from the distance as though thunder had torn through the gloomy skies above.

But the skies aren't gloomy. Not anymore.

Thomas looked up to see a dazzling brilliance, brighter than any sunlight he had ever witnessed. But the brightness did not hurt his eyes. Instead, it drew him, pulling him higher, as it lovingly whispered his name.

"Thomas? Thomas, my love?"

Thomas looked sharply to his right, his pulse quickening. He *knew* that voice.

"Isabella?" Laughter—spontaneous, uninhibited, breathless laughter—erupted from his chest. "Isabella?"

Isabella stepped out of the light, young, with a freshness he had never before seen. She was exquisite, radiating an indescribable beauty. He had always sensed that she had been near. But to *see* her!

He held out his hands. There were no wrinkles. "Isabella, what has happened?"

He didn't see her move, but in an instant she was at his side.

"I've waited so long for this moment, Thomas," she said.

Thomas looked back at the prison compound. His body sagged at the post while blood collected in a dark pool at his feet.

In that moment time lost its hold, falling like invisible shackles at his feet.

"Thomas?" Isabella placed her hands in his. "We must go."

He withdrew from the shadowed scene behind him, turning back toward the light.

"Go?" His heart pulsed with anticipation as he gripped her hands. Like his own, there were no wrinkles. They were soft. Warm. Pulsing with life. "Go where, my love?"

"Why . . . home, Thomas." Isabella pointed to the light, then touched his cheek. "We're going home."

PART 3

December 1918

Chapter 26

Berlin, Germany

The luxurious black Maybach glided off the crowded streets of Berlin. The car's engine purred as it nosed its way onto a cement driveway that coiled around a lifeless garden and waterless fountain toward the Reichstag—the meeting place of Germany's parliament.

Barren tree branches jutted upward like the skinny arms of a scarecrow, strikingly black against the snow that whitened the ground. Although decorated with small, glittering electric light bulbs, no artificial beauty could hide the fact that the trees, like the country itself, were dying.

Fritz Haber, feted chemist and father of the chemical weapons that had slaughtered hordes of Germany's enemies, clucked twice, shaking his head as he took in the winter landscape.

Everything is wrong!

Just before the guns of the Great War had fallen silent as the armistice went into effect, Kaiser Wilhelm II had been forced by his generals to abdicate his throne. Like a criminal, the erstwhile emperor had fled his own government, escaping to the Netherlands. With his departure had come a civil war that paved the way for Germany's new government—the Weimar Republic.

"As if the death of millions of soldiers is not enough." Fritz heaved a deep sigh as his eyes drifted to the crinkled newspaper he clutched in his left hand. Unfortunately, he could personally identify with the idea of civil war. Angling the paper so the light from the courtyard's lampposts spilled across his page, Fritz read the bold headline once more.

WILL THE CHEMIST'S SECOND MARRIAGE GO DOWN THE TUBES?

Fritz crumpled the newspaper and tossed it to the car floor. "God, I *hate* the press!"

When his driver opened the door, Haber heaved his bulk outside with another groan, then quickly pulled on his black top hat as the frigid air ambushed his bald head.

"*Danke.*" He jerked his chin downward in a brisk nod, then walked slowly toward the palatial Reichstag, his feet crunching over soft snow. With each step, a memory surfaced. He had met Charlotte in a place much like this. At first, she had been supportive and adoring. Their relationship had soon become intimate although he was still married to his first wife at the time.

Crunch. Crunch. Fritz closed his eyes as regret swelled within him. The words Charlotte had whispered in his ear before he left home this evening wrapped themselves around his mind like a garrote wire.

"This is your last chance." Venom had dripped from Charlotte's voice. "Pull genius from that eggy head of yours! Enough to make a success out of us. I want the world, Fritz. The world, do you hear me?"

Fury made his chest tight. How dare she talk to him as though he were a slave!

Where is the woman who once offered me words sweeter than honey?

A shudder slid down his spine. She was still here. But she had finally revealed the raw ugliness her seductive charm once concealed.

"Welcome, *Herr* Haber." A porter opened the door and took his black coat and hat. Handing them to an assistant, he motioned for Haber to follow him. "General Hindenburg and the others are in the ballroom."

Haber's eyes roamed over the lavish decorations and ornate furniture as he followed the porter toward a ballroom at the far end of the carpeted hall. Hindenburg and his Weimar Republic might have done away with the monarchy, but there was too much of the old ways in their blood to sanction a complete divorce from luxury. Rulers—be they kings or elected officials—had to maintain certain standards.

As such, General Hindenburg, head of Germany's military during the war and now a shaper of the country's republic, had arranged for a winter gala to be attended by Germany's key politicians and their spouses. Haber knew that the gala's true purpose was to convene the minds responsible for the assassination plot that would rewrite the course of western civilization.

Haber's brow creased as he plowed ahead, ignoring the murmured greetings that followed him. Charlotte had obstinately refused to come, deliberately leaving him with the awkward task of being a bachelor at a soirée for couples. With the newspapers touting details of his private life and Charlotte's conspicuous absence, tonight promised to be nothing short of an emotional crucifixion.

He stepped through the ceiling-high, double-leaved ivory doorway as the porter's baritone voice carried easily over the crowd. "Announcing *Herr* Fritz Haber."

There was no need to say anything more. Everyone in this room knew who he was. They also knew he was married. Speculations as to why his wife had not accompanied him to such a formal event would run rampant.

His cheeks burning, Fritz edged into the room, shoulders drawn together and head lowered.

"Ah, there you are, Haber." General Hindenburg, a tall, fleshy man with short-cropped, graying hair, rested a small glass of sparkling champagne on a moss-green marble table. Detached himself from a small group of high-ranking military officers, he extended his right arm. "*Wilkommen.*"

Like most of the attendees, Hindenburg was out of uniform. Pressed black pants contrasted sharply with a crisp white shirt and red cravat, all toned down by a black waistcoat.

"*Danke.*" Fritz hurriedly shook the general's hand.

Hindenburg looked around Fritz's shoulder. "Is your wife not with you?"

"She . . . had a headache." Fritz covered the lie with a short bow. "My apologies."

"Ah, yes." Hindenburg took Fritz's arm, leading him away from the main entrance as the murmurs of the crowd floated above the gentle strains of a waltz played by a small orchestra. "The infamous female headache. Strikes the fragile creatures at the most awkward of times, don't you think?"

Fritz just nodded, unsure of how to respond.

"I tell you, women are trouble." Hindenburg picked up two full glasses of champagne from a passing server, handed one to Fritz, and tilted the other to his lips. "With the exception of my own good wife, of course." He jerked his chin toward a plump, matronly brunette who was surrounded by a small circle of women.

Fritz scrutinized the bubbly contents of his glass. "Of course."

"I've read the papers." Hindenburg shook his head. "You have my complete sympathy."

Fritz downed half the champagne in one gulp. "I don't need sympathy, General." He drank again.

"True." Hindenburg raised a plump index finger and eyed him sternly. "You need a divorce."

Fritz choked. Drips of champagne spilled onto his black shoes. Heat flooded his face as heads swung in his direction once more. "I- I'm sorry." His words were more a twisted croak than intelligible speech.

Hindenburg arched a sardonic eyebrow. "Don't die, Haber. Not just yet. Your country still loves you—even if your wife doesn't."

"I'm not dy—" Fritz heaved a final ragged cough, then pulled in a deep breath to clear his lungs. "A divorce?" He lowered his voice. "That would be the worst humiliation I could imagine. It is not done. Not among our class, anyway."

"Is it worse than another suicide on your hands? You almost lost your mind after Clara killed herself. A good commander knows when it's time to make a strategic retreat." The general shrugged. "Now is such a time."

"Y-you don't understand. I promised myself that I would make this marriage work." A sour taste filled Fritz's mouth as the thought of divorce sank its claws into his mind. He verbalized a response that sounded weak even to himself. "Besides, Charlotte is a very different woman. She wouldn't *kill* herself."

"Your guilt over your last wife's death almost drove you to madness. I don't like mad scientists." Hindenburg emptied his glass and set it down with a bang. "So for the sake of your sanity, let us pray you are right."

◆◆ ● ◆◆

"Announcing . . . *Fräulein* Elsbeth Schneider."

Elsbeth sauntered into the Reichstag's brightly-lit ballroom, her brown eyes and sharp mind cataloguing observations with each step. The room itself was not too large, a fact which allowed the crowd of about thirty to easily fill the space.

Overhead, several gilded chandeliers dangled from a wood-paneled ceiling, scattering light across the glossy hardwood floors. The cream walls sported the newly-formed Weimar Republic's coat of arms, the black *Reichsadler*, or Imperial Eagle.

More like an imperial chicken!

Disdain made her lip curl as Elsbeth eyed the bird's upraised wings and squawking beak. It was the symbol of a traitor—Hindenburg. Loyalty had once been the lifeblood of Germany. Apparently, Germany's blood had seeped out on the battlefields of France and Belgium.

Loyalty. Her mind shifted to Leila. Of all the betrayals she had experienced, this one stung the most. Following protocol, Mercedes had sent word that Leila had carried out her mission. But the next day, Malcolm Steele had managed to rise from the dead so he could testify at his father's trial.

A mistake by Mercedes? Possible but unlikely.

Elsbeth hid the violent fury that roiled within her behind a calm smile. In failing to kill Malcolm, Leila had written her own death sentence. If Leila had corrupted her second-in-command, then Mercedes too would pay the price.

One thought governed Elsbeth's every waking thought—justice. Justice that would be served on two fronts.

First, she would instigate a chain of events that, given time, would unravel this pseudo-government General Hindenburg had created. She could not hope to see Kaiser Wilhelm II reclaim his throne, but she *could* destroy the man who had spearheaded his downfall.

Second, she would crush Leila. In every sense of the word. Emotionally. Mentally. And when Leila lay broken at her feet, Elsbeth would snuff out whatever life lingered in her ungrateful body.

Chin erect, Elsbeth strode down the long, plush red carpet, her eyes fixated on the man whose duplicity had orchestrated the Kaiser's downfall.

Hindenburg stood with his back toward her, the only man still oblivious to the fact that she had entered the room. Her nostrils flared. She was a patriot, one of the few women to ever earn the coveted Iron Cross, a medal given by the Kaiser himself.

No amount of pandering to the people could hide the fact that Hindenburg and his pack of dogs had long coveted the Kaiser's power while lacking his qualities. Like a coward, Hindenburg had profited from the Kaiser's diminishing popularity, establishing a new order that had the strength of a chicken bone.

Aside from General Hindenburg, no one knew her identity. Her clandestine operations throughout Europe were shrouded in secrecy. But tonight she would take the first step toward the most covert operation of her career. And, to succeed, she would need to be nothing short of stunning.

A black satin gown shimmered beneath the light cast from the chandeliers, clinging subtly to her toned figure, while a strand of Bulgari diamonds curled about her slender throat. A sidelong slit offered easy access to the concealed Luger strapped to her inner thigh.

The musicians—all men—lost their place in the score, drawn by the predatory magnetism that radiated from her every movement. Elsbeth focused on her prey, ignoring the rush of speculative whispers from the women and wistful stares from the men.

Alerted by the mistimed music, Hindenburg turned around. His piggish eyes bulged. "Ah, *Fräulein.*" Running a hand over his short-cropped hair, he cleared his throat. "I've never realized how lovely you are."

"There is a reason for that, General." The pencil-thin heels of her black stilettos clicked on the hardwood floor as Elsbeth stepped off the carpet. "I've never let you close enough to notice."

"That *is* a problem." Hindenburg proffered a glass of champagne, which she accepted. "Perhaps a little later I can get even closer, hmm?"

"You know I never mix business with pleasure, General." A trace of scorn tinged Elsbeth's light laughter. She wasn't here to seduce Hindenburg but to distract him.

Hindenburg considered her remark. "Well, at least I'm glad that you consider being with me a pleasure. It is a possibility, no?"

At your age? Not likely.

Elsbeth shoved the words back down her throat. As much as she despised the man, she needed to remain in his inner circle if she wanted to engineer his downfall.

But that doesn't mean I can't scratch him a little.

"You misunderstand me, General. I don't consider being with you a pleasure." She sipped at her champagne. "Just business." She leaned forward, her voice dropping to a whisper as her lips curved in a vicious smile. "Besides . . . I don't like men who wear red *unterhosen*."

"Red?" Hindenburg stared at her, jaw unhinged.

"Hmm, yes. There's a small hole in your pants on the left—"

"Enough!" Hindenburg's face turned the same color as his underwear.

"Don't worry. Everyone else will pretend not to notice." Elsbeth tossed her head, making the diamonds dangling from her earlobes sway back and forth. "It just stands out against the black pants, you know?"

She turned to Hindenburg's pudgy, sad-eyed companion. "You are Fritz Haber."

"Y-yes." He stepped back, a wary look on his face. "Have we met?"

"Only by way of reputation." Her mind flashed through the files she had skimmed on her way here. Fritz Haber was the brains behind the covert operation codenamed *Hubris*. Originally called *Herkules*, the operation had been renamed in an attempt to mislead Leila in the event that she had shared intelligence about the plot with the British. But the plot had also been expanded—as the stakeholders gathered here tonight would soon learn.

"I'm afraid my reputation is not what it once was." Fritz spoke again, his voice that of a man twice his age. "I seem unable to solve the most basic of problems."

Hindenburg clapped him on the back, rocking the shorter man on his feet. "We are about to fix that. Come, let's go to the adjoining meeting room where we can discuss our *business*." He glared at Elsbeth, then stood with his back rigid and made a curt gesture toward a nearby doorway. "*Fräulein*, you go first."

"With pleasure, General Hindenburg." Still smiling, Elsbeth deposited her empty glass on a nearby table.

A sense of grim satisfaction swirled within her chest. Hindenburg might be angry, but he did not suspect her. If he did, he wouldn't have admitted her into this meeting. The snake had no idea that she had already begun to saw away at the foundations of his empire.

A muscle worked in Elsbeth's jaw. *Phase One—done.*

Chapter 27

Berlin, Germany

Paul von Hindenburg closed the door behind him, entering the small confines of the wood-paneled boardroom with a tight smile on his lips. He kept his back to the wall as he made his way to his seat, trying to ignore the humor that glinted in Elsbeth Schneider's eyes.

Treacherous vixen!

Knowing Elsbeth's strong devotion to the Kaiser, Hindenburg had ordered she be watched while in Germany. A series of clandestine meetings with a radical socialist named Adolf Hitler confirmed Hindenburg's belief that the lovely *Fräulein* no longer deserved the nation's trust.

Elsbeth had served the old Germany as no woman before her, aiding the flow of coveted intelligence through her network of spies across Europe. But that had been under the old order. Now she was a threat.

Hindenburg's eyes narrowed as he took his place at the head of the table. Truth be told, he needed Elsbeth—for the moment. Without her, *Operation Hubris* didn't stand a chance. So he tolerated her barbed words and insolent disregard for his authority, letting her think he was blinded by her sensuality until the time came when she was no longer needed. Then—if

Elsbeth survived the pending operation in France— he would ensure she never gave another order.

"I will come straight to the point." Hindenburg's gaze probed each of the four sober faces at the table. To his left sat the president of the Weimar republic and the chief of its army, both of whom answered to himself. Across from Hindenburg, Elsbeth yawned without covering her mouth while Fritz Haber wiped at his sweaty bald head with a white handkerchief on her right.

"Let us begin with what you do not know." Hindenburg sat and pulled his chair close to the table. "In a few months, I will retire from politics."

Silence met this unexpected declaration, but Hindenburg noted that Elsbeth's gaze sharpened as though this news offered an unexpected possibility.

"Before I leave office, I want to make one last sacrifice," he said, "one last *gift* to the country I love."

They waited, doubtless anticipating the direction of the conversation.

"Germany has left the outdated notion of absolute monarch and become a modern republic. But our nation also faces significant challenges. Internal revolution spawned by the socialists. Unemployment confronts the returning soldiers. Hunger."

Hindenburg paused, letting his words sink into their minds. "We need bold, precise action to unite us. And I will take that action in one decisive blow against the enemy. *Hubris.*" He said the word reverently.

"Here is what Germany will soon face. Our enemies—the British, the French, and the Americans—are drafting a treaty that will be signed at the palace of Versailles in France."

Hindenburg turned to the man on his left. "President Ebert, what have you heard about the treaty?"

Ebert answered without hesitation. "I hear the demands made by the enemy are insupportable. *We* must accept full responsibility for the war. *We* lose much land and territory. *We* must pay staggering war costs. It is a travesty! We cannot accept."

"Yet accept we must." Hindenburg leaned back in his chair. "It is the only way that *Herr* Haber's plan can succeed."

"Oh, *Operation Hubris* is not *my* plan." Fritz Haber mopped his sweaty brow with a handkerchief. "It was all the Kaiser's idea. Since he is no longer in power . . ." Fritz ended his flow of words with a shrug.

He started as though a thought had occurred to him, then added, "B-but I believe it is in the best interests of my marriage—" He colored. "I mean, it is in Germany's best interests to carry out the plan."

"I disagree." Groener, the head of the army, folded his arms across his middle. "It is not wise to proceed. Our armies have been disbanded."

"And they will be recalled," Hindenburg said, turning to him. "We did not lose the war because our armies were defeated. We lost because of politics and Allied propaganda."

"But can we mobilize enough troops in time to punch through whatever resistance we encounter and seize Paris?"

Hindenburg propped his elbows on the table, wove his hands together, and tapped his index fingers against his lips several times before answering. "I would ask you a question—what do we have to lose?"

All eyes were glued to his face.

"If we do not accept these terms, the armies of the world will come storming through our gates. They will throw us back into a war that will be fought on *their* terms." He paused again. "If, on the other hand, we pretend we are willing to sign this treaty—albeit grudgingly—they will not suspect any treachery. When we strike from *within* France, the enemy will be taken totally off guard."

Hindenburg rapped the table twice with his knuckles. "General Groener, how many men do we have in the *Reichswehr* at this moment, ready to fight?"

"Only about a hundred thousand."

"And there are hundreds of thousands more across the country who could be mobilized soon after." Hindenburg paused as the old hunger for battle stirred within him, making his bones momentarily forget their dull ache. "The corrupt politics of the Kaiser drove us to defeat. But we will rise again."

"Did not the Kaiser's generals urge him to begin this war?" Elsbeth Schneider leaned back in her chair, draping one slim leg over another. "A war that cost him an empire."

The vixen bares her pretty teeth!

The edges of Hindenburg's sharp moustache bristled. "Just what are you implying, *Fräulein*?"

"Implying?" Elsbeth arched a pencil-thin, dark eyebrow. "I imply nothing. I only want to know which version of truth will be recorded by history. Will it be yours—that Germany's defeat in this war was all the Kaiser's fault—or the real story?"

Hindenburg decided to ignore her thinly-veiled insinuation. "The past no longer matters. It is the future we must consider. I say that we go ahead with *Hubris* as planned."

"But can it be done?" The president rubbed his jaw.

"We have made significant modifications to the plan."
Hindenburg jerked his chin in Elsbeth's direction. *"Fräulein.*
Tell them where we stand."

"There is no question as to whether the operation can happen.
In fact, it has already been done." She waited until the startled
murmurs that filled the room died down before speaking again.

"Several months ago, *Herr* Haber synthesized a liquid form
of a deadly nerve gas. It is colorless. Odorless. Without taste.
Yet it kills within seconds if swallowed or inhaled. A few drops
on the skin can end a life within minutes." Elsbeth uncrossed
her legs and leaned forward, making eye contact with each
of them. "Twenty-eight Germans will be sent in small teams
throughout Europe. They will be angels of death."

"We will not only destroy the leaders of enemy nations."
Hindenburg's voice was animated now. "We will decimate
their armies."

The president eyes went wide. "How?"

"By targeting the major towns and villages," Elsbeth said. "We
will disperse the poisonous vapor on crowded British railways
and contaminate the water reservoir in Paris. Our agents will
also strike at other vital areas such as Calais, Etaples, and Dover,
which are still likely to have high numbers of enemy soldiers."

Hindenburg reclaimed the floor. "We can kill tens, maybe
hundreds of thousands in a day. It will be ten times better than
Ypres!"

The president swallowed. "When will this terror begin?"

"With the attack on Versailles," Elsbeth said. "The death of
the Allied leadership will be the signal to begin. If something
goes wrong at Versailles, I will get word to our . . . esteemed
leader."

Hindenburg ignored her cynicism. "In the chaos, we will strike with all our might. Britain and France will be unable to mount a formidable counter-offensive. Like lightning, we will mobilize small units of soldiers who will crush all opposition."

"And civilians?" Groener rubbed his jaw. "There will be many civilian deaths. Women. Even children."

Silence gripped the room. The silence of men ready to shed whatever conscience the war had not yet killed.

"So be it," Hindenburg said.

"And . . . what of the Germans within the palace?" It was Haber who spoke at last.

"I will lead a team inside the hall where the documents will be signed," Elsbeth said. "All you need to do is make sure each of us has the antidote." She jutted her chin. "Leave the rest to me."

Hindenburg scanned the faces in the room. They all wanted this. But the plot was so unprecedented, the cost so diabolical that they hesitated to act.

That is the true burden of leadership. To act when others tremble.

"Once the leadership is dead and the general population deaths begin to mount, our army will swiftly advance in the confusion," Hindenburg said. "We will establish command centers throughout Europe before the enemy is able to recover."

"And the Americans?" General Groener spoke again, hiking his shoulders together. "What about them? They will not remain idle while this happens. They will retaliate with full fury."

Hindenburg slanted him a glance. Groener was an effective leader, but his caution could be galling. "Not since Switzerland's financial clout is on our side. As you know, we have already established a financial understanding with Switzerland."

A humorless chuckle slipped passed his lips. "The *almighty* American dollar can soothe even the most tender of consciences. Since the Americans are a major Swiss trading partner, they are not likely to jeopardize such a relationship—especially as they too feel the effects of a recession. Once money is involved, they will tread lightly."

"But—"

Hindenburg cut off Groener's protests with an upraised palm. "We will negotiate terms of a separate treaty with them once Europe is secure."

"I see." The president gave a thoughtful nod. "This is why you have been courting Switzerland's favor for some time. Very good, General. Very good."

Hindenburg grunted. "This is not the first time we have used biological weapons to our advantage in this war. You all remember the white powder, anthrax, we used to infect the Allied horses." He glanced at each one. "We have become more efficient. Now we will infect an entire population. When this is over, the souls of our dead will be avenged, and the Fatherland will be greater than ever before."

He rose, signaling the end of the meeting. "You will receive further instructions in the following months. Are there any questions?"

Silence fell.

Hindenburg motioned toward the door. "Then I hope you all enjoy the rest of the evening's festivities."

Hindenburg waited until all but Elsbeth had filed out of the room. Then he closed the door. "A moment, *Fräulein*."

Elsbeth paused, one hand on the door's handle. "I already rejected your offer, Hindenburg."

"This is not about you," he said curtly. Her self-importance bordered on the brink of obsession. "It is about what happened in Switzerland."

"You think I failed." Elsbeth tilted her head back, looking up at him.

Hindenburg decided to go on the offence. "Yes. You failed. And miserably at that."

"I don't know what you mean."

"Leila Steele has a general idea of our plans. By now, I expect she has shared that knowledge with her government."

"Do you think they would believe her?" Elsbeth folded her arms across her chest. "They just executed her father-in-law. I think that says something."

"So why isn't *she* dead? Don't tell me you still hope to win her back to the fold." Hindenburg lowered his voice, struggling to hold his rising temper in check.

"*Nein.*" Elsbeth shook her head. "Once I did hope that using her son would be motivation enough, but it appears that I . . . miscalculated."

Hindenburg made a slight *humphing* noise in the back of his throat. It was the closest the woman would ever come to admitting she was wrong. "She betrayed you."

"I will take care of Leila," Elsbeth said. "In fact, if you hadn't summoned me back to Germany, her son would already be a cuddly corpse. Thanks to you, my good general, the brat gets to live a little longer."

"You will be in Germany for the better part of two weeks." Hindenburg's eyes narrowed slightly. No doubt Elsbeth would spend part of that time plotting with her neophyte, Hitler. "When you leave, your priority is to find that traitor and see that she is destroyed."

"Oh, never fear, General. I have a thing for traitors," Elsbeth said. Her eyes smoldered with a dark intensity that made him shuffle back a step. "Sooner or later they always get their due. By the time I'm finished, Leila will beg me to end both her life *and* her child's."

Hindenburg snorted. "And they say we men are brutal."

"It's a matter of practicality." The smug lilt had returned to Elsbeth's voice. "Leila will die when I am ready. As I said before, she is at this moment more valuable to us alive."

"Stop speaking in riddles, woman!" Hindenburg pounded the table with his fist. "We old men have no time for them."

Elsbeth sighed, turning fully around. "With Thomas dead, there is only one remaining loose thread in the Steele scandal—Leila. What would you do if you were Robert Hughes?"

"My job."

"And if, while doing your job, you were to stumble across a trail of breadcrumbs that hints Leila Steele will be at Versailles when the treaty is signed?"

"But Leila won't be there."

"Perhaps. Perhaps not." Elsbeth idly traced a spiral pattern onto the table. "All that matters is whether Robert Hughes *thinks* she will. And that he personally comes to Versailles."

"Hughes will die with the others." Hindenburg nodded as illumination set in. "Without him, Britain's network of spies will crumble."

Looking up, Elsbeth gave the condescending nod of a patient teacher speaking to a slow student. "When the next war comes, Britain will find itself behind the times."

"The next war?" Hindenburg went rigid. "What are you talking about?"

"Oh, come now, General." Elsbeth's laughter was tinged with scorn. "Don't tell me you actually expect this little plan of yours to succeed."

"Of course I do! Why else would I bother?"

"General,a global war was sparked by one assassination. What do you think will happen if *all* the leaders of Europe are murdered? How long do you think your precious republic will last when faced with the righteous anger of those nations? Have you thought of that?"

Elsbeth snorted and shook her head. "No? I thought not. *That* is why we lost this war. Because no one took the time to think."

"That's preposterous!" Hindenburg barked out a contemptuous laugh, his face darkening. "A supreme Germany will mean the end of a divided Europe. Think of Charlemagne. Or even Bonaparte. Peace can only be won by the sword. And my peace will reign from the Mediterranean to the Black Sea."

"No, Hindenburg. That is only a fanciful dream." Reaching up, Elsbeth placed a soft hand on his wrinkled cheek. Her voice gentled, taking the edge off his anger. "Just like my body, it is something you want . . . but will never have."

Hindenburg withdrew, stung despite himself. "If you don't believe in the plan, then why are you doing this?"

"Because I am a patriot." Elsbeth lifted her chin. "Because I believe in what my country can achieve. If we strike hard enough, we may gain a few years in which we can develop our strategic advantage. Robert Hughes will die, and when the next war begins, *we* will be victorious."

"You seem confident the spymaster will meet his end. But this mission to France is fraught with danger. What if you are the one who dies?" Hindenburg drilled her with his eyes. "Have you thought about that?"

Elsbeth tilted her head to one side, lips curved in the faintest hint of an enigmatic smile. "Have you?"

Without waiting for a reply, she opened the door and glided out of sight.

Chapter 28

Berlin, Germany

Fritz Haber puttered about his laboratory, mumbling a liturgy of chemical formulas. It was late, but he didn't want to go home. Only here, surrounded by his potions and poisons, could he find a measure of peace.

A knock made him jerk his head up.

Waddling to the door, Fritz opened it and stepped back, jerking the safety goggles from his eyes. "General Hindenburg?"

It had been three hours since the gala at the Reichstag had ended, and—Fritz glanced at his watch—it was now well past midnight. Despite the hour, the aged general didn't look as though he had slept. Perhaps he too could not find peace.

"Are you going to stand there gawking like an old woman, or are you going to let me in?" Hindenburg brushed past the stunned chemist, shutting the door firmly behind him.

"I-I'm sorry, General, I didn't expect—"

"When you're as old as I am, Haber, you learn not to waste time. Hindenburg wheeled about, pinning Fritz with a steely gaze. "Now, this conversation must never be mentioned outside this room. It is of the utmost secrecy. Do you understand?"

Fritz nodded. "Y-yes."

"I ask again, do you understand?" Hindenburg loomed over Fritz, silver brows knit together.

"I do, General. I do."

Hindenburg heaved a sigh, then turned and gestured to the vast array of tubes that covered Fritz's workspace. "So many ways to manipulate nature. It seems almost obscene."

"It is my life's work." Fritz edged closer, defensive now. "It is my legacy."

"But can you manipulate one person's death?"

For a moment, Fritz just stared at Hindenburg, unsure if he had heard correctly. "You are asking if I can—"

"Create a false antidote," Hindenburg finished. "A member of our party is an enemy of the state. During the operation, I want this person removed."

Fritz's mind reeled with the implications of Hindenburg's question. He had no qualms about taking life, but so far his poisons had been used only for war. This was altogether different.

"Yes," he said slowly, ideas coming together in his mind. "Yes, I can synthesize a placebo."

"How does it work?"

"Well, instead of containing the main ingredient, the vial would be simply fluid. Sugar water, perhaps." He paused, unsure of how the general would react to his next words.

"What is it, Haber?"

"Well . . . I don't want to be associated with executions."

"You?" Hindenburg barked out an unfeeling laugh. "The man whose gas slaughtered thousands at Ypres? Who developed mustard gas that killed tens of thousands more?"

"I—" Haber's shoulders drooped. He moved toward the table and nudged a sealed petri dish. "I hope to create a cure of a disease. Tuberculosis, perhaps. To make something that can"—he faltered—"help humanity."

"I see. You're trying to redeem yourself in the eyes of the international scientific community." Hindenburg rocked back on his heels, thrusting his hands into his pockets. "The world's brightest minds reject you because of your alleged abuse of science."

"Yes." Fritz again stared at the floor. "If I had known then how much it would cost me, I would never have done it. My wife. My reputation. My self-respect." He looked up, desperate for someone to understand. "I made knowledge my god. It demanded everything but gave me nothing in return. I—"

"Oh, shut up!" Hindenburg cut him off. "There's no time for this nonsense. Your country needs you. The Weimar Republic needs you to deal in *death*, not life."

Fritz expelled a long, heavy breath. It would be most unwise to refuse as powerful a man as Hindenburg. "What do you want me to do?"

"Instead of making a placebo—or whatever it is you called it—put more of the poison itself inside the vial that contains the antidote."

"Whose vial?"

"The woman who joined our meeting yesterday—Elsbeth Schneider."

Haber's head jerked up. "The leader of the *Kriegsnachrichtenstelle?*"

"As I said, she is an enemy of the state." General Hindenberg's steel-gray eyes hardened. "I want her dead. Do you understand?"

Fritz nodded mutely.

"Good. Elsbeth leads a very powerful organization. If her followers were to learn that she was assassinated, things would become very complicated. I need this to look as though she is a victim of the operation."

"You want it to seem as though my work has failed?" Fritz drew back, his cheeks reddening. "Hasn't my reputation suffered enough damage?"

"Not as much as it will if you fail me now."

"B-but you must understand what is at stake, General Hindenburg." Haber removed his round wire glasses and wiped them on the edge of his white sleeve. "If she dies, this mission may fail. If *Hubris* fails, my marriage will be over. I do not want my children to grow up in a shattered home."

"Our mission will not fail, even without Elsbeth Schneider." Hindenburg drew himself to his full height. "And you will have enough glory to satisfy any woman. Serve your country well, and your fame will long outlive you. Can I count on you?"

Hindenburg paused, his words hanging in the air between them. Then he spoke again. "We are still putting out the last fires of civil war. The Republic is too fragile to risk more internal division. If *Hubris* fails, Germany will be forced to sign the ridiculous French treaty. We will swallow our pride until we are ready for another war. But Elsbeth must be removed. No matter what."

Fritz was silent.

"Can I count on your continued loyalty?" Hindenburg straightened. "Or will you too betray the Fatherland?"

Fritz swallowed, hearing in Hindenburg's words an implicit threat. Traitors had no place in the new republic. Neither, for that matter, did dissenters.

Hindenburg placed a hand on Haber's shoulder. "Good. Your talent for death is a gift, Haber. It is not a curse. Do you understand?"

Fritz's gaze shifted from the general's face to the petri dish and back again. Life offered no chance for redemption.

Not for men like me.

"Yes. Yes, I do."

Chapter 29

Geneva, Switzerland

Leila hunched over a table in the corner of *Café du Bourg-de-Four,* forcing her tired eyes to pore once more over a small map of the city. *"Rue de Veyrier,"* she muttered, stifling a yawn. "It's got to be here somewhere." Blinking rapidly to clear her vision, Leila sat up and took a long draught from her steaming mug of black coffee. Seventy-two hours without sleep was taking its toll.

The café was not very crowded. Cloth panels decorated with swirl patterns lined the top half of the walls while glossy cherrywood panels continued to the floor. Leila held the hot liquid in her mouth for a moment, her gaze shifting to the door at the far end of the room, then swallowed as her sluggish mind replayed the events that had brought her here.

She and Mercedes had agreed to separate in London. Leila would go to Geneva to continue the search for her son while Mercedes headed to Berlin. After returning to Geneva, Leila had contacted Giovanni, Pierre's second-in-command. Now she was forced to wait until Pierre chose the time and place to meet. But each second lost was a nightmare of twisted scenarios that continued to slam against her mind. Was Michael still alive? Would she find him before time ran out?

Rubbing the grit from her eyes, Leila leaned over the map again, this time starting from the northwest corner of the Geneva canton. Pierre was a valuable lead, but Mercedes had possibly stumbled across another. It was possible that a gatekeeper in Geneva coordinated Michael's transient locations. The fragment of the address Mercedes had provided was *Rue de Veyrier*. If the street *was* in Geneva, Leila would find it.

A blast of cold smacked her forehead. Leila shivered, looking up again. Not for the first time she missed her long hair. She'd cut it short so it curled around her ears, then dyed it a dark-brown before leaving London. Whatever it took to be unrecognizable.

The café door closed behind a heavy-set man with short-cropped dark hair. Black pants hung tight beneath a slight paunch that rebelled against a gray collared shirt. A black leather jacket hung open despite the frigid temperatures outside. The man caught her eye and nodded once.

Sipping her coffee again, Leila leaned back. As he passed her table, the newcomer tucked a small, folded slip of paper on top of her map without looking at her, then moved on to the bar.

Leila waited a few seconds before sliding the note close and opening it. When she did, every part of her body turned to ice.

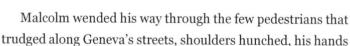

Malcolm wended his way through the few pedestrians that trudged along Geneva's streets, shoulders hunched, his hands tucked into the pockets of his black greatcoat. A light dusting of snow dulled the thud of his boots on the cobblestone streets. The afternoon sun did little to warm him. Malcolm paused to adjust the small Kodak camera dangling in a leather case around his neck, then resumed walking.

It had been a year since he had last been in Switzerland. But in that brief space of time, his world had gone through an orbital shift more times than he could count. His heart still bleeding after his father's execution, Malcolm had leapt straight into the hunt for his son as soon as Thomas's body had been lowered into Northshire's frozen earth. He ran his hand over the growth that clung to his cheeks. The beard and a pair of false spectacles were easy changes that dramatically altered his appearance.

Malcolm's jaw clenched as the café where he was to meet Leila came into sight. They had lost much and gained little. But now, if God would help them, everything was about to change.

Pulling open the door, Malcolm stepped inside, grateful for the sudden warmth. He stood in the corner of the room and rubbed his hands together as he skimmed the area with his eyes. The café was mostly empty now with just a few couples and one or two men.

His eyes shifted to the corner. Then he saw her. With her hair now brown and curling around her ears in the modern trend, anyone looking for Leila could easily pass her by.

Malcolm walked directly passed her and headed for the counter.

"Can I help you?" The bartender, a bubbly woman with dark hair and brown eyes, wiped a glass dry then set it down.

"Coffee, please," Malcolm said in French.

A few moments later with the miniature cup of steaming brew in hand, he made his way slowly toward Leila. She looked up at his approach, her expression wary. "Can I help you?"

She had clearly not recognized him, a good sign. Leaning back against the wall, Malcolm commented quietly, "It's a cold night for a lovely lady to be out alone."

As soon as he spoke, the slight furrow in his wife's brow vanished. It felt awkward, pretending to be a stranger when all he wanted was to crush her to his chest. But the attack on his father in Geneva and the attempt on his life in London had been well-coordinated. Elsbeth had access to an extensive network. It was best to assume he was being watched wherever he went. For both their sakes.

Leila paused a moment, head tilted to one side. "Who said I don't like being alone?"

"Fair enough." He tilted his cup to his lips. "In the odd chance that you'd like company, may I join you?"

Leila motioned toward the chair. "As long as you promise to behave."

"I'll do my best," Malcolm said with a slight grin. He removed the camera from around his neck, placing it carefully on the table as he sat. "So what do they call you?"

"Annabelle LeClerc," she said. "What about you?"

He smacked his lips as the bitter edge of the brew sank into his taste buds. "Paul DuChevalier." Under different circumstances, he might have enjoyed this sort of charade. After all, why should a man stop courting his wife after marriage?

She raised her eyebrows, continuing the charade. "So are you from this area?"

"From Alsace in France. Just here visiting a friend now that travel is a little easier." Malcolm tapped the camera. "I'm a photographer, as you can see. Spent the day snapping pictures, and I thought I'd warm up before giving the cold another run. What about you?"

"I'm on the job." She made an almost imperceptible nod toward a heavy-set man in a black leather jacket. His back was toward them, but Malcolm could see he nursed a beer at the bar.

"Oh?" Malcolm sipped his coffee again. "What kind of a job?"

"I'm a journalist for the *Zeitung*," Leila said. "I'm following up on a lead."

Malcolm's pulse quickened. Clearly, Leila had learned something. It was also clear that the man at the bar was somehow connected to whatever she had learned.

"A journalist? Impressive."

"Why, thank you," Leila said. "Most men I meet don't seem to think so." Her eyes glinted. "I think I scare them."

"Well, journalists are useful," Malcolm said with a shrug. "But it takes a *camera* to really bring out the story."

"Now that's debatable."

"For some reason, I get the feeling that debating with you is not good idea." Malcolm placed his cup on the table and leaned back, hands spread wide. "So, is it a big story?"

She laughed—a rather convincing sound that belied the desperation they both felt. "Not really. The war is over. Everything from this point on is going to pale in comparison."

"Well, that's a good thing, I would think," he said, avoiding the urge to look down as Leila slipped a scrap of paper across the table. "What kind of a story then?"

"Oh, nothing interesting." Leila waved flippantly. "Just a missing person piece. A page filler, you know?"

"Oh, in that case, perhaps we could meet again." Malcolm slanted her a speculative glance. "Just how busy is your schedule?"

Leila hesitated. "That's rather forward, coming from a complete stranger."

Leaning forward slightly, Malcolm stared deep into her emerald-green eyes. "But I have the feeling you're not offended. After all, the best stories come up rather unexpectedly, don't they?"

"I . . ."

"Who's to say this encounter happened by chance?" Malcolm pressed, taking her hand in his. She didn't pull away. "Perhaps it was all meant to be."

Leila looked at him for a few seconds. "I have an interview in an hour," she said. "Perhaps we can meet afterwards at the Fountain?"

"The Fountain?" The Geneva fountain was one of the city's main attractions—in warmer weather. "It'll be freezing."

Leila drew back, a serious note in her voice contrasting with the smile that played about her lips. "Then you'd better come prepared."

Malcolm held her gaze. "I can't wait."

Draining her cup, Leila stood and ran a finger over his arm. "I'll see you soon. Don't be late."

She made her way through the tables toward the door, but Malcolm waited. As he expected, about a minute after Leila left, the hefty man at the bar rose, tossed some cash on the table, and followed her.

Heat crawled up the back of Malcolm's neck, and he fought down the urge to pound this man who was stalking his wife into the floor.

Easy, Malcolm.

There could be another watcher Leila had missed. Malcolm waited, his mind filtering through the information Leila had shared.

Leila would soon meet someone who knew something about their son's whereabouts. But the situation would be dangerous so Malcolm should be prepared—or armed—in case things went wrong.

Questions churned in the back of his mind. Who was she meeting? And where was Mercedes?

After another few moments, he palmed the paper Leila had pushed across the table.

Three o'clock. 1780 Rue de Veyrier. Carouge. -P.

Malcolm downed the rest of his coffee, then rose and moved over to the roaring fireplace. Spreading his fingers as though warming his hands, he let the note fall and watched until it was reduced to a spot of ash.

Then, shrugging on his coat and slinging his camera around his neck, he shoved the door open and stepped onto the snow-dusted street. Just ahead, Leila's stalker lumbered around the corner into a rather narrow alley on his left.

"Good thinking, Leila," Malcolm muttered as he broke into a brisk trot. She would have deliberately chosen that road, figuring there would probably be few witnesses in a back alley. And that suited Malcolm's mood perfectly.

"Right, Fat Boy." Malcolm flexed his knuckles. "Time to find out what you know."

◆◆●◆◆

Leila walked down the alley with brisk steps. It was a narrow street. A dead-end, really. Empty and shadowed by windowless buildings on both sides, it was the kind of place she would typically avoid for fear of being ambushed. It was also the kind of place she would deliberately choose if she wanted to ambush someone else.

Large, overflowing bins of trash lined the right side of the road. She stepped around a pile of refuse, sending a protesting rat scurrying.

Leila was halfway down the street when she stopped and confronted the man behind her. "You delivered your message. What else do you want?"

Her stalker slowed down but still shuffled closer. "What any man would want." He sniffed, wiping his nose with the sleeve of his black jacket as his eyes roamed over her body. "Who's going to deny Victor his fun, eh?"

Victor was large. Too large for her to handle alone. Unless of course she killed him. But that would be a waste. If she could just keep him busy until Malcolm arrived . . .

"I wouldn't do that. Pierre will have your liver for   dinner if you lay a finger on me." Folding her arms across her chest, Leila ignored her spiking pulse and planted her feet shoulder-width apart.

"Oh . . . I don't think he'll mind." Victor licked his thick lips. "Not too much, anyway."

He inched closer. Leila took a half step back, her mind dissecting his words. What would make this animal so bold?

Where is Malcolm?

Her left hand inched toward the gun tucked in the small of her back. "What do you mean?" she snarled, legs bending into a slight crouch.

"I just think the boss has other things on his mind." Smirking, Victor swiped out, reaching for her hair. Leila dodged his paw, then moved to one side.

"Lay a finger on my wife, and I swear I'll ram your entrails down your throat *before* I kill you!"

Malcolm's stentorian voice sliced between them, jerking Victor to a skidding halt. He pivoted—just as Malcolm's fist shot forward. The big man reeled, staggering backward. He jerked a gun from his pocket.

Malcolm moved in a blur. He stepped inside Victor's reach. Grabbing his enemy's arm, he squatted and jerked. Hard.

Victor flew over his shoulder, slamming his back on the stones.

In an instant, Malcolm loomed over him. Pulling a blade from his boot, he knelt on Victor's chest and pressed the edge of the blade against the other man's throat.

"Malcolm!" Leila darted forward. Scooping up Victor's fallen weapon, she grabbed her husband's shoulder. "Malcolm, stop!"

Malcolm looked at her, and Leila shrank back. She'd seen her share of violence. But the look in Malcolm's eyes chilled her to the core.

"This beast wanted to assault you." Malcolm grunted, tightening his hold on Victor's shirt. "And you want me to let it live?"

Reaching out, Leila gently touched his cheek. She understood. His rage stemmed from his love. As did his need to protect her. She couldn't deny him this right. He was a man. He was *her* man. But there was something Malcolm didn't know.

"Malcolm, listen to me," Leila said urgently. "I think this man can tell us something. Something about our son."

"This just keeps getting better," Malcolm said through gritted teeth.

"I . . . I won't say anything," Victor spat through clenched teeth.

"Do you know how many men I killed during the war?" Malcolm said in a quiet voice. He didn't wait for an answer. "Seventy-two. Seventy-two confirmed kills. And do you know why I killed them?" Again, he didn't wait. "Because they were German. They never did anything to hurt me. Some were good men. But I killed them. Just because they were on the wrong side of the trench."

"P-please!" Victor squirmed, but he couldn't escape Malcolm's iron grip.

"First you assault my wife." Malcolm leaned closer. "And now you refuse to tell me where *my infant son* is being held a prisoner. If I killed those men who did me no harm, what do you think I'm about to do to you?"

Grabbing the prone man's collar, Malcolm twirled the blade so it dangled a half-inch from Victor's bulging eyeball. "Last chance."

"Stop!" Victor's eyes rolled in wild circles like a man possessed. "I-it's LaRue. He has him. H-he has your son!"

Malcolm increased the pressure on the man's chest. "Where?"

"I-in a barn." The words gushed out like flowing blood. "In the woods. East. East of his house in Carouge. W-where she's going to meet him tonight."

"How many guards?" Leila squatted beside him.

"Two. Sometimes three."

Malcolm bared his teeth. "And how do we know you're not lying?"

"He isn't lying," Leila said in a quiet voice. "Remember the address Mercedes found? It's the same address Pierre gave on his note."

It made sense. Pierre maintained strong connections to the 'Ndrangheta, an Italian mafia. Carouge with its strong Italian

284

culture was a logical haven. But Pierre had her son. And Elsbeth had written his address beneath the word *warden*. Which could only mean . . .

"Pierre was in league with Elsbeth all along," Leila said, rising slowly as though she had suddenly aged four decades. She shivered as something cold bit at her core.

Pierre had sat across the table from her. Talking. Laughing. Hearing the desperation in her voice. And all along, he had been playing her. Pretending to be her ally while working hand-in-glove with her nemesis.

Why?

"We have to go, Malcolm. Now."

Malcolm's gaze flickered to her briefly. In that moment, Victor made his move. Slamming his fist against Malcolm's wrist, he shoved forcefully while rolling free. The knife skittered out of Malcolm's hand as he crashed hard on his side. Regaining his feet, Victor closed the gap between himself and Leila in two strides.

He grabbed her.

"Back off or I'll break her neck," Victor spat, wrapping his arm around Leila's neck in a chokehold.

Malcolm scooped up the knife and sprang to his feet. "If I stay back, you'll kill her anyway."

Leila fought down a jolt of panic as an ugly laugh belched out of Victor's chest. The man's thick arm was crushing her windpipe.

"Not till I've had my fun." Victor's groping paw dropped to Leila's breast, an ugly chuckle spilling out of his mouth. "Maybe I'll even make you watch. Who knows? She might even enjoy it!"

Leila writhed in the bigger man's grasp, struggling now to breathe. But Malcolm shook his head slightly, and she became motionless.

"And you get another notch in your belt, is that it?" Malcolm took a few steps closer. The look in his eyes swore to Leila that the criminal was a dead man walking.

"Drop the knife or she dies now!" Victor pulled her tight against his chest. She could smell his perspiration. Feel the harsh dominance of his body. She made a croaking sound as spots began to dance before her eyes.

"All right. All right." Malcolm stopped a few feet away. He lifted his hands, spreading his fingers wide. The knife blade dangled between his fingers. "Let's make a deal. You let my wife go and I—"

In a blur of motion, Malcolm flipped the blade and sent it speeding forward. A puff of wind punched Leila's face as the blade sliced through the air less an inch from her cheek.

Schthunk!

A small spray of blood and gore spattered Leila's left cheek. A short-lived screech sounded against her ear. The hands that had crushed the air from her lungs relaxed, then went altogether limp.

Leila turned, shrugging off Victor's deadweight, and doubled over, sucking in deep breaths as his body hit the ground with a dull thud. Ignoring the ache in her throat, she eyed the corpse. Malcolm's knife was buried deep in his left eye socket, its edge lost in a pool of blood.

Malcolm hurried forward. He pressed two fingers against the side of Victor's throat, seeking a pulse. A moment later, he grunted in satisfaction and jerked the blade free. Wiping it clean on the dead man's pants, he tucked back into his boot, then turned around.

"Are you all right?" He touched Leila's face tenderly. "I'm sorry, I shouldn't have let him do that. I—"

"Stop," she said, laying a hand on his mouth. "It's not your fault."

Her voice was raspy. Malcolm drew her close, not saying a word. She clung to him for just a few seconds, then pulled free. "I suppose I should swoon, but I'm really not in the mood."

Malcolm picked up Victor's discarded gun and tucked it into his belt. Squatting, he jerked the dead man's jacket off his shoulders. "I think this devil has done enough swooning for the both of you."

"All the same, you were magnificent." Leila bent to press her lips lightly against his.

"I'll put him in the dumpster with the rest of the trash." Breaking free from her kiss, Malcolm stripped the shirt off the corpse. "Where's Mercedes?"

"Back in Germany," Leila said as Malcolm jerked Victor's belt off and rolled him onto his belly. As he began tugging off his victim's pants, she turned around. "She's trying to find out if Hindenburg still plans to double-cross the Allies at the signing of the treaty."

"Good," Malcolm said. "We don't have much time. If Pierre is working with Elsbeth, he won't hesitate to kill our son either."

"I just can't bear to think that Michael was within reach all along," Leila said. She blew her cheeks out in a ragged breath. "What could Elsbeth have *possibly* offered Pierre to get him to cooperate? She betrayed him!"

This was what repulsed her the most about her old life. It was nothing but a vicious cycle of backstabbing piled upon betrayal. When would it end?

"The war has changed everything, Leila," Malcolm said. "Allegiances now are as stable as the wind. As the world tries to define a new normal, none of us can take anything for granted."

He moved around and faced her. His stormy eyes were gentle now. Focused. He wore Victor's clothes and jacket. They were too big, but from a distance Malcolm could be mistaken for the unconscious criminal.

"You didn't know." Malcolm tenderly laid his hands on her shoulders. "So don't blame yourself. We'll get him back."

"I know we will." Leila's voice sounded as brittle in her ears. Raw like her emotions. "But what then? Where can Michael be safe when the whole world wants to kill us on sight?"

"Then we'll disappear," he said, pulling her close. "But first I need you to be strong. Strong enough to take down Pierre LaRue. I know you can do this."

For a moment, Leila just stayed still, listening to the rhythm of his heart, drawing strength from his faith in her. "All right," she said at last, jaw tight. She straightened and turned to the road, pent-up fury melding into resolve. Her son was close, almost close enough to touch. Heaven help whoever stood in her way.

"Let's finish this," she said.

Chapter 30

Carouge, Switzerland

The afternoon sun barely reached *Rue de Veyrier*, thanks to the thick stretch of plane trees that lined the gravel street. For Malcolm, the cover was a welcome gift, one of which he would make full use. Even when stripped of their leaves by winter's breath, the dense motley trunks offered ample opportunity for an experienced soldier to make his way forward unseen.

Crouching in the shadows, Malcolm watched through the tree line as Leila strode up the long, winding lane toward the massive brick house that dominated the center of a clearing. From Malcolm's vantage point, he could see four guards. And their eyes were all on Leila.

Rising to a half-crouch, Malcolm stalked forward on cat's feet. Their plan was simple as the best plans always were. While Leila engaged Pierre LaRue, Malcolm would rescue Michael, then immediately return to Geneva, where Leila would join him.

Pushing naked branches aside, Malcolm followed a narrow, snow-spattered game trail that wove its way east. Damp leaves muffled his steps. He was grateful. It was possible that LaRue had men scattered throughout the woods.

I know I would.

Pierre expected Leila, but their advantage lay in that he had no idea that Malcolm was here as well.

Malcolm paused, seeing a flicker of motion to his far left. Movement crystallized into shapes. Shapes that moved in his direction.

He squinted.

Two men. Armed.

Malcolm shrank back, pressing his shoulders against the thick trunk of a tree, and waited.

"I didn't sign up for this, Giovanni." The man in the lead shifted the rifle slung across his shoulder and looked in disgust at a baby bottle in his hand. "I didn't leave the 'Ndrangheta to become a nanny!"

"No," the older man in the rear said calmly. "But you *did* sign up to follow orders."

Malcolm's gut clenched. These men had Michael. So they would lead him to his son.

He waited, immobile, for five heartbeats after they passed by. Then he prowled after them, a ghost among the trees.

A sudden bend in the trail led to a small clearing. At its center, a small wooden barn contrasted with the white snow on the sloping hills behind it. Pulling a pair of smoke-gray field glasses from his pocket, Malcolm crouched at the edge of the tree-line and scanned the perimeter.

One man huddled near a small fire, his weapon propped behind him against the barn wall. The two men Malcolm had followed nodded once in the third man's direction, then hurried inside.

Malcolm flexed and unflexed his fingers, barely feeling the biting cold. *My son is in that building.*

His pulse beat out a steady tattoo as he put away the field glasses. These men were all that stood between himself and the son he had never seen. That was about to change.

Rising, Malcolm eased Leila's gun out of its holster. Knowing Pierre's guards would search her, she'd gone in unarmed. Unlike his own revolver or the gun Malcolm had confiscated from Victor, Leila's Luger was equipped with a silencer. And that fact might determine if Malcolm succeeded ... or died.

Turning up his collar, Malcolm pulled the brim of Victor's black hat low over his eyes, then stepped out into the open, mimicking the gait of the criminal he'd left dead in a dumpster.

He was about halfway to the barn door before he was noticed.

"Hey, Victor! Where've you been?" The man at the fire spat, then grabbed his rifle. He sauntered forward. "You're late. The boss is angry. He wants us to let him know as soon as you get back." He froze, eyes narrowing, as he jerked his rifle upward. "Wait! You're not—"

Pfft!

The thug sank downward, a neat circle in his forehead.

Malcolm dragged the corpse to the side of the barn, then made his way to the back of the building. Maybe, just maybe, there would be a back entrance.

There!

Midway along the barn's side, he glimpsed the rectangular shape of a door. Instead of a handle, the barn door had a rusty hook-and-eye style latch that lifted up and down. The outside latch hung loosely down, but Malcolm saw through a crack between door and frame that a similar latch was in use on the inside.

Shifting the Luger to his left hand, Malcolm eased the long trench knife from his boot. Sliding the blade between door and jamb, he maneuvered it to lift the latch, praying there would be no additional padlock.

The latch rose freely. Malcolm eased the door open just wide enough to fit through, then let it close soundlessly behind him.

Malcolm waited as his eyes adjusted to the gloom. It was a relatively small space. Neat cubes of hay were stacked in neat piles along the sides of the barn walls, but the area near the main entrance was clear. Directly to his right, rows of neatly stacked grain sacks rose above his head, preventing the two men inside from seeing him.

Malcolm stalked forward, moving toward the sound of murmuring voices. *Michael . . . Michael.*

His heart punched against his ribcage. Any second now, he would finally see his son.

"You look different every time we meet, Madame Steele." Pierre LaRue pointedly eyed Leila's cut and dyed hair. His gaze roamed over her body, taking in her loose gray skirt and white top. He clasped his hands behind his back. "A different face for each occasion. None of them true yet all of them ravishing."

Leila's eyes skimmed the room. They were alone—which meant his men were probably hidden in the next room.

"I am what I need to be to get the job done," she said.

"Ah. And therein lies the problem. The job. You see, we had an agreement." Pierre lifted his index finger, and the sleeve of his caramel-colored suit jacket fell back. She caught a glimpse of a gold watch.

"Why did you ask me to come here?" Leila asked, every sense on high alert. "Have you found my son?"

"We had a deal," Pierre said. "You would find the identity of this anarchist who seems bent on complicating my life, and I would provide you intelligence concerning the whereabouts of your son."

"What have you found out?" Leila edged closer. Pierre did not move.

"Something rather interesting. But I am a true gentleman. You go first." His smile held the warmth of an ice block.

"Elsbeth is behind the attacks," Leila said.

"Really?" Pierre slipped his hands into the pockets of his chocolate-brown slacks. "And what would lead you to that conclusion?"

"It's the only thing that makes sense. Germany stands to gain from an alliance with Switzerland. This is more likely to happen if the pro-German factions feel targeted. This anarchist is pushing Switzerland into bed with Germany." It was as much of the truth as Leila dared reveal.

"Elsbeth." Pierre turned away, pacing slowly. "Who would have thought? And all this time I thought it was . . . you."

Leila leapt in front of him, every muscle in her body poised for combat. "Enough games, Pierre!"

His brown cravat dangled a few feet away. She grabbed it.

Jerking him forward, Leila slid a thin blade from her boot. "The next time you have someone search me, have them do it properly!" She pressed the tip against the hollow of his neck. "Now tell me *why* you cooperated with Elsbeth."

Pierre's face reddened. "Isn't it obvious? Money covers a multitude of sins. You know that. Building a criminal empire is not a cheap business." He swallowed.

Gingerly. "Elsbeth and I settled our differences rather amicably . . . before you showed up at my door."

She pressed harder, and a trickle of blood stained the collar of his white shirt. "Since you knew I was working for Elsbeth before I came, why did you let me leave alive?"

"When games are played in the shadows, one never knows who will win. Sometimes it's best to sit back and see who will come out on top. I get the money, and you kill my enemy. Everybody is happy." A pained smile split his reddening face. "Besides, it wouldn't do to kill the possible future queen of the *Kriegsnachrichtenstelle*, now, would it? But . . . this time it seems you've overplayed your hand."

Leila tightened her grip. "Your life is between these hands."

"Oh dear," Pierre said. His eyes slanted down as he strained to see the blade. "I almost think you're serious."

"I am."

"I . . . thought you might say that."

The doors on the far end of the room swung open. Two men burst inside, their revolvers aimed at her.

Leila pivoted, putting Pierre in front of her but keeping the knife at his throat. "Back off!" She took three slow steps to the door on her left. "I'll kill him!"

"No, you won't!" Pierre hissed through gritted teeth. "If you kill me, my men will blow you to pieces!"

"Then let me go, and we both leave here alive!" Heart slamming against her ribcage, Leila kept easing Pierre backwards toward the door. Had Malcolm found Michael? Were they on their way back to Geneva? Perhaps—

She froze as a voice sounded from behind her. "Release my husband. Or I promise that you will die where you stand."

Malcolm heard his son first. A babble of sound that electrified his soul. Words, mispronounced, yet more powerful than anything he had ever felt.

"Da. Da. Da."

"Eh, Giovanni. The stupid rat thinks I'm his father!" Coarse laughter followed a muttered curse.

Malcolm crept closer, Luger back in his right hand, knife held loosely in his left. The man called Giovanni came into view and offered a glass bottle to his chunky comrade. Malcolm noted that neither had guns, though a rifle like the one the first guard had carried lay tossed carelessly across a stack of hay cubes.

"That is because you are the one who feeds him. Just be glad he doesn't call you Mama!"

"What?" The other thug sat up straight on his stool, eyes wide with horror. "A bullet in the filthy creature's brain would fix it. If I had my way—"

Malcolm was already rushing forward, Luger raised. *Pfft!*

Giovanni's eyes went wide a split instant before his forehead exploded into red. The bottle fell from his slack fingers, shattering, as he crashed backward onto the hay, his lifeblood soaking the ground.

Malcolm had already pivoted toward the other animal cowering in the straw-laden corner. He raised the Luger again.

"*Ave Maria, piena di grazia!*" It mumbled the words, staring at Malcolm, white-faced, hands raised.

"A dog like you, praying?" Malcolm said. His voice was the growl of a stalking lion.

"W-who are you?"

Malcolm stalked forward, glancing at the child on the barn floor only long enough to be sure he was out of reach of the second man's grasp. "The harbinger of justice."

"L-look, I was just following orders."

The child on the floor started to cry. The sound twisted something inside Malcolm, unleashing a mix of emotion and rage. He took another step closer.

"A bullet in his brain?" Malcolm's chest heaved as though he'd been running. "You would threaten a *child? My* child?"

"Your—"

The beast suddenly jerked a revolver free from where a grain sack had hid it from Malcolm's view. Aimed it at the squalling boy.

Chut! This time it was Malcolm's knife that sped through the air. It bit deep into the man's wrist. With a scream, he dropped the revolver. Malcolm pounced. Hooked his left fist into the criminal's square jaw.

"My orders are to protect my own," Malcolm said, grinding the Luger against the man's temple. As the   suppressed echo of the shot died away, a hush claimed the small barn. And in the stillness, Malcolm heard the voice again.

"Da . . . da?"

Turning from the spread-eagled corpse, Malcolm staggered over to his son. "Michael?"

It was a hoarse whisper. A prayer. A cry all mingled into one.

Michael lay propped against a sack of grain, wrapped in a matted dark-blue sweater and stained, thick gray pants. A leather cap lined with wool had slipped off the swath of fuzzy brown hair on his head. His eyes, glistening from his recent tears, were startlingly like his mother's with the exact emerald shade of green. As he looked at his father, Michael's face reddened and screwed into a tight ball.

"It's okay, son." Malcolm wiped his bloodied hands on his pants and scooped Michael up. "Don't cry. Daddy's here. You're safe now. You're safe." He pressed Michael gently against his chest, and at that moment, his world experienced a dynamic shift.

For the first time, Malcolm knew the power of a parent's love. In that moment, he understood what had driven his own father to expel him from their home, then welcome him back with open arms. He realized what had driven Thomas to sacrifice everything so that his son could lack nothing.

"Michael," he whispered to the warm bundle he held in his arms. "Daddy loves you."

Michael pushed himself up against Malcolm's chest, then cocked his head to one side. "Da?"

As the boy touched his bearded cheek, Malcolm broke down sobbing, the weight of his struggles crashing upon him.

Over. It's over.

But it wasn't. Not yet.

Wiping his eyes with his free hand, Malcolm glanced around. He grabbed the cap that lay crumpled up in the straw. Sliding it over Michael's head, he wrapped his son in his own coat, tight against his chest.

Cocking the Luger, Malcolm kicked the barn door open. "Let's get out of here, son."

The unfeeling barrel of a pistol jammed hard against the back of Leila's skull. "Bernadette?"

"Let my husband go or I'll kill you."

Leila barely breathed. "Bernadette, I saved your life. Don't you remember?"

"I'm not likely to forget." The voice was cold. Detached. "But that buys you no credit. To kill my husband is to kill my soul twice over."

"Oh, I . . . love you too, my darling," Pierre said, gushing now. "I have always loved you. Adored you. Do not let this devil come between us!"

"Bernadette." Leila ran her tongue over her lips. "Bernadette, listen to me. Your husband kidnapped my baby. My child is here, somewhere on your property. Pierre's been holding him hostage."

"And now you slander him?" The gun's hammer clicked back, loud as thunder. "You lying witch! Pierre has some faults but—"

"Would I be here if it weren't true?" Leila tightened her grip on the knife. "He's lied to you! He's not the man you think."

"Oh, I know why you're here." Bernadette pressed harder on the gun. "You're here because you're in league with that devil Elsbeth. She's always wanted my Pierre dead! She's the reason we had to flee Germany."

"No. No, I—"

"I don't want to kill you, Leila. I really don't. So I will give you one final warning." Bernadette slid in front of Leila, keeping the barrel against her temple. "Let. Pierre. Go."

Leila's gaze flickered from the men on the other side of the room to the middle-aged woman before her. The moment she stepped away from Pierre, they would open fire. But if she refused to back down, Bernadette would kill her anyway.

Her eyes drifted toward a distant window. By now Malcolm should be on his way to Geneva. If God was merciful, he would have found Michael. She could ask for nothing more.

"Are you . . . ready to die?" Pierre sniggered, a laugh that was a strange combination of a whine and a snort.

Leila's gaze snapped back to Bernadette's unfeeling blue eyes. "No."

She released her hold on Pierre. Shoved him against his wife. Leila dropped and slammed her right heel into Bernadette's ankle.

They collapsed in a heap. Bernadette's gun roared.

"Pierre?" Bernadette's scream was muffled.

Leila ducked as two bullets sped overhead.

I need a weapon.

Hysterical, Bernadette rolled out from beneath her husband's deadweight. "Pierre? No, it can't be!"

Wrenching the gun from Bernadette's loose grip, Leila pulled the trigger.

Missed.

She fired again.

One of Pierre's guards went down.

"Pierre? Oh God—Pierre! Talk to me, my love." Dragging herself next to her husband as bullets gauged holes in the walls, Bernadette shook his lifeless body. "Talk to me!"

Keeping the wailing Bernadette directly between her and the remaining guard, Leila ran in a half crouch to the door, then turned and pulled the trigger.

A short-lived scream.

Then Bernadette's shrieks were the only sound.

"I've killed him!" The woman crouched over her husband's body, rocking back and forth on her haunches.

Tucking the gun into her waist, Leila stepped around the broken glass and debris. The beauty of the room was gone, shattered like the life of the woman before her by senseless violence, greed, and corruption.

"My fault." Bernadette convulsed. "It's all my fault."

Leila opened the door and paused, her hand on its gilded handle. Love sometimes had a way of playing the cruelest of games, blinding those who should be best able to see the truth—no matter how ugly.

"I'm sorry, Bernadette," Leila said quietly. "I'm truly sorry."

Then, stepping outside, she closed the door with a soft *thud*, leaving a world of brokenness behind her.

Chapter 31

Hôtel LeVillier, Paris, France

A steady rain sluiced down from the pre-dawn sky. Leila stepped back from the window of their cramped hotel bedroom, letting the damask curtain fall back into place. She breathed deep as a sense of peace washed over her.

On the bed next to his father, little Michael slept deep, arms flung upward as though he wanted to embrace the whole world. His little chest rose and fell as miniature snores escaped his perfect mouth.

Thank you, God.

The miracle of the moment didn't escape Leila. In one night, her world had been transformed once more from utter brokenness to sheer beauty. Tiptoeing over to Malcolm's side of the bed, she eased back the coverlet and snuggled in beside him.

He stirred. A few seconds later, his right arm slipped around her shoulders.

"Can't sleep?"

This early in the morning, Malcolm's voice was a deep bass that made Leila's spine tingle.

"I'm too happy to sleep." She settled back against his chest. "You, me, and Michael all together. It is all too wonderful. As though the first light of dawn has kissed the sky after a long, dark night."

Malcolm leaned over and kissed her.

"Um, morning breath," Leila teased as she pulled away.

"Not like yours is any better," he responded, chuckling

Reaching up, Leila pulled her husband close. "Thank you for arranging all this. False identity papers?Choosing Paris as our hiding place since Elsbeth's still on the loose? You're a natural, Malcolm."

"Well, I learned from the best." Malcolm shifted onto his side, propping himself on his elbow. "Do you know what today is?"

"I could never forget."

"We were married five years ago today."

"This is the first anniversary we've spent together. Ever. And now we have our son with us." Leila sat up, leaning back against the wooden headboard. "Faith can truly still move mountains."

Malcolm pulled himself up beside her and laid a gentle hand on their son's stomach. "It seems that some mountains are more stubborn than others."

"Malcolm, we'll find a way for us all to go home. Thomas's death won't have been in vain."

"I know that," Malcolm said. "But it's hard sometimes, you know? I just can't believe he's gone. It's bad enough when you lose a fellow soldier or a subordinate. But when it's someone who's a part of your heart . . ."

"Thomas lives on through you, Malcolm. Somehow, we'll make his vision come true. I know it."

"Well," Malcolm sighed, running his fingers through her hair. "The fact that you managed to get the prime minister's tacit permission to spy for Britain is a godsend."

Leila leaned her head on his muscled shoulder. "Mercedes knows to contact us through Grayson if she discovers anything new in Berlin."

"We'll stay in Paris for the next few months. We'll have to move around a bit, but all that matters is that we'll be together."

Leila traced a spiral pattern on his neck with her finger. "Hm . . . an extended vacation in the city of love?"

"Only the best for my queen."

She clasped his hands to her lips, serious now. "Malcolm, I love you with every breath I take. With every beat of my heart."

Leaning over, Malcolm rested his forehead against her own. "I know. And I promise you that nothing will ever separate us again."

PART 4

June 1919

Chapter 32

Paris, France

Malcolm pressed his way against the steady flow of pedestrians. Tourists, soldiers, and journalists clogged the narrow walkways while motorized traffic and horses competed for the streets themselves. A historic treaty officially ending the "war to end all wars" was about to be signed at nearby Versailles Palace. Now it seemed that everyone and his brother was thronging Paris.

"Any more people and the city will explode," Malcolm said under his breath. The additional crowds were a mixed blessing. The prices of everything had surged, but more people made it less likely that he and Leila would be recognized. On the other hand, there was also increased risk of Elsbeth's agents moving more easily into the city.

Spying an opening in traffic, Malcolm darted across the street, then turned down a quieter alley. Halfway down the street, he exited another quick left toward the small flat he was currently renting. They rarely stayed in a location more than a few weeks at a time.

A rueful smile slipped over Malcolm's face. Once he would have considered this kind of transient living barbaric. But life in the trenches had taught him to adapt. For the moment, adapting meant doing whatever it took to keep his family was safe.

Shifting a small cakebox into the crook of his left arm, Malcolm fiddled a key out of his right pocket. Once it had felt strange to purchase his own food. Servants had taken care of those duties his whole life. A cake for his son's first birthday would have been handled without his knowledge. But the world had undergone a cosmic shift, and he felt an odd sense of pride in being involved.

The old order was over. Malcolm accepted that. Even agreed with it for the most part. For the past four years, he had been denied the privileges associated with his social rank. He had slept in the muck and mire with men who in some cases barely knew how to write. Yet Malcolm had found them to be among the truest hearts in the empire. The world had changed on many fronts.

And so have I.

"*Monsieur* DuChevalier?" A boy's voice, breaking in adolescence, piped up from his right.

"Yes?" Malcolm twisted as the sandy-haired teen held out a cream envelope.

"A telegram for you, *Monsieur.*"

"Ah!" Malcolm laid the paper bag to one side, outwardly betraying no emotion though his pulse spiked. Only one man knew his precise whereabouts. And if he had sent a telegram, it meant his world was about to change once more.

"Thank you, young man." Malcolm flipped the messenger a coin. When the teen had darted off, he glanced about, opened the door, and stepped inside.

"Where's my angel?" Leila dangled a tiny stuffed brown bear above Michael's face, smiling as the giggling child swatted at the toy. "Where's my angel?"

Leaning forward, she planted a kiss on his upturned forehead.

"Mama," Michael said. He stuck a finger in his mouth. "Mama."

Leila's heart melted as her eyes soaked in the sight of her son's stocky build, his bright green eyes, and straight chestnut hair. A few light freckles sprinkled his dimpled cheeks.

"Yes," Leila said, wrapping him in her arms. "You're here with me." Tickling him, she held him close, as he squealed and wriggled in her arms. "And you're not . . . going . . . *anywhere!*"

Michael finally broke free, tottered a few steps, then fell on his rump. His eyes suddenly widened. "Da . . . da?"

Leila turned as Malcolm stepped in from the short corridor and gently placed a brown box onto the table. "I didn't hear you come in."

"That's because our son had you at his mercy." Malcolm pulled her into a tight embrace. For her part, Leila wrapped her arms around his neck.

Not once had she ever imagined life could offer such happiness. The darkness of the recent past had been exchanged for something incredibly wonderful. Her lips drifted to his mouth. Malcolm filled her days with joy . . . and her nights with bliss.

"I love you," her husband whispered, burying his face in hair that now dangled about her shoulders. His words touched her soul, but there was something in his tone, a slight catch that didn't match the intimacy of the moment.

"Malcolm?" Leila pulled back, holding his face between her palms. "What is it?"

Malcolm didn't answer. Instead, he turned and held out his arms to their son. "What a day to celebrate." He tossed a giggling Michael in the air. "One year old and ready to conquer the world!"

Leila stepped over to the small wooden table at the center of the room. A cream envelope peeked out from beneath the corner of the cakebox. She tugged it free, then slid a finger beneath the seal.

Leila read in silence, her heart beating out a muffled tattoo. Then she looked up and met Malcolm's gaze. "Mercedes has contacted Greyson."

He moved next to her, Michael on his arm. "I thought so."

"She'll be at the Arch of Triumph at noon today."

"I'll get her," Malcolm said softly. He reached out and stroked Leila's cheek with the backs of his knuckles. "It was only a matter of time until reality found us, Leila. We both knew that."

"Yes."

"We've let the madness slide by for a little while. But it's caught up with us."

A lump rose in the back of Leila's throat, choking off her words. "I . . . I've never known such happiness." She stepped into his arms and clung to him as though he were life itself. "But you've given me something so precious. It's a dream I don't want to end."

"I know."

Straightening with a sigh, Leila folded her arms across her chest. "But we can't live in hiding forever. One way or another, everything has to end." Her gaze drifted from Michael to the birthday cake. "For his sake as well as ours."

"I just wish it weren't today."

A grandfather clock struck eleven sonorous notes, breaking the silence.

"I'd better go," he said.

"Yes." Leila held out her arms, taking Michael. "It's time."

◆◆●◆◆

Mercedes sat across from Leila, hands pleated. To Malcolm, it seemed the small bedroom had become even smaller. It wasn't the physical presence of this slight, blonde-headed girl in a navy-blue skirt and white shirt that constricted the space. It was the knowledge that their dream-world was about to be shattered.

"I'm so glad you're safe." Leaning forward, Leila squeezed Mercedes's hand. "All these months with no contact? I didn't know what to think."

"It was dangerous." Mercedes's face twisted in a wry grimace. "You see, Elsbeth was in Berlin when I arrived."

"Was there any trouble?" Leila asked.

"Not exactly." Mercedes looked down at her hands. Malcolm noticed there was a thin band of gold on her ring finger. "But we're facing something bigger than any of us thought possible."

"Why don't you start from the beginning?" Malcolm suggested.

Mercedes drew in a deep breath. "Shortly after I arrived in Berlin, I became friendly with a member of the *Reichswehr*, Hindenburg's army." She twisted the ring. "I-I didn't expect anything to come of it, but it just . . . happened!" Mercedes glanced at Leila, a slight flush on her cheeks.

"Believe me, I understand," Leila said, looking at   Malcolm.

"Well, Lars—that's his name—and I became very close. He lives alone and . . . we were to be married. Today."

The sound of Michael blowing raspberries filled the abrupt silence.

Malcolm spoke first. "What happened?"

Mercedes looked at him, serious now. "Two days ago, Lars told me he had been chosen for a specific task."

"*Hubris?*" Leila said, leaning forward.

Mercedes nodded once. "But worse." Bending, she carefully withdrew a small, dark steel canister. A square cage clamped down over the canister's screwed on lid. "This is Fritz Haber's latest gift to mankind—a colorless, odorless liquid that kills within seconds."

Malcolm moved closer. "What do they intend to do?"

"Wipe out tens of thousands across Europe. Political leaders. Soldiers. Even civilians."

"Dear God." Leila's face was ashen. "He'll release this in Paris?"

"Not just Paris." Mercedes's eyes darkened. "London. Calais. Etaples. Anywhere there may be a high concentration of soldiers. It will all begin after they get word that the attack on Versailles has succeeded."

She paused, her gaze shifting to Leila. "There's more. Lars's unit was supposed to rendezvous with the strike team from Versailles. That team will be headed by Elsbeth."

"Why did your fiancé tell you all this?" Malcolm said.

"Lars didn't know anything about *Hubris* until his commanding officer briefed him two days ago. Lars was furious because he hated being part of the army and thought the war was over since the armistice was signed six months ago. These orders to move out came on our wedding day—yesterday. Lars knew he owed me some kind of explanation."

"So he violated his oath to secrecy?" Leila exchanged a glance with Malcolm, and he read the unspoken message in her eyes. If anyone identified Lars as the leak, it would be just as well he had no family.

"We love each other," Mercedes said in a quiet voice. "We decided to get married that same day. We spent our wedding night in his small apartment. Before he woke up the next morning . . . I was gone—with the poison."

Leila pulled Mercedes into a tight embrace. "It was the right thing to do."

"The right thing?" Mercedes shoulders shook as she leaned into Leila's shoulder. "All I can think about is the hurt he must be feeling right now. I keep imagining the pain in his eyes"—her voice broke— "knowing the woman he married betrayed him. He'll think it was all a lie."

"But it's *not*, Mercedes," Leila said. "You'll both find a way to move past this, I know it!"

Malcolm caught Leila's eye and nodded toward the door.

"It'll be all right." Leila held the other girl close a moment longer, then followed Malcolm outside, closing the door behind her.

"I need that canister," Malcolm said, reaching for his hat.

"I'll get it. You're going to Versailles?"

"The Big Four have been there for months finalizing negotiations. If I can get David Lloyd George to look at what Mercedes brought, it will change everything."

Whirling, Leila jerked open a drawer and grabbed a small slip of paper. "This is the telegram he sent to me in Switzerland. Show it to him and tell him everything."

"The French will be more than happy to listen. They just want an excuse to carry on this war." Malcolm forked a finger through his dark hair. "God help us, Leila. Do you realize how far we've fallen as a human race? Millions of civilians dying—for what?"

Leila touched his arm gently. "A world without God is a world without a conscience. But we still must do our part to help."

Malcolm pressed her hands to his lips. "And we will. Do you trust Will and Eleanor with our son's safety?"

"Yes," she said. "I'll get a message to Greyson and ask him to have them come right away. Mercedes and I will join you in Versailles. I have a plan that the French prime minister, Clemenceau, will want to hear."

Pulling her close, Malcolm whispered, "Be safe. I need you alive as does our son. Whatever happens, just . . . stay alive."

After a moment, Leila pulled back, her eyes glittering with fierce determination.

"This ends at Versailles, Malcolm. I will find Elsbeth. And when I do, I'll make sure our son never has to fear the night again. Whatever happens . . . it all ends here."

Chapter 33

London, Great Britain

Robert Hughes drummed his fingers in a staccato rhythm on the glossy surface of his cherrywood desk. His eyes shifted to a fly that landed on his blue trousers, then buzzed onto his starched white shirt.

Distracted, Hughes waved the pest aside, then glanced at Lord Curzon, a leading member of the prime minister's war cabinet. While David Lloyd George was at Versailles hammering out the treaty's final details, Curzon served as his immediate point of contact.

Curzon held a sheaf of papers that detailed security protocols for the treaty that would officially end the Great War. There would be multiple security sweeps by both French and British military personnel. Ramped-up squadrons of Allied soldiers patrolling the grounds. There could be no mistakes. But a question wormed its way into his gut with dogged persistence. *Is it enough?*

"Well, out with it, spymaster." Curzon shoved the papers back into a cream folder and tossed it onto Hughes's desk. "God knows I have enough on my mind. So what's the problem?"

"Problem?" Hughes arched an eyebrow. "Who says there's a problem?"

"You've stopped frowning," Curzon said pointedly. "For most people, that would be a good thing. In your case, the lack of a frown worries me."

Hughes leaned back in his chair, choosing to ignore the jibe. "It's nothing, really. Just that my agents on the continent recently intercepted a message."

"Not a birthday message to our gracious sovereign King George, I presume?" Curzon squared an ankle over one knee.

"No," Hughes said tersely. "It was a message that indicates Leila Steele will be at Versailles.

Curzon scoffed. "Still gnawing away on that bone, are we? A plot to assassinate the world's leadership, wasn't it? I thought all that died with Thomas months ago. Yet here you are, the illustrious Sir Robert Hughes, still thinking about the rambling of a German spy."

"Not thinking. Just . . . remembering." Hughes pursed his lips. "It doesn't matter, really. The security will be tight enough to catch a German fly, let alone an assassin."

"I—"

The piercing ring of the black telephone on his desk amputated Curzon's reply. He leaned back in his chair with a *humph*, motioning for Hughes to take the call.

Hughes picked up the phone.

"Sir Hughes." The shrill voice of his secretary made him wince. "I have Prime Minister George calling from France. The line is secure."

"Thank you, Margaret." Hughes straightened up in his chair. The prime minister never called from overseas unless something was wrong. Very wrong.

"Hughes." David's voice was as cold as steel. "I need you to listen carefully."

"Of course."

"I have received credible intelligence that the Germans are about to unleash a weapon that will eliminate the leadership here at Versailles and the civilian population in Allied nations across Europe. Liquified gas is the method."

Silence fell, a silence so complete that Hughes was certain David could hear the suddenly erratic *thud, thu-thud,* of his heart.

"What?" It was more of a mangled croak than an intelligible question.

"The plot, Hughes." Menace laced David's voice. "The plot the girl tried to warn us about. Well, it's real. Only it's worse than even she expected." He was silent a moment, then added, "Hughes, they intend to kill us all."

"What is the source of this intelligence?" Hughes's mind reeled, but even as David's voice filled his ears, his mind began conjuring up several counteroffensive maneuvers. If just one spy could be apprehended . . .

"I engaged the services of Leila Steele last year. She obtained a sample, snatched out from beneath the noses of the Huns themselves. Her husband, Malcolm—you remember the man, don't you? Of course you do!—got the sample to me. Clemenceau, my French counterpart, had his best scientists examine it. The threat is real. Within a few hours, thousands of civilians could die."

"God help us," Hughes said.

David barked out a bitter laugh. "Well, He better help you. You were wrong on all counts."

Hughes was silent for a moment as the implications of David's words sunk deep into his mind.

Wrong?

Thomas. Leila. The assassination plot.

All wrong?

He shrugged off an unexpected barrage of self-acrimony. There would be plenty of time for that later. Now he had to save the empire.

"I need whatever information you can get me."

"Details will arrive at your door within the hour."

Hughes felt Curzon's eyes on him. He gestured impatiently for the man to leave, but Curzon ignored him.

"I'll get right on it, sir," Hughes said. "We *will* find them."

"You've got twenty-four hours. Clemenceau is a gnat's twitch away from invading Germany at this point. Can't say as I blame him. Fail me, and the killing we've seen so far will be a tea party compared to what's coming."

"I understand, sir."

"Do you? Do you indeed?" David was shouting, but Hughes remained unflinching. This was just. He had failed his government. His king. Himself. He deserved every scrap of shame that would be heaped upon his reputation.

Hughes's eyes snapped to the map of Europe on his wall. "I will find them."

"Twenty-four hours. Then we prepare to invade."

Click.

"Well, that seemed rather unpleasant." Curzon shifted in his seat.

Hughes slowly turned toward him, dazed. "Malcolm Steele had news for the prime minister."

"You're flogging a dead horse, Robert." Curzon leaned forward, his eyes boring holes into his face. "I went along with your scheme to eliminate Thomas because he was a threat to the social order. After all, what message would it send to the rabble if one can challenge the Crown itself and get by with it?"

"I—"

Curzon lifted a finger. "But his son does not share the sins of the father. Don't ask me to stand idly by while you tarnish Malcolm Steele's reputation. I happen to like that young man."

"I plan to do nothing of the sort." Hughes pushed the words through clenched teeth.

"Then what is the problem, man?"

"This information must not leave this room," Hughes said.

Curzon rolled his eyes. "Of course, Robert, of course!"

"Steele—Leila Steele—was right. There is a plot."

Curzon stared at him, his face the color of bone. "When I showed you Leila's letter before the trial, you insisted that it was all a ruse." His tongue flickered over his lips. "You told me Thomas had been corrupted by German gold. That it was my *duty* as a patriot to expose him."

"I assure you—"

"Shut it, Robert!" Curzon's face set into a series of rigid lines. "Your bungling has placed a thousand years of British dominion in jeopardy."

Hughes was silent. The empire meant more than life to Curzon. And to himself. Now it could end . . . because of him.

"You do realize the implications?" Curzon said.

"Yes." How could he not?

"Leila was innocent. She was working with Thomas against the Germans. Just as he said." Curzon fell back, clapping a hand to his forehead. "Dear God! We forced the man to take drastic measures because of *you*."

"Thomas was guilty." Hughes struggled upright. "The details are negligible."

"Bah!"

Fury roiled in Hughes's gut, adding to his volatile mix of emotions. "I have no time to debate the guilt of a dead man when so many others may soon share his fate. If there is nothing else, Lord Curzon?"

"This war has turned you into a legend." Curzon picked up his tweed hat as he stood. "Fail, and I will show the people that their hero is nothing more than a twisted man who has outlived his usefulness to King and Country."

"If I fail," Hughes said evenly, "like as not, I'll be dead."

Curzon jammed his hat onto his head. "You're finished, Robert. My advice is to resign. Gather whatever scraps of dignity you can muster and get out. Or I swear I'll destroy you."

With a parting contemptuous glare, Curzon stormed through the door.

Chapter 34

Versailles Palace, France, June 28

Elsbeth inhaled, savoring the scent of roses wafting into the air as she sauntered down the elongated parterre that led to Versailles's celebrated Hall of Mirrors. Versailles was a sprawling complex of masterful French architecture that spanned more than a thousand acres. Its central point was the stunning castle itself.

Masses thronged the castle grounds, which were open to the public. The crowds were largely made up of French, British, and American soldiers. But there were also journalists as well as hundreds of civilians. In short, it was the perfect mix for the four other German agents on her team to remain invisible until Elsbeth was ready to unleash havoc.

She rolled her shoulders, relishing the warmth of the summer sun on her back.

"A dreadful day, is it not?"

Elsbeth turned, shading her eyes against the afternoon sun. Framed in its rays was the moon-faced buffoon that Hindenburg had commissioned to sign the treaty, Germany's recently-appointed foreign minister, Hermann Müller.

With a shudder, Müller tugged at the lapels of his dark suit. "A black day for the Fatherland." He moved to stand beside Elsbeth, lowering his voice as his eyes skittered over the crowds. "I still don't understand why Hindenburg insisted you accompany me. And under the pretext of being my wife?" He snorted. "I already have a wife."

"Yes." Elsbeth looped her arm through his and steered him toward the looming palace. The heels of her black pumps clacked against the concrete steps. "You also have your orders. If you want more than that, I suggest you take it up with General Hindenburg when you return to *Deutschland*."

"That may be true, but I demand an explanation." Müller came to a stop. "Should I be aware of something that is happening?"

"We both know that certain affairs of state cannot be shared, even with other members of the government." Elsbeth wanted to strangle the idiot. Instead, she straightened his crooked tie and spoke in low, measured tones.

"But—"

"But I can tell you this. Eight days ago, you were promoted to the position of foreign minister. Few people here know your face. No one knows what your wife looks like. I too am unknown. So as far as you are concerned, this weekend you have a new wife."

Müller slanted her a glance as a French soldier wearing the uniform of the Republican Guard jerked his head downward in a stiff nod and pulled open the massive doors. "Well, since you put it that way, does that mean—?"

"You men are all so alike." Elsbeth's chuckle cut him off. "You know, I remember the last time a politician asked me that question. I was in London, and a French diplomat made the same proposal."

"And how did you answer?" Müller squeezed his bulk through the door.

"I agreed." Elsbeth said. "He knew of a secret room in a crypt beneath a cathedral in London. It was very discreet."

"A crypt?" Horror tinged Müller's voice. "Barbaric. Leave it to the lascivious French! What sort of relationship can occur among corpses?"

"Hm, a deadly one." Elsbeth's lips curved upward."The next morning—when I had the information I wanted—I left him with a smile . . . on his throat."

Müller froze. He stared, mouth agape. "Y-you mean . . .?"

"Take my advice and stay focused, *Herr* Müller." Elsbeth gave his hand a tight squeeze, eyes shifting beyond him to the French soldier who had opened the door. "Anything else might prove fatal."

With another tight smile and pat on the shoulder, Elsbeth released him and took a step back into a corner of the immense hall. At least a thousand men filed into rows of chairs that had been set apart from a table on a raised dais at the far end of the hall. That was where the actual treaty would be signed.

Elsbeth glanced through the glass panes on her left to see dozens of others climbing on chairs and dressers to catch a glimpse of the proceedings. Her other four agents were scattered at equidistant points around the hall.

Elsbeth's mind ticked through the details of their plot. Their mission was rather simple, really. Each agent would discretely open the flasks and let a small amount of Haber's poison spill onto the floor. Then they would discretely move to another spot in the room and start again.

If all went well, the first victims—ideally the assembled heads of state, who were seated closest to the dais—should begin to react. In the ensuing chaos, she and her agents would empty whatever remained in their flasks, escape, and move on to the next city on their list. If plans went awry, each was equipped with a small syringe and needle of Haber's antidote.

This is a black day—a day on which all scores are settled.

Müller was right. The French sought to avenge their wounded national pride. Little did they realize the Germans were not yet defeated.

But Elsbeth too had a private vendetta.

Leila.

Elsbeth's hands balled into fists, her fingernails digging into her skin. The news of Pierre LaRue's death and the Steeles's dramatic rescue of their whelp had been a shock.

"I leave for just a few weeks, and everything falls apart!" Elsbeth sighed as she adjusted the silver chain of a black fur purse encrusted with small diamonds over her left shoulder. The purse sported a floral silver pattern. Beauty that concealed death.

How appropriate.

Elsbeth's eyes skimmed the room once more. The security around the place was tight.

That was to be expected.

What *was* unusual was the sudden arrival of an additional thirty French soldiers at the far end of the hall. Barking out orders, they jerked startled onlookers roughly to their feet, demanding identification and forcibly opening bags. Elsbeth glanced outside the immense glass windows.

More soldiers trotted rapidly toward the hall's rear entrance! Members of the press protested and snapped pictures, but the French doggedly continued, dividing the crowd into small groups and inspecting anyone with a bag or purse.

Elsbeth's lips pursed as the soldiers lining the walls snapped to attention, their rifles at the ready.

This wasn't just a tight security operation. This was a search!

Something's wrong!

Elsbeth's mind skimmed through possibilities. Perhaps the French had somehow caught wind of the operation. If the Allies suspected a conspiracy, luring her into the Hall of Mirrors would be an effective way of trapping her team.

Elsbeth lifted a small pair of black field glasses to her eyes. None of the Big Four—as the American president plus the French, British, and Italian prime ministers were dubbed— had come to the table. Only a handful of unimportant political representatives were present. Elsbeth had initially taken this as a minor delay—global leaders were busy people, after all—but what if the men were deliberately absent?

She lowered the glasses, thoughts streaming like flight-crazed starlings through her skull. In a place as large and crowded as Versailles, the only way of finding assassins would be to lure them into a trap. Since that clearly was the case, someone must have warned them. Someone with evidence. And access to the most powerful men in the world.

Who?

Elsbeth's eyes swung to the other German agents. They were in the crowd near the methodically-searching French soldiers. If they were found, everything was finished. It was time to disappear.

Shrinking back, Elsbeth turned and made her way out of the Hall of Mirrors. Passing through a pair of massive double doors, she slipped into the *Salon de Guerre*—the War Room. Her footsteps echoed on the glossy wooden floor.

The salon was largely empty. Most observers were either inside the Hall of Mirrors itself or on the castle grounds waiting for the salvo of firearms that would follow the treaty's ratification.

Elsbeth bit back a curse as she passed a relief of Louis XIV on horseback. The attack at Versailles was the heart of the European operation. Agents scattered across the continent waited for this attack be carried off to strike their own targets.

Elsbeth stalked forward. They had planned for this contingency. If the attack failed at Versailles, she was to notify Hindenburg immediately, and the other operations would continue.

Her teeth clenched. The entire operation had been meticulously planned. Small teams. Few people involved. Details shrouded in secrecy. The individual agents had been kept apart. They were under a sworn death sentence—as were their families—if they talked.

The War Room boasted a series of ceiling-high windows on three sides with the fourth side leading into the Hall of Mirrors. Each window was covered by thick scarlet drapes that fell from top to bottom but were parted in the middle to allow light into the room.

As Elsbeth strode toward a small door leading outside to the parterre, she took idle note of a woman who stood at one of the tall windows. Her body was partially concealed behind the long drapes, but the tilt of her head made clear that she was gazing down at the crowds below.

Soldiers patrolled those crowds, but Elsbeth knew she could evade them easily enough. She passed a black marble bust crowned with laurel leaves and approached the door. She would get to Paris within a half hour and—

The woman pivoted. "Hello, Elsbeth."

Elsbeth froze for just the fraction of a second, but in that brief moment, something hard jammed up against her spine. Her lip curled up in a sneer.

"So I was right, then. The little lapdog *has* switched mistresses. You're not clever enough to spin this web yourself. I see Leila's hand in this. She's here, isn't she?"

"Give Mercedes the bag." Leila's voice was quiet, but as she pressed the barrel of the gun into the small of Elsbeth's back, there was no doubt of her intentions.

"I'll take this." Mercedes was already slipping Elsbeth's purse off Elsbeth's shoulder and onto her own arm. She flanked the other two women so any observers across the salon wouldn't see Leila's gun as Leila again prodded Elsbeth in the spine.

"Now start walking toward the door," Leila said coldly. Elsbeth spied a narrow door in a section of the salon wall not covered by windows. "Keep your hands visible!"

"And if I refuse?" Elsbeth queried softly. "Will blood stain the floor of the Hall of War?"

"I'm sorry." Leila's voice was iron. "Is that a question?"

Elsbeth considered. Her gun was strapped to her left inner thigh and a knife was tucked into her right. Having trained Leila, she knew her protégé would not turn her over to the French. Leila would want her dead.

However, Elsbeth knew Leila would prefer to get her alone before executing her so as not to draw attention from the handful of people loitering in distant corners of the large salon. But Elsbeth also had no doubt that, if given no other choice, Leila would gun her down where she stood. The French would certainly be on her side.

Elsbeth gnawed on the corner of her lower lip. For the moment she would comply with Leila while watching for an opportunity to access either of her weapons. Especially since she too preferred a private arena in which to make these two traitors pay for the insult of turning on their mistress and maker. She was still better at this than either of her surrogate "daughters."

"You know, if I'd been in Switzerland, you would never have found your son." Elsbeth chose her words carefully as she allowed Leila to prod her toward the small door in the paneling. "Pierre was a fool to bring you to his house. If it were me, just one step too close and *boom.*"

She mimicked an explosion. "Bye-bye, baby!" She eyed Leila in her peripheral vision, hoping for a reaction.

There was none.

Mercedes moved ahead to open the door. Through it, Elsbeth could see a small room dimly illuminated by daylight filtering in from a window high above, highlighting suspended particles of dust. The room was spartan compared to the salon they'd just left, an uneven stone floor, piles of dusty wooden crates against the walls, and no other furniture. Probably some type of storage or workroom for the servants who maintained all the costly beauty surrounding them.

It was also empty of people and by the dust accumulation long unused. So this was where Leila thought to end Elsbeth's life. Ignominious. Like a rat in a cellar.

"Move!" Leila shoved Elsbeth forward toward the open door. Mercedes quickly stepped back out of the way.

It was Elsbeth's opportunity, and she seized it. Pretending to stumble against Mercedes as she passed through the doorframe, Elsbeth slid her left hand through the slit on the side of her dress. Easing her knife free, she flattened it against her wrist as she straightened.

Mercedes latched the door the moment all three women were inside the room. Her gun still digging into Elsbeth's spine,

Leila used her left hand to search Elsbeth for weapons. Tugging Elsbeth's gun free, she held it out to Mercedes.

As Mercedes stepped forward to take the take it, Elsbeth spat in her face. "I trusted you! Promoted you. And this is how you repay me?"

"You see, that's just it." Mercedes wiped the spittle from her face. "You've always treated me like an unwanted mongrel, using me and giving nothing in return. No affection. Not even appreciation."

"I promoted you," Elsbeth said coldly. "That's affection enough."

"Maybe in your world. But Leila showed me the truth."

"What, that you're an incompetent whore who doesn't deserve to live?"

Mercedes lifted her chin. "That my life has value."

"Oh, I see. She's baiting you with more of her religious prattle, is that it?" A scornful laugh dripped from Elsbeth's lips as Leila continued her search. "Face it, Mercedes. You're just another fallen woman hoping to find redemption in a tangled web of lies! Nothing can change what you've done."

Mercedes moved closer. Elsbeth waited, arms limp, head slightly bowed. She knew what would happen next. She'd trained them both.

"You took everything from me," Mercedes said, teeth clenched and nostrils flared as she stalked closer. "My childhood. My freedom. And for what?"

One.

"How many other lives will you ruin if you walk out of here alive?" Mercedes stepped closer, her index finger pressed against her chest. "What we do today, we do for the good of humanity."

Two.

"Where's the knife, Elsbeth?" Leila's voice cut in. As she spoke, Elsbeth felt the gun's pressure ease from her spine, sensed Leila taking a half-step back, knew when the other woman shifted her gun to her left hand to check Elsbeth's right thigh for the knife Leila knew Elsbeth always carried.

Now!

A growl ripped out of Elsbeth's throat as she leapt forward, knife extended. Her blade sliced through Mercedes's right cheek, gauging out a chunk of flesh.

Mercedes screamed. Staggered back. The gun confiscated from Elsbeth went flying as she raised her hands to cover her face. Blood spurted through her fingers.

Elsbeth pivoted just as Leila shifted her own gun back into her dominant hand. Before Leila could raise it, Elsbeth snapped out a swift kick. The gun clattered on the floor.

Elsbeth lunged forward, intent on slashing Leila's throat.

Leila swerved. Chopped at the base of Elsbeth's neck. Fire snaked down Elsbeth's spine as the knife flew out of her hand and she landed hard on her stomach.

"It ends today, Elsbeth." Leila grabbed Elsbeth's dark hair. Pulled back. She slammed Elsbeth's skull against the floor, sending sparks forking through the woman's body.

Prostrate, Elsbeth panted, pushing herself to her knees. Blood streaked from a gash in her forehead, trickling down her chin.

"Now that's the spy I remember. That's the woman"—Elsbeth lashed out, slamming her heel into Leila's ankle— "I trained!"

Leila cried out as she crashed onto her side. Elsbeth rolled. Grabbed the blade. Swiped downward.

Leila's hands shot up in front of her face. The blade sliced deep into both her palms. Blood flowed, making the knife's blade slick.

Elsbeth bared her teeth, then glanced at Mercedes. The girl struggled upright, pressing a torn off corner of her shirt against her face. Despite the dim lighting, Elsbeth could see it was already dark with blood. "It wasn't supposed to end like this."

A quick glance around spotted Elsbeth's gun on the far side of the room. Tossing the slippery knife after it, she scooped up Leila's gun instead and pointed it at Mercedes. "Get back!"

Mercedes shrank against the door, hands trembling as she pressed the cloth against her face.

Elsbeth leveled the gun with Leila's forehead. "You poor deluded girl. You really thought you could defeat me, didn't you? What a disappointment you've turned out to be." Her finger curled around the trigger. "You brought this on yourself. All of it!"

"What choice did I have? You would have killed my son. Murdered thousands of innocents!" Leila pushed herself upright, then clutched the edge of her shirt in her bleeding palms.

"They'll die anyway!" Elsbeth coughed. The air was dry, and her lungs burned. "Your son. Your husband. They won't escape." She stalked closer. "So what have you *really* accomplished?" She coughed again, violently this time.

"What have I accomplished?" Leila lifted her chin, still defiant. Odd for one about to die a failure. "What I wanted to accomplish."

"Really?" Elsbeth blinked rapidly to clear her watering eyes, then pressed the heels of her left palm against her skull. "And what is that?" Her head clanged as though it had been shattered by a bullet. It was probably a reaction from Leila's futile attack.

"I've saved my son," Leila said. Her words seemed garbled, lethargic.

Something's wrong.

"What's ... happening?" Elsbeth staggered as the room began to swing in a slow arc. She closed her eyes for a moment, then opened them, sucking in a series of short breaths.

Leila smiled—a tired, wan smile. "Ask Mercedes."

Elsbeth pivoted, her blood turning to ice. Mercedes lay in a heap a few feet away.

The poison flask was open beside her. The ground between her and Elsbeth was soaked.

"No. No!" Reeling, Elsbeth lurched for her discarded purse.

The antidote. Haber's antidote!

Fumbling for the syringe, she jerked off the leather sheath, hiked up her skirt, and rammed the needle into her thigh.

"You've failed, Leila. I have an antidote." A low, wheezing laugh leaked out of Elsbeth's lungs. "You've forgotten what I taught you. Hope ... for the best. Plan for the worst."

The drug coursed through her body, pumping Haber's life-saving medicine to her cells with each beat of her heart. Elsbeth waited as the seconds yawned into a minute. Then two. But her chest continued to tighten, and her pulse became more erratic.

Dub, dub. Dub ... dub.

Her heart slowed as though it were tired of life. Fire wormed its way throughout her entire body as though some evil spirit twisted inside her. Had Haber's antidote also failed?

"Failed? I don't think so," Leila said slowly. "I've won."

"*Arrêtez-vous!*"

The stentorian command came from the other side of the door. A second later, it slammed against the wall, and soldiers poured in. Gas masks covered their faces, and their weapons were at the ready.

"*Vite!* Quickly!" The group's leader pointed urgently to Leila and Mercedes. "Get masks on them. Get them out of here!"

"No!" Lips pulled back in a snarl, Elsbeth shoved herself upright as bitter realization crashed into her mind. Leila had spun a tight web, one that included collaboration with the French. But Leila was unarmed. Elsbeth could still shoot her before the soldiers got too close.

"Put down your weapon. Now!"

Ignoring the Frenchman, Elsbeth swung back to Leila, raising her gun.

Pough!

A bullet slammed into Elsbeth's chest, unleashing an inferno of pain. She blinked, unable to understand why her fingers were suddenly too weak to hold the gun any longer.

Leila stood, leaning against the wall, as a whisper of smoke curled from a small pistol in her bloodied hand. Elsbeth crashed onto the floor, arms and legs akimbo.

Leila had brought a second weapon.

"Hope . . . for the best," Leila wheezed, pulling herself upright. She coughed, but the light of triumph glittered in her eyes. "Plan for the worst." She coughed again. "I'm . . . a good student."

"Madame Steele, put down the weapon please!" The words were distant. Wrapped in fog. "Our orders were to capture the woman alive."

Dimly, Elsbeth felt someone slip an oxygen mask onto her face. It would do no good. Haber's antidote had failed. But the most bitter truth was that *she* had failed. And with her would die the hope of Germany's ultimate triumph. But it was better to die than to see her beloved nation so humbled.

"*Deutschland über alles.*" Elsbeth tried to force the words out of a jaw that was too slack to obey. Germany above all others.

But now Germany would lie crushed beneath the boots of its enemies. Her heart slowed its rhythm to a crawl.

Dub. Dub . . . dub.

Fear left an iron taste in her mouth. Was this death? No. It was sleep. The unending sleep for which her body ached.

But the darkness! An oppressive darkness, so thick it could be felt. For the first time, Elsbeth feared the shadows. She had always managed to cheat the Boatsman. But this time, the oncoming night was inescapable. Filled with terror. Deep. Endless.

Cringing, she shrank within herself, trying to escape the darkness that tinged the edge of her vision, swallowing the room's feeble light.

Then came the cold. It struck her feet first, then slowly enshrouded her entire body as the night spread across her vision.

Distant wails—unearthly and discordant—shrieked louder in her ears, splintering her soul into jagged fragments. Elsbeth tried to fight the horror, but her hands refused to move. She wanted to scream but found she could not speak.

Vanity.

The word wrapped itself around her dimming conscience, sapping whatever strength she had left.

Everything is vanity.

Then, as a lingering breath rattled through her parted lips, the darkness in Elsbeth's soul overcame its prison and swallowed her whole.

Chapter 35

Versailles Palace, France, June 28

"Well, there you have it." David Lloyd George's voice sounded tired, as though he had aged thirty years in the past twenty-four hours. "Four German agents captured here at Versailles. Their leader—Elsbeth Whatever-Her-Surname-*Was*—is dead. My man, Hughes, has spearheaded an international counterterrorism operation that has already begun to yield spectacular results with twenty operatives already in custody."

He fished a thick cigar from the breast pocket of his dark-gray suit, then lit it. "Things turned out smashingly well. Once we got our hands on two or three of the reprobates, our combined intelligence networks proved rather effective at stopping this threat."

David grunted as he leaned back in his chair, tendrils of smoke curling upward from the cigar poised between his thick fingers. "I almost wonder if we could make a go of our American dreamer Wilson's League of Nations."

Malcolm glanced at the faces of the four men seated around a dark wooden table in the French prime minister's office. They were the Big Four—the leaders of the world's most powerful nations. For the past three hours, they had remained in seclusion under heavy guard.

Malcolm had been ordered to remain with the men until the premises were secure. He had spent the past hours answering the same questions from the Big Four. On any other occasion, Malcolm might have felt honored to be included in such company. But at the moment, he only wanted to be at his wife's side.

"Have it?" The drooping white moustache of Clemenceau, the French prime minister, bristled. "I'll tell you what we have—the answer to my most fervent prayers!" Clemenceau crossed his hands then swiped them outward in a decisive chopping motion. He was a short, balding man whose tuft of white hair made Malcolm think of a stuffed owl. "This is the excuse we need to wipe Germany off the map."

Squeezing Malcolm's shoulder, he said, "I admit that I had my doubts when your pretty wife approached me with her plan of trapping this Elsbeth Schneider. That is why I had to make sure we had an ample supply of soldiers nearby—in case things went wrong. But she succeeded!"

Clemenceau lifted both hands in a gesture of adoration. "I assure you, she and her friend are receiving the best medical care France can provide. The very best. From this moment, you shine among our brightest stars."

Malcolm jerked his head downward in a stiff nod. "Thank you."

Clemenceau paused, then shook his head. "My only regret is that Madame Steele killed the she-devil before we had the chance to—how do you say it in English?— erm . . . *interrogate* her." He grimaced. "Not that I blame her. The officer in charge

reported that the German was about to shoot your wife so . . ."
He ended his words with a shrug.

"But you do see the need to sign the treaty," David said.

"*Sign* it?" Clemenceau clenched a fist and closed his eyes as he looked up at the ceiling. His anger thickened his French accent. "For the first time in many years, I believe in God again. Here we have an opportunity unlike any other—a real *raison* to strike at our enemy until there is nothing left but dust and rubble. Why on earth would I spit on such a blessing?"

"I understand your anger, Clemenceau." The American president, Woodrow Wilson, spoke softly as he removed his wire spectacles from his beaklike nose. "In fact, it's just about how the zealots felt about the Romans in the time of Christ. But isn't it better to *forgive* this latest atrocity and rebuild in the name of charity?"

Clemenceau threw his arms in the air. "Oh, spare us your self-righteous platitudes, Wilson! Must you turn everything into a sermon? There is a time for war and—"

"There is a time for peace," David cut in. "That time is now."

Clemenceau glared at him. "Let me be sure I understand. The wicked Huns come here ready to kill everyone in *my* palace—a relic from the reign of Louis XIII, mind you—and you say to me that it is a time for peace?" Rushing backward, he rested a pudgy hand on Malcolm's shoulder. "Were it not for this man—and his ravishing amazon of a wife—none of us would be alive!"

"We are all aware of the part Malcolm Steele played—"

"*Ah, oui.*" Clemenceau snorted, stepping forward again. "So aware that you had his father shot to death! Imagine if Leila Steele had been captured, huh? Or killed? Where would we all be today?" He jabbed a finger under David's nose. "*Morts!* Dead, that is where, dead!"

Malcolm leaned forward as he waited for the British prime minister's response, every muscle in his body taut. Clemenceau was right. So very right. And he wanted to rub that knowledge into David Lloyd George's face until it bled. But that wouldn't help his cause. In the end, practicality won.

"Stay focused, Clemmy," David spoke around his cigar.

"I *am* focused!" Flecks of spittle flew from Clemenceau's mouth. "I am focused on one thing—eliminating a threat to my people. I will go to the press. The world will eradicate Hindenburg and his sham of a *république*. Then I will agree it is time for peace." He mopped perspiration from a balding head and reddened cheeks.

David rounded on him. "And how many more must die for that to happen?"

"As many as it takes!"

"Forget this emotional claptrap. Think politics, man!" David pulled his cigar free, allowing wisps of smoke to climb into the air. He gestured toward the door. "No one out there knows exactly what's going on—not even the other representatives who are here to sign."

"That is about to change." Clemenceau folded his arms across his chest.

"Clemmy, if you grass about this to the press, whatever other agents that are still out there will go to ground. You think they won't carry out their orders?"

"He's right," Wilson said. "Anything other than sticking with the plan will just upset the apple cart."

"Go ahead, give a statement of how some pro-German extremists tried to sabotage the treaty. Let your lot give the press something to gab about." David leaned back in his chair.

"But don't reveal the full truth. Don't fuel public passion that could reignite a war none of us—I said none of us—is prepared to fight!"

"I agree with David," Wilson spoke again. With a sigh, he looked down. "My dream of a league of united nations appears to be stillborn. But I still hope that we can all rise above our fallen natures and aspire to higher heights. France should pioneer this vision."

"Shut up, Wilson." Clemenceau spoke through gritted teeth. "God gave us ten commandments, and we broke them all. Now you expect us to keep your Fourteen Points of a new world order?"

Wilson's smile was pained. "If you could just—"

"The Germans have not blown *your* country to pieces. *You* have not suffered through four years of war. *You* have not seen your national pride destroyed."

"But we Italians have." Vittorio Orlando, the Italian prime minister, spoke for the first time. "My people are not happy with this treaty. We have also suffered. The loss of our lands. Our pride." He shrugged. "But to reveal the entire truth would be to invite disaster."

Clemenceau gaped at him. "But we all know this is not a true peace. I-it is an armistice for ten, maybe twenty years. If we break Germany now, we may spare the human race yet another deadly war."

"Look, Clemmy, none of us wanted this dastardly affair. It's not as though we planned it."

"But you ignored the warnings," Clemenceau shouted.

A long silence fell as eyes turned toward Malcolm.

"I realize that things should have been handled differently," David said. "But the real question is, where do we go from here?"

Prime Minister Orlando shook his head. "Italy is not in a position to return to war."

"Britain wants peace," David said.

"I am the only American targeted here at Versailles." Wilson steepled his fingers together. "While America is ready to defend itself, I'm ready to forgive the Germans. Unless I am overruled by Congress, my position in support of peace will stand."

"Is France ready to take on the Germans singlehanded?" David arched a thick eyebrow.

"Very well!" Clemenceau drew himself up to his full height, giving the lapels of his navy blue suit a sharp tug. "You want me to sign? I will sign. There is nothing left to say. Nothing except that I hope you will be happy when millions more lie cold in the ground—victims of a war that you could have prevented!"

David rose, wincing after sitting for several hours. "But today is not that day."

With a huff, Clemenceau turned to Malcolm. "As for you, if your country is too blind to reward you for your devoted service, be assured that France will welcome you with open arms!" Twisting, he glared at the other politicians. "Let us end this barbaric assassination of justice."

David approached Malcolm as the others filed toward the door. "The world owes you and your wife a debt. It is one I intend to pay."

A muscle jerked in Malcolm's jaw. "With respect, there is no atonement for some sins, Prime Minister."

"Perhaps not." David tossed the still-burning cigar onto an ash tray. "But I believe a measure of grace can be found in the empire's heart."

"You know what I want," Malcolm said. It was goading to think of his father as needing grace, but he stifled the urge to retaliate.

"Yes," David said. "I rather think I do." He began walking toward the door but paused and looked back. "You think battle is difficult? Try Whitehall. In war, you gamble with the lives of men. In politics, we gamble with the lives of nations. Think on that, Lord Steele, before you judge me too harshly."

Then he turned to the leaders of the nations behind him. "Let us go, gentlemen. We have history to make."

Chapter 36

London, Great Britain

The atmosphere of the Red Lion pub was one of celebration. Glowing chandeliers dangled from wainscoted ceilings illuminating the faces of a nation that had gone to war and won.

As Joseph's eyes flitted over the men and women who ate, drank, and danced on its freshly-glossed floors, he saw sadness but also hope. Joseph rubbed his chin thoughtfully with the ball of his thumb.

How long has it been since we've had hope?

"Ah, there is nothing like lamb and leek pie to stimulate the mind." Across the table, England's new Lord Chancellor, Frederick Smith, dabbed his thin lips with a red cloth napkin, then reached for his glass of Merlot. He had a round face, with dark hair and heavily sloping eyebrows. Young, he wore a tailored suit in a modern style with a vibrant red tie that offset his white shirt.

The two men sat apart from the pub's clientele in a secluded booth. It had been years since Joseph had taken Frederick under his wing as an apprentice. But the younger man radiated a contagious energy that the nation would need in the years to come.

"It was a good choice." Joseph picked up his own fork and carved off a piece of tender chicken.

Frederick set his glass down. "The lamb?"

"You." Joseph chewed thoughtfully, eying him. "You'll have your work cut out for you, no doubt. You're one of the youngest men to hold the office of Lord Chancellor. And readjusting to peace sometimes brings as many problems as war."

Joseph leaned back, pleating his hands across his gray waistcoat. Knowing that Frederick was a fashion afficionado, Joseph had worn an immaculate white Savile Row double-breasted suit and matching shirt. "The public will scrutinize your every move."

"And you'd know all about that, wouldn't you?" Frederick scrutinized his half-empty glass of wine.

"Yes."

"You know, when I served as your apprentice, you drilled the importance of speaking for the voiceless into my head. I can't imagine how many times you told me,"—he mimicked Joseph's heavier voice—"the law was not given to prosecute the guilty but to protect the innocent."

Joseph arched an eyebrow while reaching for his own glass. "I'm glad you learned something."

"Right lot of good it did when you took on this Steele chap's case. For a while I thought you'd gone barmy."

"That case gave me something greater." Joseph leaned forward, eyes intent on his face.

"And what's that?" Frederick spoke around a mouthful of lamb.

"Peace of mind. A clear conscience." Joseph shrugged. "In our line of work, those two things alone are worth their weight in gold."

"So you say." Frederick swallowed, then carved off another slice of lamb, causing a thin stream of blood to leak onto the white plate. "Let's cut to the chase, shall we? This isn't just about catching up, is it? You want something."

"No need to look for evidence. I confess that I'm guilty." Joseph loosened the knot of his crimson tie. "Guilty of wanting you to follow my example."

"You know of another traitor that needs defending?"

"No." Joseph lowered his voice. "But I do know of a German spy who needs a royal pardon."

Frederick chewed thoughtfully, his face expressionless.

"You've been in contact with the prime minister, Frederick. You know that she worked on behalf of the empire with his knowledge. At the beginning of the war, Leila served the enemy. But it is clear that the intelligence she gathered was vital in saving our nation."

"Thomas Steele was executed for treason less than a year ago." Frederick tossed his napkin onto the table with a shake of his head. "And you want me to ask the King to pardon his daughter-in-law so quickly?"

"Let me ask you one question." Joseph leaned forward, pointing a finger a Frederick's face. "Who taught you the nuances of the law?"

Frederick's brow tightened. "You did."

"Do you honestly think that I'd waste my valuable time and reputation supporting a family of traitors?" Joseph forced himself to calm down. "Now I can see that experience has hardened you. You can't have risen so high without making some hard choices."

"Somehow I believe I'll have to make yet another one tonight."

"I am asking you to go approach our sovereign with a request for Leila Steele's pardon."

Frederick tilted his head to one side. "No. What you're asking is that I use my influence on your behalf. By your own admission, Leila Steele served the enemy. Granted, she's done a good turn. But that's not enough in my mind. I'm new to this post. I must protect *my* reputation."

He folded his arms across his chest. "So what's in it for me? Aside from peace of mind and a clear conscience, of course."

Joseph fought off a wave of bitter disappointment. He had so hoped the student he had nurtured would become a man who embodied the spirit of the law, using its power to improve lives rather than serve as a political tool. But innocence was the price of achievement.

"You speak of justice as though it were a game of politics." Joseph stalled for time, mentally analyzing the man before him. Frederick was ambitious. Ruthless. While the two traits were a dangerous combination, they suggested Frederick might be persuaded to take a strategic risk that another man would shun.

Frederick mopped up the gravy in his plate with a piece of bread. "We both know the two words are synonymous."

Joseph slanted him a shrewd glance, inspired by Frederick's previous comment. "True, but politics is a game that none can be sure of winning."

"I'm listening."

"The country needs to move forward." Joseph straightened, dabbing at his mouth with a napkin. "There is no better way for our government to show its greatness than by issuing a pardon for a woman who has *proven* her loyalty at risk of her own life. A woman who saved the life of our prime minster. A woman whose personal intelligence network operated under the shadow of the enemy's nose in Berlin to thwart a plot that would have devastated the world as we know it."

"I'm still waiting for my answer," Frederick said.

"Our social order is changing by the moment. It's no longer enough to have the support of the upper class."

"Yes? And?"

"Reduce the opposition you'll face in your new role by showing our country that you believe in clemency. Show yourself to the public as the greater man, one who rises above the past, while also strengthening your position by making a strategic alliance with Malcolm Steele. He is not one to forget a good turn." He let the thought work its way into the ambitious politician's mind.

"I understand Malcolm has retained his father's title," Frederick said. "He is now the Earl of Sussex County."

"That is correct. I think friends are always less expensive than enemies, don't you?"

"And I thought I was Machiavellian." Frederick's gaze held more than a tinge of respect. "All right. I'll speak to the King. But I can't promise he will listen. Like as not, he'll confer with the prime minister, who didn't help much when that Steele chap was on trial."

"That was before Versailles," Joseph said, his lips curving into a tight smile. "Everything has changed."

"Perhaps. One never knows with politicians."

"There is something else."

"Don't tell me." Frederick pointed the tines of his fork in Joseph's direction. "You want me to petition to clear Thomas Steele's name."

"That was a complete miscarriage of justice, and you know it." Joseph shot him a glare. "The exculpatory evidence completely vindicates Leila Steele. That same evidence must be presented to the Crown on behalf of the late Earl of Northshire. He sheltered a valuable agent who saved the nation. The man should be given a posthumous medal!"

"I cannot guarantee that the Crown will reverse its opinion of a man it recently executed."

"All I want is that you present the situation in as favorable a light as is possible."

"Right." Downing the contents of his glass in one swallow, Frederick blew out his cheeks in a long sigh, then smacked his lips. "And all *I* want is another glass of Merlot. And since you're paying . . ." With a smile he snapped his fingers in the air. "Waiter? More wine!"

Chapter 37

Berlin, Germany, July 1919

The black telephone on General Paul von Hindenburg's desk sounded its piercing cry, making him start. He sat with Fritz Haber in his office at the Reichstag, doing the most difficult part of any failed operation—minimizing collateral damage.

The telephone rang again, screeching like a Valkyrie come to claim his soul. Hindenburg leaned back in his chair, brow furrowed, his index finger lightly tapping his peppered, short-cropped moustache.

It was over.

The glory. The dreams of a republic that would span a thousand years.

Brringg!

Hindenburg scowled at the telephone. Maybe if he ignored the screeching noise it would stop. Hindenburg grunted. If only he could silence Germany's rising star—a psychotic named Adolf Hitler—as easily.

Brringg!

With a sigh, Hindenburg reached out. Battles were not won by ignoring the enemy. His hand shook as it hovered over the telephone. Whether it trembled due to age or fear, Hindenburg refused to consider.

He picked up the telephone. "*Das ist* Hindenburg."

"I don't speak German. Thanks to our intelligence networks and the pluck of our lads in the field, I never will." The voice on the phone was cold. Unforgiving. Ruthless. "This is David Lloyd George, prime minister of the British empire."

Hindenburg switched to English. The words dropped like lead balls from his tongue. "I know who you are, Prime Minister."

"I'm sure you also know why I'm calling."

"And how could I know that? I am not a—how do you say?—a psychic."

"Don't play games with me, matey. We both know what happened in France. Obviously, since I'm making this call, your lot failed." He chuckled, a gruesome sound that grated in Hindenburg's ears.

"I have absolutely no idea what you mean."

"Since you didn't feel the need to come to Versailles yourself, I thought it would be best if we had ourselves a little talk by telephone."

"What is your point?"

"My point is that your republic is going to honor the treaty we signed. Break it and Germany will be devastated." David Lloyd George waited a few seconds, then added, "Believe me, there's nothing Clemenceau would like better than to grill you like the *bratwurst* you lot eat. A few phone calls from me, and we'll have your defeat at Amiens all over again. Only this time, it'll be Berlin that's left in ruins. Have you got that?"

Hindenburg closed his eyes, fury massing in a tight ball in his chest. How dare the Allies expect his proud nation to honor a treaty that ripped away its territories, slashed its army to nothing, and saddled it with an insurmountable debt?

Protests against the treaty had erupted across the republic. Some government members who had supported the bill had been assassinated by their own people.

One day . . .

"I know you're getting up there in years, old man. Perhaps you're going hard of hearing as well. Do you need me to repeat that?"

Hindenburg tightened his fingers around the telephone, wishing they were wrapped around the throat of the man on the other end of the line.

"The Weimar Republic will keep the treaty. I am *ehrenmann*—a man of honor. Do not fear, Prime Minister."

"Oh, believe me, I'm not afraid. We leave all that on your part of the continent. One wrong move, and your country will be extinct."

Click.

Hindenburg slammed the telephone receiver in place, then covered his face with his hands. He remained unmoving for several long moments, mangled waves of shame and fury threatening to choke him. One word echoed in his skull, pounding like the repeated thumps of a muffled drum at an execution.

Over.

Haber laid a hand on his shoulder. "We did our best, General Hindenburg."

"But our best was not good enough, *Herr* Haber." Hindenburg looked up. The chemist's eyes were red-rimmed, his face pasty. "Have you ever devoted your life to a dream only to discover that some dreams are not meant to come true?"

Haber looked down. "Yes. Many times."

"I am not speaking of marriage, Haber. There is a difference between that and war!"

"Is there?" Haber met his gaze. "Odd. Somehow I never noticed a difference." He sighed. "I shudder to face my wife. She was clear that our marriage depended on the success of this mission."

Hindenburg waved dismissively. "Who has time to think about such a tiny detail when the world is on fire? I staked everything on *Hubris* and now . . ." His voice dropped. "Now I fear that my fledgling republic will not outlive me."

He had no illusions. The people of Germany were starving. Starving for food. Starving for revenge. His government offered complacency whereas the masses wanted blood. *He* wanted blood. But Hindenburg had lived long enough to know that revenge would come at too heavy a price. So it was over.

"*Ja,*" Haber said in a sober voice. "You are probably right. The people will support a man who offers change—radical change."

Hindenburg bared his teeth. "A man like . . . Hitler."

"*Ja,*" Haber said again, but this time his voice trembled. "And we who are Jews have every reason to fear."

With a groan, Hindenburg stood and shuffled to a window that overlooked the Reichstag's stone plaza, clasping his hands behind his back.

"With the stroke of a pen dies the dream of a nation." He hung his head. "Yes, my friend. Life as we knew it is . . ."

352

"Over!" Charlotte slammed the last piece of clothing into the brown leather suitcase and jerked the leather strap into place. "Our marriage is over, do you hear me?"

Fritz Haber stalked toward his wife, every fiber of his body rigid. "How dare you? You know the fault wasn't mine."

"Then whose was it?" Charlotte glared at him, hands clamped to her hips like the crooked arms of a boiling teapot. "Mine?"

"Charlotte—"

"No wonder Hermann left home to study abroad. He probably couldn't stand looking at a father who reeks of failure."

"I created the gas, woman! That and the antidote. Neither had a flaw. Once that was done, the whole affair was out of my hands."

A sneer worked its way across Charlotte's face, deforming her brightly-painted lips into a garish leer. "Oh, you'll always find a way to blame someone else. You know what? Your real genius lies in making excuses!"

"You . . . you viper!" He whipped his hand back.

"Go ahead, Fritz." She leaned forward, taunting him with her mocking smile. "Hit me. Show me just how much of a man you are."

A feral grunt escaped his mouth, but Fritz forced himself to resist the temptation to slap the silly grin off her face. Instead, he wiped the back of his hand against his lips, wishing he could eradicate the first kiss they had shared—a kiss that had sent him down the path of infidelity and ruin. "You never loved me."

"*Loved* you?" Charlotte threw back her head, cackling like an insane hen. "What about you could possibly inspire love? Your eggy head? Your bulging stomach?"

The laughter died as suddenly as it began. "I loved what you could do for me." Storming forward, her loose black slacks allowing her the stride of a man, Charlotte gestured toward their bed. "I endured your repulsive touch. I gave you two children. And all the while, I hoped I would finally hold true power in my arms. Was that too much to ask?"

He gaped at her.

"Don't do that, Fritzy! You look like a fish gasping for its last breath. You're ugly enough as it is." Charlotte flicked back the evenly-cut dark hair that dangled about her thin shoulders.

"But—"

"This was our chance for a new beginning. To gain more than we've ever had before."

"You mean *your* chance," Fritz said flatly.

"That's what I said." Charlotte reached into the red clutch that dangled from her wrist and withdrew a thin cigarette.

Fritz gritted his teeth.

She knows I hate to see her smoke.

Just like his first wife Clara, this woman pushed him to the brink of insanity. The unexpected thought drew him up short.

"Clara! Clara warned us this would happen." Pulling his pince-nez from his eyes, Fritz passed a moist hand over his face. "S-she called God's curse upon us before she died. Now look what's happened!"

Charlotte exhaled, sending a stream of smoke in his direction. "So, the great Fritz Haber—a man of science— is scared of a dying fool's last words. Pitiful!" Her laughter mocked him, and in that moment, Fritz realized he could take no more.

Screaming with rage, he grabbed an ornate vase off a pedestal in the corner and smashed it onto the tiled floor. "Wretch!" His chest heaved. "Everything I've done has been for you! I indulged you. Put up with more of your nonsense than I ever stood from Clara."

"And why is that, Fritz? Huh?" Charlotte's eyes gleamed as she thrust her face inches from his own. "I'll tell you why."

The stench of tobacco on her breath clawed at him, making bile rise in the back of his throat. "Because every day we've been married, you've been trying to atone for Clara's death." Her voice dropped to a merciless whisper. "But you can't do it. Why? Because you're a failure. And that's all you'll ever be!"

Smack!

Fritz couldn't help it. Before he realized what he had done, Charlotte was on the floor, looking up at him with a bemused expression, the imprint of his hand on her otherwise pale face.

"I'll kill you!" He jerked open the drawer of a nightstand and pulled out a revolver.

Charlotte regained her feet slowly. "The same gun that killed Clara. You remember the night. You were with me in the garden. Rutting with me on the grass like the beast you are."

"Stop."

She ignored him. "Clara found us. Saw what we were doing."

"Please . . . stop!" It was a mangled cry. A twisted plea that Fritz barely recognized as being his own.

"And then Clara blew her heart out." Charlotte stepped toward him, her mouth slightly parted. "Why not end your second marriage with the same weapon?"

"Stop!" He glared at Charlotte, then at the gun in his trembling hand. He wanted, oh how he wanted, to pull the trigger.

Just one little squeeze.

But words had always been the weapon Charlotte wielded best.

With a groan, Fritz let the gun clatter to the floor, then buried his face in his hands, sobbing.

"Old habits die hard, don't they? Or maybe they weren't dead at all. Just buried alive. Just like your guilt."

He looked up, lips trembling. "Charlotte—"

She probed her bruised jaw with her fingers. "I'm going back to my family with the children. Don't contact me. Unless it's to finalize a divorce."

Fritz sunk to his knees, howling. "You ruined my life." He slammed his fists against the unfeeling floor. "You're the worst thing that's ever happened to me!"

Charlotte paused at the bedroom door. "No Fritz." She spoke without turning around. "*You* are the worst thing that's ever happened to you."

Then she slammed the door.

Chapter 38

Northshire Estate, Great Britain, August 1919

Sunlight skipped across Northshire's verdant fields, kissing away the lingering fragments of a long, dark night. For Greyson, the dawn itself presaged a new chapter in the estate's tumultuous story.

It had been just over a week since the Steele family and their friends had returned from France. Greyson rubbed his burning eyes. In all that time, he doubted if any of the household staff had slept more than a few hours. Between the estate's daily needs, attending to the various needs of the small army of doctors and nurses that had arrived with the returning heroes, and making suitable arrangements for the young master Michael, they had all been on their feet for days on end.

But things will quiet down now, I'm sure.

At least, that was his hope.

"Mr. Greyson?"

The butler turned from the library's expansive window. "What is it, Jenny?"

The dark-haired maid bobbed out a curtsey. "Lord Malcolm's barrister Mr. Mara just rang. He'll be up at half-past three to discuss somethin' of great importance."

"Thank you. I will inform his Lordship."

"Also, we have a letter for Lord Malcolm." Jenny proffered a slim cream envelope, then said in a conspiratorial whisper, "It's from the prime minister."

"From the prime minister, is it?" Greyson hiked his silver eyebrows together as he cast stern eyes on the young woman. "And how would you know *that*, pray tell?"

Spots of color rose in her cheeks "I, um, couldn't help but take a gander at the name on the envelope."

"Examining his Lordship's private correspondence now, are we?"

"I . . . I didn't mean any harm."

Greyson harrumphed, barely managing to hide the laughter that bubbled in his chest. "Yes, well, neither did Eve. You know how *that* all turned out."

Jenny wrung her hands together. "Um, will you be needin' me for anythin' else at the moment, Mr. Greyson? I-I think Cook might like some help."

Greyson raised his index finger. "Hm . . . I do realize that the arrival of the young master has us all a bit off the mark, but let us not forget the basics of British propriety. It is by our own standards that we are to be judged, after all."

"Yes, Mr. Greyson." Jenny curtsied and hurried to the door. It was only when she was gone that Greyson allowed the smile he had been hiding to slip across his face. As the heavy door closed behind Jenny with a soft thump, he cast a cursory glance at the slim cream envelope.

"She's right! It *is* from the prime minister."

With a new spring in his step, Greyson left the library, striding over the foyer's white tiles in the direction of Thomas's study.

Lord Malcolm's study now.

Six months after the earl's death, Greyson still struggled with the sight of Malcolm in his father's high-backed leather chair. His only consolation was that the boy-prodigal had indeed become a man worthy of his father's name. And for that he was grateful.

Peering through the mahogany French doors inlaid with glass, Greyson cleared his throat and rapped twice.

"Enter."

He pressed down on the curved handles and stepped inside. "Good morning, Your Lordship."

"Greyson, come in." Malcolm leaned over his large, walnut-stained desk, fists planted on either side of a neat set of drawings. The young man had insisted on throwing himself into making changes on the estate with an energy Greyson found nothing short of exhausting.

"Mr. Mara is on your schedule for half-past three on a matter of some importance." Greyson pulled the envelope from the breast pocket of his black suit. "Also, this arrived not too long ago, sir."

"Thank you, Greyson." Malcolm didn't look up. "You can leave it on the bureau." He tapped a spot on the map. "Here, look at this."

Greyson stepped around the desk. "You mean this spot of land near the village, sir?"

"It's where our new hospital will be built."

"A hospital?" Greyson stared at him. "In Sussex county?"

"Well, isn't it a smashing idea? Think of it, man."

"Is there a need for a hospital?"

"There is." Malcolm sat on the edge of the desk, describing his plan with his hands as well as his words. "The times are changing, and we must change with them. Our old order of master and servant is a relic of the past. A hospital on Northshire's grounds may open the door to new prosperity."

Greyson rubbed his chin. "Well, with the men back from war, the village is likely to have more, ahem, little ones about."

Malcolm threw back his head and laughed. "Right you are, Greyson. Furthermore, Sussex county is a prime position to attract the best and brightest minds."

"So you plan to donate land on which a hospital will be built?"

"Not just donate land." Malcolm's eyes were bright and animated. "I'm going to finance half the building costs. The rest will come from private donors in the Bank of England." The light faded from his eyes, and his voice took on a sharp edge. "Donors who will, no doubt, be eager to make amends for their failure to stand by my father in his hour of need once they see that I have the prime minister's favor."

"Well." Greyson adjusted his necktie. "Your father would be proud of your interest in the locals."

With a sigh, Malcolm turned to the large marble hearth over which a portrait of both his mother and father hung. "Each day, we make a choice to either see the strength of the goodness around us or that of the challenges which confront us." His eyes flickered from the portraits to the older man. "Our choice will determine the outcome of our lives."

The butler stared at him, stunned. "I-I couldn't have said it better myself, Your Lordship."

Malcolm turned and slanted him a wry smile as he picked up the letter and tucked it into his breast pocket. "Speechless, Greyson? Now that is news indeed."

◆◆●◆▶

Leila laughed as Michael squealed at the sight of a robin perched on their windowsill. She sat in a rocking chair at a window that faced the eastern horizon. Her hands were swathed in bandages up to her wrists, ending at the sleeves of her loose, sky-blue housedress.

Balancing Michael on her knee, Leila nodded to the bird. "I think he wants to play."

"Bud?" Michael reached out, cupping his fingers as he called the bird. "Bud!"

The bedroom door opened, and Michael twisted in her lap, craning to see over her shoulder. "Dada?"

Malcolm's warm voice caressed Leila's heart. "And is this what you call resting?" He came to stand behind her, kissed the side of her neck, then scooped Michael up into his arms.

"Mm, I've had all the rest I can take." Leila reached up, clumsily brushing her hands against his smooth cheek. "Besides, Michael and I have so much time to make up for." Leaning backward, she let her eyes wander over his body.

A square black beard neatly framed his mouth, accentuating the angular slant of his jaws and the smoky blue of his eyes. His white shirt, crisp and unbuttoned at the collar, lay below a vibrant blue waistcoat that snugly fit his strong chest and abdomen.

"I must say, Lord Malcolm, that fatherhood takes you quite well." Her husband had a maturity about him that Leila found both attractive and admirable.

Taking her left hand in his own, he gently kissed the bandages that crisscrossed her palm. "Motherhood takes you even better."

Swatting Michael playfully on his rump, Malcolm deposited him onto their bed, then withdrew a letter from the pocket of his black pants. "This arrived from the prime minister."

"Oh?" Leila straightened, her heartbeat suddenly irregular. "Is it about me?"

Malcolm shrugged. "More or less. It's just a brief note of gratitude. Two medals from London are forthcoming. He also mentioned that there will be no public accolades due to the confidential nature of our service to His Majesty's government."

"Oh," she said again. Leila didn't know whether she was more relieved or disappointed. "Is-is that all?"

"Hm . . ." A smile played about Malcolm's lips. "Now that I think about it, he did mention you by name."

She went rigid. "What?"

"He also says . . ." He glanced at the letter, squinting.

Leila made an impatient gesture. "Well?"

"Well, he handwrote it, and the print is a bit dodgy." Malcolm tilted the paper toward the light as though he were genuinely having a hard time making out the words.

His teasing made her want to scream, but she was at his mercy. She couldn't exactly *snatch* the letter from him, not with her hands encased.

Arching an eyebrow, Leila glared at him. "I am *not* amused."

"All right, all right." Malcolm sobered. "The prime minister writes that King George has determined you were indeed working for the empire's interest throughout the latter part of the war. Your loyalty has been undeniably proven by your recent activities on the continent."

Malcolm paused, then pulled in a deep breath as he read slowly, "Lady Steele's devotion has persuaded the Crown to pardon all former crimes committed by her against the British empire."

Leila drew in a sharp breath. "A-and Thomas?"

"Father has been issued a posthumous pardon." A muscle jerked in Malcolm's jaw.

"So . . . what does this mean? For us?"

"I'll know more after consulting with Joseph this afternoon. But from all appearances, we're free, Leila." Malcolm sighed. "Free."

"Are we?" Leila sobered as memories rose fresh in her mind. "I still have the nightmares. Still jerk awake at night to make sure Michael hasn't been stolen."

Malcolm pulled a chair beside her. "Things will get better."

"For who? When?" The muscles in her face tightened. "I-I'm immensely grateful for the pardon. I can't tell you how grateful! Especially knowing that Thomas's name has been officially cleared. But when I think about the cost of it all. To us. To Mercedes!"

"Leila, you can't hold yourself responsible for that."

"That poor girl upstairs has to live with the fact that she betrayed the man she married. The first man she's ever really loved."

"But her sacrifice saved countless lives."

"*We* know that, and Mercedes knows it too. But knowing the truth isn't quite the same as being free from the lies that sometimes haunt us." She paused, then added. "Elsbeth scarred that girl in so many ways."

"At least Mercedes is alive. She almost didn't make it." Malcolm gently touched her cheek. "And neither did you. If it weren't for the Clemenceau's soldiers, the world would have lost what little goodness it still possesses."

"I understand, Malcolm. But Mercedes has a hard time understanding the value of living when her beauty has been stolen. For a girl who grew up in a world where physical beauty defines her personal value, a scar like that is devastating."

Malcolm lifted her chin. "I've seen the war at its worst, Leila. Talk about devastating? Shattered limbs. Shattered lives. Shattered minds. They were everywhere. I wondered how God could let it all happen."

He pulled in a deep breath, then exhaled slowly. "One day I realized God is an author who crafts a story out of each of our lives. There are parts we don't like."

"Like Thomas's death?"

"Yes. There are dark parts. Scenes we'd rather forget or have removed altogether." He took her hands in his own. "But the darkness of those moments—the pain and scars that linger on—they're all needed to show what was in His mind before our lives began."

Again, he kissed her bandaged palms. "Leila, before going to the cross, Christ knew the scars would be permanent. But the love for His lost children made Him go anyway." Malcolm glanced at their son. "And did He succeed?"

Leila just nodded, unable to trust herself to speak.

"Yes." Malcolm rested his forehead against her own. "There are dark places. Times in the great story that made even God feel pain. But every moment plays a part in the greater picture. So don't hold yourself accountable for what's written in the story of Mercedes's life. In time, she *will* understand."

Unable to say another word, Leila just slipped her arms around his neck, pulled him close, and cried.

Chapter 39

Northshire Estate, Christmas Day, 1919

If Joseph Mara had to describe life in one word, that word would be miraculous. There was no other possible way to express the power of this moment. Leaning against one of the massive pillars that lined the castle's foyer, Joseph let his eyes flit over his surroundings.

This was the first Christmas since the end of the Great War, and Northshire had much to celebrate. Like the great ballroom and much of the castle's exterior, the foyer itself was festooned with glimmering lights. The staff was much smaller than he remembered, but judging by the sheer beauty around him, it appeared that Leila and Malcolm were prepared to adapt.

In one corner of the great hall, a small hired orchestra filled the castle with carols. Dozens of silver candelabras added to the magical atmosphere inside while a roaring fire at the far end of the hall kept the wintry chill outdoors.

Fresh wreaths curled around the bannisters of the double-wide staircase leading up to the veranda, spicing the air with the pungent scent of spruce. At the base of the staircase stood an immense Christmas tree that glimmered with all the brilliance of the stars that twinkled outside.

Joseph glanced at the happily chatting crowd, comprised mostly of villagers and neighbors. Like himself, they had come to this Christmas celebration at Malcolm and Leila's invitation, and the crowd itself was a curious conglomeration of social classes.

A miracle.

Joseph's gaze fell first on Will, who stood with one arm curved around his wife's waist. The lanky soldier, who now wore a sharp brown suit, had shared his incredible story of imprisonment, escape, and reunion with his wife, Eleanor. It was nothing short of miraculous.

Next, Joseph caught sight of Colonel Stewart, who smacked his lips while clutching a miniscule cup of white china in one massive paw and a plate loaded with beef pasties in the other. Turning to his wife, Stewart whispered something in her ear that earned him a blushing smile and a quick peck on the cheek.

The aged soldier had survived a war that had taken many younger men. It was a paradox. "Something unbelievable yet true."

A soft chuckle slipped past Joseph's lips.

"What are you looking at, Papa?"

Joseph straightened as his twelve-year old daughter approached with a white mug of apple cider in each hand. She tilted her head, eying him with one brow raised, and Joseph felt a lump rise to his throat.

Just like her mother.

"At a miracle, Hadassah. I'm looking at a miracle."

Hadassah handed her father a steaming cup. "Show me."

"Well, miracles are all around us if we just take the time to look." Joseph warmed his hands on the cup. "Take that young lady, Mercedes."

Mercedes, dressed in a pale-green dress, made no effort to hide the thin white scar that on her right cheek.

"Mercedes came to Northshire believing her true value came from a pretty face," Joseph said. "When that was taken from her, she became bitter. But now that she understands a woman's beauty comes from her character, Mercedes smiles and even laughs from time to time."

"That's not a miracle, Papa." Hadassah crinkled a brow. "That's because she's in love."

Joseph arched an eyebrow. "Oh? And how would you know that?"

"I have my methods," Hadassah said, tossing him a smug smile. "Observe everything. Make logical deductions from the evidence. Isn't that what you taught me?"

Laughter bubbled out of Joseph's chest. "I did indeed. But what evidence do you have?"

"I'm an eye-witness." Hadassah lowered her voice to a conspiratorial whisper. She frowned. "Or maybe it's an ear-witness since I . . . um . . . overheard her talking to Lady Steele."

"Hadassah? Your mother would not approve of eavesdropping."

"I wasn't eavesdropping!" Hadassah's eyes widened. "I was collecting evidence."

"I see." Joseph hid his smile by sipping his cider. "And what did you discover?"

Hadassah's eyes lit up as she grabbed his arm, sloshing the caramel-colored drink wildly in his cup. "Miss Mercedes is leaving tomorrow for the continent. She's going back to Germany to look for the man she married. Isn't that *so* romantic?" Hadassah heaved a drawn-out sigh. "I'm sure she'll find him, and then they'll live happily ever after. They'll probably be newlyweds forever. Or at least for a few months."

"A few months? I'll have you know your mother and I were newlyweds until . . ." Joseph's voice trailed off as he lost his way in the sudden fog of a distant memory.

"Until?"

"Until God took her."

Clearing his throat, Joseph sipped the cider. "Um, it's good. Well, then there's Lord and Lady Steele's miracle."

"Ooh . . . doesn't Lady Steele look simply *gorgeous*?" Pulling her father forward, Hadassah pointed to the staircase. Dressed in a shimmering red evening gown, Leila mounted the spiral stairs toward the veranda. "Just look at that dress! The color and the way it glitters. Can I get one like that, Papa? Please?"

Joseph followed his daughter's outstretched arm with his eyes. "Hmm." He smiled as he tugged at his graying beard. "Perhaps when you're older, Hadassah. *Much* older."

Leila climbed the last step, then turned. Malcolm, dressed in a spotless white tuxedo and a red waistcoat that matched her dress, ascended behind his wife as their son toddled alongside him.

"Finding little Michael and receiving a pardon that brought them all back to Northshire," Joseph said. "That must be the greatest miracle of all."

But on the heels of that thought came another. The return of Malcolm's son and the written approval of Leila's pardon had indeed both been hallmark moments. But the greatest miracle had actually been . . . himself.

"Pastor Elijah." Joseph broke away from his daughter as he glimpsed the slight, balding farmer who ministered to Northshire's community. "A word?"

Elijah Farrow's brow creased as a warm smile broke out across his weathered face. "Ah, Joseph. It's been several months since I've seen you."

"Yes." Joseph returned his smile as a surge of excitement coursed through him. Never had he felt so inspired. So free! "It's not that I haven't wanted to come and hear you speak, but I needed time to search out the truth for myself."

"No need to apologize." Elijah gave a relaxed shrug. "I'm glad that you've taken my words to heart. Faith is not a decision to be quickly made."

Joseph set his empty mug of cider onto a nearby serving tray. "I've now taken the time to examine the evidence. Beginning with the Torah and continuing with the prophetic writings, I have compared hundreds of references to the Messiah with the accounts given by Jesus's disciples. Furthermore, I have done extensive research into the historical accounts of the times in which He lived, going so far as to cross-reference them with statements made by those who opposed His teachings."

"Well done." Elijah folded his arms across his chest, nodding in approval. "If only others in my congregation were as diligent."

"Well, I *am* a barrister. One can only come to a reliable conclusion after examining all evidence in an objective manner."

"And what is your conclusion?"

Joseph gripped Elijah's shoulder. "Young man, I am convinced that Jesus *is* the Messiah. In the light of the evidence, there is no other possible rational conclusion. Every prophecy, every element of symbolism in the law and the history of the kings of Israel points to one man: Jesus of Nazareth."

Straightening, he gestured toward Malcolm and Leila, who now stood at the top of the terrace. "I have seen His power in the lives of my friends. And I am ready to say that I have accepted Him as my Messiah."

"You know what I think?" Elijah tilted his head to one side, studying Joseph's face for several moments.

"What is it?"

"I know someone who needs you to speak on his behalf. His name has been slandered. Unjustly, of course. He would be grateful if you'd take the case."

Joseph stepped back, hands open. "Who is he?"

"Christ," Elijah said simply. "He needs you to be His voice to others of the Jewish faith. Tell them what you've discovered, the *evidence* as you call it."

Joseph rocked back on his heels, stunned by this suggestion. But the thought appealed to him. How many did he know—Jew and Christian alike—who were caught in a cycle of religious ritual, never looking up from rote ceremonies to face the naked truth? So many never experienced the sheer exhilaration that stemmed from knowing sins could indeed be forgiven. That final atonement *was* a possibility.

I can be His voice.

"Perhaps I shall, young man." Joseph nodded, holding Elijah's stern gaze. "Perhaps I shall."

———— ◆◆ ● ◆◆ ————

Malcolm slipped an arm around Leila's waist, pulling her close, as he kept a wary eye on Michael, who leaned on the dark banister spindles for support.

Turning back, Malcolm drank in the sight of his wife. Her golden mane spilled out beneath a silver leaf-shaped tiara, cascading in a waterfall of curls midway to the back of a vibrant red satin gown that shimmered beneath the light of the chandeliers.

White gloves reached up to her elbow, leaving the rest of her arms bare beneath a short, tapered sleeve.

"Leila, why are we here? It's a bad host who leaves his guests."

"Oh, it's all for a purpose, my love." Leila winked at him. "Besides, the guests are busy catching up." She pointed to Mercedes, who took a step back, then jumped forward, grabbing Eleanor's arms. "Looks like Eleanor just told Mercedes the news."

"News?" Malcolm tilted his head "What news?"

"Eleanor is pregnant."

"What?"

"Haven't you noticed that Will is wearing a new suit?"

"Uh . . . no. I'm not really in the habit of committing Will's clothing to memory."

"Well, neither do I, and *I* noticed." Leila laughed, lightly punching his arm. "It's not just because of tonight's event. The Thompson family is expanding."

"I see."

"Do you?" Leila sidled next to him, bringing with her a dark musky scent. She traced a spiral pattern on his chest with her gloved finger, turning his blood to fire. "The war is over, the men have come home, and everyone is in . . . a certain mood. Sometimes moods result in happy surprises."

"I see," Malcolm said again. How was it that she could still make him lose his focus with just a few words and a touch? He shook his head, trying to clear his mind. "I suppose I shall have to give Will an increase in his wages."

Grabbing his red cravat, Leila pulled him closer. "Be sure to keep a little something for yourself. Just in case."

Malcolm froze as her words sunk into his mind. He gaped at her, jaw slack. "What?"

371

"Hm?" She blinked at him innocently as she took a step back, making the diamond strands that dangled from her ears sway gently. "Did I say something?"

Tingles ran down his spine. "You just said—"

"Ladies and gentlemen." Leila slanted Malcolm a mischievous smile as she turned toward the milling guests below. "May I have your attention for just a few moments?"

Conversation died to murmurs, then petered out altogether as the guests became aware of their radiant host. Leila stood like a queen—poised, graceful, and head high. Pardoned, she saw no need to hide from the public but remained determined to face life's storms with the same resilience that had drawn them together one fateful night six years and a lifetime ago.

"Thank you for your presence in our home," Leila said. "Tonight, all of Northshire has much to celebrate. God has been good to us. We have seen the end of a devastating war, the safe return of many of our loved ones, and the hope of a new beginning."

Leila paused. When she spoke again, there was a slight tremor in her voice.

"But the blessings we enjoy came with a heavy price. On nights when we gather with friends and family, our minds go to those whom we have lost. There is someone missing, a man whose courage and faith was the bedrock of Sussex County. I ask you to join me in lifting a glass to my father-in-law, the late Sir Thomas Steele." She turned and lifted a fluted glass high. "To Sir Thomas!"

His name echoed on the lips of family, servants, and guests alike. Leila waited until the noise faded away, then spoke again. "I am doubly privileged. Not only am I the daughter-in-law of a great man, but I have the honor of being wife to an even greater one."

Malcolm gave a demure nod as applause filled the foyer.

What is she doing?

"It is the Steele tradition to have a portrait of the heir hung in this great gallery. One year ago in Switzerland, Sir Thomas unveiled a portrait he wanted hung next to his own here at Northshire. His last request, detailed for me in a letter, was that I ensure the portrait came home. Tonight, my father-in-law's desire is fulfilled." She picked up one end of a long, silver cord that dangled over the banister's edge.

Leila looked up. Along with the crowd, Malcolm followed her gaze, realizing now why she had insisted he stay out of the foyer all evening.

"Ladies and gentlemen, I give you Lord Malcolm." Leila pulled on the cord to remove the cloth that covered the portrait. Thunderous applause swelled behind them, ringing off the ancient walls.

Incredible realism was detailed in Malcolm's portrait, capturing his personality in the brushstrokes. He had been present when Thomas first unveiled it. But seeing it here hanging next to his father's portrait overwhelmed him. This line of portraits was more than art. It was a visual depiction of a trust. A heritage that embodied Northshire's soul.

His portrait was one of four that lined the wall—each an immortalization of the men in the Steele family. The line began with his great-grandfather's image and ended with himself.

His mind rolled back to a dark night when Thomas had sworn that Malcolm, then a wild prodigal, would never take his place among the men who had built this estate with their blood and sacrifice unless he proved himself worthy of the honor.

Clutching the railing behind him, Malcolm took a step back, overcome by a myriad of emotions.

Pride at this treasured moment.

Regret that his parents were not here with him.

Apprehension at the responsibility that lay on his shoulders.

Malcolm's gaze shifted from his father's portrait to his own, then back again. Only now did he realize how much they resembled each other. Could it be that their personalities were similar enough for him to carry on his father's legacy?

Leila's hand slipped into his own. "This is your crowning moment, darling. *This* is what Thomas wanted. Us all home together and your portrait on the wall next to his own so all the world will know he trusts you with this heritage."

"I-I only wish he were here . . . with us." Malcolm could barely speak past the lump in his throat.

"Oh he is, Malcolm." Leila squeezed his hand. "I believe that Thomas and Isabella are both here, celebrating this new beginning with us as a thousand angels look over their shoulders."

Leila held his hand for just a moment longer, and he quietly clung to her, needing her touch. Then, releasing him, Leila glided back to the tray and turned to face him as she lifted her glass once more.

"A toast to Lord Malcolm, Earl of Northshire. I know you will lead us all successfully into a bright, new, beginning."

Her emerald eyes glinted, hinting at forbidden secrets that were his alone to discover.

Leila raised her chin, pride radiating from every inch of her beautiful face. "To my husband. My lover. My friend. My heart. To Malcolm."

Epilogue

Northshire Village, Great Britain, January 1, 1920

The dark skies above Sussex County proclaimed to all the world that the new year had come. Variegated fireworks ripped through the darkness in brilliant arcs of flame. It was as if they in their own right had risen to challenge the power of the night.

For the first time in six years, Britain and the rest of the free world had reason to celebrate. Instead of tolling doleful liturgies for the dead, church bells rang out the joyful proclamation of new hope for the living. The war was over. Freedom, at long last, had prevailed.

Leila gave a contented sigh as Malcolm pulled his ivory Rolls Royce over to one side of the long, winding road that ran along the crest of the hill overlooking Sussex village.

Propping one elbow on the walnut paneled door, Leila rested her head on her hand and turned to admire her husband. Malcolm carried himself with an easy confidence. His shoulders were set back, and his right hand effortlessly controlled the steering wheel. The aura of leadership clung to him like the refined beard that framed his face. In some ways, it was as though he was a completely different man from the one she had married.

Yes, she had loved him when he was nothing more than a selfish profligate. But the passion that had drawn them together would not have been enough to build a lasting marriage. They had needed something more. And they had found that. Christ. Time. Adversity. All had come together to transform them.

A thought struck her. "Malcolm?"

He gently slowed the car to a complete stop and turned, giving her his full attention. "Hm?"

"Thank you," she said.

"For what?"

"For becoming the man you are today. For not giving up on yourself. Or on me."

He blew out his breath with a sigh. "You had as much to do with it as I did, Leila. Without you, I don't know what would have happened. We've come full circle. Six years ago on this very night, we were on this very spot."

Leila slid into his arms, inhaling the scent of his cologne. "Things could have ended so differently. I'm so glad it all turned out right in the end."

"So am I, darling." Malcolm rested his head on her shoulder. "To be honest, I try to put everything in a sort of mental box that I hide somewhere in my mind. It's the only way I can live with it all. The things we've had to do. The people we've lost."

"I understand." Her nightmares had slowly become less frequent, but some nights she still kept watch around Michael's bed.

Malcolm pulled back, and the light of the fireworks revealed a glint in his eyes that surprised her. "You know, there are times when I'm afraid."

This was unexpected. "Of what?"

"Of the future." He gently placed his hands around the small bulge in her abdomen. "I worry that our children will face a world much darker than the one we've known. This war took more than immense human life. Somewhere in the trenches of Europe, we lost our innocence."

Leila interlaced her fingers within his own as the child within her womb stirred. "We don't control the future, Malcolm. It's out of our hands."

"How did my father survive, knowing I was hiding in a trench or dodging German bullets?"

"I'm sure Thomas worried. Every parent would. But rising above all our fear is faith." She looked up at the sky as a firework exploded, releasing a waterfall of glittering light. "It's the faith that, somehow, whatever light we possess will be enough to scatter the night."

He was quiet for a moment. "Sometimes I forget that."

"Just one more reason you should be thankful for your wife," Leila teased.

"As if I needed another!"

"Come on." She sat up, slipping her black shawl off her shoulders and tossing it onto the backseat. "Let's go outside."

Malcolm's chuckle was a deep bass that made her spine tingle. "Still braving the cold, are we?"

"Cold?" Leila wrapped her fingers in his dark hair, pulled him close, and kissed him. Hard. At length, she pulled back, breathless. "Who's cold?"

With a light laugh, she threw open her door and stepped onto the snow-spattered ground. A gust of wind swirled around her, turning the bare skin of her arms into gooseflesh. Lifting her chin, Leila spread her arms wide, embracing the exhilarating sensation of freedom that the chilly bursts of air ignited.

Together, they made their way toward the crest of the hill and gazed down on the small corner of the world that belonged to them alone. The moon played games of hide-and-seek behind scudding clouds, bathing the village and the forested acres in a stunning white haze.

Boom! Pop! Pop! Pop!

The echo of exploding fireworks was overshadowed by their colorful brilliance. The light illuminated the castle's crenelated spires, which stood like silent heralds, proclaiming the end of one age and the birth of another.

Malcolm stood behind Leila, wrapping her in his arms.

"Yes, the world has changed, Malcolm, but so have we. We're Christians now." She leaned back into his embrace, tilting her chin upward to look at him. "In the dead of the night, *we* are the sparks of light that defy the darkness. As long as our faith endures, we will shine on. No matter what tomorrow brings."

Leila rested her head against Malcolm's chest, and they held each other tight as a fresh gust of wind-driven snow swirled around them and fire rained down from Northshire's heavens.

The End

A final word from the author

I can't begin to express how much this novel and, in fact, this whole series has meant to me. It is the most intricately woven plot I've compiled to date with over two hundred hours of research behind it. While some of the plot may seem incredible, most of it is true to the historical record.

The Germans did launch an anthrax attack that targeted the horses of the Allied cavalry in 1917-18. The unnamed gas—which we now know as sarin—was also developed by the Germans, though this discovery actually happened about two decades after the end of the war.

Like Thomas Steele, several British nobles, including royalty, did lose their titles due to the *Titles Deprivation Act of 1917*.

The 'Ndrangheta remains a powerful multinational mafia that traces its heritage back to the days of Napoleon while becoming visible in the 1860s. Though Pierre LaRue is a fictitious character, Swiss and Italian police have reported joint action against the organization in Switzerland as recently as 2020.

The planned attack of Versailles is purely a figment of my imagination. But I believe it captures the spirit of nationalism that gripped Europe and set the stage for a much deadlier conflict just twenty years later. I drew realistic detail for this event from the 1994 Matsumoto attack in Japan and the ongoing Syrian civil war.

My hope is that you've gained as much pleasure from reading *Northshire Heritage* as I have in writing it. Most of all, I hope that the interwoven stories give a fresh perspective of the power, love, and breathtaking scope of God's plan for all His children.

Share your thoughts about the series online: JPRobinsonBooks.com or on social media.

About the historical characters

David Lloyd George remained prime minister of Great Britain until 1922, when he became involved in a political scandal comprised of selling knighthoods and peerages. Although he remained active in politics, his reputation suffered damage. In 1944, he received the title of Earl. He passed away in 1945.

Fritz and Charlotte Haber officially divorced in 1927. Fritz Haber found himself increasingly ostracized from the scientific community due to his part in the development of poison gas during the Great War. Burdened by guilt over the German defeat, Fritz's life after the war was one of misery.

With the rise of Adolf Hitler's regime, Haber's Jewish roots made him the target of Nazi aggression. He resigned his position with the Kaiser Wilhelm Institute and fled Germany. Much of the remainder of his life was spent wandering Europe, looking for a place to call home.

In 1934, he died of heart failure in a Swiss hotel, bitterly regretting the role he had played in developing poison gas. In a historical irony, some of Fritz Haber's extended family were murdered in Nazi concentration camps that used Zyklon B, a poisonous gas developed at the laboratory Haber once ran.

Charlotte and the two children she bore to Fritz Haber immigrated to England. Her son Ludwig became a prominent British economist and wrote a volume of history entitled *The Poisonous Cloud*. Charlotte's daughter Eva lived and worked in Kenya for many years. She died in the United Kingdom in 2015.

Hermann Haber, Fritz's son by his first wife Clara, immigrated to the United States with his wife and family. There in 1946, he committed suicide.

Arthur Hoffmann left a cloud of uncertainty behind him when he left politics. As noted in *In the Midst of the Flames* (Northshire Heritage Book 2), the real Arthur Hoffmann tried to forge a separate peace with Germany in conjunction with Robert Grimm. It is unclear why exactly he took such a political risk. Hoffmann died in 1927 in disgrace.

General Paul Hindenburg led Germany's Weimar Republic until Hitler's rise. When the Nazis seized power in January 1933, Hindenburg appointed Hitler as Chancellor, albeit very reluctantly. Hindenburg died at a very convenient time for Hitler in 1934. His death paved the way for Hitler to declare himself *Führer* of Germany.

Robert Hughes is a fictional character heavily inspired by the historical icon Sir Mansfield Smith-Cumming. Smith-Cumming feared that he would be forced into early retirement due to his lack of linguistic and other qualifications. This tension is reflected in the relationship between David Lloyd George and the fictional Robert Hughes.

As was the case of the fictional character depicted in Northshire Heritage, the real spymaster suffered from ill health and died in 1923.

Elsbeth Schneider is a fictional character inspired by the enigmatic Elsbeth Schragmüeller. The real Elsbeth did not die in France. Much of her life remains shrouded in mystery. But historical records indicate that she returned to Germany after the war and continued her academic career, becoming an assistant chair at Freiburg University. Her family had ties to the Nazi party.

Elsbeth's active role in espionage and her strong character set the stage for my depiction of an aggressive patriot. I believe that she would have been in favor of Hitler's regime, despite its anti-Semitic slant, as Hitler offered the promise of bringing Germany back to a place of European dominance. Her father and brother were killed by Hitler's associates during the infamous Night of the Long Knives.

Elsbeth died of bone tuberculosis in 1940.

About the author

JP Robinson is a minister and a Black author of historical and political suspense. He is also the president of Lancaster Christian Writers Association. A tenured educator of history and French with fifteen years of experience in education and marketing, JP's high-adrenaline novels have been praised by Publishers Weekly and other industry leaders.

Bilingual in French and pursuing a degree of Master of Education, JP frequently speaks at writers' conferences and church groups across the nation. He has been happily married for over fifteen years to his high school sweetheart.

Other exciting books by JP Robinson

Northshire Heritage
In the Shadow of Your Wings

Leila Durand, an elite German spy charged with infiltrating the home of British icon Thomas Steele, sees the war as a chance to move beyond the pain of her past. But everything changes when she falls in love with Thomas's son, Malcolm.

Is there a way to reconcile her love for Germany and her love for the enemy?

In the Midst of the Flames

Estranged from his wife, and haunted by a lie, Malcolm wonders if he can ever find forgiveness as he begins the long journey home.

Leila desperately searches for a way to escape her past life as a spy—and the German agent who has been sent to kill her—as she struggles to prove her innocence.

Determined to save his family, Thomas risks everything in a high-stakes political gamble, bringing Britain to the brink of obliteration, as spymaster Robert Hughes plots his downfall.

Secrets of Versailles

Twiceborn

Versailles is the center of European power, but the court of King Louis XIV is also a hotbed of intrigue and political manipulation.Despite the rigid structure of Angélique's upbringing, temptation proves stronger than her principles. She gives birth to twins, Antoine and Hugo, who are ripped apart by their mother's shadowed past. Can anything restore her honor?

Bride Tree

The year is 1789. France is reeling under the impact of a civil war between its social classes. When a secret agent from Rome joins forces with a vindictive politician bent on revenge, the stage is set for an explosive outcome that will shake the country to its core. Meanwhile, Queen Marie- Antoinette engages the help of her lady-in-waiting, Viviane de Lussan, in a desperate battle to keep her throne . . . and her head. But how can she win a struggle she seems fated to lose?